M000103941

a dream within

a pastor butch gregory novel

JAMIE GREENING

Also by Jamie D. Greening:

Novels and Anthologies:

The Haunting of Pastor Butch Gregory and Other Short Stories
ISBN: 9780982277669

The Little Girl Waits

ISBN: 9781936830657

How Great is The Darkness

ISBN: 9781936830831

Short Stories:

The Land Begins to Heal

Jolly Rogers

The Last Message

Speculation

a dream within

a parker butch mystery novel

By

Jamie D. Greening

Published by

ATHANATOS
PUBLISHING GROUP

A Dream Within
By Jamie D. Greening

A Butch Gregory Novel

ISBN 978-1-947844-98-8

Published by Athanatos Publishing Group, 2019. All Rights Reserved.
www.athanatos.org

This is a work of fiction. None of the characters or characterizations correlate to actual people living or dead. Nevertheless, this story is filled with truth. Let the reader understand.

For my father, Jack Greening.
The field is plowed, the corn laid by,
and the peas are picked.
Rest in peace.

Acknowledgements

Thanks, is not enough, but alas, it will have to suffice.

I begin my gratitude with you—dear reader. There are so many other things you could be reading today, but you chose my novel and for that I am thankful. You will never know how much I appreciate that act of trust.

I also deeply appreciate Athanatos Publishing, specifically Anthony Horvath. His belief in Butch Gregory, from the very first short story in 2009 all the way to this volume, has been an encouragement that feeds my soul. I also owe a debt to the other writers in the Athanatos 'stable'—specifically Joseph Courtemanche, Joe Shaw, Robert Cely, and Derek Elkins. After you buy two or three more copies of this book to give as gifts, you should immediately go buy their books. The same can be said of my little writer's group: Patrick Shaub, Iris Macek, and Amber Jones continually remind me to shorten my overcomplicated, comma infused, compound, run-on, and pretentious sentences; avoid the echo of word echoes, as well as to not swing for the fences on fourth and goal by mixing my metaphors. My writing would be exponentially better if I listened to them more often.

Many people have read through this work at various stages, and I deeply appreciate their labor. My writing and grammar are always in need of improvement. This is particularly true of plane old homophones. I am convinced this was a section of grammar in grade school covered by my teacher when I had my tonsillectomy. If you find one or more in this book, it is no one's fault by mine. These eagle-eyed people include Joe Courtemanche, Pastor Barbara Agnew, Sheila Cochran, and Elisha Pile. Another thanks to Pastor, writer, and theologian smart guy John Duncan for his assistance with tricky Greek transliteration.

A Dream Within is the most pastoral book I have ever written, and as it pertains to that I wish to express my deep appreciation for Joe Chambers and David Caddell, both of whom share in the very difficult work of shepherding my soul even if they don't know it. Related to this, the three churches I have been blessed to pastor—Walnut Springs Baptist Church, First Baptist Church of Port Orchard, and now Fellowship Baptist Church, have helped me more than I have ever helped them. I owe these three congregations so much, and I am thankful the awful things that happened to poor Butch at Sydney Community have never been my own experiences. Although, there was that one time . . .

I am a crazy, insecure, neurotic writer, yet somehow my wife and daughters love me anyway. I can't even imagine life without them. Thanks, FamSquad. I love you.

Jamie Greening
Texas Hill Country
May, 2019.

While I weep—while I weep!
O God! can I not grasp
Them with a tighter clasp?
O God! can I not save
One from the pitiless wave?
Is all that we see or seem
But a dream within a dream?

From "A Dream Within a Dream"
Edgar Allan Poe

PART ONE

The crucible is for silver
The furnace is for gold, and
The Lord tests the heart.

Proverbs 17:3

I

Pastor Butch Gregory felt as dark and blue as the necktie he kept tugging.

The tie wasn't tight. Tightness squeezed his throat from the inside out. It had been a long time since he'd felt this uncomfortable. It was warm, temperatures in the upper seventies. The sky was clear and blue. The sun felt good on his black suit.

The weather was not the reason for his discomfort.

Something wasn't right.

Of course, things weren't right. He was standing at the graveside service for a sixteen-year-old boy. A boy who had everything going for him. It was not just any boy, either. He was the boyfriend of his daughter's best friend. The boy had been in his house. He had eaten at his table. He had watched countless movies in his living room. He had driven his daughter around town.

He was a boy who was almost a man.

And now he was dead.

What part did Butch expect to be alright, anyway?

He grunted as he tugged. The necktie loosened; the tightening increased.

Funerals are always tough, but he wasn't the officiant at this graveside. Here, he was a mourner.

Butch's wife, Lucy, stood with one arm around their daughter, Sarah.

What pain Sarah must be going through. Why hadn't he spoken with her about it?

Sarah was between Butch and Lucy. Paul, their son and youngest child, stood on Butch's other side. It was their normal family seating order at public events: parent, child, parent, child. Sarah always between her mom and dad, and Paul to the right of his old man. It was how they sat at movies, concerts, football games, airplanes, and now funerals.

The chapel service had been scriptural and uplifting, and his colleague from First United Methodist Church had done a good job dealing with the difficulties and trauma involved. Butch knew she would. Here, at the graveside the minister was reading a sobering and reflective text from Ecclesiastes. He listened, looking for hope. He'd always found hope in the Scriptures. Not necessarily the hope he

11

wanted, but always hope. He listened with his aching heart, hoping to hear something positive. Anything to help.

He worked hard to not conjure the passage from memory, but instead to listen with fresh ears as each word was released into the air.

> To everything there is a season, and a time to every purpose under the heaven:
> A time to be born, and a time to die;
> A time to plant, and a time to pluck up that which is planted;
> A time to kill, and a time to heal;
> A time to break down, and a time to build up;
> A time to weep, and a time to laugh;
> A time to mourn, and a time to dance;
> A time to cast away stones, and a time to gather stones together;
> A time to embrace, and a time to refrain from embracing;
> A time to get, and a time to lose.

The familiar text from Ecclesiastes should've comforted him. He could remember times when it had. It was the exact same set of verses he'd read at his own grandmother's funeral. That was in the past. Today, though, the Bible agitated him. It mocked him. He felt as if he was always losing. When was it his time to win? His turn to get? When was his family allowed to dance? Why was their laughter always tempered with the weeping? And pain? Was the Gregory family ever allowed to heal?

God felt a million miles away.

He tugged at his necktie.

Sniffles and sobs filled his ears. Butch felt like the entire high school student body was at the funeral. He knew some, most he didn't. He'd baptized a few of them. His heart ached for them and the world they lived in. This was not the time in the lives of these children when they should be weeping. They should be laughing, dancing, studying, exploring, dating, learning, and living. They should be asking big questions about their place in the universe, thinking about love and God and eternity and politics and philosophy, and what college to go to. It wasn't fair. The young man would never experience these again, and Sarah would have to face life's bitterness far too soon.

His heart hurt for the boy in the coffin. A coffin which would soon have pall bearer boutonnieres placed upon it. Then dirt. And then not a small number of tears.

Butch looked at the sky through his sunglasses and imagined how he might be more comfortable if Roberto had died in a car crash. Or kidney failure. Or a sudden aneurysm. None of those would have eased the grief, but any one of those horrible things would have at least made some sense. People die. It was part of life. Accidents happen. Illness steals away years. Medicine fails everyone, eventually. Even kids. It was the human condition.

But Roberto didn't die in a car crash. He didn't have kidney failure. His brain was fine—there was no aneurysm. The limitations of medicine or science had nothing to do with why Roberto would not be in class Monday morning.

Roberto had opened the veins on his wrists with a razor blade. He bled to death on the floor of his bedroom. His mom found him when he didn't come down for dinner.

What a horrible experience it must have been for her.

Butch tugged at the necktie.

The more he stared upward into the sky, the more bothered he became. He'd been bothered since it had happened, but he'd blocked the whole unpleasantness from his thoughts. The ability to compartmentalize came in handy for pastoral ministry, and he'd successfully used this skill to shelter himself from thinking about Roberto. Instead, he thought about work, the landscaping of his backyard, and the book he was reading. He diagnosed himself with classic denial.

He'd not even taken the time to sit with Sarah and talk to her about her friend's death. How could he have neglected her spiritual needs? Was it a mental block? Defense mechanism? Professional distance? Why had he ignored her? Had she been anyone else's daughter, he'd have made an appointment to specifically speak to her as she went through this. Yet under his own roof was a teenage girl with enormous pain, and he hadn't even talked to her. That this girl was his daughter made his heart even sicker. His shoulders slumped. His left knee buckled. Failing his family had always been his fear, and now he saw he'd done the exact thing he'd never wanted to do.

Butch drew his left hand from his pocket; he draped his arm around Sarah's shoulder.

He moved to pull her close to him, but Sarah stepped to the side, pulling away. Without ever looking up at him, she clutched her mother's arm instead. Only two feet separated him from her, but it was an emotional Grand Canyon.

Butch's arm fell empty to his side He looked at her; she never looked at him. He felt as though he gazed at a stranger.

He clutched at his necktie, but this time he didn't tug at it. He tightened it.

After the minister had declared the sure and certain hope of the resurrection to eternal life and the funeral director gave brief instructions, Sarah and Lucy stepped up to the casket. Sarah took a necklace from around her neck and placed it atop the silver casket. Lucy held her daughter tight. Butch stood helpless beside Paul. He didn't know they'd planned that. When had they talked about it? He tried to remember if they'd talked about it, but he couldn't focus.

The car ride home was quiet. Butch held Lucy's hand, but neither spoke. Sarah and Paul doubled down on their parents' silence.

The weather outside was warm for a spring day, but the atmosphere inside Butch Gregory's home was cold.

II

Tommy Bothers brought the meeting to order. "As you know, this is a special board meeting called to discuss the sorry state of our church."

"Come on, Tommy!" Dr. Gerald Land said. "You've not made a fair characterization at all of what our situation is. Your pejorative term is not appreciated."

"Appreciated or not," another voice chimed, "Tommy's words are spot on. Things ain't good."

Tommy enjoyed this moment. He'd anticipated it, or something like it, for years, for as long as he could remember. It was his destiny. Tommy carried a mood about the whole arrangement. Last year he was elected board chairperson. His father and mother had politicked hard for him to earn the position, and their work paid off. He had endured the troublesome Butch Gregory long enough. Tommy knew how church should work. He knew what Sydney Community Church needed. He knew the solutions to their problems, and the solution started with removing the old preacher and finding a new one.

A younger one.

A smarter one.

A professional one.

A sensible one.

A compliant one.

But he had to be careful. There were difficult waters yet to navigate. Tommy knew he needed to be cautious. It couldn't look as if he was working solely to get Butch fired. He had to make a logical case for a change in direction. It must look as if he was doing the hard things and saying the hard things for the church's sake. Most people in the church loved Butch more than words could express, and the old guy had allies on the board. But the preacher's power had waned since Miss Betsy died. She had thrown him cover, and now she was gone. Two other ardent supporters had moved away to live near children and grandchildren. The only real anchor Pastor Butch had left was the dentist, Gerald Land. Tommy knew the time was now. If he played his cards right, he could persuade the rest, even those who loved Butch, it was right for him to go. Nothing negative and no slight, only a painful recognition new leadership was needed, and needed immediately.

His most powerful asset in this task was the numbers. Numbers, they say, don't lie or have an agenda. But they could be manipulated to serve an agenda.

Tommy cleared his voice and spoke up. "Let's stick with the facts. I admit my word choice was a little strong. I didn't mean any offense by it. But I've been pouring over the numbers for the last month, and what I found is shocking. Let me share with you a handout I have made to demonstrate the urgency we face." Even as the word, "urgency" came out from his mouth, Tommy was pleased with his words and tone. It all happened as he'd practiced.

It took some time for the single page handout to circulate around the somber room. At most board meetings laughter, stories, and the conversational filler of groups filled the room. Not so tonight. Tonight, the smell of nervous sweat tainted the air.

On the piece of paper there was a simple list of declarative statements, many had percentages, dollar signs, or hard numbers. The heading was "Summary Statements of Our Present Situation" and at the bottom was a single sentence which read, "Compiled using church approved documents and statements, all of which are available for review with Mildred." Tommy had been specifically pleased with the last sentence. Mildred had all of the data, indeed, but he knew no one would check his work. The appearance of transparency was all he needed. No one would verify it.

"You will see," Tommy began, "attendance has dropped fifteen percent from 2016, and that is only in worship services. For small groups, attendance is down twenty-two percent. Those numbers are bad enough if we were merely talking about one year. But if we go back to 2012, the year before our pastor drug our church into a murderous conspiracy, attendance has slipped right over forty percent. I don't need to tell you what a dangerous number forty percent is. It is a church split, really. Half the church has gone, even if they didn't all leave at the same time nor did they go to the same place. The result is effectually the same."

"Tommy," Lisa Rickover interrupted. Her voice was strong and confident. "These statistics are a tad bit misleading, don't you think?"

"Lisa, I don't quite know what you mean. Numbers don't lie."

"Of course, they do!" She pounded the table with her fist. "Your numbers fail to account for the fact the aircraft carrier that had several families in our church on it relocated to San Diego in 2015. We've had the situation here for years—military movements have always had a Yo-Yo Effect on our church. I have been here since I was a kid, and I can tell you it's just the way it goes, and blaming it on Pastor Butch is ludicrous."

There were two or three affirming noises.

"What's more," Lisa said, "We've added several new families in the last two years, but because they are new Christians, their attendance is sporadic." She picked up the paper and considered it further.

"And another thing, we've had a large amount of deaths since 2015. It is natural to expect a dip in attendance numbers when you bury as many people as we have. We have indeed added new, younger families, but they are not as regular in attendance as the older people were."

Another voice chimed in. "Don't forget also, when Pastor Philip left to take his own church in Kennewick, we took a hit in attendance, especially with the youth."

"I hear what you guys are saying," Tommy smiled as a politician would, waving his hand to metaphorically sweep away their words. He pointed his sharp tongue to diffuse them with his practiced response. "This is true, but behind each of these rationalizations there are legitimate problems we need to examine. Why haven't we recovered at a faster pace when the carrier left? I have been here my whole life too, Lisa, and it always hurts when people we've built a relationship with up and leave because Uncle Sam needs them somewhere else." He brought his hands to the tabletop and clasped them.

"The point you're missing is we've always recovered faster in the past. The Navy takes away, but it also gives. Do you not remember the carrier that left was replaced with another one? That's the way it works." Tommy nodded his head up and down the way his father practiced with him the night before.

"As to the new members, yes, those have been nice, and we all celebrate people who have found new life in Christ. However, we can all agree, can't we, that it is the pastor's job to disciple people and teach them about consistency in church attendance. It might be possible," Tommy shrugged his tiny shoulders and put a doubtful expression on his face before he continued, "very possible, perhaps, or at least I ask you to entertain the thought, that a key reason these new people have not been more consistent in their attendance is because they are not being taught to be. In other words, what we have here is a failure of leadership."

Someone, Tommy couldn't tell who, said, "Surely you don't—" but Tommy cut the protest off and didn't let the person finish the sentence. He did so not in a rude way, but in a manner which emphasized his position as leader and as the one who had the floor. He was working doubly hard to not be rude, for his normal temperament was ill-mannered.

"Surely, I do," Tommy said, "It tells us something that when Pastor Philip left to take his own congregation some folks left our church. It could be powerful evidence to support the claim of a failure of leadership from our pastor. All those people were here because of Philip, and when he moved two hundred miles away, they slowly dropped out and found somewhere else to worship. Somewhere else to serve. Somewhere else to give their tithe." Tommy clasped his hands together. "Perhaps Pastor Philip held us together more than we realized. More than Butch did. Or does."

Tommy picked up his papers from the table, "Now, let's continue to look at the evidence. Right after the information on attendance you will find the financials are not much better. Revenue has dropped by almost thirty percent since 2014. But check the next line, and you will see Sydney Community Church has been in the red for eight years. I admit, I was shocked to put the pieces together. We have not had a balanced budget since 2009. I didn't realize it was so bad, and I've been on the Finance Committee. If I didn't see the whole picture, I doubt many members do, either."

"But Tommy," a deacon named Morgan said, "you're only looking at the general fund. When you add in the designated giving, there has been plenty of revenue."

"Plenty of revenue, Morgan?" Tommy raised his eyebrows in surprise. This was another manipulative trick his father taught him. "No impartial soul would ever say we've had plenty of revenue. Last year we had to dip into the savings to make payroll in September and August. Does that sound like plenty to you?" What Tommy didn't bother to tell them was this was something they'd done every year for almost twenty years because giving dips in the summer but picks back up in the winter. He also omitted the fact there had been such surpluses in December of 2016 and January 2017 they could not only replace what money they took out but also add to the general fund.

His mother always told him it is not what you say, but it is what you don't say. Besides, if someone wanted to look it up, Mildred had all the notes.

No one would look it up.

Tommy continued prosecuting his case against Butch Gregory. "In addition to these numbers, there have been numerous complaints and emails some of us have received about our pastor. Most are benign, but some are pointed. If these were isolated, or rare, we wouldn't consider it an issue, but there are quite a few of them."

"Emails!" Gerald Land shouted so loud Tommy winced. "What kind of emails?"

Tommy fought back the smile which formed at the corner of his mind. The good dentist had fallen right into his trap. He couldn't afford, at this critical moment, to let a little smile of pleasure corrupt his otherwise perfectly somber face. Not yet, anyway. He would allow himself to enjoy this later. "Dr. Land, I hadn't wanted to be that specific, because some are embarrassing. But I thought someone might want some hard evidence, so I printed a few to share." Tommy pulled out a manila envelope from underneath a stack of papers. He shuffled them before he read the words on the crisp pages.

> I can't believe you let our historic church be disgraced with the antics of Butch Gregory. The Scriptures teach us we should live quiet, peaceable lives. Our pastor does the exact opposite as he continually drags our good name into the mud.

"Another email reads," Tommy said, shuffling his papers to give the appearance there were many to choose from.

> My grandmother was in the hospital for two days before Pastor Butch came to see her. Two Days! What a joke of a pastor is that? What if she had died?

Tommy looked up from his paper and repeated the last line with an emotional zing that would have made Tom Hanks envious. "What if she had died?" He brought a hand to his eye to wipe way an imaginary tear.

"There are several more." He held up a stack of papers as evidence. "I don't feel the need to read all of those along these themes. There are also several letters that complain, if I could put them into a general category, about the direction of the church. I picked a sample to stand in for the lot of them:

> Our wonderful church has lost its way. We do not have a slogan, a motif, a catchphrase, or even a logo. Our music is lazy, the worship services have no pep or pizzazz, and the people are all going over to the Lutherans, Presbyterians, and Pentecostals. If we don't do something, and soon, I'll be looking for another church to attend.

Tommy could feel the board being swayed his way. Not one of them suspected the emails were all from him, his parents, or his inner circle of friends. He and his particular tribe of troublemakers had intentionally left a paper trail of supposedly unhappy people for this moment. He had one more card to play. That it was a half-truth didn't matter.

No one would look it up.

No one would check.

No one would verify.

Even if they did, it would be far too late to do anything about it. This was going to happen, and it was going to happen right now. He could feel it. With each innuendo and falsification, he felt himself getting stronger. It was now time to play the trump card.

"It is not an email, but one of our young people, Bobby Bowman, told me about a troubling encounter he had with our pastor. Earlier this spring, right after Easter, Butch and his family went away for a week during Spring Break, which was fine. But this young man, who is only sixteen years old, was asked by Butch, originally, to come by his house and mow it while he was gone. Butch said he'd pay him and everything. The young man dutifully came by and mowed the grass, but when Butch got home, and saw the young man in the hallway at church, he berated him for what a horrible job he'd done and refused to pay him. Bobby was heartbroken and came to me. He adores Butch, but he has found his hero has clay feet, and it has left him with mud all over him."

Tommy collected all the emotional and spiritual energy he could muster before he spoke the magical incantation that could bring his hopes and dreams to reality.

"Some of us have been praying about this and thinking about it for a while now. We feel the Lord is leading us to change leaders. Butch Gregory is an honorable man who has served the church and the Lord well, but times have changed, and we need to adapt if we are to keep pace with the other churches in our community. He is stuck in a world where people come to church to hear the Bible, but the world has changed. People come to church to be a part of a growing organization with a dynamic vision for what we can be. 'Where there is no vision," Tommy bowed his head in prayer as he misrepresented the exhausted old verse from Proverbs, "The people perish.' We are perishing because Butch Gregory has lost his vision for ministry, for God, and for Sydney. He is more concerned about chasing off after glory, being busy keeping time with gun-toting heathens, and dragging our good church time and again into the news and headlines for things that do not glorify God. The result is far too many people have left. They want a church where they feel safe and secure with a steady leader who has business skills and marketing acumen. It wasn't his intention, but Butch Gregory has made Sydney Community Church another casualty of his escapades. It is time for new leadership, and I call for an immediate vote, right here tonight, whether to retain his services any longer."

"You can't do that!" shouted Lisa Rickover.

"Yes, I can," Tommy said. He repeated the line his mom coached him. "This doesn't make me happy at all, but I do indeed have the authority. As the chairperson of the board, and with the whole board present, I can call for a vote of no-confidence. It takes three-quarter majority to pass. This rule was put in the church by-laws by our forefathers for a reason. They knew sometimes hard choices have to be made. In their wisdom, they wanted us to be able to discretely take care of serious personnel and leadership issues without all the histrionics and handwringing that would occur if the whole church were involved in the process. Our work as guardians is to protect the people in the pews from the hard decisions. Most would never make the call to remove Butch, but their inaction would be a death sentence for the church. We don't have the luxury of being sentimental about our beloved friend and brother. We have to put the congregation's needs ahead of our own feelings."

Secret ballots had been prepared ahead. It was a simple measure. The top box was next to the word CONFIDENCE and the bottom box was next to the words NO CONFIDENCE.

No prayers were offered before the vote.

Gerald asked to table the vote, but Tommy ruled him out of order pointing to Roberts Rules and something about how he'd missed his opportunity to table earlier in the meeting. No one in the room was sure if Tommy was right or not, but he tossed in enough official sounding legalese no one questioned it.

And no one would look it up, either.

The ballots were passed around the table. Tommy Bothers gave a brief set of instructions and informed the group again three-quarters majority was needed to remove Butch Gregory from his position as lead pastor of Sydney Community Church. He said the full board—compromised of the ten deacons, eight program leaders, and the only current ministerial staff, which was Butch—totaled nineteen. It would take fifteen votes to remove Pastor Butch.

Ballots were quickly scratched, folded, and returned around the table.

No one spoke.

Tommy collected them. He read the ballots out one at a time. The first vote was CONFIDENCE. He put that on his left. The next twelve were NO CONFIDENCE. Those he piled on the right. Then there were two CONFIDENCE votes. One more NO CON-FIDENCE, then two more marked CONFIDENCE. Tommy Bothers held the last ballot in his hand. This is the one that would determine the fate of Sydney Community Church and its beleaguered pastor.

Tommy opened it and said the words, "NO CONFIDENCE." He put it in the much larger pile to the right. He took a deep breath and said, "By a fifteen to four vote, the board has voted no confidence in Pastor Butch Gregory. By tradition and decree it is thus decided Butch Gregory is terminated as pastor of Sydney Community Church."

* * *

Butch Gregory had sat silent to the left of Tommy Bothers during the meeting. Like Christ before his accusers, Butch was deaf before the shearers. It was not his choice. He wanted to defend himself. He had a defense for every single point, as well as ideas on how things would improve. Being silent was what he had to do, though. It wasn't his idea. For some reason, God wanted him to be silent. He was certain.

When the vote was finished, Butch stood up and looked around the room. He looked at men and women he'd prayed with. He looked at people he'd married. Three of them he'd baptized. He'd counseled more than a few of them through marriage difficulties and out of divorce litigation. He thought of them as friends. No, it was more. He'd thought of them as family.

His eyes met every one of them until he at last came to Tommy. Butch had expected to feel anger at Tommy, but instead he was surprised by pity. The pastor wanted to cry, but he couldn't. It was a luxury he shouldn't take. Not here. He could cry later. He held their gaze as a hypnotist might, turned, and walked out of the Fellowship Hall and straight to his car.

III

Lucy Gregory knew what had happened in the meeting before Butch ever opened his mouth. It was the way he looked.

His forehead drooped. Crestfallen eyebrows rested atop weary eyes. He was sad, but it wasn't only sadness. The sadness was varnished with thick anger. His face flushed red with rage he could barely control. Pathetic eyes tried to hide his injury, but his countenance was as a lover who'd been betrayed. Hurt. Wounded. Rejected. Scorned.

Lucy Gregory saw a pain she'd never seen before on her weary husband.

"I thought it'd make you cry," Butch said.

"It should," Lucy said. "But it doesn't. Actually, I thought you'd be crying."

But there were no tears in the Gregory home that night. In fact, through the whole ordeal, Lucy would later recall she never shed any tears over Sydney Community, which was hard for her to believe given the blood and sweat she'd poured into the people. Her husband would have his moments of grief in the days to come, but here, on this night, he was stoic. The word 'brave' came to her mind at the time. She loved her brave husband more in this moment than ever before.

Butch had skipped dinner before the meeting, so he sat in the living room and ate the sandwich Lucy made for him and drank coffee.

"Tommy Bothers doctored the evidence." Butch was halfway through his sandwich before he spoke.

"Does it surprise you?"

"No."

"Did anyone argue for you?"

"Gerald tried."

"Anyone else?"

"A couple. None fought too hard, though."

"Do you want to talk about it?"

"Not really."

"How do you think the church body will react?"

"I don't care."

"Sure, you do."

"No, I don't."

"Why? How could you not care, after all you've done and all you've given of yourself?" Lucy felt the need for answers. The question was, did Butch have answers?

"Because." Butch glanced away.

"That's not an answer."

"Because they are in God's hands, not mine. I did what I was supposed to do."

"I don't understand. What were you supposed to do?"

"Take it," Butch scratched his chest.

"Take what?"

"Take whatever they did. For some reason, this was God's will."

There was a knock at the door. Lucy glanced at Butch. "Are you expecting anyone?"

"No," Butch said. "But I'd bet almost anything it is Gerald. I perceived he was more upset than I was."

Nothing was said as Lucy opened the door. Gerald reached in and enveloped her in a giant bear hug. Butch sat down his empty sandwich plate and walked to the doorway.

After the hugging finished, they took familiar seats in the living room. Gerald's mouth opened and he spoke as soon as his bottom hit the loveseat cushion. "The good news is the board is giving you a year's salary, lump sum."

"What is the bad news?" Butch said.

"You have to have your office cleaned out by the end of the week."

"Can I come to church Sunday and say goodbye?"

"No." Gerald was direct in his words while his eyes darted to the ground. "It is probably because they know if you show up, the people will rebel against their decision. With you absent, Tommy and his henchmen can control the narrative."

Lucy shook her head. Her breathing became shallow. She looked straight ahead.

"I've never been fired before," Butch said, after what felt like a year of silence. Lucy came to herself, and fidgeted with the coffee pot, pouring more into the three cups, even though they were all full.

"Not even as a teenager?" Gerald said.

"No, not even then. I was always quickly promoted and given responsibility. This is a new experience for me. The sad thing is, I'm here in my early fifties and fired. I am unqualified for anything other than the one job I got canned from. I'm just like the man in the story Jesus told in the gospel of Luke. Remember?"

"Which one is that?" Lucy said.

"The one that is called the shrewd manager. He gets fired and realizes he is too proud to beg and too flabby and comfortable for labor, so he makes quick friends with his boss' debtors. That's me. I am too old to start over, and too comfortable to go without. I don't know what I will do."

Lucy hit her husband's arm. "You're not too old for anything!" She stomped her feet a little as she said it, waving her hands with emotion. She loved her husband, but she knew he had a tendency toward depression, and she didn't want to relive 2007 all over again. Being fired was bad, but she didn't want the darkness again.

"Well," Gerald said, "you don't have to make any decisions yet. Take some time. You have the money to let your mind clear out. At least you own your home. Back in the old days—and I remember when I was a kid and the church's pastor lived in the parsonage next to the church—they fired him one Sunday night while he was on vacation and they all showed up the next morning and put his furniture, clothes, and books all in the front yard for him to find when he got back."

"Because that is exactly what Jesus would do," Lucy said. Her chin sharp. Eyes narrow.

"Look," Gerald said, "I didn't say it was right. I'm saying it could be worse."

"True," Butch said. "I suppose I could be homeless as well as unemployed. If only my pickup truck was broke down, I'd be a country music song."

"I guess it is good you can keep your humor about you." Gerald sipped his coffee. "However, you mistook my meaning. There have been times when you've spoken truth into my life. Let me speak a little into yours. Will you open your heart and listen for a moment?"

Lucy and Gerald awaited a reply.

"Oh, that's not a rhetorical question, is it?" Butch said.

"No, it is not." Gerald's head shook and his eyes widened in expectation. "Before I tell you what I think, I want to confirm that you're willing to listen."

Butch said, "You know I will. I'm hurt, confused, and as I analyze myself from a clinical perspective you both should realize," he glanced at Lucy and continued, "I may not be open to big picture thinking right now. I'm not in my right mind, and I know I am still in the shocked stage. However, you have been one of my closest friends. I trust no one more than the two people I'm here with right now."

He reached out his right hand and put it on Lucy's.

Gerald nodded. "Well," he held out his hands as if he were beginning a briefing before a general or a pitch to a Hollywood director for a movie idea. "Here is what I was alluding to. Both your children are older now, considerably older. Maybe you and Lucy can take some time off and travel this summer—either alone or with the family; you won't have many more years when you are all together. Trust me, I know. I spent those last years working myself nearly to burn out. Why not go overseas, tour the east coast, or cruise to Alaska? Or Hawaii? I guess I want you to find a way to enjoy this season in life as a blessing."

"That's not a bad idea." Lucy's eyes were on her husband's heart. "We've always talked about going to Germany, or maybe Greece. Wouldn't it be lovely to see those beautiful blue islands in the Aegean?"

Butch nodded his head. "And while we're there, we can tour all the cities where they stoned the Apostle Paul. We can even see where all the martyrs were burned." He gave out an insincere chuckle, "It'd be a hoot."

Lucy's head sagged.

Gerald ignored Butch's gallows humor. He said, "I keep thinking about the passage from Joseph you preached a couple of years ago. It came to my mind while I was driving over here. Remember, Joseph told his brothers that they had meant it for evil when they sold him into slavery, but God meant it for good. You told us God doesn't do bad things to us, but through faith he takes the bad things that happen to us and makes them redemptive. Do you remember?"

"Now that is a rhetorical question, because you know I would remember my own sermon." A smile flirted with Butch's lips, but then ran away to hide.

Gerald said, "There is no doubt in my mind Tommy Bothers is a snake. He is cut from the same cloth as his mom and dad. Once, their regular dentist was away on vacation. Tommy was a kid back then, maybe ten or twelve. He had a cavity that was hurting him. They came to me to fix it. I'd swear I saw scales down that boy's gullet."

Gerald shuddered as if remembering a horrible nightmare.

"Anyway, those people are evil, and I apologize I didn't fight harder years ago to keep him away from power positions. I thought we could appease Tommy and his gang, but I see now we were playing

25

with fire the whole time. We all got burned tonight." He gathered his thoughts, "The Lord will deal with him. But you are God's vessel of redemption. He has always worked through you. Not like Jesus saves, but in the name of Jesus you have worked at a ministry of redemption ever since you came to Sydney. The same is true now. God is going to use this as good in your life. You wait and see. This is not the last page in this book."

Butch nodded. "I know in my heart you are right." He opened his mouth to say more but closed it and looked away.

IV

Butch's phone began ringing early Monday morning. He answered the first four calls. They all went along the same lines. The person calling would say something similar to or with the effect of, "I am so sorry" and fidget around with small talk and eventually ask, "Is it true," to which Butch could only say, "Yes, I was fired," and the person would ask, usually in long paragraphs of hemming and hawing, the obvious question of, "Why" to which Butch would say, "I don't exactly know. They wanted new leadership, I guess. Or maybe they just didn't want me." The second caller, a woman named Margaret, bluntly asked Butch, "Who did you sleep with?" and she would not believe Butch when he told her no one, other than his wife. Margaret told him this was God's punishment for his sin. He assured her he was indeed a sinner, and she might be right about the punishment part, but he had not been fired for moral failure, or for any lurid things she'd imagined. She didn't believe him. The third caller had finished his sympathy speech by suggesting the names of four different lawyers Butch should consult. The fourth caller went through the same questions then finished his call by saying he'd personally front ten thousand dollars to help Butch start a new church in town. He'd already figured it out, he said. They could meet in the old abandoned Albertsons. Butch declined by telling him, "I don't know if I will ever be able to pastor again. Ever. So, no." Butch didn't tell him how he didn't even have enough spiritual energy to put his pants on, much less open his Bible or pray. The idea of leading anyone to do anything exhausted him. Starting a church was a ridiculous proposition. How could he plant a church when what he wanted was to sit with Jonah under the vine and wait for the end.

Butch stopped answering the calls after that one. He changed his voicemail message to reflect his current situation. Previously it said, "You've reached Pastor Butch Gregory of Sydney Community Church. I am not available, so please leave a message and I will get back to you as soon as possible. This is the day the Lord has made, let us be glad and rejoice in it." He recorded a new message: "I will not be answering my phone for a long time. I don't want to talk about it. If you want to talk to somebody, call Tommy Bothers."

Lucy told him his voicemail greeting was meanspirited. Butch grunted.

On Tuesday, he received a phone call from Curtis Moore. Butch didn't answer it, his phone told him who was calling. Curtis was in his early forties and in the midst of a messy divorce from his wife. Butch felt guilty for not answering. He knew Curtis needed to talk.

Curtis left a voicemail that Butch did not listen to.

Then Curtis called back. He left another voice mail.

Then again.

Again.

He sat at the dining room table and drank coffee, watching his phone ring over and over as Curtis kept calling. He was determined not to answer. His determination left him as he pushed the green button.

"What?" He mumbled into the phone.

"Pastor Butch, thank God. I need to talk to you."

"What's wrong?"

"Melinda wants to reconcile. Can you believe it?"

"That's great."

"Can you meet with us?"

"I can't."

"We can meet you at our house."

"I told you, I can't."

"But we need you. No one else can help but you. You understand us. You know us. You're the pastor, you've got to help us."

"Curtis, I love you both, but I'm in no condition to help anyone right now."

"But what about us? We need you."

"You'll be fine. If you two will be honest with each other, forgive, and move forward, you'll be fine. I always knew you'd work it out. You love each other, but things got in the way. Sometimes it happens. Things get in the way and we forget what matters. Sit down with Mel and talk it through. Look at the old photographs from your wedding. Talk about your kids. Dream about the future you can make together

27

by building on your shared past. You'll find love is a near inexhaustible source of strength and hope."

"See, Butch, that is what we need you to say, that stuff. The good stuff."

"That is all I can give. Curtis, I can't help you or anyone." Butch closed his eyes, squinting under the pain in the words he was saying. Each syllable cut him. "I am not a pastor any more. I have given you all I have to give. Please tell Mel I said hi."

"What are we supposed to do?"

"You don't need me. Nobody does. You'll figure something out." He hung up.

Later that night he tried to say a prayer for Curtis and Mel, but nothing came from his mouth or his heart. He was empty. Butch's heart was dry. His soul was a desert.

* * *

When Sunday came each week, so did the pain.

He sat in the Adirondack chair in the backyard all morning.

It had been six weeks since Butch had been at a church worship service, or even set foot in a church building. The first Sunday after he was fired from Sydney Community, he had every intention to go to church somewhere. He even told his family the night before to be ready in the morning. He told them they would find somewhere to attend. He put a positive spin on it by saying at least they could go to church and worship together as a family and not have to worry about leading anything.

By sunrise, his steely resolve turned to grief. So, they stayed home. Lucy made pancakes and sausage, and they listened to praise and worship music in the kitchen. Butch never came in to eat. He sat in the backyard and watched the sky.

He only left the house that week to go to the hardware store and buy supplies for the garden he was building in the backyard. For reasons he couldn't explain, he had the strongest desire to build a koi pond. Never had he raised fish, not even a goldfish in an oversized glass bowl when he was a child. But the need for the fish was overwhelming. Lucy had taken the role of therapist in the relationship. She told him there was something subconscious going on in his noggin. She said the symbolism of fish, fishers of men, casting nets and all of the other biblical imagery was stuck inside looking for a way out. Butch did not deny the possibility. He didn't argue with her. He didn't care. He knew he had to build a fishpond.

The next Sunday he thought he'd be ready to go to church, but when he woke up, he went through his mind of where he and his family could go. He certainly couldn't go to Sydney Community, even though it was the only church his children had ever known. That was a particularly acrid thought that stuck in his throat. Not only had he lost his job, but his children had lost their network of support. Forever.

He made a list of the other churches in Sydney. He either knew too much about the pastor of each church or too little. Too much information meant he'd prejudge everything. Too little information means the pastor is a recluse, and/or the church is too inbred for his liking. Besides, everyone in Sydney knew him. His firing had made the front page of the local paper and the public affairs program for the NBC affiliate. There was no church he could attend where there wouldn't be a thousand questions from well-meaning people.

Lucy suggested Terence's church. It was a tempting thought, and his old friend would no doubt make him feel comfortable, yet even there—and maybe especially there because of the many friends—he knew it would not be a peaceful moment. It wouldn't be fair to Terence or Muriel.

These thoughts, and sometimes even more desperate ones, dogged him every weekend. He wanted to go to church. He wanted to worship. He wanted to sit with his family and make his prayers. He wanted to go.

He couldn't go.

The fourth Sunday after his firing, he seriously contemplated attending the Jehovah's Witness gathering so he'd have someone to argue with.

It was the fifth week after he'd packed the last books from his study at Sydney Community when he got the phone call from Steve Bremer. Steve wasn't a friend, but they had been acquaintances for a long time. Colleagues was a better description of their relationship. Steve recently had retired from ministry, but he found himself giving leadership and support to denominational churches in the area. One of the problems Steve encountered was reliable pulpit fill for congregations that were either pastorless or whose pastor was on vacation. Steve wanted Butch to preach the upcoming Sunday at a small church near Olympia.

"Which church is it?"

"Lighthouse Church."

"I don't know that one. Is it new? A church plant?"

29

"No, not new. Old, in fact."

"How old?"

Butch realized he sounded elitist and snotty. He also realized he didn't care if he sounded elitist or snotty.

Steve answered Butch's question without comment on how ugly and inappropriate the question was. "Old enough to pay the bills, but too old to appeal to any pastor looking for a chance to grow a congregation through family ministry."

"I see." Butch rubbed his hands through his hair and snapped off his glasses. The easy speed and quick reply Steve had given him indicated to Butch he'd fielded those questions before. He worked to activate his memory, which was ever faulty and untrustworthy, but he nevertheless managed to recall a conversation he had once with Steve, and he thought this might be the church Steve had mentioned way back when. Butch couldn't remember if it was in Portland at an evangelism conference or was it a board meeting in Yakima. But he thought he remembered Steve politely called this particular Lighthouse Church a retirement church—where pastors go to draw a supplemental salary until someone dies, either the pastor or the church. Sometimes they died about the same time.

Not much work is required in these churches, other than to show up, preach an old sermon from file, and make sure you don't rock any boats with crazy new ideas. You also couldn't say curse words while preaching, which is what the previous pulpit fill for Lighthouse did. He dropped an excrement bomb during a vivid illustration about falling out of a kayak on the Columbia River.

"Are you interested?" Steve asked.

"Is this your way of putting me out to pasture? Because maybe I have more left in me before I hang it up and start doing funerals every weekend." Butch thought this might have been a lie. He wasn't quite sure if was true. He might be a washed-up has-been, only good for weekend funerals, and sermon illustrations so old they are in black and white.

Steve exhaled into the phone. "Far from it. This is something for you to do right now, and to help me out at the same time. Look, I need help out there, and if I could find someone else, I would. But there is a need and you're available, so I am working here, doing my job by pairing up a pastor with nothing to do on Sunday and a church with no pastor on Sunday. You need to see things from my perspective. You're the highest qualified person to come around in a long time. I'd be negligent or foolish to not try and get you on the team."

"How long of a commitment is this?"

Steve pounced at this apparent yes, "Why don't we say you do it for six weeks at two-hundred dollars a Sunday? We will call it pulpit supply, not interim. All you have to do is show up and preach. Deal?"

"Sounds fair," Butch said. "Let me talk to Lucy and the kids about it. They might have some input. But for now, let's say yes. Send me a text with the exact location, what time the worship service starts, and a contact name."

The two men made small talk for several more minutes, but the next instant he was sitting in the parking lot of Lighthouse Church in Olympia. In reality, it had been five days since he'd talked to Steve, but it all jumbled. Lucy, Sarah, and Paul had been indifferent as to whether he did this, but he was insistent they not come the first time. He wanted to get a feel for it, so he could prepare them later. He knew how these small churches could be. He cut his teeth pastoring one of these nearly thirty years earlier when he was a soaking wet-behind-the-ears seminary student. If only he'd known then, what he knew now.

He wished he could be excited as he drove to Lighthouse Church in Olympia. His mind wandered so much he ran a red light in the sleepy town of Shelton. It was after that he noticed the sticker in his rear windshield. He remembered when he'd put it there. It was a decal that had Sydney Community Church wrapped around a glowing sun hovering over the mountain range. He pulled over into the Wal-Mart parking lot and tried to peel it off. It was stuck so well and for so long it wouldn't budget. He pulled out his car keys and scratched it off, bit by bit. He finished the job by pouring some of the coffee from his travel mug on it and wiping it clean with a spare jacket he kept in the trunk.

His first impression of Lighthouse Church proved worse than he possibly could have imagined. Moss covered so much of the roof it looked purposeful, the way they make those ecological buildings in Seattle with a grass roof to offset sunlight and cool the atmosphere. But this moss wasn't on purpose. It was neglect. Rust ran down the side of the building where downspouts had once been. Someone had removed the "H" in Lighthouse on the church sign and replaced it with a spray painted "M" indicating this was "LightMouse" Church. Trash littered the gravel parking lot, which was torn up with doughnuts and brake skids. The only sign of friendly life was a gigantic smiley face painted on the sidewalk near the front steps. Some trickster had painted a bullet hole in the forehead with blood spurting out.

Steve had sent him incorrect information. This was something

Butch made a mental note to scold him about. The start time he'd been told was ten. Butch assumed ten was the worship service. It was not. It was the Sunday School hour. When he'd walked into the building, he was greeted by a man who looked like the love child of a lumberjack and a serial killer. A red beard adorned his face the way strings hang from a dirty, overused mop head. He wore a blue and black flannel shirt, unbuttoned, with a Harley-Davidson motorcycle T-Shirt underneath. His jeans were clean, but the boots he wore were covered in mud. The man didn't speak as he shoved into Butch's hand an old-fashioned denominational Sunday school book, the kind people used to call a "Quarterly" because they came out four times a year. The silent man took him down a dark hallway with a low ceiling to a room that smelled of antiquity.

The room was tiny but filled with people. Butch shuddered. His psyche rejected the enormity of how uncomfortable the situation in front of him looked.

A typical round folding table was in the middle, completely filling the room. The space between the people, table, chairs, and the walls was below minimal. Twelve or thirteen people sat smashed in their chairs. Their Bibles were opened. Each person had either a cup of coffee in Styrofoam or energy drinks with cans of various colors. Butch was certain the thermostat was set to a hundred and twenty degrees. A hum came from the obscene brightness of the fluorescent light on the ceiling. The closest end of the light fixture dangled two inches from an asbestos relic.

"Hey, Daddy, I found the preacher." It was the first thing the one-man welcome team had said.

"I see that; tell him to have a seat. We are about to get started."

Obediently, the welcome team looked at Butch and said, with no sense of irony, "Have a seat. They are about to get started."

Butch said, "I don't see an extra chair." He pointed around the room, "Also, there isn't much room in here."

"Daddy, he says there isn't much room. And there isn't an extra chair."

"Go get one from the storage closet," Daddy said.

"I'll go get one from the storage closet," Mr. Welcome Mat said.

Butch decided to interrupt the pretend world where he needed a go-between. He extended his hand toward the man who was called Daddy and said, "I'm Butch Gregory. Steve told me to look for a man named Rueben Field. Are you Rueben?"

"Yeppers. Folks around here call me Rue, though."

"Or Daddy, apparently."

Rue laughed at the joke. "Yep, that's my boy, Frank. He's the welcome committee. That over there," he pointed across the table, "is my daughter Nicole, who we call Sprocket, and that is my wife, Diana, but everyone calls her Suzy." Rue continued to point at people and name them, "That is my brother Robert, but we call him Bobby, his wife Maggie Mae goes by Emcee, then Paul, who's not married, beside him is Deena, Diana's sister, the tiny blonde beside her is her daughter Chloe, but we call her Lo." He continued on through all the people until he'd introduced everyone. Butch leaned across the table to shake hands with the first two but transitioned to a smile and wave for each one thereafter.

Butch didn't even try to keep the names straight in his head or how they were all related. He'd figure out who was who if it was important. Besides, he'd never figure it out. It would take an Excel spreadsheet to keep track of everyone's real name and nickname along with how everyone was related. His throat tightened, though, and he had the feeling of being trapped. He fought down the anxiety, looked around the table and said, "It is a pleasure to meet all of you." He took a step backward, "My name, as I said, is Butch Gregory and it is a joy to be with you here today." He made a broad gesture with his hands. "It looks cramped in here." A tiny, psychosomatic cough forced its way from his mouth. "Perhaps it would be better if I helped with the children or youth today? Or better yet, maybe there is a place I can look over my notes and pray before the worship service." Butch didn't need to look at any notes and he certainly didn't want to help children or the youth. What he did desperately want was to get away from this room. Grasping at these ecclesiastically appropriate straws was a perfectly acceptable option to him when faced with such a terrifying situation.

"Well, there are only three children, and the mommas got them, and the youth group has got the strep throat today."

"I see," Butch said. "The whole youth group, huh?"

His question hung on the air until the chair arrived. Somehow, in a miracle akin to the widow's never-ending oil, there was enough room for him to sit on the circle's outside edge by the opened door. Butch was glad the door was open. It made his momentary claustrophobia manageable. In his heart he prayed, 'Thank you, Lord, for the open door. It will be enough.'

Butch nodded at Frank. He'd be okay now. He told himself all would be great now. He'd gotten over the awkwardness and had

33

adjusted to the cramped feeling. Parked here in a familiar church chair by an open door would be fine. Not perfect, but fine. He would survive.

"Frank, remember to make another pot of coffee and put the bulletins out," Rue said, "and don't forget to shut the door behind you."

Panic rose in Butch's throat as the door gave a creak. Wind rushed over his cheeks as the death hatch sealed shut. His eyes darted around the room. There was one window, but the blinds were drawn closed. Errant light beams crawled around the outer edge of the portal out of the Sunday School dungeon. Butch felt an almost uncontrollable and irrational desire to rip off those blinds and kick the window out. The room was beyond stuffy. It felt to Butch something akin to the way an airplane feels when hot and sweaty travelers have boarded the plane in Phoenix or Atlanta or Houston, somewhere hot and steamy, and the plane pushes away from the gate but doesn't take off, but instead sits on the runway tarmac for what feels like forever plus a day with no air circulating in the cabin at all because the engines are not engaged while everybody is smooshed together, smelly, and foul in both appearance and temperament because of the extremely uncomfortable situation but also from the slight nervosa most everyone feels right before takeoff; therefore, all those human bodies are excreting untold hormones, fighting subconscious phobias, creating a situation that, although perfectly logical, makes an individual almost insane with the need to escape.

This was how Butch felt in the Sunday School room.

Rue took prayer requests from the small group. It was a typical organ recital: spleens, kidneys, livers, brains, lungs, hearts, colons, and two prostates. It was after the last organ—a request for someone with kidney failure—when the first surprise of the morning came. Rue made eye contact with Butch from across the table and said, "I bet you have a lot for us to pray about, don't you, preacher?"

Butch didn't know if Rue was making a snide comment about his recent dismissal from Sydney Community, or if it was a sincere statement about the guest preacher knowing about things which needed prayer. The dichotomous thought came at him fast. Along with the cynicism, crept a memory. There was something in the way Rue said, "Preacher" that reminded him of Amber, who had called him, "Preach." Consequently, he trusted Rue's intention and dismissed the dark thought.

"Thank you, Rue." Butch said. Then it happened. His mouth

opened, then he said, "It would be kind of you to pray for my daughter. Her name is Sarah."

Several people wrote down Sarah on their prayer lists. One woman, it might have been Lo or it might have been Sprocket, he couldn't remember, asked, "Anything specific for Sarah?"

It was a thoughtful question, the kind he'd asked many times himself.

"No, nothing specific to share. Just pray for her to put all the pieces together."

Why had he said that?

The group bowed their head in prayer and spent several minutes going around the room as different people spoke aloud to God. Butch spiritually couldn't participate. Instead his mind raced. Why had he asked for prayer for Sarah? It was as if someone else had formed the thought and borrowed his mouth to say it when he wasn't paying attention. He hadn't made a conscious decision to ask for prayers about his daughter. It was far too personal. There were a thousand generic or deflecting things he could have said to the group, everything from prayers for the sermon later to healing for the many people he knew were ill. But no, this incredibly personal request came out of his mouth against his will. What's more, he didn't even know it was on his heart. He knew Sarah was in a bad way, but he hadn't seriously thought about her as someone who needed special attention. And here he was asking a room full of strangers to pray for her to 'put the pieces together,' whatever that meant. Butch Gregory valued control, and he felt out of control.

There was another surprise yet lurking on Butch's horizon. It happened in the sanctuary after the worship service was over.

Butch was happy with his homiletics, especially considering the psychic trauma of the Sunday School hour. The song service had been a disturbing endeavor. A man who clearly was suffering from what sounded to Butch as end-stage COPD tried to lead the sixty or so gathered saints in hymns which were being played electronically from a box plugged into a speaker amp. It sounded the same way hymn karaoke does at a nursing home or something from a story about Pastor Ingqvist in Lake Woebegone. The song leader liked "Love Lifted Me" so much they sang it three times, and each time it got worse. Butch managed to live through it. In fact, he preached what he thought was a fine sermon from Paul's second letter to Corinth about the treasure God has placed inside all of us as earthen vessels. It was one of Butch's favorite images for humanity in general, and people of faith in specific. He elaborated on the creation of human beings from dirt, emphasized the use of earthen vessels as storage containers, and moved into a brief talk about the image of God and the human experience all placed inside something as fragile as baked mud. He finished the sermon with a flourish regarding the deposit of faith in Christ which God seals within us as human beings through the power of the Holy Spirit. In the sermon, he quoted Langston Hughes, referenced Einstein, and challenged his hearers to see themselves as a repository for the secrets and mysteries of eternity. He'd preached the sermon before in several different ways and contexts over the years at Sydney Community, and he thought it was effective here at Lighthouse Church this morning.

The second surprise came after the sermon. Butch stood at the front of the worship area, near the altar. He put on his coat and prepared to leave. He'd talked to Rue before the service started and they both agreed it was better if he didn't take the pastor's spot at the backdoor because that was where Rue always stood. Butch didn't care, so he let it slide. It'd be easier for him to get away if he wasn't at the door. Besides, Rue was right, the backdoor was where pastoral ministry happened and he wasn't the pastor of this church. Or any other church. Not anymore. He was the supply preacher for the morning. He was only a temp. A hired hand.

The sanctuary was almost empty. Rue was at the back door, and Frank had given Butch an envelope with his name handwritten on the front. It was a tad bit mercenary, but Butch peeked inside to see a check for exactly two hundred dollars. When he turned to pivot out of the front row pew, a woman stood waiting in the aisle. He didn't recognize her as someone one he'd met. In fact, he couldn't remember her being in the sanctuary during the service.

Butch tried to smile, but it was hard coming. He was emotionally ready for a break. In his mind, he'd already checked out, and was ready for the recliner and a bowl of Lucy's award-winning chili she'd promised to have ready when he got home.

The woman didn't smile back. Blonde hair hung around her shoulders. Her face was thin and long, but her nose was tiny. She stood a foot taller than Butch. Her hazel eyes narrowed upon his countenance, lips turned downward. She held up her hands, palms out, even with her shoulders and said, "A daughter's love is precious." The words hissed from her parted lips, and the sound increased in intensity beyond what one would imagine possible. The woman repeated the phrase again, "A daughter's love is precious." She brought her palms together in a folded position of prayer and added, "But her trial is severe."

The spoken words pushed him backwards. He stumbled over his feet and found himself falling slowly onto a pew. His face turned forward to the chancel area. His eyes became fixed on the large wooden cross nailed to the wall behind the platform. Butch gasped for breath because his chest tightened. A heat wave flushed across him; his feet tingled, and he thought his heart might leap out from his body and fall onto the floor.

Eventually, he found himself. It took a herculean effort to stand up and catch his breath. By the time he did, the oracle was gone.

V

He shook all the way to his car. He'd found a way to tell Rue, "Goodbye," and "See you next week," before he left the building, but he barely made it to the safe confines of his car.

The woman's words ran through his mind over and over.

A daughter's love is precious, but her trial is severe.
A daughter's love is precious, but her trial is severe.
A daughter's love is precious, but her trial is severe.

He didn't have the wherewithal to start the engine. Instead he kept mumbling the words over and over. The shuddering which started in the sanctuary grew into a tremble. The tremble became a breakdown.

He knew what God was telling him, but he didn't know where to start. The worst part was the heartache. The first priority he and Lucy had was to protect, love, and nurture their children. He had failed. He had failed his family. He had failed his daughter. His failure was complete. In his devotion to serve the church and do the work of ministry, he'd forgotten what was important. Now, at the pivot point of his life, he'd lost his ministry and he knew his daughter's relationship with him was in trouble.

He needed the forty-five-minute drive home from Olympia to think. By the time he arrived, he knew what to do. What he didn't know was who the spooky woman was. He had a sinking feeling that he'd either never know, or when he did find out, it wouldn't be the most pleasant of circumstances. He knew she was an oracle from God. He didn't know whether it was a condemnation or a warning. He prayed with desperation to Almighty God that it was a warning, and that there was time to fix it.

Butch kept his emotions in check through lunch. It was a quiet meal. Paul wolfed down his chili and ran out of the house to the city park. Spring fever had hit Butch's youngest hard, especially his love for baseball. Lucy asked a few questions about the Lighthouse Church, and Butch relayed the humor of the welcome he received and talked about how it was a good church but needed some pastoral skill to bring it around. He didn't say anything about the surprises.

Sarah did the Sarah thing—she silently sulked while she ate, then politely recused herself from the table to go hide in her room. It was a habit which had been developing for the past several months. The moodiness was so gradual neither he nor Lucy had taken special notice. Butch felt Lucy was probably more in tune with what was going on than he was, but he perceived not by much. Sitting here at the table, what bothered Butch most was how he suspected these things now, but he and Lucy had never talked about it. They'd simply accepted the cold shoulder from Sarah as inevitable and moved on.

That ended today. It had to. The omen demanded it.

He helped Lucy clear away the table and load the dishwasher after lunch.

"We can have chili dogs tomorrow night—with cheese and onions," he told her as he put the leftover chili into a storage container. "I was thinking maybe tomorrow night we could play a game like we used to, you know, Monopoly or Yahtzee or something and eat cookies and ice cream sundaes?" Butch closed the refrigerator door and sighed. "It has been a long time since we had a family night." He leaned against the kitchen counter beside Lucy. "We lost our family fun when we lost Sydney Community. We need to get it back. A pallor has fallen over all us because one aspect of life changed. It's my fault, I know, and I've got to fix it. I lost my job, but no one died."

Lucy, who knew her husband better than anyone else this side of eternity, gave her husband a hug and a peck on the cheek. "It's not the only thing you need to fix."

"I know," Butch said. "I got the message from God this morning about what was going on. Or at least he told me what the problem was. The problem is me. It is not her as much as it is me. I'm going upstairs right now to talk to her."

"Before you do, listen to me for a moment," Lucy dried her hands on a dishtowel before taking a drink from her water glass. Butch could tell she was preparing her thoughts because her hands were not wet.

"You can't fix things with a game night."

"I know," Butch said.

"No, you don't." Her head shook back and forth. "You can't fix it with ice cream. Sarah, and Paul too for that matter, are not little children. Sarah is seventeen-years-old. Do I need to remind you, as you've so often reminded me, you were seventeen when you preached your first sermon? Sarah is a woman, not a child. Paul has his own life, too, with his own friends, passions, and ambitions. Sarah even more so, and you've barely said four words to her since the funeral. Which reminds me, you said a few moments ago you lost your job, but no one died. That's not exactly accurate. Someone did die, and that someone was a close friend of our daughter's."

"I—" Butch started to protest, but Lucy cut him off.

"You're right." She took his hand in hers. "You need to fix things with Sarah, but the solution is not to treat her like a child. Your daughter has changed. Your relationship to her has to change, too. She is a woman. That reality demands an attitude change from us. You must give her the same respect and care you'd give someone at church who needed you." Lucy crinkled her nose and drew up her mouth. "Actually, it's more. She needs more attention than a church member. A church member at her age would have a pastor and her father. Sarah only has you, so you have double-duty."

"I'm sorry," was all Butch could say. The words never sounded so useless and hollow to him.

"I know you are, honey. And I don't say this stuff to attack you. I say it because, sometimes, we feel cheated."

She walked toward him, and Butch thought she was going to hug him and say everything would be alright. Instead, she moved right past him in the narrow kitchen and turned toward the backdoor. "I'll be outside on the patio reading. Good luck."

Butch nodded his head up and down. He knew his wife was telling him, "You're on your own with this one." She was right. Lucy couldn't do anything about this. It was up to him. He left the kitchen and headed upstairs.

* * *

It had been a year since they moved into the refurbished home. Sandra Bennett's pressure-cooker-internet-special-bomb hadn't destroyed their house completely, but it ruined enough. The opportunity to redesign the majority of the upstairs and master bedroom area was too good to pass up. What had been a narrow stairway to tiny bedrooms carved from leftover attic space was turned into a wide stairway visible from the ground floor. A balcony walkway added an impressive aspect of size to the upstairs, and the skylight in the middle poured natural sunlight into the living area. Butch had worried it was too fancy. In the end, his wife won the argument because the endeavor had cost them nothing out-of-pocket. The various insurance companies involved in the settlements were more than happy to keep the whole thing out of court, especially those representing Blackjack County.

He hadn't been upstairs in a while. It was the primary abode of his children. As he neared the landing, he felt butterflies in his stomach. The last time he was in Sarah's room was the day they moved her furniture in a year ago. Why hadn't he been up here? No wonder things were tense. He would have felt more comfortable going to a hospice patient's bedside in a crowded city hospital than his own daughter's bedroom.

He cursed himself for his lousy parenting.

Butch stood outside her room. A *Hamilton* poster decorated the front. When did she become interested in musicals?

> Dear Lord, I have failed. I want to be a better daddy to my daughter, and through the voice of strangers you have rebuked me. Please forgive me and help me not to fail again. I want to make things right. In Jesus' Name. Amen.

He felt better after the prayer. He always did. Except that one time.

The knock on the door was louder than he intended it to be. Must be nerves.

"Go away, you toad." Sarah screamed it through the door.

"Excuse me?"

The door opened quickly.

"Sorry, Dad. I thought you were Paul. He's been pestering me all day and I'm in here trying to finish *Cry, The Beloved Country* before Wednesday."

"Oh, I understand. But Paul is at the park." He looked down at the floor and returned his eyes to her.

She looked at him, her eyes telegraphing confusion, screaming, "What are you doing here?"

He stammered a bit. "Do you like the book?" He shifted in the doorway. He noticed she hadn't invited him into her room. "It is one of my favorites."

"You've read it?" Sarah's eyebrows raised in surprise.

40

"Sure. It's a classic. The way it describes the plight of people trapped in the gears of society—the gears holding them down—yet who have hope— is encouraging and inspiring. It is also a fair representation of the struggle we Christians have in trying to work out our faith, live our faith, in the face of such systemic gears of oppression and control." He cleared his throat, "They also made a movie about it back in the fifties, starring Sidney Poitier."

Sarah tilted her head sideways. "How do you defeat evil?"

Butch cleared his throat. "Don't ask a hard one or anything."

"I suppose it's a hard one, but you've been fighting evil your whole life, so I figure you're an expert. How do you defeat it? Surely you know."

"The best answer is our beliefs guide our actions. If we focus on the evil, then the evil wins. If we focus on ourselves, then the evil wins. But if we focus on our beliefs and who we believe in, evil doesn't have a chance." He paused for a moment. "We can't beat evil. We can only be tools through which evil is defeated."

Sarah, standing in the doorway before her father, slid her hands into her back pockets. "In the book, it feels as though Kumalo is going through the motions, though. And what is it with the father? He is wandering around haplessly moving from one tragedy to another?"

Pain tremored through him. He said, "Well, that is how most parents feel. We don't always know what to do. The Dad loves his sister—I can't remember her name—and he loves his son. His name is Absalom, right?"

Sarah nodded her head.

"You realize Absalom's name is chosen on purpose." The conversation had not gone where he intended. It had turned troublesome and was heading toward danger.

"Sure, Dad. It is from the Bible. Right?"

"Yes, but you know why the author – Paton, right? —you know why he probably picked this specific name from the Bible, from all the names in the world? Do you know who Absalom was?"

"Wasn't he one of David's sons?"

"Yes. He was David's son—the brightest and the best. But he, or perhaps it was his father, let bitterness, injustice, and violence overtake their father/son relationship and they ended as enemies. Absalom died in a rebellion against his dad."

"Maybe it was both their fault? David and Absalom were both to blame." Sarah walked back into her room and sat down on her bed.

Butch felt this discussion was not about Paton or the Davidic

41

dynasty any longer, and they both knew it. He took a gamble and entered her bedroom. He sat down on the roller chair at her desk. He noticed her MacBook was powered on and she'd been taking notes from the book. A certain academic pride swelled up in him. In many ways, she reminded him of himself. Always studying something. Eager. Ambitious. Hungry.

Butch took a deep breath, sighed and brought his hands together in his lap. "Sarah, every parent feels lost sometimes. There is no guidebook on what to do, and there is no one to teach us in the middle of things. When it hurts us, we mask the pain away and pretend it isn't there. I wonder if that is not what the father in Paton's book did. He knew his son was troubled growing up, but he pretended it wasn't real. Later, when the son grew up, it was too late."

Sarah attacked. "Is that why you never even talked to me after Roberto died? One of my friends sliced his wrist in the middle of a weird pentagram, and you never said a word to me directly about it. Why? Why are you always there for everyone else in the whole world—if Mrs. Such-and-Such has a loose bowel movement you're in the car right away to go pray for her to recover. But not me. I'm in the deepest agony, and I get nothing from the great and mighty Pastor Butch. Only silence. Never-ending silence."

She flushed red. She wasn't screaming, as her mother would have, and as he would have expected. She was calm and pointed in her words. Measured. The same way she'd practiced them in front of a mirror. Butch had an ancient memory of practicing a similar speech once in the mirror toward his own father not long after Shark died. How had he let this happen to him and his Sarah?

He was about to answer her accusation with a weak apology, but she turned on him again. "It's not fair. I needed you and you were not there. I hear all the time about how you're a great spiritual healer— how you helped the church heal old wounds, rescued the little girl, or fought off crazy church ladies masquerading as domestic terrorists, but we get your leftovers, and this time I didn't even get leftovers. Not even a crumb!" Sarah's arms spun in motion as she spoke. "Mom won't say anything to you because she is the charter member of your fan club, and Paul is too young to notice. He will someday. Someday soon he will figure out where he sits in the grand scheme of things. He will realize the position he holds is somewhere behind the property committee and whatever mean old lady is being rushed to the hospital tonight. We all know where we stand with you, and it's not high."

The rebuke was brutal. All these years he'd thought Sarah and Paul were protected. Here, with stinging acumen, his daughter told him he'd failed in that endeavor. He hadn't protected them; he'd isolated them. Abandoned them. Minimized them. Taken them for granted.

Butch rose from his chair. His eyes were dry. Oh, how he wished he could cry, but he'd reached a sadness deeper than tears. He told his daughter, "I'm sorry. What more can I say? I didn't mean to. I thought I was doing the right things." He turned around and walked toward the door. He turned back toward Sarah and said, "I really am sorry." He stared at her, looking for a sign of hope. She drew a breath, raised up her head, and brought her lips together as if she were going to say something—to offer a healing balm, an olive branch, a bridge for relationship, a kind word, or perhaps another salvo to kick him while he was down. But nothing. She said nothing. She looked down at her bed, rejecting her father's pathetic face. Butch heard her silence, and it sliced his soul.

He left her room wondering if he'd ever be able to be a father to her again.

VI

It was some time later when Butch opened the backdoor and walked down the steps toward the giant green trash bin. The garbage bag from the kitchen was only half-full, but he didn't want the smell of salmon in the house. He was on his way back up the stairs when he caught whiff of a different odor. It was a familiar stench that warned of the presence of an old friend. Butch walked back down the steps to the backyard. He followed his nose around the corner, knowing exactly who would be there.

Wyoming Wallace gave no greeting. "Koi, huh?" The failing daylight caught the cigar smoke's blue hue, creating an otherworldly aura. "You know the birds and the neighborhood cats will eat all your fish."

"Actually, I hadn't thought so far along yet," Butch said as he sat down beside the smoke encased figure. "Tell me, Wyoming, when did you become an expert on backyard gardening?"

"I'm not an expert. What I do know is fish are easy targets. If you're lucky, maybe you'll see a bald eagle swoop down and eat one of your pets."

Butch said, "To see it would almost be worth the effort, then, I think."

"Yeah, it would." Wyoming said. "Predators, true predators, are something to behold. You never see them coming. They attack with a swift violence impossible to prepare for or mimic. The suddenness of their action undermines the fact they've been planning the moment of attack for some unknown amount of time. Sitting. Waiting. Plotting. Preparing. Creeping. Easing. Looking. At the perfect time, they fly in out of the sky, jump out of the woods, or pop out of the ground. The whole thing is over before the victim even knows what happened."

Butch could only see Tommy Bothers in his mind's eye.

The two men sat, neither talked. Wyoming smoked. Butch smoldered.

Butch hadn't seen Wyoming since he'd been terminated from Sydney Community. They had swapped texts two or three times, and Wyoming knew what happened, but he was off on some business in Florida.

Butch trusted Wyoming. If pushed, he'd even admit he loved Wyoming. He also knew he needed Wyoming. Yet, when he thought about it, it surprised Butch how little he knew about his tough-guy friend. After all this time, he had no idea what it was Wyoming Wallace did for income, what all his trips were for, or how Wyoming always turned up at the right time. He always thought to ask, but somehow never did.

There, in the darkening back yard, Butch reasoned in his heart and mind he probably didn't want to know the answer to the questions, which is why he'd never asked. It was one of many peculiarities of their relationship. Wyoming Wallace was a mystery Butch felt he might not ever solve. He assumed Wyoming wanted it that way.

A part of the enigma of Wyoming was figuring out what he was really talking about. He didn't know how long his friend had been sitting in his backyard, or even if his friend knew he'd eventually come outside to take out the trash. He did know, though, the language about the predator was not a nature lecture. Something else was on his friend's mind. The real question Butch had to answer was whether he would pick that brain or let the thoughts stuffed deep inside it slowly bleed out with each painfully slow word Wyoming spoke.

"It is good to see you," Butch finally said. "How was your trip to Florida?"

"It was profitable." Each word was a slow-moving cloud drifting through the air.

The sun fell behind the horizon. The normal gray which covered the heavens during the springtime over West Sound had been replaced with unseasonably clear skies. God's black canvas rolled out from the east toward the west as the last rays of sunshine slid behind the Olympic Mountains. Butch had a shuddering thought—was the sun setting on his ministry, and was Wyoming Wallace the messenger? Was he the prey to the predator's swift action?

Butch shoved the thought away like a child pushes an unwanted toy. He knew that wasn't true.

"What is on your mind?" Butch asked.

"Do you remember the day we first met?"

Butch held his breath for a beat. How could he forget the day they met? He and Amber had stood on Wyoming's porch asking for help; they received none. What they got instead was bullied. Butch considered reminding Wyoming of the threats he'd hurled at them. He decided now might not be the time. Instead, he played along, knowing Wyoming's introspection was going somewhere.

"Yeah, I remember. It was back in 2012 when we were looking for Tamara Rey. Amber knew you from around town. She introduced us on your front porch. Your dog tried to eat me."

"Olalla hates you." Wyoming laughed. It was a true laugh, not a forced conversational grin done out of politeness. When the laugh faded, a frown came back to Wyoming. "It is hard for me to believe it was that long ago. Has Amber been dead so long?"

"I'm afraid she has." Butch frowned. He wished Wyoming hadn't used the word dead.

The porch light came on and interrupted the dark thoughts in the backyard. Lucy stepped out of the house opposite from where they were, the side Butch had come down originally with the garbage. "Butch, where are you?"

He looked at Wyoming, shrugged, and shouted, "I'm over here, Hon."

"What in blue blazes are you doing out here? It doesn't take a person this long to take the trash out—" Lucy was full tilt as she came around the corner of the house toward the backyard right up until she saw Wyoming sitting in the chair beside her husband. She shifted gears. "Well hello, Wyoming. Butch, why didn't you tell me he was here? Are you hungry? Want some coffee or tea? We've finished dinner, but there were plenty of leftovers. I've got baked salmon, green beans, some of those delicious Hawaiian rolls, and mashed potatoes. I've even got a cookie if you want it."

"No thanks," Wyoming's sheepish grin showed a tinge of embarrassment.

45

Telepathy is the best word to describe what happened next. Butch reached out, not in a mystical way, or at least not for him, and did what couples who've been together a long time do. He spoke to her without words. The bridge on his nose crunched up. His lips pursed. His eyes narrowed. He tilted his head to the left. These were all unconscious maneuvers that told his wife he was in the midst of a serious conversation. His look gave her a complete dossier on the mood. It told her Wyoming was in full Wyoming mode. It also intimated to her she was welcome to stay, but she needed to turn the cheer down. His glance wasn't a rude look or an upset expression. It was an update on the situation which Lucy needed if she was to handle it properly. He said it all without ever opening his mouth.

Lucy received the message, and for a moment Butch thought she would politely dismiss herself and go back into the house. She didn't, though. She stayed, and he welcomed her presence. Now things were getting interesting.

A clash of someone's trashcan lid and the loud curse word that went along with it echoed around them. Dim headlights along with the hum of a small car went down the alley behind them. Mrs. Evan's mastiff barked. None of them spoke. Butch couldn't tell if it was relaxing or eerie. He decided it was both.

Directly overhead came the call of an owl. The sound of the nocturnal hunter snapped Wyoming back into the moment.

"Do you remember, Reverend, how I told you it was a dream? It was a dream about Iraq?" His words came at an excruciatingly slow pace, typical of Wyoming when he was thinking.

"Yes, I do. You said it was a dream about the little girl."

"Exactly. It was about the little girl who was at the wrong place at the wrong time. No one meant to hurt her, but she ended up a casualty of war anyway."

"Are you feeling guilty again?"

"No. Well, not anything new." Wyoming waved his hand. "I suppose I will go to my grave with guilt on me. You've helped me work through most of it, and I appreciate that. I know it wasn't my fault specifically. I think I've finally accepted it wasn't anyone's fault. It is just one of those things. But I will always carry her with me. Her face, her broken and bloodied body. Those will never leave me. Neither will what Amber whispered on the pier as she looked over into the other side."

He took a long pull on his stogie. "But that's not what I'm wanting you to focus on. Remember the dream? I told you it was a dream, but it was also different. In the dream, I wasn't reliving moment by moment what happened. I was outside of it. Watching it. And I wasn't only me in the dream, somehow I was different people." He stuck his cigar between his teeth, lifted his ball cap off his head, and ran his hand through his curly hair. "Reverend, I was her. I felt the bullet. I heard the confusion inside her brain. The questions. She didn't understand what happened. Do you remember me telling you?"

Butch's stomach churned. "Yes, I remember."

"Well, I'm having dreams again, but different."

"How different?" Lucy scooted the chaise lounge she was in toward him. She put her hand on Wyoming's shoulder as she probed.

"I don't know." He sighed. Butch had never heard despair come from his friend before. "In the dream, I am somewhere far off, but near. I can't explain it. I am wandering, looking."

"Is it from your past?" Lucy leaned in more.

"No, it is somewhere I've never been before. It looks the same as here, but different. It feels like it is here, but I don't recognize it."

"Here?" Now it was Butch's turn to lean in. "You mean Sydney?"

"Yeah, Sydney—Western Washington—Sometimes it seems like it is even in your backyard or on your neighborhood streets. It feels familiar."

"Our backyard?" Lucy sat upright, removing her hand from Wyoming's shoulder.

"There is a koi pond there, too, but your house is not there. At least I haven't been there yet. It is hard to tell. When I wake up it is hard to remember. Each dream was a brick in my hand that suddenly turned to sand and sifted through my fingers. The memories of the dreams are solid, but they disappear grain by grain."

Butch asked, "How long have you been having these dreams?"

"The first one was the night those jackals at your church fired you."

"I didn't tell you about it until a week after it happened."

"I know. Weird? I knew before I knew. But a different kind of knowing. Since then I've only had one ever so often, until this week. I've dreamed this kind of stuff for the last five nights."

"Wyoming," Lucy said, "tell us more about these dreams. Are you alone in the dream? What are you doing? I know sometimes when I dream, I have emotions I remember after. Do you remember how you felt?"

Wyoming grunted. "I wake up lost. I feel detached and disconnected." He scratched his beard. "I'm not afraid in the dream, but I am worried. It is not the same dream over and over. Each one is different. But I always get the feeling I'm looking for something or someone."

It was a moment of insight Butch later regretted, because it couched the situation too neatly. However, the truth remained. He asked Wyoming, "In the dream, were you the predator or the prey?"

"Good question, Reverend."

"You mean you don't know?" Lucy pulled her legs under her bottom and brought her sweater around her midsection, stuffing her arms inside it against the chill. "It strikes me you would know, one way or another, whether you were hunting or being hunted."

"Me too," Wyoming said. "Only two or three times in my life have I felt I was the one personally being targeted. Once was with those crazy ladies a couple of years back. Remember?"

"We remember," Butch and Lucy said in unrehearsed unison.

Wyoming grinned.

"You know, almost always in every situation of my life, I am the one doing the hunting. That is how it was in Florida a month ago, down in Texas last summer, and over Christmas in Maine. I am the hunter. But in these dreams, it feels different. Something is missing."

Butch rubbed his chin. "If we talk about your dreams from a classic psychological perspective, it is pretty easy to evaluate. You're at a point in life where you are ready to make a transition, to add more to your existence and experiences. There is a natural desire inside most people, including you, to be a part of a family with a wife, children, steady home, and friends. You almost had it with Jennifer, but you let her slip away because you weren't ready to commit. By nature, you're a loner. Those loner ways have served you well. Now, though, deep inside there is a longing for something else. The dreams feel 'here but not here' and are a desire to be somewhere else but maintain your liberty. The uncertainty is your fear. You could beat down a hundred tough guys in impossible situations with no sweat at all. By contrast, facing your own inadequacies as a human being terrifies you."

"I will not deny," Wyoming said, "the possibility some of what you are saying might be true. There is a part of me who wants to have what you and Lucy have. I do regret, often, the way things ended with Jennifer. I loved her. I don't know what went wrong."

Lucy said, "She knows you love her, but you wouldn't let yourself be loved. A relationship is about being vulnerable. Vulnerable is not something you wear well."

"Perhaps," Wyoming said. He hesitated. He turned to look at Lucy, and back to Butch. His eyes were focused. His face set in an intensity few living people have seen from Wyoming. "But neither of you understand what I am saying. I am not saying I am dreaming normal dreams. I am saying I am going there. It is real."

"Define real, please." Lucy tilted her head sideways.

"I mean, it is something somewhere occurring, in real time. I don't know the right word for it."

"Parallel?" Lucy asked. "Is your dream parallel to us?"

"Sorta, but that isn't exactly right either. It is more overlaid than parallel. You know, on top of it. Parallel lines run alongside each other, but do not occupy the same space. I get the feeling, in my dream I am occupying the same space, but perhaps not at the same time."

Butch felt lost in this conversation. The intensity his wife had for it piqued his curiosity. Did he know her at all? This woman he'd shared life, a home, and a family with all these years amazed him. Who was she? What other secrets did she keep from him?

Lucy raised her eyebrows, "You say you've had this more than once?"

"Yes, many times. And now it is every night."

"What are you thinking?" Butch asked Lucy.

"I'm not sure yet. When Wyoming first started, I wondered if he was experiencing some kind of hypnagogia. But the more I listen to him, I don't perceive that is what is happening. Not exactly, anyway."

"What is hypnagogia?" Butch asked.

Wyoming nodded.

"It is the moment when you first wake up but you're not fully awake. It is this state of sleep some people feel their dreams are more real or lucid. Medication, stress, or anxiety can add to this. Sometimes, it is so strong people hallucinate. Hypnagogia is such a strong phenomenon, some have speculated it is usually where most alien abduction stories originate. It is simply a hypnagogic hallucination." Lucy brought her hands down to her knees and straightened her back. "But this isn't what Wyoming is experiencing. This has more to do with the Lord."

"The Lord?" Butch almost shouted the question. He realized this, and so brought his tone down. "In what way?"

"This is spiritual." Lucy pointed at Wyoming. "At least, it is my opinion this is spiritual. These things are always hard to know for certain because it is nebulous. But I firmly believe something mystical is happening when Wyoming closes his eyes to sleep."

Butch shook his head. "No, probably not. This is probably only a dream. Dreams are random and unexplainable neurological activities of the brain." Butch felt a tremor down his leg. He knew it was the Holy Spirit reminding him about some of his dreams in the past. But he ignored it. He didn't want to do this anymore. Pushing down on his very soul, he quenched that feeling and said, "Don't overanalyze things, Lucy."

"You're a fine one to talk, Mr. Pastor-Man."

Wyoming almost choked on his cigar laughing as Lucy ripped into her husband.

Butch raised his hands shoulder high in surrender. "Yes, ma'am."

The moon was up now. Three quarters of it lit the heavens. The light cascaded over them. The owl called again. This time it sounded closer.

"I assume you are not pregnant, Wyoming Wallace?"

"Lucy!" Butch shouted.

"No," was all Wyoming said.

"I didn't think so, but these days, you know, you can't be too sure." She reached over and patted Wyoming kindly on the hand. "I'm teasing. But the truth is pregnant women often have crazy dreams. What's more, some women have dreams when they are pregnant which come true."

Butch stroked his chin, "You mean prescient?"

"No, that is not what I meant at all, and you're using the word prescient incorrectly in this context. If you mean is it predictive, yes. I have a cousin, Cecilia who lives down in Coos Bay. She has four children, and with each one she had such vivid dreams when she was pregnant, she would wake up every morning and write them down. For each child she predicted hair color, eye color, gender—long before ultrasounds were as sharp and clear as they are now—she even knew and recorded what month the child would start walking." Lucy shivered. "She had a fifth pregnancy, but they lost that child in the third month due to a miscarriage. She still dreams about it. The child is a boy whom she named Eli. He has brown hair, green eyes, and likes red popsicles."

"Reverend, is this true?" Wyoming's said.

Butch opened his arms, palms up. "I've never heard the bit about the dreams before. Lucy's cousin does live in Coos Bay, Oregon, and she does have four grown children. About fifteen years ago, she miscarried her fifth child. I can confirm those details." Butch looked at his wife, "I've never heard about the dreams, though, or this dreamscape log she's kept. These are details in the story previously hidden from me."

It was Lucy's turn to be incredulous. "Women talk. I wasn't hiding it from you, dear sweet husband-of-mine. I knew you would respond the way you are right now, with cynicism and doubt. Men don't believe in certain things women know to be true. God talks to us in different ways and more often than he does to you narrow-minded men. All us gals know it. We all talk, and we never tell you."

"Reverend," Wyoming took a long drag, "I believe she just called us a couple of knuckle-dragging mouth breathers."

"You're right, my fellow Neanderthal. Maybe we should leave now and kill a couple of wooly mammoths or a saber-toothed tiger then go draw on a cave or two."

"Look," Lucy wasn't exactly protesting their accusation, but she was not about to be minimized, "I'm not saying that at all. What I am saying is women are differently connected and differently wired to the Lord and to spiritual things than most men are. Some believe it is hormonal. You wouldn't believe the kind of things that happen to some women when they get their first period."

Butch and Wyoming both made a grunt in reaction to what Lucy said.

"See. This is what I'm talking about. You men don't want to hear certain things." She paused and continued. "Others believe it has something to do with the chromosomal makeup of women or it might be in the brain. But whatever you do with the reasoning of it, the truth—and I mean truth, Wyoming Wallace—is women are more mystical and more spiritual than men are. We often perceive the world differently."

"But he's not a woman," Butch said.

"Thanks for the ringing endorsement of manhood." Wyoming stared at Butch. "So far, we've established I am not pregnant, and I am not a woman. This is a banner night for me." Wyoming flicked his cigar nub across Butch's patio and into the neighbor's yard. The orange glow streaked in the night the way a meteor flames out in the atmosphere of the earth as it plummets from the heavens. It reached apogee over the cedar fence. Gravity pulled it back until it thudded against a rhododendron. Embers ejected from it in every direction as the butt fell to earth and died atop a thin layer of beauty bark.

Lucy said, "My point, Wyoming, is I believe your dreams are not dreams in the traditionally accepted sense. I believe, from what you're telling us and from when they started, these dreams are something else besides normal sleep activity. Something important, even. Given your

51

history with God, and the way he has used you, and how, for reasons clear to me and Butch, it should be assumed Jesus has a unique plan for your life. You are his instrument; therefore, it is logical to assume there is something else going on with these dreams."

"But what?" Wyoming sighed.

"Sometimes, in our dreams, we are solving problems. Many, many times I have gone to bed thinking about a problem with no apparent solution. I wake up knowing the answer. The brain works when we don't know it is, and sometimes it works better if we get out of the way. Sleep appears to be an active time for our subconscious self rather than a dormant time. Dreams have important work to do."

"But I'm not aware of any problem to speak of. There is nothing particularly bothering me."

"Not true," Lucy did not hesitate. "When you found out about Butch's problem, it became your problem. The subconscious kicked into overdrive. You and Butch are bound together by the Lord. It is like family, but in a way, it is deeper than family. Your experiences, your losses, and your callings have woven you together. When he was in trouble, you felt it."

"I can see that, and you're right." Wyoming leaned forward and put his head in his hands.

Butch was content to remain quiet, for now.

"When we sleep, the brain also processes information. It's why students who are studying for a test should look over their notes before they go to bed. The brain does much of the work for them while they sleep. Part of your dreams could be you processing something. Of course, I don't know what your dreams are and so far, you've been so vague it is hard to analyze them."

"I don't mean to be vague, but it is difficult to explain. The way I feel—no feel is not quite the right word. It is more see, but I also know." Wyoming spit on the ground. "I am walking around Sydney, except, there is no traffic. The roads are more like trails. The homes and buildings are shadowy—everything is in a heavy fog until you walk up to it. But it is not fog as we normally understand it. It's a fuzzy picture. But when you walk up to something, it clears up. In these dreams, I'm never at my house, though, I'm always wandering around. I am looking for something. Or maybe I'm lost."

"Not all who wander are lost." Butch said. "And not all that glitters is gold." Butch looked at his wife shaking his head, "And when did you become Sigmund Freud?"

"Not exactly Freud." Lucy tilted her head sideways. "Freud was

52

more into symbolic representation in dreaming. But to answer your question of when, after the horrible incident with Tamara and Amber, and the way both of you spoke about dreams and visions, I did some research. That was when I pieced together stories I'd heard from my family, from church people, and from friends. Take Becky, for instance."

"You mean Becky Springer?"

"That's the one. A couple of years ago, she and I were talking at a church picnic—it was Labor Day. She told me she kept having these startling dreams that woke her up every night. Of course, I followed the trail and discovered she kept dreaming about her child being in a fatal car wreck. She said it upset her so badly she called him in Virginia where he was working and asked if everything was okay. Everything was, so she let it go and tried to stop worrying about it. Yet, the dreams kept coming."

Butch said, "You're not about to say what I think you're about to say, because I remember."

"I am," Lucy said. "Exactly eleven days after she and I talked her husband, Donald, was killed in a horrific car accident going through Snoqualmie Pass on his way back from a business trip in the Tri-Cities area."

"You never told me that part. No one did." Butch sat back in his chair, stunned. "I mean, I did Donald's funeral. I spoke with Becky, her children, and everyone as we prepared and planned. I prayed with them. I cried with them. But no one ever said anything about the dreams. I can't believe Becky wouldn't have told me about something like that."

"We usually don't." There was an edge to her words. "We know we are not taken seriously, and we know every excuse under the sun will be given other than simply believing us."

"Wait a minute, though. I've got to work on this." Wyoming Wallace pulled out another cigar from the inside pocket of his blue jean jacket. As his Zippo clinked open, he said in an interminable, slow way, "She dreamed about the kid in a crash, but he was fine. It was her husband who died in the crash? Something doesn't exactly make sense to me. Why would the dream get it wrong?"

Wyoming was looking at Butch when he asked the question, but Butch shook his head. "You take this one, Honey. You can answer it better than me."

Lucy nodded at her husband. "Yes, I can. Dreams can be predictive, I believe, but they are also ambiguous and vague.

53

Sometimes what they record is something similar to the event, but not the exact event. They are not precise reflections of reality."

"Why?"

"Good question, Wyoming." Lucy's left leg bobbled, and the speed of her words came faster. "The answer, as I understand it, is about the unseen reality around us. The spiritual side—whatever that exactly is— interacts with our own psyche which in this understanding is not to be confused with the soul. I'm talking about our unconscious self, a part of our biology. So, in Becky's case, she was getting 'car crash' from the dream, but her greatest fears are about her children, so, in the place where our heart intersects with our head, she interpreted 'car crash' as being about her son. It is not that the dream was wrong, or the spiritual touch was wrong, but the way her brain handled the information from inside her, moving it through her own unique mélange of fallibilities, weaknesses, fears, hopes, and defects. Butch and all his theological friends would say this is the evidence of the fall of humanity. God made us to connect this spiritual side of our dreams and subconscious self in a more perfect way with the Lord, but because sin and our own weaknesses have entered in, we don't often handle it correctly." Lucy paused to catch her breath. She said, "We do the same thing, I think, with our emotions. The data is before us, but our emotions often interpret it in a skewed way. The result is we don't logically see all we should or assess the information properly. Sometimes the result is confirmation bias. If you already believe something, you will inevitably understand anything that happens filtered through your belief system regardless of what the facts are actually saying."

Butch added, "In the same way, we don't handle the scriptures the way we should, either. We always run those through our own fallibilities, fears, and weaknesses. It is a fault inevitably leading to misunderstanding and problems."

Time ceased. The three of them sat in the moon-bathed backyard. Listening. Breathing. Thinking.

The owl called again. Her perch was now in the alder tree over their heads. The tire swing Sarah and Paul had played in as little children swung from the lowest branch.

VII

"Where are you going?" Sarah called to Jessica from across the

54

hall.

"Nowhere." Jessica's cheeks blushed as she put her head down.

"Liar!" Sarah said as she walked up alongside her friend. "Your eyes always shift to the left when you are lying."

"They don't," Jessica shouted.

"They do. You've always done it for as long back as I can remember—all the way back to Mrs. Johnson's class in fourth grade. I noticed it when you'd have candy in your lunch. If I asked if I could have a piece, you'd say 'no' but your eyes would dart away and then you'd always have candy on the playground later."

Jessica glared at Sarah and whispered a crude phrase at her friend.

"So, where are you going?" Sarah asked again.

"Fine. If you must know, I'm going to see Mr. Raba."

"Yuck! He gives me the creeps." Sarah feigned vomiting. "There is something about him that bothers me."

"It's all in your head."

"No . . ." Sarah stopped walking and grabbed her friend. "It's in your head. You're the one going to see the psychology teacher."

"Ha-ha" Jessica replied, clearly not humored by Sarah's joke.

Sarah tilted her head sideways, "Did you do something wrong? Are you in trouble? Do you have to do some more make-up work?"

"No, I want to ask him a question. You remember yesterday, in class he talked about Freud, and Jung, and psychoanalysis?"

"Again?" Sarah said. "Didn't you go see him last week?"

"No," Jessica said. "But I should have. Last week he talked about how the brain sometimes fills in gaps to deceive us and make us think things happen when they really don't, and how this is why people remember the same events differently. Remember how he told us it explained why even eyewitness testimony to something isn't foolproof. Wasn't it interesting?"

"Wow, Jessica. You've taken to this psychology thing. You usually watch cat videos during class. And that," Sarah's eyes opened wide in mock surprise, "is why you have a solid C average in AP History, Pre-Calculus, and English Lit."

Sarah was only partly kidding. Her friend's lack of scholarship or devotion to academics disturbed Sarah. Jessica wasn't stupid or dumb. Her problem was laziness. She didn't study. She never had.

Sarah, on the other hand, loved psychology, but she didn't like the teacher, Mr. Raba, or as most students called him, The Rab.

"I'm thinking about majoring in psychology in college." Jessica started walking again.

"You mean, if you get into college?" Sarah felt a twinge of guilt at her indulgence in the conceit of the joke. She should be encouraging her friend, not ridiculing her. Jessica needed her support. She didn't need her sarcasm. Especially now. Especially without Roberto. She hated how she sometimes didn't know when to let a joke go. Sarah had a flashing memory of her father and the way he always put people at ease. He could make the most miserable soul comfortable. The words he spoke, the way he stood, his posture when he sat, the look in his eyes, how he put his hand on someone's shoulder—it all made people feel better. She'd seen him do it a thousand times. She wished she'd had the same ability to be comfortable with people. But she didn't, and because she didn't, her anger sparked at him all over again. Why did he have to be so perfect?

The two students came to a T-junction in the hallway.

Sarah said, "Well, have fun with the sketchy Rab. I'm gonna watch the boys' varsity baseball practice. I love to look at them warm up. Especially Josh Fairbanks. Why don't you come with me, instead?"

"Nah, this is a conversation I need to have." Jessica's chest tingled with craving.

"Suit yourself," Sarah said. She gave Jessica an air kiss and turned right toward the baseball diamond while Jessica turned left toward the science wing.

Jessica saw The Rab through the window in the door. He was at his desk working on his computer. She took a deep breath as she opened the door. "Do you have a minute?" Jessica said. She stood in the doorway with expectant eyes. Her body physically arched before it swayed toward the man sitting at the desk in the middle of the room.

The Rab looked up and flashed a perfect smile. His olive skin and curly black hair made her weak at the knees. She was drawn to him like a moth to the flame. He was too old for her, of course, but she'd told herself there was nothing wrong with an innocent crush. So what if his Middle-Eastern features and charismatic personality were such a turn on? What did it matter?

"Sure," he said, closing his laptop. "What is on your mind?"

Jessica sat down in the chair he kept on the opposite side from his desk. She plopped her heavy backpack down onto the green tiled floor. "Well, this is kinda embarrassing, and I don't even know where to start."

"How about you just say it, put it out there, and we'll go from there. Nothing to be embarrassed about here. Embarrassment is society's tool to keep people mired in their guilt and shame. Religions use shame and guilt, but this is a room dedicated to science."

Jessica smiled. "Okay." She looked down at her shoes and pushed her ginger hair back behind her ears. "I found yesterday's class interesting—you know, about dreams and what different people say they mean and how we should interpret them." She paused and looked up at The Rab. His eyes affirmed her. They told her to keep going; there would be no judgment here. His eyes told her this wasn't church where you had to watch everything you say. This wasn't home where your parents might turn your own words against you. This wasn't friends who will scorn and mock you behind your back. This wasn't the mirror, which told her she was flawed and ugly. His eyes told her this was a safe place. He was a safe person and he only wanted to help her discover who she was. His eyes told her no one understood her the way he did. The Rab cared about her. This knowledge gave her the courage to continue. With each sentence, she felt more and more comfortable with him. She belonged with him. He knew her in a way no one else on earth did or ever had. Not even Roberto. His eyes, large and dark, roamed the vast expanse of Jessica's mind. She belonged with him. She belonged to him.

Jessica squeezed out another giggle. She said, "I found it interesting because of the material we covered, but because—I've been dreaming weird things lately. I don't know if they are dreams which everyone has or if something is wrong with me."

The Rab sat back in his chair and folded his hands in his lap. "In your dreams, are you falling? That sometimes means a person has a fear of failure. You are at a time of your life when failure could be on your mind and your subconscious is processing it. Are you dreaming you are late for class, or taking a test you haven't studied for? Many high-quality students such as yourself have these types of dreams as they near the end of their high school career and get ready for college. In fact, I have variations on that dream now and again. Is it any of these?"

"No, it is not those."

"Hmmm." The Rab gave Jessica a thin smile. "Are you dreaming you don't have any clothes on?"

"No," a school-girl giggle came from her mouth. Her eyes finally broke from his as she looked down at the floor again and brought her left hand up to her mouth.

"Are you sure?" The Rab said. "Those are common dreams," he chuckled. He finished the thought with a suggestive tone. "Given the right circumstances, those are the kinds of dreams which can be fun."

57

Jessica's pulse quickened. The Rab's flirtations excited her, and she scooted restlessly in her chair. She nibbled the right corner of her bottom lip.

The Rab didn't respond to any of her overt physical cues, as he continued. "Let me ask a harder question, Jessica." Her eyes found his again; they were as deep as the Pacific. "Are you dreaming about Roberto, because that would be perfectly understandable? We often dream about what we've lost, especially when the loss is a tragedy."

The question stung.

"No-no." She leaned back, putting her hands in her lap. Shifting her weight, she said "I do miss him, but the dreams are not about him." She paused, "I suppose I should feel guilty, shouldn't I? If I loved him, I should be dreaming about him. Maybe if I'd loved him enough, he would be alive today. True love could have kept him from killing himself, right?"

"It's not your fault," The Rab said. "I understand why you might say that, but it is not your fault. Remember, there is no guilt or shame here. However, as to the original statement, I confess my interest is piqued. I'm having no luck guessing what you're dreaming, so would you please be kind enough to end my speculation and tell me what you perceive you are dreaming."

Jessica took a deep breath, her eyes locked on his. "I am somewhere like Sydney, but there are no people there I can see. I am all alone, but I can feel other people are near, as if they are in a different dimension from me. I know it sounds too *Stranger Things*-ish, but it's the best way to describe it."

The Rab said, "Don't worry about using whatever you need to describe your dream. I can't tell you how many times I dreamed variations on *The Matrix*. It is the way our brain works. It is possible you saw some episode on television, and your neurons and axons are using the paradigm from the show to help you discover something about yourself. This is how evolution has made us. Those big bulks of gray matter between our ears are mysterious marvels of natural selection."

Jessica giggled again. It made her feel so good to have someone tell her she was right, and nothing was wrong with her. She'd lived her life assuming she was broken and different. Being affirmed and accepted by such a great man as The Rab felt right. Very right.

"What are you doing or feeling in your dream?" The Rab asked.

"I don't know. I feel empty, but I also feel pressed for time. I've got to hurry to get through everything. There is some task I must complete, but I don't know what the task is. I am frightened in the dream."

"It's the future." The Rab folded his hands under his chin. "Emotionally, you're ready to be rid of Sydney High School and the fakery of high school life. That is the task you feel you need to hurry up with and complete." The Rab snapped his fingers simultaneously on his right and left hand, three times in quick succession. The snap was loud and vibrated off the sheetrock walls. The rhythmic echo transfixed Jessica. The spell he'd been weaving since she sat down had now taken hold. He caught her eyes again with his, and it was as though she stared into the wonders of the universe. She lost sense of herself, where she was, who she was, or when she was. Time and place evaporated into the ether of his persona. His words were not coming through her ears any longer, but into her mind. Through her eyes.

She could hear him inside her brain. "Jessica, you are afraid of the future and of what might be. But you don't have to be. You are smart, strong, and beautiful beyond compare. The silly girls who prattle on are beneath you. The boys who chase you are but gnats flying around your head. Trust in me and put your childhood away. I will help you become the woman you are meant to be—free from your parent's infantile superstitions—a strong woman—as strong as any woman in your generation—whole of mind, body, and soul. Give yourself to me, and I will teach you how to shine with the radiance of a thousand sunrises and exult in the freedom of a million erotic moons."

An electric thrill started in the base of her neck. It built momentum as it shot down her spine into the cradle where her womanhood remained secret. It was a feeling she'd never experienced. It startled her. Her breath quickened.

"I can give you everything you've ever wanted," The Rab said to her mind, sending another shiver of delight through her. "Do you enjoy it? Do you give yourself to me?" The two questions he spoke came into her mind but were one idea. He asked for her complete surrender to him. To sweeten the question, The Rab again gave her a warm caress from the inside out.

"Yes," she whispered through her trembling lips. Barely able to speak, she pushed the word from her mouth. Why wouldn't she, for he understood her. He knew. He knew her. To be known in that way was more than she could imagine. What more could she want in life than to know and be known, to feel this good?

Again, The Rab spoke directly to her mind. "Are you sure this is what you want? I need to be sure." As he queried her heart, he dimmed his charm and took some of the bliss he'd imparted to her. "Because if you don't want to, I can withdraw and leave you to figure out your dreams and fears by yourself. You can go back. You can be all alone again, if you want me to."

Panic jumped into her eyes as he diminished his psychic touch on her mind. "I'm going to leave you now, and you will not remember this conversation in your front brain, but in the back of your mind you will remember this moment. When you close your eyes tonight for sleep, you will long for the feeling only I can give you. You will crave me—crave this moment—crave these feelings. Longing will replace every other thought until you come see me again, and on that third time, you will willingly give yourself to me. You will do so because it is what you want. It is what you have always wanted. It is what you need, and I am the only one who can give you what you need." The Rab lowered his voice to a deep resonance below the human vocal register. "And we can be together, forever. Nothing will come between us. Do you understand what I am commanding you to do?"

"I do," She said as her breathing came back to normal, her eyes took on their healthy zeal, and the blush in her cheeks subsided.

The Rab snapped his fingers again, and when he did, Jessica was walking to her car in the far parking lot. She had no recent memories. She was confused by the missing time. The last thing she remembered was air kiss between Sarah and her in the hallway, and how she thought negatively about Sarah going to watch the boys practice baseball. She'd been going somewhere when it happened, but she couldn't remember where. Apparently, her mind had been preoccupied with thought—funny how the brain does that—puts you on autopilot while your brain works on other things.

Maybe next week I'll go see The Rab and talk about this kinda thing, about how complicated the brain is. Yes, The Rab is who I need to talk to. The Rab is who I need. The Rab has all the answers.

VIII

Ten days later, Sarah sat at the group table and worried. She was supposed to be helping the group build a presentation on Franklin Roosevelt's New Deal measures and then present an argument as to whether or not it was effective in dealing with the underlying causes of the Great Depression. The group had come to the conclusion Roosevelt's attempts were more about power grabbing than actually solving anything. Sarah loved these discussions. Except, today her heart was somewhere else.

Jessica was the only thing on her mind. It wasn't at all odd Jessica wasn't at school. She wasn't exactly famous for her attendance record. What was odd was she hadn't texted Sarah. When Jessica ditched classes, she would text Sarah all day long about what fun stuff she was doing, or how late she slept, or links to all the YouTube videos she was watching while lying in bed. On more than one occasion she had video called her from Pike's Market or the Tacoma Mall.

Not today.

Jessica wasn't at school, and Sarah's phone had been silent.

As soon as the 3:45 bell rang, Sarah headed to her car. She drove too fast to Jessica's house on the other side of town where all the rich kids lived. Panic climbed into her throat when she pulled into the driveway. Her hands were clammy. In her head, she could see Jessica in trouble, drowning in a choppy sea. There was no logical reason for Sarah to be afraid, but it was genuine.

Sarah ran around the house to the backyard. She burst through the patio door which she knew would be unlocked.

"Jessica," she cried out. "Jessica, are you here? I see your Mustang in the driveway." She looked around and saw nothing. She crossed through the TV room to the stairs. "Jessica! Jessica!" she shouted. When she got to the landing on the second floor, she heard the music.

Her knees buckled. Her left hand came up to her mouth.

"No, no, no!" she shouted. Her impulse was to run to Jessica's bedroom door, but again fear and panic took over. She wanted to run, but she could only manage a slow walk. She didn't want to see, but her mind betrayed her, and her spiritual eye saw water crashing over Jessica's head. She saw blood. She saw fire. She saw darkness.

She felt darkness.

She tasted blood.

She smelled fire.

She gasped to breath.

The closer she got to Jessica's door, the stronger she felt evil pressing against her nerves. She passed through a grotesque veil of pain that covered the hall. Every insecure thought she'd ever had taunted her. She felt ugly, alone, fat, and isolated. Negative emotions combined with doubt in new ways to remind Sarah she was different and being different was bad.

Sarah took a deep breath and rebuffed those feelings. This was 'it', whatever 'it' was, trying to keep her away from the door. She didn't have a name for 'it', but the ominous feelings felt personal nonetheless.

This was no general oppression she was feeling, the way she sometimes felt whenever she passed a homeless person on the street or saw photographs of malnourished children overseas. She was experiencing something specific and individual. It was a private attack designed uniquely for her. It knew her name and called her by it. Sarah shook her head in defiance. "No," she whispered. She put her hand on the doorknob to Jessica's bedroom.

That was when she felt the cold, slimy tentacle of malevolence wrap itself around her spine. She could feel it work through her body toward her brain. She no longer felt fear or inadequacy. She felt neediness. Every desire of her heart was laid bare. The darkness around Jessica's room wanted her. It wasn't trying to keep her away, it wanted her to belong to it. It called to her, whispering "Sarah" in her mind. It knew her.

Maybe it would be for the best to surrender. Why fight?

Sarah's soul was in its greatest despair. She wanted to give up. Every insecure thought from her life came to mind. She would never live up to her father's expectations, so why try? Her mother didn't understand her. No one did. Boys didn't notice her because of her plain looks. Jessica was her only friend, and Sarah already knew what Jessica had done on the other side of the door. The burden of living squeezed her.

Somehow her ears filled with babies crying in lands far away. Babies sitting beside the bodies of their mothers who had been executed for fun. She felt hunger's sting in a famine not caused by weather or pestilence, but by corrupt, greedy governments. She smelled flesh burning on the altar of war, fueled by hate. She whimpered as, for one fleeting moment, she experienced life through a girl trafficked by her family, sold into prostitution and pornography. Sarah heard the cry of people dying and moaning from disease in a place where the only comfort is the sweet release of death.

Life was meaningless. Only pain and atrocities remained. Her emotions plummeted.

Death was the only answer.

Darkness surrounded her. She physically, literally, couldn't see anything. She felt the slither of despair and death curling around her backbone settling into the base of her neck. At the moment of surrender, spiritual light flickered in her chest. It was a real light she saw with her eyes. She could feel the darkness wrapping her like a blanket, but now she could see the light. It flickered one more time, and pulsated. In the light's slow rhythm, she saw the gloom filling the hallway, and now she was bigger than the gloom. It did not, in fact, surround her or own her. It was quite the opposite; the gloom was small and petty, a mosquito fluttering around a potential victim.

Her hand on the doorknob, she screamed, "I will not give up!"

She turned the knob and opened the door.

What she found was not what she'd imagined. It was worse.

Jessica's body lay on the floor. Blood soaked into the white carpet, and the residue of life was absorbed by it to form a pattern that resembled an eyeball. A song played from the speaker. Sarah recognized it, and knew, as all the students at Sydney High had known, that it was the same song which had played in Roberto's room when he died.

Jessica was on her side, facing the door, with her legs twisted underneath her. It looked as though she had been kneeling. There was a tiny hole in her chest, right where her heart was. A gun was in her hand. Jessica's face was gray. Her eyes were opened wide, but her mouth had drawn in on itself. The light and beauty of youth were gone.

The girl who'd been her friend since kindergarten was dead. The hideous scene she beheld couldn't stop her from kneeling down and holding her friend. When she did, she realized Jessica's back was nearly severed. Later she regretted it, but she looked to her right and saw blood, bone, and what she was sure to be heart muscle stuck to the wall like a grotesque and cruel Jackson Pollock painting. Pieces of spine stuck into the sheetrock wall like partially hammered nails.

As her eyes moved from the wall to Jessica's corpse, she noticed the blue paint. She assumed it was paint, anyway. The paint formed a pentagram that surrounded Jessica's body. The circle around the pentagram was made from grains of salt.

"Why?" was all she could mumble. It was a rhetorical question. She knew the reasons why. Jessica was a victim. Life was cruel. Depression can be powerful. She knew the reasons. Yet even so, the question formed on her lips again. "Why?"

"Because I am the destroyer," came an answer so loud and clear Sarah jumped. The music became quieter under the boom of the voice. It was not an internal thought, like the ones she'd had in the doorway. It was audible. Her eyes darted around to find the owner of the deep voice, but she saw no one.

"She was mine," it said again. "And so are you, Sarah Gregory." The disembodied voice mocked her with laughter.

The song, stuck on repeat, started over again.

Sarah didn't hear the voice again that day. She told the paramedics she didn't know how long she had sat there on the floor holding Jessica's body. She only knew the song kept repeating until she found the wherewithal to pull her own phone from her pocket and called 911. After that, she texted her mom and dad.

Sarah sat in the swinging bench on Jessica's porch while a Blackjack County paramedic asked her questions about what she saw and how she found Jessica. By the time Butch and Lucy Gregory arrived, a police officer had sat down on the other side of Sarah and was taking notes and asking more questions. "What time did you get here? Why did you come? Had you and Jessica been fighting? Do you know anyone who would hurt Jessica? Was anyone else here?"

Those last two questions gave Sarah pause. The young woman was in a deep state of shock. Her eyes were swollen red from crying. Her breathing was irregular. Yet, she was aware enough that she couldn't tell the police officer something was in the house, and that something killed Jessica and was after her. They would cart her off in a straitjacket. She wasn't experienced in the world, but she'd seen *Girl, Interrupted*. She knew what happens when you're a girl and the system thinks you're crazy.

"No, officer. No one else was there in the house. I came in after school, like I've done a thousand times. Jessica wasn't at school today, so I was checking on her. I never dreamed anything like this could happen." Sarah's conscience pinged. The whole spiel was a lie. Something was in there. The exact reason she'd come to Jessica's house was because she was afraid something like this might have happened.

Butch and Lucy stood on a perfectly manicured front lawn, looking at their daughter. Two other Sheriff's deputies had caught them when they walked up and asked them to stay back while the officer asked questions. Butch protested at first, arguing his daughter was a minor and the officer had no right to question her so aggressively. Lucy calmed him down by holding his hand. They watched at a distance.

Not too much later, Jessica's mom and dad arrived. They had been at the country club playing a round of golf on this otherwise picturesque spring day. The weather had been gray and rainy for a week, but today the sun emerged from behind the haze and the temperature climbed to almost seventy degrees. Jessica's parents were avid golfers, and both had left work mid-morning, enjoyed elevenses, a large lunch, and a two o'clock tee time. It was one of many pleasures they took in life.

The carefree, pleasant afternoon turned to excruciating agony. An unearthly scream came from the silver Mercedes. Jessica's mom opened the door of the SUV and leapt out. She ran up the street, pushing aside EMTs and darting around emergency vehicles. She charged the stairs and through the front door. Her hallowed scream trailed behind her in one long, constant siren undulating up and down. Everyone knew when the wailing woman reached the top floor. It was apparent when she saw Jessica's corpse. The intensity of the howl increased tenfold.

In contrast, Jessica's father, Ben, marched in a slow and purposeful manner from his car. His head bowed, as one already moving toward the cemetery in his head. His face was pale. The Titleist visor on his brow and preppy Polo shirt with smart white shorts were a startling contrast to the morbid defeat scribbled across his face. Each step he took got heavier and heavier. He glared at Butch and Lucy when he walked by but didn't say anything or make any physical signs of recognition. He plodded onward through the doorway, up the stairs, until he reached the bedroom where his wife of twenty-five years pleaded for their dead daughter to wake up.

But Jessica would never wake up again. Her mother and father would never again see her smile or hear the sound of her voice.

The EMT's and deputies finally allowed Sarah to go to her parents. The three of them hugged there on the lawn for what felt to Sarah like three hours. She needed every second of the embrace to replace the spiritual and emotional trauma of the experience upstairs.

A clanking sound and the voices of people trying to be hushed but also needing to be heard broke the intensity of their hug. The six Gregory eyes looked up toward the house and saw the stretcher coming through the door along with a woman from the coroner's office. A person in the doorway, not coming through it, but behind it, halfway behind the door, inside the house, in the shadows, was talking on a cellphone. When Butch Gregory noticed this, he pointed with his eyes so that Lucy could see the man in the dark suit and sunglasses. Lucy didn't stare but got a good look. Sarah saw her parents share the moment and then formed a question with her face. Butch looked at his daughter and his eyes said, "Later."

Such was the nature of meaningful conversations in the Gregory household.

Moments later they were in Butch's car. "I wonder what the FBI was doing here, and so soon?" Butch said as he drove away from the flashing lights in the cul-de-sac with the house that used to be where Jessica lived. "It doesn't make sense an FBI agent would be on the scene of a teenage suicide." He scratched his head. "And so soon."

"Is that what the look was about?" Sarah said. She was rattled, but alert and aware of what was going on. It was helpful to her to talk about something procedural rather than the snuffed life of her dearest friend. "How do you know it was an FBI agent?"

Lucy turned her head toward the backseat to see her daughter. "We know. I wish we didn't, but we do."

"Federal agents stand out like sore thumbs pretty much everywhere they go," Butch said. "It is something Wyoming taught me. I've noticed it more often since he gave me the run down on how to spot them. Last year, at the annual Christmas Tree lighting downtown by the old Harbor House, I spotted at least four agents in the crowd. I never did figure out why they were there."

Lucy said, "Maybe they solved whatever the problem was. Maybe they did their job so well no one knew what danger we'd been in. Instead of suspicious, maybe you should be grateful."

"Perhaps," Butch nodded. "They make me nervous." Butch adjusted his rearview mirror to see Sarah. "This one at Jessica's house might be FBI. That's who I've had the most dealings with. But for the record, they could also be Homeland Security, ICE, or maybe even INTERPOL." He glanced back at the road as they came out of the neighborhood and onto the major thoroughfare. "It makes no sense for them to be at a teenage suicide victim's home. No sense at all."

Lucy looked back at Sarah, smiled, and then whispered to her husband. "Unless they are suspicious because of the situation. Teenage girls don't shoot themselves."

"I can hear you," Sarah said from the backseat. "Paul and I have always been able to hear you when you whisper. What are you trying to say, Mom?"

"I'm trying to say," Lucy blushed a bit, "is perhaps more has been going on in Sydney than Roberto's suicide. Perhaps someone is keeping an unusually close eye on Sydney."

"Maybe," Butch nodded. "Maybe."

Nothing more was said on the ride home or in the next half-hour after arriving. Lucy put on a pot of coffee. Butch made a phone call.

Sarah took a shower. She threw away the blood-soaked clothes and put on leggings and a hoodie. When she came downstairs, her hair was wet. A towel hung over her shoulders.

"Tell us what you want to tell, Pumpkin." Butch said. "And nothing more."

Sarah took a deep breath and relayed to her mom and dad the events of the afternoon—from the feeling she had after school all the way to when she called 911 and texted them.

Sarah was focused and clear as she explained, relating every detail. When she finished the story, however, she broke down. "Daddy, it felt like shame. Everything I could be shamed. I felt ashamed of the good things I'd done as if they were too little and insufficient to make a difference. I felt ashamed of you and mom. I don't know why I did, but I did. I felt ashamed of being a Christian because it was so narrow-minded, backwards, and un-enlightened. I felt the shame of being a girl, of womanhood. I felt ashamed because of my gender. I felt ashamed of my race. I felt ashamed of my nation. I felt ashamed of our church—well, what used to be our church. I even, if you can believe it, felt shame for daring to be alive while Jessica was dead."

Lucy rose from her chair at their large oak dining room table where they had gathered. She sat down beside her daughter and hugged her. Butch was sitting to Sarah's right at the head of the table, and he reached out and grabbed Sarah's left hand.

"When did you feel all of this, exactly?" Butch asked.

Lucy released some of her hug, freeing Sarah to sip her peach oolong. She dabbed her eyes with a towel. "The moment I reached the top of the stairs. I could hear the music from her room and saw the door was closed. Somehow, in my mind, or maybe it was with my heart, I saw danger. I could smell death. And I heard the taunting voices." She took another sip. "What was that, Daddy? Tell me, please."

Fresh tears flowed. "Was it in my own head?" She slammed the table. "It can't have been in my own head, because I heard him with my ears. Am I crazy, Daddy? Am I?

"No." Butch said. He fidgeted his hands and turned his body in his seat. He realized he'd answered a series of vital questions too fast. "Let me clarify. It was in your head insofar as your head is who you are. But you didn't imagine it, which is what I perceived you were asking. It was real, Honey. I am so sorry you felt those things. I've felt them too, and your mom has as well. Don't believe those voices. They are lies." He squeezed her hand. "You are not crazy."

Now it was Butch's turn to gather his thoughts and try and put them into words. "Sarah, I don't know if other people always experience what you did today. As I said, I have, more times than I care to remember, seen things, heard things, and experienced things which can't be explained." He pointed at Lucy, "The same goes for your Mom. Most people don't realize the spiritual dynamic in the moments that pass through our lives. What you experienced today was nothing less than the Evil One oozing out his evil all around you. But because of who you are—our daughter—and how we raised you—you were able to perceive it. You also recognized it for what it was. What it is." He swallowed hard, then added, "What it will continue to be for the rest of your life."

Lucy had long since released the hug and was in the chair to Sarah's left. She played with Sarah's hair with her right hand and said, "There is a power at work in the world that has malevolent purposes, namely he wants to kill, and he wants to destroy. He killed your friends, and he wants to destroy you as well."

Sarah jumped when Lucy said the word destroy.

"What's wrong?" Lucy said.

"Destroy. Destroyer. It is what the voice said when I found Jessica. The voice said, 'I am The Destroyer.'" Sarah's lips shook. Her head quaked.

"What else did he say?" Butch said.

"He said Jessica was his." She looked at her father, "And he said I was, too."

"See?" Butch said, "Another lie right out of the pits of hell. You don't belong to him. Jessica let herself be taken, but she didn't always belong to him. You belong to the Lord, and the Lord has set you free from the powers of this earth. This voice is lying to you."

"But, Daddy, for a moment I believed he was right. I mean—I almost—I don't know—I wanted to die, too. It was the most logical and natural thing in the world was to give up and die. Like turning out the lights and going to sleep. I felt so tired, used, and drained. I only wanted to be free from the pain. From the doubt. From the struggle. Death and dying felt the only way out."

Lucy said, "Oh sure, he wants you to believe it, and he will lie to you, try to get you to destroy yourself. It happens every day all over the world. But you do not belong to him. You can make your own choices. You have a power inside that is greater than him."

"It was a light," Sarah sipped again. The heat from the tea felt good on her lips. There was a comfort in it; a familiarity which gave her a sensation of safety and peace. Those two feelings, safety and peace, had been absent from her for a long time, longer than she could remember.

"What kind of light?" Lucy asked without any sense of wonder or anxiety, continuing to twirl Sarah's hair in her hand.

"Before he announced himself as The Destroyer, I had my moment of doubt at Jessica's door. That was when it felt the worst. If I'd had a gun, I might have shot myself. The feeling, the icky icky feeling was so strong and tangible. I loathed myself to the point of wanting to end it all. Life was tragic, worthless, useless, futile, and empty. The feeling around me promised pleasure and bliss if I gave in and trusted it to fulfill me. It was a tempting promise. It sounds silly saying it out-loud right now, but it made sense at the time. I bet those were the same things Jessica was feeling when, you know, when she killed herself." Sarah looked down into her tea cup the whole time she talked, trying to stay focused. Her nerves were shot. Her concentration was falling apart. The memories of the event were already beginning to fade and run together. She squinted her eyes. "I felt the same way she must have felt. Like killing myself. But then I saw the light. Literally, mom and dad. Literally. A glowing light came out of my chest. The gloomy oppression around me lifted. I knew it was Jesus helping me. He helped me say no. Without the light, I would have died today."

Lucy kept playing with Sarah's hair. Tears formed in the corner of Butch's eyes. He wiped them away with his shirtsleeve.

"I didn't just see the light, Daddy." Sarah tapped at her chest. "I felt the light. I didn't only see it, I felt it. Inside me. I was about to give-in. It felt useless to fight to live anymore. There was such a combination of despair but also of pleasure I didn't see any sense in living." Her voice cracked, and she gasped for air as she sobbed. "I can't explain it, I don't have the words. I wish I could make you feel what I felt. It wasn't that I wanted to give up, there was a sense," and now she was crying so loud her voice was nearly shouting to get the words out, "I would actually enjoy it. It would feel good." She wiped her face and nose with her towel. "And now I feel pathetic. Dirty. Small. Inadequate."

"Pain often has a twisted pleasure to it." Butch nodded. "But that is not the story for us to focus on right now. The big deal is what you saw. You actually saw light?"

"Yeah, from inside. It was tiny at first, and it flickered. It started to almost dance in me. It gave me the strength to fight and open the door."

"That was the Holy Spirit." Butch said. "You belong to the Lord. He is always with you, and he wasn't going to give you up without a fight. The Bible tells us, 'Greater is he that is in you, than he that is in the world.' As your mom said, there is a power inside you evil can't overcome."

Sarah turned toward her father, "Does that mean Jessica didn't have the light? Does that mean she wasn't a Christian? That she is not in heaven?"

Butch took his glasses off. "Not necessarily." He looked up and took a deep breath, "Even people who follow Jesus sometimes give into the darkness. It probably means she had been playing with the darkness, inviting it in, and liking it. She believed the lies. Over time, she'd cultivated the darkness more than the light. She didn't nurture her walk with the Lord, therefore, in the weak moment, the time for battle, she was unable to mount a defense. But don't judge her too strongly. Today was your first encounter with this evil. We don't know how many times it had come for her. The Evil One is nothing if not relentless. Don't forget the death of her boyfriend. Death begets death. Jessica was a victim in this, and yes Christ-followers can be victims."

"So, Jessica is in heaven?"

Butch saw his wife's uneasy shift when Sarah asked the question. But the question didn't bother him. He knew it was the next, logical progression in this conversation and Sarah was enough like him that he knew where her mind was going. "I don't know," he said. "Let's examine the facts. We know Jessica said she believed in Jesus. We know she and her family attended church, although not what used to be our church, but it is a good one, nevertheless. We know she had shown in the past some fruit of discipleship—by her behavior and by her words. And, ultimately, we lean on the grace and mercy of God. He makes these decisions, we do not, and there is good reason for it. What happened to Jessica is a tragedy, a tragedy that will hurt her family and friends for the rest of their lives. Nevertheless, God loves her, as he loves you. He knows the heart of human beings. He knows all about our frailties and faults. Jessica is right now as she has ever been, at the mercy of God. We can trust his mercy." Butch raised his left hand as if he were telling a cab driver to slow down, "However, Jessica did something terrible, and something that cannot be undone. She has robbed God of the one thing she could give back to him: her life. Life is a gift God gives. She has thrown his gift away. She has desecrated the image of God within her. She also has absconded her future in an act of violence. Whatever the circumstances, that is something I believe she will somehow be responsible for. She will answer for it. Someday."

The front door swung open, startling them.

The oddity of the scene must have shocked Paul, as he threw down his baseball bat and glove and asked, "What happened?"

IX

Butch didn't know what to do.

His chest contracted. It squeezed the breath out of him. He panted. His eyes darted up and down and all around. Every muscle in his body tightened. He squeezed the steering wheel so hard his knuckles were cotton white. Sweat pooled at the base of his neck. His pasty skin blotched.

An hour earlier he'd left his home to buy a bag of gravel and stone for his koi pond at the local hardware store. He stopped for a scone and coffee at Starbucks on the way home.

But he didn't go home.

Muscle memory, or some kind of unspoken need to punish himself, took possession of his movements. Without the knowledge of his conscious self, Butch had driven someplace he never intended to go. His heart had guided him to Sydney Community Church, a place which had been home to him. He pulled into the driveway of the church before he realized what he was doing—as natural as ever—going to what used to be his office.

Awareness returned to him halfway across the parking lot. His car lurched when he slammed the brakes. He pushed the lever into reverse and accelerated hard. The back tires squealed in hurried desperation. Butch wheeled the car around, changed gears to forward, and again spun his tires as he drove away.

If he'd been in control, he'd driven home.

Butch was not in control.

He obsessed about the control issue, muttering to himself as he blocked around three times before he parked on the roadside opposite Sydney Community Church.

That was when the sweat, the shallow breathing, and the constriction on his torso came. It wasn't a heart attack. He knew that. It was an anxiety attack brought about by his experience. How many times had he been on the other end of the phone conversation with someone in the middle of these episodes, and when they had them, he was the person they called. He was the person everyone trusted. He was the person who could help. Butch knew exactly what was happening to him, because he'd seen it many times. But it was always someone else.

Even though he knew the clinical symptoms of what he was experiencing, it didn't help. The feeling came nonetheless. He'd never felt it before, something between fear and paranoia, blended with regret then topped loneliness.

He turned off the car's engine. With all the willpower he could gather, he forced himself to get out. He'd counseled people dealing with fear, and he'd always told them it was important to face the fear. A person had to look into what they were afraid of and work through it. Running away didn't help. Running away only made it worse. Now here he was, petrified. His subconscious had driven him here because he knew he needed to face the fear. But he didn't want to. It was time to take his own medicine, and a bitter pill it would be.

He stood with the car between him and the church building. The sedan and its metal served as a shield around his thin psyche. It protected from the full blunt trauma whipping toward him from this specter of his past. The protection proved to be woefully insufficient. The building he stared at taunted him like a schoolyard bully. He heard the steeple's scorn, "The church is better off without you." The windows became eyes. They squinted at him. The ghost whispered, "They never loved you. No one loves you." The glass doors yelled invectives: "Wimp," "loser," "pathetic," and "failure." The church sign that once had his name on it laughed. All the sounds came at once. Every word sounded to Butch as if it had been spoken by Tommy Bothers.

Time evaporated. It might have been a minute, or it could have been an hour. A mail truck drove by and broke the trance. The barrage over, he glared at the building. He thought about all his friends in that church, or people he'd thought were friends. Betrayal's bitterness made his knees buckle. The relational knife they plunged into the soft flesh between his shoulder blades burned so hot he reached to pull it out.

Images in his head formed of funerals held for beloved souls, weddings with happy brides and grooms in love, baptisms for new believers overjoyed by their commitment, infant dedications and anniversary celebrations. The sweet moments of prayer and worship he had taken for granted for so long now were gone forever. He smelled the lemon cleaner used on the altar furniture and it took his breath away. The taste of communion bread and cup filled the back of his mouth.

72

How he missed it! How had he never realized someday it wouldn't be there. If only he'd have known his days were numbered, he would have taken better care with the crucial moments, savoring each bite as a sweet dessert or a sip of hot cocoa on a snowy morning. More than anything he'd ever wanted, he yearned to walk across the road and enter the building. If only to put his hand on the door. It was a mere building made with stick and steel, yet he longed to feel it, to touch it, to be near it. To be in it.

The hole in his heart bled; only Sydney Community could clot it. He was in prison, looking through the chain-linked fence at the liberty denied him. Exiled, like Cain into the land of Nod, he could go anywhere but home. His spiritual home. It was his promised land, and he wasn't allowed to enter.

All that remained was to find Mt. Nebo and die.

His soul stirred again, and he regained some composure. Getting in his car, he knew he should go home. But he couldn't. Not yet.

Instead, Butch drove around the block another two times before he turned right onto a side street. He followed the tree lined neighborhood road to the city park he knew so well. In the past, he would often take his lunch and walk to this park from his office. Other times he would take a Bible and notebook along with strong coffee in a thermos to work on sermons and lessons under the tall trees. More than once he'd used the short walk from Sydney Community to calm himself before an important meeting or after a confrontation with someone. The stream that ran through it was his personal Gilead, and the time beside it a balm for the pain of ministry. In this place, Butch had always felt free to spiritually center and pray, even when the weather was cold and gray. Today the weather was a perfect eighty degrees, bright blue sky, and clean fresh air typical for Puget Sound this time of year. It was his soul that was cold and gray. The air in his heart was putrid.

Before he realized it, he was sitting at the picnic table under the alder tree and talking to God.

"I don't know what to do?" Butch prayed. "I've never felt this way before. This feels so different. My spirit is stirred in a way that is personal, as if someone is sticking Voodoo pins in me." The emotional pain of being fired was severe, but not as severe as not feeling connected to a church. "I feel alone!" Butch shouted to God. He vented this pain upon the only person he knew who could help. It was there in the park he rambled the gut-wrenching prayer of the godforsaken.

Oh Lord, I know I am not alone, but I feel so very alone. Nothing in my life feels right. Why? Why did you do this to me? I have done the best I knew to do to serve you, and now I am abandoned and kicked to the curb. I have been left to drift off into irrelevancy. I hate this feeling. I hate this feeling. And why are you suddenly so silent? Why don't you help me? Where is my deliverance? Why do you seem to help everyone else but those who give the most of themselves to you? Is it because I have nothing else left to give? What more do you want from me? Do you want me to open my veins and bleed for you like the prophets of Baal? No, you don't want my blood; you want my flesh and blood. That's it, isn't it? You want to take my daughter away from me, too. Why does Sarah hate me so much? Can't you fix her?

In the midst of his prayer, he realized his thoughts had turned from Sydney Community to Sarah. He remembered the oracle at Lighthouse Church who'd warned him. The freshness of Jessica's suicide made his heart hurt, but not for Jessica. His daughter had seen something she should never see. He hurt for her, and his prayer pivoted.

Jesus, if you will not help me, at least help her. I don't really matter that much. I'm just an old man who is now a has been, but she has her whole future in front of her. Could you do that for me, please? Heal the wounds I've caused her. More than that, bring us together again. I miss her. I miss holding her in my arms when she was a tiny baby. I miss her needing me. I miss her being innocent. I miss being her hero. I suppose, Lord, what I am asking is to give me clarification as to why I had to leave the church I loved in such a horrible way, and why in the process my daughter has turned on me. Even as I pray it, I realize the prayer about the church is not what matters most. Forgive me for my angry words a few moments ago. I know better. I know you love me, like I love my daughter. I ask you to do whatever it takes to heal my relationship to her, and to bless her by allowing her to truly see things as they are. Send people into her life to help her, because I don't think I have any credibility left. I'm only her dad. Maybe others can help her. Probably others are better anyway, as I have proven to not be much of a leader or teacher. Send her a pastor to help her. Send her a protector to guard her. I have failed in both these areas of her life, so please redeem what I've messed up. In Jesus' name. Amen.

PART TWO

As the sun was going down,
A deep sleep fell on Abram.
And behold, dreadful and great
Darkness fell upon him.

Genesis 15:12

X

Wyoming Wallace opened his eyes, but he didn't know if his real eyes were open or not. He took a big breath and realized his real eyes were not open. He was here, again, in the fuzzy world of his dreams. He could see the road beneath him, and a misty glow came from above. It wasn't quite sunlight, but it wasn't a cloud bank either. The light was almost green in color. It reminded him of the color of a trailer yard for long haul truckers in West Texas he visited once with his mom and dad when he was around six or seven years old. He remembered standing there in the hot summer night, drinking a soda, and eating a treat. He thought about how the blue RC Cola can didn't look blue in that green aura. His mind knew it was blue, but the light made it look green. For a brief moment, he could hear the low rumble of big engines idling. A whiff of diesel made his nose perk. He remembered how sweet the soda was on his lips. Everything used to taste better. Life tasted better back then, before it became bitter.

Wyoming knew he wasn't in West Texas. He was in Sydney, Washington. But he wasn't in Sydney either. He was in the dreamland Sydney that had become an unwanted second residence for him lately. The light in this Sydney was green. He was on a road again. The same road as always. It was a city street. There were buildings around him. His perception was these were homes or offices, but he couldn't see them. His vision was limited to the area right in front of him. If he left the road and walked to a building, he knew they would be vacant, abandoned boxes with no character. They reminded Wyoming of the houses and hotels from a Monopoly board game, without the garish red and green. The buildings and structures on the edge of the fog were more symbolic than actual.

His feet were shod with his typical ankle high work boots. He wore his trusted blue jeans, an Eric Church t-shirt, and a green lightweight jacket with The North Face emblazoned on the front. Atop his curly sandy blond hair was a dark blue Seattle Mariners baseball cap.

Weird. He owned the boots, pants, and shirt, and the old ball cap he'd bought at Safeco Field in 2001 was his favorite. But the green The North Face jacket was an article of clothing he'd never laid eyes on before.

His pistol felt good and right under his left arm. At least part of the universe was in good order. He knew his pocket knife was in his right pocket. But a curse came off his lips when he realized he didn't have his hunting knife on his belt. As soon as he thought about it, and wanted it, it appeared. He said, "Alright, that's what I'm talking about." His voice echoed around him, like it would in a house of mirrors with vibrations bouncing off glass or in a tiny basement with the reverberations reflecting off concrete walls. If someone had been with him to ask, he would have said the feeling gave him claustrophobia with the air squeezed around him to keep him confined. The fifteen feet of visibility was one thing, but the sounds that echoed close were something altogether different. The thought he was trapped in a small room with no way out filled his mind. He brought his right hand up and slid it into his unzipped jacket to grip the pistol. He didn't put his finger on the trigger, but he squeezed the grip and rubbed his thumb on the knurled steel.

Relax. Everything is going to be okay. It is a dream, and you have your .45 so nothing to worry about. Soon you will wake up, take a hot shower, drink some coffee, and everything will be fine. Ride it out. Nothing to worry about.

As he reassured himself, Wyoming Wallace heard a terrible screech start its descent from above. Wyoming looked up. He expected to see an owl or hawk, but he couldn't see anything. The sky was as slate gray as Seattle in November with a fog bank underneath.

The screech came again. This time it was accompanied by wind gusts.

Again, he heard the screech, sounding as if it were moving away.

Wyoming didn't know whether to get low on the ground, find a defensible position, or run. He looked down to check his watch to measure the time interval until the second attack, which he assumed was coming. The trusted Swiss Brietling he'd had since his first tour in Iraq was not there, which was odd, because he never took it off—not to bathe, work, or sleep. Wyoming closed his eyes and thought for a moment. He knew he was in bed, at home, and the watch was on his arm. He knew that to be true. He opened his eyes and looked at his wrist again.

Still no watch.

His hunting knife had appeared because he wanted it to. Why didn't it work for the watch?

Before he had time to contemplate the situational paradoxes or the peculiarities of time measurement in a dream, the second attack came.

The flying beast came from directly above. The wind around Wyoming fluttered and swirled. He reached up to hold his ballcap in place. The moment it landed, it hopped, and twirled around to face him. Wyoming rubbed his eyes. It was a giant Amazon parrot. The feathers were bright green, and the beak was as big as Wyoming's thigh. The bird was over a foot taller than Wyoming but tilted his head sideways to stare eye-to-eye. It looked to Wyoming to be the exact same parrot who shared the cab of his father's Peterbilt in his truck driving days. His dad had named the parrot Jose Cuervo. He would call the bird to his arm, and sing, "Jose Cuervo, you are a friend of mine." Wyoming was unsure whether his father didn't know the rest of the words, or if he stopped at those words in the lyrics because the bird was his best friend. Either reason was a distinct possibility.

Wyoming expected the bird inexplicably standing before him to attack with claws or beak. Jose's beak had been hard and strong. He could strip a pistachio in no time flat. He saw himself being pried open and disemboweled, his clothes and bones discarded like a nut's shell, while the giant bird chewed on the meat and sinew of his innards. Or, on the flip side, he thought the bird might carry him off to a nest somewhere and feed him, piece by piece, to baby birds waiting for a meal.

With a measured, slow movement Wyoming drew his pistol and aimed it at the bird. He didn't intend to shoot the bird, but he wanted to be ready in the event any kind of an assault came at him. The parrot responded to the weapon by raising his head up higher.

"If I didn't know better, I'd say you knew what this was." Wyoming said to the parrot.

With his free hand he rubbed his eyes. What kind of dream is this? Did I die in my sleep? Or am I going crazy? Which would be better?

The parrot said, "There is no need for weapons, Mr. Wallace. I am a messenger and have been sent to tell you two things." The parrot spoke in a formal tone, like a butler from a movie about a rich person. It wasn't European, just formal. And male.

Wyoming said, "Two things, huh?"

"Yes, two things. The first thing I am to tell you is the other two will be here shortly."

"The other two what?" Wyoming said.

The parrot ignored his query. "The second thing I am to tell you is do not look into the eyes of the gryphon. And make certain you tell the other two, beforehand." Having delivered his message, the parrot flew away.

XI

Wyoming Wallace walked, but he wasn't getting anywhere. His feet moved. His legs moved. But his position didn't change. The sensation was almost identical to a childhood memory. He and his sister were playing on the escalator in the shopping mall. There weren't many people around, or at least Wyoming didn't remember any other people, and the two of them were walking up the down side of the escalator. Each step they took only kept them in the same place.

He had the exact same feeling as back then. He could hear the sound of his boots on the ground, the rustle of his clothes, and he felt movement through his body with each step. Yet he wasn't moving. As a test, he stopped walking. He expected to start moving backwards, as if he were on a conveyor belt or on a moveable sidewalk at the airport. To his surprise, he didn't. But what did happen was stranger.

Through the fog, he saw a figure coming toward him.

Gryphon? The parrot had said to watch out for the gryphon.

Wyoming crouched low and brought his hand to his holster, but let it fall when he recognized what was coming toward him was not a mythical beast. It was a human. By the time he raised back up to full height, he recognized the other person as Butch's friend, Terence Harrison.

"Wyoming, is that you?" Terence said as he broke through the fog. The two men stood within three feet of each other. "What are you doing here?"

"I was about to ask you the same thing."

"Well, the short answer," Terence said, "I've been here almost every night for the past week or so. It has been the same dream, over and over. This time felt the same, except it's not quite the same."

"How so?" Wyoming said.

"Because I've never met anyone else in this dream."

"Me, neither. It's been going on for me regular now for about two weeks or so."

"Is that right?" Terence said. "Now that I think about it, this is the first time I've been here and fully aware of what I am wearing. It looks like this time I am dressed up a bit. Must be going to a party."

Wyoming noticed what Terence was talking about. The preacher wore nicely pressed trousers, elegant shoes with a Cuban heel, A Brooks Brothers oxford shirt, a Michael Kors silk necktie, and the whole ensemble was brought together by an expensive brown leather jacket.

"You look like you're on your way to a GQ photo shoot," Wyoming said. "Or a funeral."

"You look like you're on your way to a truck stop." Terence highlighted the obvious. "And I wish I was wearing your clothes."

Terence held out his arms, "I've got everything going on here but the timepiece. I wonder why I don't have the Rolex watch I've wanted for Christmas every year for the past twenty years?" He laughed at his own joke.

"Put your hand in your jacket pocket," Wyoming said.

"Why?"

"It's a hunch. Trust me."

Terence tilted his head and smiled his pearly whites. His lips puckered, and he kissed the air before he said, "I'll do it, because once upon a time you saved my life, and I've got no reason not to trust you." He plunged his hands into the luxurious lining of the leather jacket. Terence's face turned from smiling, to quizzical, and settled on confused as he brought out with his left hand a Rolex Datejust watch.

"It is a shame this is a dream," Terence said. "I could get used to reaching into my pocket and pulling out expensive things. How did you know?"

"I had a similar experience earlier, except I didn't wish for a watch. I wished for my knife to go along with my pistol." Wyoming opened up his decidedly more proletariat coat and showed him the trusty .45 revolver hanging under his left armpit and the knife hanging on his rawhide belt.

"Hey," Terence nodded, "your wisher is better than mine." He rubbed his perfectly cut Vandyke, then added. "I'm glad you got that, and you know how to use it."

"The odd part would be if I had to use either of them here in this dream. My other dreams have been peaceful. Yet, this one is different, don't you agree?"

"Different how?" a third voice said from the fog.

Both men jumped.

"I didn't mean to startle you," Sarah Gregory said as she came into full view.

Wyoming said, "Where did you come from?" He paused between every word, speaking at a pace that would make a tortoise impatient.

"I guess the same place you did." Sarah shrugged her shoulders.

"It might be important for us to compare our stories," Terence said.

Wyoming added, "Yeah, humor us." He folded his arms across his chest. He didn't know if this communicated his frustration with Sarah's presence or not, but he hoped it did. Terence being there might not be a benefit, but it wasn't a hindrance. Even though he was a preacher, he was a man, and in theory, responsible for himself. But Sarah, Sarah was a kid, and a girl at that. Her being there meant double duty for Wyoming. He would have to protect her as well as himself.

Sarah started, "The last thing I remember was reading some of my book for school. I suppose I went to sleep with the light on again." Sarah looked down at the ground. "Then I was here, and I heard the two of you talking."

Terence raised his left hand and his index finger, "Is this the first time you've been here, to this foggy Sydney?"

"No." Sarah didn't elaborate.

"Well, when was the first time? Because you see, it kinda matters." Terence said.

"I can't see why it matters," Sarah shook her head quickly back and forth. "But if you must know, I started coming here about six months ago."

"Six months," Wyoming said.

"Have you told anyone about it?" Terence opened his hands wide.

"No. No one except Jessica." She shuddered when she said Jessica's name, but came back to the topic at hand. "Mr. Wallace, Pastor Terence, how long have you been coming here?"

"Not as long as you, kid." Terence said.

They started walking. No one suggested they walk, and no one started walking first. Some internal signal inside them told them all it was time to move on. This time Wyoming believed he was making progress as he walked. There was a temporary feeling of *déjà vu*, if *déjà vu* is possible within a dream. He wouldn't figure out why until the end. For now, though, it was only unsettling.

"Hey," Wyoming said, "Did you ever meet anyone or talk to anyone when you've been here before? Cause this is the first time for both of us."

"No."

They walked on in silence, not knowing where they were going. Sarah grunted, and said, "Actually, that is not completely true. About a week ago I had a great conversation with a banana slug."

"A what?" Terence said.

"A banana slug," she repeated. "You know, the long slugs you find everywhere around Sydney pretty much year-round."

"Yeah, I know what a banana slug is, but I don't know about talking slugs, unless you count Republican politicians."

"Hey, watch it!" Wyoming punched Terence in the arm. "I voted for Trump."

"I'm sorry to hear that," Sarah said, in a dry tone that would have made her father proud.

"That makes two of us," Terence added as he grinned at Sarah.

Wyoming didn't surrender the point. "Like all true Americans, I'm tired of snowflakes running the country, always offended by something."

"Snowflakes!" Sarah was bouncing. "Snowflakes!"

Pastor Terence took control. "But back to the actual banana slug. You talked to an invertebrate? And more specifically, what did you talk about?"

"Yes, I did. I don't know how long we talked, because time doesn't seem to matter here."

"Actually, maybe it does. Show her the watch." Wyoming pointed at Terence's left arm.

Obediently, Terence raised the sleeve on his arm and showed her the expensive timepiece.

"A Rolex?" Sarah said. "My dad has always wanted one. He saved up once to get it, but he never bought it. He was always too worried about how the church board would take it. I guess you didn't worry about the board."

Terence raised both arms, "I don't own a Rolex. I wished this into existence."

"You wished a Rolex onto your arm but somehow thought it was okay to make fun of my talking slug."

"It happened to him, too." Terence pointed at Wyoming. "He wished his hunting knife onto his belt."

Sarah shook her head. "I'd take the watch over the knife. Every. Single. Time."

Terence frowned. "Your old man should go ahead and get the watch. He doesn't have any church boards to worry about now."

"Fools," Sarah mumbled.

"Back to the slug," Wyoming interrupted. "What did you talk about?"

"We talked about so much. We started with an elaborate conversation about the evil nature of the boy band, One Direction. The slug agrees with me. Let's see, we talked about growing up and how our parents sometimes don't understand. We talked about it for a long time, but the thing we talked about mostly was the Old Testament."

Terence chortled. "The Old Testament is a big book. What specifically about the Old Testament did you speak with Mr. Slug about?"

"His name is not Mr. Slug. It is Josiah. He was named after the child king of Israel."

"Ah, one of the good kings," Terence rubbed his head. "Is that what you talked about? Did you talk about the boy king? Was it his partial reunification of Judah and Israel?"

"No. Well, yes, some. We talked about the different idols and false gods. He spoke to me about Josiah's reforms against Baal, and how he even went so far as to desecrate the shrines of Baal. Do you know what Josiah told me? He told me Josiah in the Bible desecrated them by peeing on their shrines. Isn't that funny?"

"Funny?" Wyoming said. "I don't know about funny but peeing on something is the first thing you've said I understand. You two have me at a decided disadvantage when you start talking Bible stuff."

"Maybe we do," Sarah said. "And maybe that is one reason why you shouldn't assume you have to protect me because I am a girl. And I'm not a child."

"What did you say?" Wyoming stopped walking. "Why did you say it?"

"Because I can hear all of your thoughts."

XII

The dynamics that come to bear upon human beings when they are pushed into an unfamiliar world where the rules for everyday living no longer exist strain every aspect of personality and logic. Why Sarah, Terence, and Wyoming would think a world where a person could wish a knife in a sheath onto a belt loop or a Rolex watch onto a wrist stuck into a pocket would not also have different dynamics for the way in which the biochemical sensors inside the brain process information is not for anyone to judge. They had no experience in this dream world where parrots and banana slugs talk. Most people wouldn't, so do not judge their ignorance of actions.

Likewise, it never occurred to them they were not, strictly speaking, standing next to each other. Sarah was in her bed with the lamp on. Terence was in his favorite recliner with Biblical Archaeology Review lying open to an article about high places in ancient Israel on his lap. Wyoming was in his trailer, passed out on the couch after drinking four too many tequila shots. It was only in the spiritual, or perhaps mystical place they had tumbled into, like Lewis Carroll's famous *Alice in Wonderland*, where they existed in close proximity. They had bodies, but these bodies were detached from their usual selves.

The ability to perceive someone else's thoughts is something most people believe to be impossible, beyond the banter of married couples or trained experts who read body language. Some are able to intuit another's thoughts by force of charisma or intelligence quotients, but this is not the same thing Sarah experienced with Wyoming's stray thought about her competence. Nevertheless, in the spiritual world, knowledge can be a gift as is perception and discernment. For some reason, Terence and Wyoming take their gifts of weapon and watch as a delightful indulgence, but they reasoned Sarah's gift was troublesome. Perhaps this is so because Sarah's gift is not made from steel nor has been hammered into place by human hands.

It should be obvious to any unbiased observer of the situation neither Wyoming's knife or Terence's Rolex was actually made of steel or made of anything for that matter. Both only exist in the dream world. True, Wyoming's knife had an analog in the everyday world, but the one on his belt was more of an idea or symbol than a knife. Neither knife or watch existed, at least not in the realm of what usually passes for actual being. In stark contrast to this, Wyoming's stray thought about Sarah was an actual emotion from Wyoming. It emanated from his character, experience, and perception of how things are. There was nothing phony or symbolic about his feelings toward her. Sarah's gift is the only one of the three which is real and will matter when they wake up.

If they wake up.

* * *

"What do you mean you could hear it?" Wyoming snarled, his eyes squinted.

"I felt it," Sarah shrugged. "That is all I know. When I showed up both of you were startled, but Wyoming had a moment where he was put off by my presence." She pointed her finger at him, "You felt I would be in the way, that I couldn't take care of myself, and me being here would make your job harder. Don't deny it. I felt it."

"I don't deny it." Wyoming spit. "I don't like it."

"Me neither," Terence said. "Can you feel me?"

"Is that a request?" Sarah said, not picking up on the unintended double entendre which Terence didn't recognize until after he'd spoken it.

"No," he stammered, embarrassed. "No, I was wondering if it is between you and Wyoming or if you can feel what I feel as well."

"I can. Your feelings aren't as offensive as his." She pointed at Wyoming. "You," she now pointed at Terence, "are a nice man. A good man. You have only had one feeling since I showed up and that is amazement. You keep asking yourself over and over if this is real. I also sense you are thinking about one word in particular." Sarah closed her eyes. With her left hand, she reached out and touched Terence on the small of the back. "It is a foreign phrase. Latin. You keep thinking *mysterium tremendum*. It is how you're thinking about this moment."

"Exactly," Terence said. "Numinous. Rudolph Otto wrote about it, but he was thinking about the religious experience that makes us fall before God in awe." Terence took off his glasses (the thought never occurred to him, or his companions, as to why he would need glasses here) and wiped his brow in thought. "That is not exactly what we're experiencing, but it feels close."

"You've got to stop it." Wyoming grabbed Sarah's arm and pulled it away from Terence. "If you keep reading our minds, I'm not going to be able to think straight." Wyoming opened his eyes wide to punctuate the thought. "So, stay out of my head." He punctuated that with the foulest of swear words.

"I will try," Sarah said. "It is not something I normally do. Or have. I've never had this ability before, so have patience with me. Please."

"This is all odd," Terence said. "We're weirded out. I can see where Wyoming is coming from, but I can also understand Sarah. If we can all learn to work through this together, there is a chance we'll figure out what it all means."

"You sound just like my father," Sarah said.

Wyoming said, "You didn't read my mind on that one, but I was thinking the exact same thing. Must be a preacher thing." Wyoming started walking again, and Sarah, dressed in a maroon and gold running suit and athletic shoes fell into his left and Terence to his right. They took only a handful of steps before Wyoming spoke up again. "I need to tell you something." He hesitated, looked at them both, then corrected himself. "I am supposed to tell you something."

"What?" Terence asked.

But before Wyoming could answer, a screech came from overhead, followed by a strong gust of wind. None of them could see what it was, but they felt it move above their heads and heard it crash into the ground with a thud in front of them.

"That. I am pretty sure that is what I was supposed to tell you."

There was another whoosh swirling air around them. Wyoming couldn't see the source of the wind, but he knew what it was.

They heard it lift off again. Terence ducked onto the ground with his hands over his head. Wyoming shook his head in disgust. He glanced at Sarah, who was to his left. She never flinched. Her hair blew around her and the athletic clothes she wore whipped in the wind. Wyoming second guessed himself. Perhaps he'd overestimated Terence's value and underestimated Sarah's mettle.

As this thought formed inside his mind, Sarah looked right at Wyoming and glared at him. Never in his life had Wyoming felt intimidated. Never in battle. Never in a fight. Never in a challenge. Afraid, yes, but never intimidated. Until now. Something about the confidence Sarah carried inside her unnerved him. He'd known her for years through her father, but Wyoming had never had more than a four-word conversation with her. Now, he felt she was the most powerful person he'd ever met. It terrified him.

"I can hear her thoughts," Sarah said.

"What is that?" Terence shouted over the wind noise. "Definitely not a banana slug."

Before Wyoming could tell the two others it was the gryphon the giant talking parrot had warned him about, she swooped down on them from out of the fog and grabbed Wyoming in her eagle talons as she landed. It was done in one sweeping, fluid motion. The gryphon came to a perch facing Terence and Sarah. She held Wyoming at the front, with her head and beak pressed down against his shoulder to keep him in place.

Wyoming's Seattle Mariners baseball cap pressed down over his curly hair and pushed down over his eyes so he could not see. His arms were pinned against his side by the gryphon's strong arms as she sat on her haunches, beak pressed down over his shoulder, keeping him from adjusting his hat so he could see, and that frustrated Wyoming. But the blindness reminded him of the important omen the parrot told him.

"Don't look in the eyes," Wyoming mumbled to himself, remembering what the parrot had told him. He shouted it loud for them to hear, "Don't look in the eyes."

"Why?" Terence said. He was still on the ground with his hands over his head, his body twitching.

"Because he forgot to tell us something important." Sarah spoke with complete composure.

Terence and Sarah stared at the ground, even though Terence didn't understand why.

"I told you to get out of my head," Wyoming said.

Sarah ignored Wyoming's protest. "Pastor Terence, Wyoming was supposed to warn us about the gryphon. It was something," she paused, tilted her head sideways, and smiled, "something a giant parrot told him." A grin appeared on Sarah's mouth. "The parrot scared you, didn't it?"

But before she gave Wyoming a chance to answer, her voice lowered to a serious tone. "The gryphon is looking for something."

"I think it already found something," Terence said.

"No, that is not what I mean. For us to continue, we need to give the gryphon something."

"How about we give it Wyoming? She already has him?"

"Not funny," Wyoming shouted. "Are you two going to help me or not?"

The mythological animal was just over the size of a tall horse. The front half was visible to them and was mostly feathers. The feathers were blue, green, red, and purple. The face, which they avoided looking at, was that of an eagle. The beak crooked, the eyes sharp, and the head aerodynamically smooth. The other part of the creature had thick fur. The back legs were lined with razor sharp spurs. The legs looked like pistons, the feet like sledgehammers. A ten-foot tail with bone scissor-blades shot erect from the back. The four of them— Terence, Sarah, Wyoming, and the gryphon were all within five feet of each other.

It was hard for Sarah to not look up at the gryphon. She wanted to see it, to look at the eyes. Knowing she couldn't make her want to look all the more. She wondered if she could risk a glimpse, but as she did, she realized the gryphon read her thoughts. It sent image of fire from the gryphon's eyes exploding Sarah's body into a million light fractals.

Sarah realized this wasn't a threat. It was a warning.

She disciplined her thoughts back to where they were a split-second sooner and now, she had it. "The gryphon's name is Celeste, and she is looking for the pass-key. She needs the secret word. If she doesn't get the secret word, she will have no other choice but to kill us."

"Oh great. Riddles!" Wyoming couldn't see, but his ability to speak was unhindered. "Hey mind-whisperer, why don't you read the beasties' mind and figure out what the password is?"

"Her name is Celeste. And she can read my mind, and knows I can read hers, but unlike you, she is able to guard her thoughts. Don't you know I already thought of that? We have to find out the password on our own."

Wyoming cursed.

Terence was now standing upright, but looking down, as was Sarah. He waved his hands toward Sarah. "So, you're communicating with the thing? I mean, Celeste."

"Yes."

"Ask her for a hint, would ya? Something to help us to figure out the password, because I am betting it is not my computer password."

Sarah said, "I am pretty sure the password is not 1-2-3-4-5-6. Seriously, Pastor Terence, you need to get a better password."

"Now is not the time." He waved his hands and brought them down to his side with furious force. "And get out of my head, too!"

"The problem," Sarah said, "is Celeste is more complicated, or maybe I should say, different, than the two of you. She doesn't communicate with words. It's images, not grammar. Both of you think in complete sentences. Well, Terence thinks in complete sentences. Wyoming thinks in grunts. But she thinks in pictures."

Wyoming shouted, "Hey guys, it'd be helpful if you moved it along. I can't feel my fingers or anything below my thighs. So, a little help?"

Terence and Sarah ignored him. They worked on the communication problem. Terence had the breakthrough thought. "We are asking for help, so send her a mental image of needing help."

Before he'd finished the thought, Sarah had already solved the problem. It was a memory from her childhood. She was four years old. They were at her grandparents' home at the beach. She went too deep into the surf. A wave crashed over her head. She lost her balance and was violently tossed about in the turbulent water. Sarah remembered throwing her arms up over her shoulders and screaming for help. The word help was in Sarah's mind, but the image she sent was of her need for help. She hoped Celeste would understand.

"Pastor Terence," Sarah said. "I got something."

"What?"

"Celeste sent me an image of my father. He is standing in the dark. Wait, he is on a path, a rocky, uneven path. It is a mountainside with a switchback trail. He is on a trail in the dark, but he is holding light. It is a lantern maybe." The image vanished from her mind.

"Does it mean anything to you?" She asked.

"Thank you, Sarah, and thank you, Celeste." Terence kept his eyes closed, for fear he'd look where he knew he shouldn't. He raised his head up and his arms out wide in the direction of the guardian. He opened his mouth, made his distinctive kissing toward the foggy air, and said, "Your word is a lamp to my feet and a light to my path. Psalm 119:105."

Celeste released her grip upon Wyoming Wallace. She bowed low then lifted herself upward into the air. The wind from her mighty wings pushed against their faces. Terence kept his eyes closed. Wyoming held his hat on his head to keep it from flying away.

Sarah was a statue in the breeze, strong and unyielding.

They looked at her as she flew away.

"Why didn't you tell us about that thing?" Terence spoke those lines with the cold, stern, icy voice he'd used to question his children when they had made poor decisions.

"I meant to, I forgot." Wyoming adjusted his hat, which he had done over and over again since Celeste flew away. "Honest guys, I was about to tell you all about it when the thing landed down on us."

"So, the parrot talked to you?" Sarah smirked. "And you made fun of me about the banana slug?"

The three didn't say anything else for a long time, but they kept walking. The road was paved with black asphalt. They deemed the middle of the road safest. They stayed arm's length of each other. They hadn't gone too far until Wyoming decided they should check out the sides of the road. On each side was a cracked and damaged sidewalk. If they went far enough to the left or right, they found dim houses. Terence suggested they knock on doors to see if someone was home. Neither Sarah nor Wyoming thought that was a good idea. Wyoming shared his theory about the scenery around them—the road, the fog, the homes—was merely window dressing, or staging for a play. He said, "It has been put here to keep our minds from thinking too much about why we are here. It is a distraction of some kind."

Sarah latched onto that thought. She didn't know why they were there, and she wondered if they had any clues. Wyoming had no answer, Terence, by contrast, was definitive. He told them they were in the recesses of their own minds, three minds somehow linked together. Before the encounter with Celeste he didn't know if this place was the working of The Lord or of their own subconscious self. Now, he was fairly certain this was the working of the Holy Spirit. He said, "Only the Lord would have the password be one of my favorite Bible verses. It was either going to be that or Proverbs 3:5-6."

"But what about the monster? What was that all about?" Wyoming reached for the inside of his coat pocket, hoping there would be a cigar and a lighter. He'd repeated the exact same action four times since he had been attacked by Celeste, and each time he found nothing. He found nothing yet again. Frustrated, and jonesing for a stogie, Wyoming kept thinking out loud. Since the girl could read his mind anyway, he decided he might as well go ahead and announce every thought. "I don't understand why God would want to harass us with a monster who could vaporize us with her eyes or rip us apart with her talons. If God wanted us dead, he could kill us straightaway, right?"

"You've got a point," Terence said.

Sarah shook her head. "As is the case with most boys, you are looking at this all wrong. Celeste wasn't about stopping us or harassing us at all. Celeste was sent to help us, which, she did."

"Help?" Wyoming said. "She almost killed me."

"If Celeste wanted you dead, you'da been dead before we could have done anything about it. No, that whole exercise was for our," Sarah pointed at Terence and herself, "benefit. God wanted us to see, and you for that matter, we were not along for the ride. Terence knows things we need to know about. And I have this thing I can do here that we're gonna need, too. Celeste taught us we are a team, not three random individuals. We were chosen for a reason. We all know what, or who, the glue is that holds us, and we all have a role to play."

"The tie that binds," Terence whispered. He glanced at Sarah and said, "Do you think Butch will show up here?"

Wyoming mumbled, "I hope so."

"No." Sarah said. "Daddy isn't coming."

XIII

The three dreamers—Wyoming, Terence, and Sarah walked up the hill. There was no clear reason why they should go uphill when downhill made just as much sense, but Sarah started the motion, and the two men had fallen in behind her. "This way," she said as she moved in that direction.

"And a child shall lead them," Terence mumbled, assuming that he couldn't be heard.

"I'm not a child anymore!" Sarah snapped.

"True enough," Wyoming said, drawing out the word true, turning the simple one syllable word into nearly five syllables. "You are a grown woman. However, compared to two old geezers like us, you are young, a baby even. So, you might not want to get too defensive. No one is attacking you. At least, not yet. It is more a commentary on our age."

Sarah didn't respond, but the determined look remained.

"I didn't mean to insult you," Terence said.

There were no more words until they found themselves gawking at a man sitting on a supermarket scooter. It was parked there, on the side of the road they traveled, but was not moving. The basket in the front of the scooter, where a person might put milk or bread, had the store name *Albertsons* written in blue letters against a white background on the front. Inside the basket was a stack of books and a flask of wine. To say the man's hair was long would be an understatement. It hung from his head all the way to the ground, flowing behind him like a superhero's cape. The hair was gray, not a dingy gray but a bright, almost fluorescent gray. Later, Terence would say it was so fantastic it looked whiter than gray. An enormous nose stood out from the center of his long face, an Everest popping out from the Kansas plains. His hair hung over his ears, but two elongated earlobes hung atop of his shoulders like a tomato on the vine partially resting on the dirt. The wrinkles on his face reminded Sarah of a Pug or Shar-Pei, such was their overlapping and size. His head was tilted back as though he were watching the sky for rain, but his eyes were closed. Wyoming looked up to see what the old timer might be looking at, but he saw only the same slate gray that had been there since he first entered this bizarro alternate reality.

They gathered around his scooter.

"Is he dead?" Wyoming asked.

"I don't know," Terence replied. "For all I know, we're all dead."

"If this is the afterlife, my dad owes me some apologies." Sarah pushed the hair from her face and behind her left ear.

"I'm not dead," said the man in the scooter. He didn't open his eyes or move anything on his body except his mouth. The way his beard and mouth moved when he spoke reminded Sarah of a sock puppet show about dolphins and turtles, she once saw at a lousy vacation Bible school she was forced to attend the summer before her fourth-grade year. The tragedy that was the cursed theme song, with its soft synth sound and pre-teen girl vocals, made her grimace. Curiously, at the exact same time, Terence visualized his sock drawer and Wyoming smelled saltwater.

"Are we dead?" Terence asked, before thinking about whether he should or shouldn't.

"No, at least not yet. Although, one might be in mortal danger. Probably more so than any of you realize."

"Which one?" Wyoming squeezed the question from his mouth like a plea. He'd played that deadly roulette before. The taste of bile rose in the back of his brain.

"This is the tricky part, isn't it, Wyoming? You never know who is in jeopardy until it is too late to do anything about it."

Wyoming stepped back, but before he could the man in the scooter reached out and grabbed his arm. Long fingernails wrapped around his jacket and the old man's strength pulled him closer. "Let it go, son. She doesn't hold it against you. She made her own choice."

Sarah and Terence only saw the action. They didn't hear the words form. They only heard what sounded like a long exhale. But Wyoming's heart heard every syllable.

The old man let go, and opened his arms wide in a welcome gesture. "My name is Mel. We need to tête-à-tête before you three go any further on your quest. I have some things to share with you that matter quite a lot and knowing this information will help you on the descent."

"Where exactly is this?" Sarah said.

"This is where the now and the nowafter mingle together."

"Not much of an answer," Terence shook his head. "Is that a riddle?"

"No," Mel said. "Not a riddle. More like a liquid answer to a concrete question. You see, the maiden wants a place on the map with an arrow to show YOU ARE HERE, but this is not that type of place. There are no maps here, only personalities and ideas. So, perhaps the best answer to her question of where is this is to say she is located within a thought, and you three must turn the thought into an idea if you are to succeed."

The enigma of Mel's answer swam in and through their minds, but he continued with more information. "There are entities and powers at play in the world, and have been since time began, and will be until the Almighty Judge brings everything to an end and makes all things new. Of course, there are countless unclean spirits, but there are only seven powers—seven principalities—seven dominions."

Mel then gave them a lecture on these seven principal powers.

93

* * *

The first, and perhaps the oldest, is The Lord of the Flies. I say, 'perhaps the oldest' because it is hard to put the timeline straight. Much happened in the distant past which no human ever saw. No one knows for sure all that went on, not even me. I suspect some day we will know—even as we are known—but until then we will have to work with partial knowledge. But I can tell you with full confidence The Lord of the Flies is probably in the top two or three of all malevolent beings in the cosmos. That distinction alone makes him old, as in part of the original rebellion.

The Lord of the Flies has several pseudonyms including Beelzebub, Baal, and Ra. He is most famous as the harrier of ancient Israel. He is particularly fond of totems and tall trees. The Lord of the Flies likes to show off with the weather and finds pleasure in turning the beauty of creation into a spectacle of death. He was the great tormentor of ancient Israel and often confused the people into thinking he was actually Yahweh, the One True God, blessed be his name.

The second is Kali Ma. She is the demon goddess whose most famous location is India, but like the others she gets around. Kali Ma is also known as Molech, Planned Parenthood, and a thousand tribal and river deities throughout history. She has a particular appetite for the blood of children. Her *modus operandi* is to whip up followers into such a frenzy they destroy the next generation in their own greed and lust. It's a clever trick, and all too easy. All seven demons use superstition, witchcraft, and the lower elemental powers to manipulate, but Kali Ma is the master. Whereas Beelzebub poisons the minds and spirits of individual people, Kali Ma poisons one generation into believing they ought to destroy the next, thus accomplishing a societal two-for-one.

Incubus is a particularly nasty demon who comes in the night. He physically assaults his victims in unique ways, distinct from the others. I say he, but Incubus also takes the female form of Succubus. Incubus enjoys violation. You see, the Lord God made human beings in his image, and Incubus hates the image of God, so he violates the image whenever possible as an attack on the Holy One. He rapes the soul when opportunity allows, and he even kills and desecrates the body. Incubus is a monster, and as such he is known as Dracula, Jack the Ripper, Mictian, and Lamashtu. Incubus prefers to target the vulnerable, such as pregnant women, newborns, and young families.

The fourth is Djin. Djin is so clever people have always assumed

94

this to be a category, as if there were many. There is only one, and one is enough. He is a trickster demon who has fooled the world into believing he wants to give three wishes to anyone who finds magic lamps. Fools! Djin gives nothing except chaos and despair. His primary weapon is to divide and conquer. As with all these characters, Djin has aliases including Ekwensu, Aunt Nancy, Pan, and Loki. Djin murders hope and ravages dreams. He leaves his victims naked and cold on the floor at the moment they thought they would be warm and safe at the top of the world.

Then there is Grendel. Grendel is not a character from an old Anglo-Saxon mead hall story, regardless of how much truth is in the story. And believe me, it is mostly true. But more significantly, Grendel is a monster who kindles the fires of war. Also known as Ares or Mars, he turns otherwise reasonable people into bloodthirsty killers, usually with patriotic, religious, or nationalistic fervor. Blood and soil—*Blut und Boden*—as the Nazi's called it. Grendel destroys the body at places like Iwo Jima, Gettysburg, Cambodia, Rwanda, and Trafalgar. He destroys the lives and potential of young people, usually men, by seizing their bloodlust and playing the same song he sung to Cain before he was sent to the Land of Nod. His main destructive focus is upon civilized society. If there were no war, the human condition would be infinitely more improved. The irony of Grendel's deception is how he pushes the violent agenda through the haughty halls of power and prestige among old men and women who send the young to do the killing and dying for them.

Gaea is the false goddess of mother earth. Her primary gambit is to deceive people into thinking somehow creation itself is the source of awe and wonder over the Creator. As if things magically appear from nowhere. I tell ya, to be so smart some people can be really stupid. Things don't create themselves.

Gaea is a noxious rust. She corrodes the connections between human beings and the Lord, as well as the connections among people. Gaea often uses science as one of her tools, not that science is inherently evil. However, as with anything else, when placed in the wrong hands, it becomes polluted with arrogance. Arrogance breeds destruction. If you don't believe me, just ask Oppenheimer.

Gaea has alternately been known as Vishnu, Mother Nature, and Marduk by the ancients.

The Rab-Shakeh is the particular name of the power and principality you find yourself up against right now. The Rab-Shakeh has taken a physical dominion in your home village of Sydney. They don't always do that—take a physical dominion. They try, but they are not always successful. One exception is Grendel. Grendel has had a dominion set up over the central interior and eastern coast of Africa for the last four centuries. They all try to do this, but usually they are not successful. But The Rab-Shakeh has easily I might say, taken hold of your dwelling. His power grows every day.

* * *

Mel took a deep breath when he finished the lecture. He nodded his head in satisfaction for having finished the primer before he explained further. "These seven often set themselves up as idols, false gods for adoration. They feed off of how quickly others submitted to their cheap parlor tricks and dazzling diversions. By the time people figure out they are frauds and phonies, it is too late. I have found they use three primary tools in their work of destroying things. First, and most powerful I think, is superstition. Unlike the One True God, these demiurges want people to cower in ignorance, lore, and fables. They want you thinking about solstices and auras and crystals and totems and magic. It is a slight of hand move if there ever was one. There is no power in those things, as if a full moon meant anything other than the passage of time, but when people ascribe power to it, then the people can be easily moved the way we do cattle or sheep."

"Sheeple," Terence said. He said it so loud Mel jumped in his grocery cart scooter.

"Sheeple?" Mel asked. "I've never heard such an odd word before? But if it means what I think it means, I like it. You are a clever soul."

Terence took this as a teachable moment. "The word sheeple is a product of a unique linguistic phenomenon of our age called a portmanteau, where one word is combined with another word to create a new word that has a different meaning and connotation."

"I thought," Mel said, "portmanteau was a type of luggage."

"It is," Terence said. "But you should recall the luggage piece called a portmanteau has two equal pieces to make one larger piece. That usage is the derivative of the verbal usage. Two separate words come together to make a larger, different word combining the various meanings." Terence's eyes opened wide as an idea came to him. "Motorcade is another example—it combines the antiquarian word cavalcade with motor. Motorcycle, actually, is a portmanteau, combining motor and bicycle. Portmanteaus are most common in politics and popular culture. A recent example was the word Brexit, which referred to the British exit from the European Union."

Sarah, Wyoming, and Mel all three looked at Terence with the same face; their heads tilted askew, bottom lip separated from the top, and their cheeks upturned in a grimace of pain. "Thanks for the word lesson, Pastor Terence," Sarah said. It was a bold move on her part, to make a joke at his expense. She'd always been intimidated by him. Somehow, here in the dream world, that intimidation, as well as most feelings of inadequacy, had lessened. Not disappeared but lessened. At least for now.

Sarah asked Mel "Are these demons locked into a specific geography?" She rocked on her feet. "You mentioned Baal. Was he tied only to Israel in the Bible or was he in other places too?"

Mel said, "Good question, my lady. They are partial to taking a geography and claiming it as their own, the way a dog will mark his territory with the stench of his urine. Yet they are not bound by a geography and are able to be in two places at once. For example, Kali Ma nurtured her cult in both India and amongst the Sea Peoples of Phoenicia at the same time. This is why we imagine them as dominions and not kingdoms. They take dominion over a people or a land, but such dominion is neither permanent nor spatial."

"No dragon, huh?" Wyoming mumbled in sudden, flippant way that surprised even Sarah. "I would have thought there would certainly be a dragon in there somewhere."

"Shut your mouth, Wyoming—Son of Wallace. You know not what you speak. If you did you wouldn't be so careless with your words. A dragon there is, and a great terror it most definitely is. The dragon is not one of the seven, but instead he is the ancient dragon of old from which all evil spreads. The dragon was the serpent in the garden, the thunderbird in the desert, the hoarder of gold in the cave, and the deceiver of Mayans, Kukulcan. He is greater than the seven, and it is his attention you desperately do not want to attract. His hatred is so great, and his powers so filthy, it was nothing to him to burn six million Jews through his possession of Hitler. His conniving was so foul he used the people of God in an abominable doctrine of manifest destiny to commit genocide of indigenous peoples throughout North America.

"Now, though, the dragon immerses himself more in systems of thought. Evil is always personal. The Evil One has worked for the past two centuries to create and legitimize the systems of oppression, injustice, and materialism spawning ever growing numbers of people either propagating evil or victimized by it. Turning one man into a religious zealot isn't his thing so much anymore. Instead, he creates the society that proliferates it in ever growing generations and iterations of religious zealots itching to behead someone or blow themselves up in the name of Allah or throw an Anabaptist in the river to drown. The dragon is the king of all that is wrong. Every theft, fornication, blasphemy, and violent thought can trace its lineage back to him. He's the father of evil. The Father of Lies."

Mel scowled at Wyoming. "So, watch your mouth, boy. I know you don't understand, and your heart is good. Adonai has revealed it to me. But spiritual things are important things, and we ought not joke about what we don't understand. You are a strong soul, but your strength is temporary, and your confidence is misplaced. May he who has preserved your life thus far open your eyes to see the whole truth."

Wyoming did not defend himself or talk back to the old man. He stroked his beard with his left hand, as if in deep thought.

"I've got a question," Terence said, raising his hand as if he were in a classroom.

"Is it a question, Terence, Shepherd at Ebenezer Church? Because what I feel from you is contention. You want to argue. You are truly your father's son." Mel stood up from his scooter while he spoke. He approached Terence until he was standing only five inches apart. It was an aggressive act of challenge so strong Wyoming actually put his hand on the butt of his revolver.

Terence did not flinch.

"Your perception is true," Terence said. "And I pray my thoughts and actions honor my father's memory. But my question is one of history. Six of your seven make some kind of sense to me. But The Rab-Shakeh was the title of an Assyrian military officer. Equivalencies are hard to do, but it was some rank parallel or synonymous with the Chairman of the Joint Chiefs of Staff or something along those lines. The Assyrian army was terrifying, however The Rab-Shakeh was only a part of an apparatus which laid waste to a great many cities and nations."

"That is not the whole story." Mel didn't move or adjust his stance. The preacher and the priest stood nose to nose. Mel continued. "However, you at least know the biblical reference. What else do you remember from your studies, Dr. Harrison?"

"You mean to ask what do I remember of The Rab-Shakeh's role? Biblically, he was the one who taunted Judah when Assyria laid siege to Jerusalem. He stood out and yelled. If memory serves, he teased the Judahites in their own language of Aramaic not his native Assyrian. It was a type of psychological warfare. It was The Rab-Shakeh who told the Hebrews if they thought Yahweh would deliver them, they were mistaken. He claimed it was Yahweh who had empowered his master, I forget his name, to undergo the military raids he'd taken. He claimed Yahweh wanted Assyria to beat Judah. He argued no other cities had been protected by their gods, and Jerusalem would be no different."

"Well done," Mel said. "It was a religious test. The history of humanity can be boiled down to such tests. Was it not a religious test what happened between Moses with his holy staff in the confrontation with Pharaoh? Or from Elijah when he smote Ahab and The Lord of the Flies along with his prophets on Mt. Carmel? The struggle for Nehemiah was nearly identical as well when the wall was rebuilt. Also remember when our Lord Jesus stood against Ha-Satan in the desert."

The recitation of victories was obviously pleasing to Mel. A tiny, but sincere laugh came from him. The smile vanished like the sun hiding behind clouds. His face took on a trance-like quality as he no longer looked at Terence, but looked through him into the distant past, talking to someone else who was not there, or that only he could see. "The Assyrian king's name was Sennacherib. Untold numbers of innocent people died under his whim. In all human history, there have been only a handful of power systems eviler than the ancient Assyrians. They were among the first people to organize and systematize to kill purely for sport. It took great faith to withstand their onslaught."

Wyoming had relaxed his guarded stance, fully caught-up in the history lesson. "So, what happened?" he asked. "Did The Rab-Shakeh defeat Jerusalem and drink the blood of his enemies, impaling women and children in the desert heat? I kinda need to know, especially if this is the monster we're chasing."

"I got this one," Sarah said, nodding to Terence and Mel. "The siege of Jerusalem ended exactly as the prophet Isaiah said it would. King Hezekiah stood faithful, and The Lord delivered Jerusalem by sending an angel to destroy the Assyrian camp. No longer able to mount the siege, the Assyrian army returned home. Once home, there was a revolution which eventually became a whole new empire called Babylon. Their leader was Nebuchadnezzar."

"Amen," Mel said. "Well spoken, Sarah. You have honored your father and your mother with your words. They are great heroes, well-spoken of. You would do well to follow them."

Academics must reach logical clarity, or at least some kind of balance of the facts. Until they do, there is doubt in their mind. Clarity eluded Terence. "Yes, that is my point, Mel." Terence said. "There is the historical perspective and the biblical witness, but none of it specifies The Rab-Shakeh was a demon. You could argue he, along with his entire people, were misled by demonic forces but I see nothing to indicate the position of Rab-Shakeh as a dark spiritual force any more than saying my congressman or senator is a demon."

Wyoming jabbed at Terence, "All politicians are demons, Dr. Harrison." Wyoming enjoyed the joke, but he also enjoyed using Terence's title as a bludgeon to mock Terence. From that moment on, Wyoming Wallace always referred to Terence as Doc.

Mel, inches apart from Terence, whispered, "Do you not see it was but the glimpse of the exposed power. Beneath that tip, under the waterline, submerged beneath the official story of the history is the truth of the spiritual darkness. Assyria went home, yes, but The Rab-Shakeh was just getting started. Who sowed the seeds that led Babylon to eventually burn Jerusalem to the ground? Exile was a punishment from God, yes, but the vigor, bloodshed, and zeal of the Babylonians has Rab-Shakeh's fingerprints all over it."

"I sense your question, Sarah." Mel didn't turn his head as he spoke. He was still intimately close to Terence's face. "Go ahead and ask it."

"Not to change the subject, but why is it so gloomy here? I understand it is a dream, but why so dark. It's like a Christopher Nolan film."

"I know not who this Nolan bearer of Christ is, but Abraham thought the same thing, as did his wife, who is your namesake. He always found the real action started as the sun was going down."

Mel waddled the three steps to his cart and laboriously sat down again.

"Now," Mel said, "let me bless you. It is what I do."

"You could bless us with more explanation, that would be nice," Wyoming said.

Mel ignored the wisecrack and raised his hands as a priest in a worship service. "In the name of Yah, Creator of heaven and earth, and to the good will of Jesus the Messiah, and by the power of the living Ruach who moves in both the awake and the sleeping, I bless you and ask The Almighty Three In One to grant for you to survive your quest, make peace with yourselves, and above all find purpose and meaning in life before it is too late. Selah."

Terence had kissed the air again, posing another question, but he never got the chance. Mel flipped a toggle switch on the scooter he was in and rolled down the hill away from them. He was out of sight before they could mount a protest or even catch him. They ran down the hill to find him, but they never did.

"There is no way the old geezer got away from us in a grocery store scooter," Wyoming said. "Maybe he went into one of these toy houses?"

"Nope," Sarah said. "He vanished."

"Who was he, anyway?" Wyoming shook his head in wonder.

"Mel," Terence said. "He blessed us. Remember. Sarah, does it remind you of anyone?"

"Sure does," she said. "But that is a big presupposition."

"What, what is a presupposition?" Wyoming stomped the ground, a protest for being left out of the Bible club.

"Well," Terence said. "A presupposition is when you assume something which might not actually be the case. Such as—"

"I know what a presupposition is," Wyoming said. "I mean, what is the specific presupposition you two are making."

Terence said, "There is a character from the Bible. He doesn't show up much, but he is exceedingly interesting. He was a king and a priest in Jerusalem, but long before it was Jerusalem. It was called Salem then."

Sarah picked up on Terence's trail. "My daddy told me once the name meant 'My Righteous King' but I'm not sure how he pronounced it. I'm not good with Hebrew words."

"Melchizedek." Terence laughed. He repeated the name several times aloud before gathering his thoughts. "Melchizedek was right in our midst. And he blessed us." Terence spun around as if looking for someone to share the miracle with, but he found no one except the clueless Wyoming Wallace and his best friend's daughter. "What kind of dream landscape is this? What world is this, that the ancient holy man appears to us in a grocery-store scooter and schools us on demons? What have we gotten ourselves into?"

It was a rhetorical rant, one Butch Gregory, were he there, would have recognized as Terence's processing mechanism. Deep inside his big brain, Terence would answer each question he'd just asked aloud, as well as several others that he didn't say out loud, with data from his experiences and from the scriptures. His mind had already worked through the first question before he'd spoken aloud the last one. He knew what kind of dream landscape this was. It was akin to what Paul mentioned once in the New Testament as the third heaven. It is a unique part of 2 Corinthians when The Apostle is justifying his authority. Paul references it in the third person— 'I know a man in

Christ who fourteen years ago was caught up to the third heaven'—that is how Paul said it. Terence had already decided maybe what they were experiencing was something similar. Maybe not exactly like it, because who could know, but something along the same line. The Apostle Paul spoke in third person, but he was talking about himself. Terence now wondered if maybe he didn't write it in third person because it was a dream and felt like it happened to someone else. Terence formed a new question in his mind. It was a question he didn't share. He wondered what he would remember when he woke up? Would it be like watching it through someone else's eyes? Like watching a film? That was not a pressing question, and time would tell. In the milliseconds his brain fired between rhetorical questions, he decided this one would have to wait until it happened. The question assumed they would wake up. Terence didn't even bother to ask that one, because he'd already assumed they would. Or at least one of them would. But wake up where, Sydney? Heaven? Hell? Or some other place equally bazaar as this one.

Wyoming didn't know the fertile ground of Terence's mind, nor his personality and how he worked through hard issues. So as soon as Terence finished his oral questioning which was really rhetorical, Wyoming responded. "I'm not quite sure what kind of place this is, except I feel confident there is something we're here to do, and it is not to listen to the old geezer. In other words, Doc, we're not only here for a lesson. The lesson might be good, and it might be something we need to tuck away in our minds, but that is not what we're doing here. There is something we're supposed to do, and all three of us have a distinct reason for being here."

Wyoming slowed down but strung the syllables together as he continued. "I find it odd Butch isn't with us. That he isn't with us means, to me anyway, we are here for Butch. He is the one common ground we share. We are here, but he is not, because we have to fight for him. We have to help him. We have to help the Reverend."

By now Terence's brain had caught up with his own questions and had even worked through Wyoming's rationale. "Yes, Wyoming. I believe you are right. Mel, Melchizedek, matters, but only to help us know what is going on. The Lord always gives you exactly what you need. What we needed was to know who the enemy is. This is a spiritual battle in this realm of mist and gray, but the truth is there is a demon in Sydney, and the three of us are supposed to do something in this third heaven where things are, but also are not. There is something we can do here that has an effect on what is happening there, but I

102

have a feeling it is going to be hard. He paused, then finished. "I'm not sure if it is about Butch or not, but he is a part of the story."

It was then both men heard the sobs. Sarah stood, crying. "We have to help my daddy. Please God, don't let anything happen to my daddy."

Terence stepped toward her and enveloped her into his large arms. "There, there, Sarah. Let it out. We're all a bit tense and upset. But I promise you, we will do whatever it takes to help Butch. Your daddy has been in some serious scrapes in his life, and this might simply be the next one, but as far as it depends on us, he will make it out of this one, too."

"We promise," Wyoming added. As soon as he said it, he regretted it. He knew better than to promise anything. The memory of Amber came rushing over him. He pushed it away, but it wouldn't completely leave. The memory of her death always hung on his mind, for that tragedy had never left him.

"So, what do we do?" Sarah said as Terence released the hug and let her regroup her emotions.

"We go up the hill." Terence said this without hesitation.

"Yes," Wyoming said. "This is a battle, and we must take the hill."

"I was thinking more along the lines of climbing Jacob's Ladder." Terence pantomimed climbing as he said it.

They walked up the hill, not knowing what was ahead or what it meant. All they knew was they must go. Butch's life depended on it, and Butch Gregory was one thing, perhaps the only thing, these three very different souls, who didn't understand each other or even particularly like each other could agree was worth fighting for. Worth dying for.

XIV

None spoke as they walked. A somber mood settled over them thicker than the fog. Butch Gregory was on each mind, but in different ways.

Terence was the first one to notice the change in the roadway. "Hey guys, look down," he said. "The ground beneath us isn't black asphalt anymore. It is white concrete, like a driveway."

"Or maybe a parking lot," Wyoming said. "Do you see any yellow lines on it? Like parking stalls or guide arrows?"

"Nothing," Terence said.

Sarah said. "Do you see the steps ahead?"

"I do," Wyoming said.

"I don't see anyth—" Terence stopped midsentence. "Now I do. You have sharp eyes, Miss Gregory." Terence smiled at her when he said it, thinking she would smile back. But she did not. Instead he got the distinct impression she preferred to be called Sarah, and she found her last name along with the cutesy "Miss" appellation condescending and trite. He felt inside his mind something which can only be described as a giant exclamation point, as if Sarah was screaming this emotion into his prefrontal cortex. He didn't process this meant Sarah could not only read a thought or a feeling, she could also send one.

Terence considered responding with an apology, which is what his years of pastoral ministry had told him people expected from all ministers—meek apologies at the slightest perceived offense, regardless of how ridiculous the offense was. But for some reason, he didn't give Sarah an apology. Instead he turned his smile into a frown, furrowed his brow, and scowled. He might not be able to read minds, but he too could communicate nonverbally.

The fog cleared when they arrived at the steps. It was not replaced with sunshine, but rain that drizzled. It was as if what had been vapor transitioned into liquid form. The rain didn't fall from above. It formed in mid-air, then hovered in its spot. As they walked through it, it clung to their clothes like sticker burrs.

"I can hear other thoughts," Sarah said. "Someone is here other than us."

"Were you able to hear Mel's thoughts?" Terence asked.

"No," Sarah said. "It never crossed my mind when we were with him. But the answer is no. I didn't. It was normal, like in the real world."

Wyoming lifted up his ball cap and ran his hand through his hair. "This world is as real as anything else in our lives. It's just the rules are different. This might actually be fun." He looked straight ahead and smiled.

Terence wished he could muster up a smile, but adventure wasn't his cup-of-tea. However, his mind was fully engaged in what was happening. "Guys, the reason Sarah couldn't read Mel is because she wasn't supposed to. He wasn't part of the operation, but the one who oriented us. I have a distinct feeling now we are on the path we were brought here for."

The steps were long, extending at least ten feet to either side. At the top were columns. To Terence, they looked like the famous steps in front of the Philadelphia public library in the movie *Rocky* when Sylvester Stallone ran to the top in the early morning hours and danced to the tune, *Getting Strong Now*. They looked about as tall as those steps as well.

Wyoming was on the fourth step before Terence fell in behind him, Sarah right beside him.

Terence expected the climb to be long, and he was certain it would wind him. He was wrong on both counts.

There looked to be about two hundred steps, but before Terence could take more than six or seven inclines, they were already at the top. To his left, Sarah was bent over and panting, and Wyoming had his hands over his head taking deep breaths. Neither perspired, but they were clearly out of breath.

"What's wrong with the two of you?" Terence asked.

A "shut up" from Sarah was the only reply he got. He decided not to push it any further. It must be an idiosyncrasy inherent in this imaginary world. Maybe, Wyoming was right, this world was as real as the one he spent every other day in. But the rules were different.

Terence could tell Sarah was excited and wanted to say something as soon as she was able to speak. "Take your time," he said to her.

"This is my high school," Sarah said between pants. "The front is a replica of my high school."

"You're telling me," Wyoming grunted, unable to get a good breath, "Sydney High School has fifteen thousand steps to the front door?"

"Don't be stupid," she said. "The steps are different. I don't know where those come from. But the front, this façade, is exactly like the façade on the high school that faces the main road. We never use the front. The students go in and out the back where the parking lot is. But the front of the building people see when they drive by looks exactly like this. Even the concrete blocks are the same."

"Does your high school have one of those, too?" Wyoming pointed up to a maroon fascia board which formed an ugly overwrought false gable on the front of the concrete building. There was writing on the board, in large gold letters.

SCHOLE TON HEPTA DAIMON

"The School of The Seven Demons." Sarah said, looking at the text.

"Did your daddy teach you Greek?" Terence asked her.

"No," she said. "You know Greek; and I," she tapped her index

105

finger against her forehead.

The preacher turned, took off his black rimmed glasses, and over-exaggerated a frown to emphasize his displeasure at being probed.

She responded with a wicked smile.

"What does it mean?" Wyoming said.

Terence opened his arms wide and said, "It is the name of this building. Given what Sarah said, it likely means this is Seven Demons High School. It is written in Latin letters, which is our alphabet. The words are Greek."

"You mean the seven demons," Wyoming pointed behind him down the hill, "the old geezer talked about?"

"Exactly." Terence shook his head. "I have a feeling we are about to be taken to school."

"You mean challenged, don't you?" Sarah said. "This is a challenge."

Terence moved closer to the building. He put his hand on the cream-colored concrete block and closed his eyes as he bowed his head. "A challenge, maybe, but I perceive this building is not coincidence or pulled from Sarah's thoughts. This building is part of the challenge."

"Perceive?" Wyoming's face scrunched as he spoke. "Perceive? Is that some kind of ESP stuff? This is going from bad to worse. First, she can read my mind, now you can feel your way through this. All I got is steel and grit, which isn't helpful here."

"Relax," Terence put his hand on Wyoming's shoulder. "I didn't mean it in that way. This is something I've always done. I didn't ESP it. I'm simply working the problem, trying to figure out what is going on. I've concluded nothing here is haphazard. Someone, and I suspect it is the Lord, has created this place for us to learn something or accomplish something. It might be more about us than it is anything else. But Mel told us about the seven demons, now here we are at a replica of Sarah's school with a plaque that says it is the school of the seven demons. It is connected—the demons and the school. That is all I am saying. I am thinking it through. There is nothing more to actions than that." Terence reached his hand out and put it on Wyoming's shoulder. "Besides, I have a feeling steel and grit is something we're going to need."

"Good," Wyoming said. "I'll keep you in the normal pile."

"What pile am I in?" Sarah said.

"There may not be a pile for you," Wyoming said this with a straight face and no glimmering playfulness.

106

Sarah ignored the jab. "We should go in." She said.

"Where is the front door?" Wyoming shrugged.

"I told you, at our school we all use the back. I say we walk around to the back and check it out."

Sarah took off before Terence or Wyoming could object or offer another opinion.

Wyoming whispered to Terence, "The kid is dangerous."

"She reminds me of her father when he was younger. He could be just as certain about things. It is only as he aged that Butch developed a more moderate stance, or some might call it a tolerant disposition. The years have tamed him a bit. But early on, you should have seen him. He was like her right now—direct, confident, and slightly confrontational."

Wyoming nodded, "I've seen a stubborn streak in him a time or two. But still, keep a watch out. It might come to a moment when you and I have to help keep her in check. And not only for her own safety, but ours."

Terence exhaled. He didn't fully agree with Wyoming's skepticism, but he understood where the warrior was coming from. "You'd make a good Baptist, Wyoming."

"Why is that, Doc?"

"Because Baptists are naturally suspicious and paranoid, just like you."

"Call it what you will, but she could be dangerous. Very dangerous."

Sarah, looking straight ahead as she walked, shouted at them. "I'm not dangerous."

XV

To Terence's eyes, the distance along the porch on Hepta High was short, but they walked a long time. He didn't get tired, but it took longer than he'd thought it should. He suspected he could live in this world for an eternity and never figure out how distances worked here. They reached the corner, then they turned right to come down the side. As they did, Sarah's arms shot out from her side as she shouted, "Stop!"

"What?" Wyoming said.

"I see the covered walkway below where the door is," Terence said.

"Exactly," Sarah pulled at her ear. "We have arrived at the back of the building. Shouldn't we be on the side of the building? We went directly from the front to the back, as if the building were a two-dimensional object instead of three. It has length and height, but no width."

"I guess it is one of those weird things about this place." Terence looked behind him, as if checking would change what he saw. "But my guess is when we walk into those doors, we will discover it actually does have depth as well."

"Not only dimensions," Wyoming said, "I bet it will be a dimension of trouble."

"That is the first thing you've said since we got here which I agree with you about." Sarah lowered her arms and walked along the cracked sidewalk. Terence moved up beside her. Wyoming stayed in the rear, his head on a swivel, seeking and looking for potential risks.

"Can you still hear the thoughts of the other person?" Wyoming said. "Because I don't see anyone."

"Yeah," she said. "But it's not thoughts as much as it is emotion."

"What emotion?" Terence said.

"Excitement. Giddy, even. Whoever it is, he or she is excited because we are coming."

"Well, maybe this won't be so hard after all," Terence said. "Perhaps we will find ready hosts to teach and enlighten us."

Wyoming chuckled. "Hardly. Have you ever seen how excited a housecat gets when it catches a mouse?"

"Why do you have to be so negative?" Terence turned around and looked at Wyoming. "I mean, why can't you be more positive? Here I am, trying to put a nice spin on this otherwise foreboding situation, and you go and crush it all with your Debbie Downer vibe. No one needs that right now, and most especially me." When Terence started speaking, he was playfully irritated, but by the time he shouted "especially me" his protest had boiled into full aggravation.

"Why don't you grow up and face reality? This is not a walk in the park, Doc."

"Pastor Terence," Sarah raised her eyebrows as she spoke. "He is right. The excitement I feel is malevolent. It feels a little like the thing I felt at Jessica's house. Whatever we find in the school, it will not be a pleasant conversation."

They walked underneath high arching windows and beside an unkempt hedgerow until they arrived at a small covered walkway. The walkway was only about eight feet long. It jutted out from the back wall at an ugly angle that looked like an optical illusion. The back wall was flat, but where the walkway met it, it was at a forty-five-degree angle, yet somehow it came out straight at a flush right angle.

Terence mumbled. "This is a crooked door, which doesn't bode well for what we will find inside."

"So now you believe me," Wyoming said. "The logic and reasoning of knowing trouble lay ahead which I laid out for you so thoroughly meant nothing to you, but one peep at sloppy architecture and you're all in on doom and gloom." He spat. "Preachers."

The walkway reminded Terence of the awning outside the dentist office where they drill his teeth when he has cavities. They went underneath the canvas covering, which Terence was sure had been a metal covering when they first spied it. The double door was typical for office buildings. Heavy glass was surrounded by a black metal frame. Two flat handles protruded on each side.

Words were etched into the glass in the spots where one might expect to see office hours and the physical address.

On the left side door:

Welcome to school Sarah, Terence, and Wyoming.

CLASS SCHEDULE
Genealogy
History
Biology 201
Choice and Free Will
Philosophy Seminar: God is Dead
War and Hate
Psychology 101

On the right side:

SCHOOL RULES
1. No cutting class.
2. No cheating.
3. No chewing guns.
4. No one gets out alive.

Wyoming Wallace pulled his .45 from the holster under his arm and shot the left side first, then the right. The sound was so loud and sudden both Sarah and Terence grabbed their ears. Sarah's mouth was wide open in shock.

Even in the moment's fever, Terence took note. Surprising Sarah should be impossible. She should have known what was coming because of her ability to read their minds. But she didn't. Terence didn't know what this little detail meant completely, but he had a guess.

The individual shards of glass fell to the ground and bounced back up into the air. Each piece turned into a separate, tiny, liquid drop. The liquid gathered together in mid-air creating a single horizontal disk. The disk stretched itself long and wide, flipped vertical, and slid back into the doorframe. Both glass panels glowed and the same etching on the left side appeared. The same thing happened to the etching on the right side, except a new line appeared:

5. Fire. Aim. Ready.

Wyoming holstered his pistol. He put his hand on the glass door. He squinted his eyes.

"Why did you do that?" Terence asked. "I nearly peed myself."

"I wanted to see what would happen." Wyoming looked at his traveling partners. "We are mice in a maze. I felt I had to do something." His voice rose to a shout, "Resist. Fight back." Now his head dropped, and he pushed out a barely audible, "Something. Anything." He continued running his hand along the smooth glass pane. "In Iraq, we were used as mice in military experiments quite often. I hated feeling that way then. I hate it now even more. The feeling someone is messing with you just to see how you'll react. Playing with your mind."

"It's not a maze," Sarah said. "And we are not mice. I know it feels like it, but it is something else. Mice don't matter in tests. It is the result that matters. I have a feeling what happens is not too important here. We are what is important, not the results. It is all about us."

Terence stepped up beside Wyoming and put his hand on the door handle. "I am reminded of a Proverb I preached back in the summer of 2014. I didn't preach it well, but the verse stuck with me at a personal level. It said, 'The crucible is for silver, and the furnace is for gold, and the Lord tests hearts.'" Terence shuddered. "The Lord is testing us."

"But that note was written by the demons?" Sarah said. "It can't be from the Lord, can it?"

"Have you never read how it was the devil who tested Job, but it was the Lord who brought Job to the devil's attention? There is much we don't understand about spiritual things. My thinking is even demonic entities serve the Lord's purpose even if they do so unawares. They are blinded by their own sin and rebellion to such a degree they don't recognize how they are being used." Terence pursed his lips, "We are facing ugly things that are definitely not from God and not a part of his plan for the world. However, I have no doubt The One True God is writing a different narrative than the one the demons are drafting. His is bigger than theirs, and far more powerful. Yes, indeed, God himself has arranged this. It is the crucible and the furnace."

"You're saying our hearts are being tested?" Wyoming said.

"Exactly," Terence nodded as he opened the door and walked in.

"Is there going to be a bell to start things off, like in high school?" Wyoming's tone could not have been any more sarcastic as he spoke in the doorway. He and Sarah stepped in right behind Terence. Fluorescent lighting hung overhead. There were trophy cases on both sides of the entryway. Sarah was drawn to them. Her face twisted as she noticed the championships and victories. Prominent in the front of the case was a bust of Friedrich Nietzsche. It wasn't a bronze bust or any other medium recognizable to Sarah. It was flesh and blood, and the face alternately smiled and frowned as the head turned from side to side. Above the bust in gold letters, pinned against the wall was a banner that read, "Nietzsche PROVES God of the Bible is dead. History may now move forward."

To the side of Nietzsche was what looked like a blown-up copy of newsprint. The headline declared, "Caesar Wins! The Other JC Kills Democracy, Founds Empire" Below it was a copy of *The Aeneid,* opened, with Latin text. Beside it was a genuine trophy, one which in any other context could have been the regional varsity championship for football or a hunk of metal going to the debate club for winning at nationals. The base of the trophy looked like a building. In front of the building, on the bottom of the trophy case there was a model car in a motorcade. The second level of the trophy, where a cup might be on a normal award, there was another building Sarah recognized as the White House. Pillars coming out of the bottom of the building held up the second tier. Atop the second level of the trophy, the final level rose to a point with a rifle.

Sarah felt this was something she should know about, but she couldn't put the pieces together. The items about Nietzsche and Julius Caesar had been obvious to her, but not this one. "Hey, you guys, come over here." They came to her side before she could finish the sentence. "What do you make of that?"

Terence whistled.

Wyoming said, "That's it. That is a 6.5 mm Mannlicher-Carcano rifle."

The pieces started to move. The motorcade on the bottom of the trophy case proceeded along a road, a road that wasn't there before. A window flew open on the bottom building's sixth floor, a rifle barrel pushed out from it and fired three quick shots. The cars down below dissolved, followed by the whole display—the base building, the White House, and the rifle. It all disappeared; a black television screen formed and flashed in silver words, *1st Place Marksmanship to Lee Harvey Oswald.*

"Disgusting," Sarah said, her face turning pale. The facetious treatment of Kennedy's assassination triggered a psychic reaction. She raised her hand to cover her mouth. She wanted to run away, but there was nowhere to run. Sarah was trapped inside her own head, and there is nowhere to escape your own head. The grainy film the teacher showed in her history class of President Kennedy's murder in Dallas rolled in her mind, the same reel looping over and over. She smelled the asphalt street in Dallas. The wind blew on her face as the car glided across downtown. Thoughts of Kennedy's wife filled her mind. The President and the First Lady had been fighting. Mrs. Kennedy was angry with her husband, but Sarah couldn't figure out why. Sarah jumped and screamed when she heard the gunshot.

Terence grabbed Sarah. Wyoming pulled his pistol, but there was no target that presented itself and nothing was amiss other than Sarah's pain. Neither man knew anything about what was going on inside Sarah's mind.

But she saw John Kennedy reach for his throat from the perspective of someone sitting right beside him in the back of the black car. She reached for him. She, Sarah, seeing this as Sarah and not Jaclyn Kennedy, knew any second another shot would rip the President's head. She reached out to grab him, thinking if she moved fast enough, she could change history. She leaped on top of the bleeding man who, in a panic himself, kept grabbing at his throat. He looked at her with dying eyes. The eyes called for help, but the eyes also knew help was not coming. The eyes spoke to her as if their owner knew this was his fate and had known it his whole life.

Undaunted, she reacted, throwing herself on top of him as the second bullet from the traitor pierced the air. Sarah never heard the crack from the rifle, for in this reiteration of the assassination, her head took the bullet; her head snapped back as it exploded.

She opened her eyes to find Wyoming Wallace holding her head in his lap with his jacket under her as a pillow. Terence kneeled beside her on one knee in prayer.

"What happened?" she said.

"You fainted on us," Terence answered her. "You fell over."

Wyoming was quiet, but Sarah was already picking up his thoughts again.

"You're right, Wyoming. I didn't faint." She rolled over onto her side before she stood up. "I was shot. In the head. Like him," she pointed to the trophy case which had reset itself to the original image of the trophy shaped like an assassin's rifle and the Presidential motorcade below.

"What did it feel like?" Wyoming said as he stood up.

"It hurt."

Wyoming shrugged. He went back to the case and looked at the display again. "Do you see the pillars between the School Book Depository and the White House?"

"Yeah, now that you mention it." Terence whistled again. "These demons don't miss a thing, do they?"

"I don't see it?" Sarah rubbed her eyes.

"Missiles," Terence said. "Nuclear missiles. The kind of missiles the United States and the Soviet Union had pointed at each other for fifty years."

"They are still pointed," Wyoming mumbled.

Sarah spun around to the other trophy case behind her. "What did you guys find in these?"

"Same old, same old," Wyoming said. He glanced at Terence. Terence received the message and tried to turn Sarah back around away from it.

"Nothing to see here," Terence said. "Boring things. You know, history and whatnot." She persisted, nevertheless, toward the case.

Sarah said, "Looks like old-fashioned Polaroids? Right?"

"Yeah, yeah, silly pictures. Nothing to waste any time on." Wyoming positioned himself between Sarah and the case.

She pushed him aside and fired a thought into his mind, "Don't try to protect me."

Polaroids were pinned to the wall behind the glass case. Each image was illuminated by a spotlight of unknown origin. The light intensified the closer the viewer stood to the case. Sarah stood close, inching herself closer.

"Daddy?" She whispered.

Each snapshot was an image of Butch Gregory. The first one to catch her eye was a picture on the beach. Her father was fully dressed, standing in about three feet of water. It looked like he was trying to drown someone. The bizarreness confused her before she realized it was four years ago. Monica was under the water. It was the day he and Wyoming saved her life. In the space where Polaroids have a white border, below the actual picture, "REVENGE" was written in all capitals with a red marker.

Another picture was her father and Terence tied up in a chair. The word "HELPLESS" was written beneath it.

There were hundreds of pictures, all with her father in some terrible situation. Accusatory words were written in red marker underneath each one.

One photograph showed him beside a river talking with a man who looked like a park ranger. "HYPOCRISY" was written beneath that one. The word "REJECTION" was written underneath a picture of Butch sitting beside Tommy Bothers in the board room at Sydney Community; ballots were piled in front.

Sarah shook her head. Another picture cried out to her for attention. This time she didn't recognize her father until she studied it for a bit. That was when she recognized the boyhood Butch Gregory climbing the tree. She could see he had climbed far up into the canopy. She spied movement. As with the trophy of John Kennedy's untimely end, the picture began to move, but it was a subtler movement. Only after the photograph moved did Sarah see someone else was in the tree with her father.

She gasped, because she knew what happened next, because she'd heard this story. Never from her father, though. Always from her mother. Daddy didn't talk about it.

The word "FAILURE" was written below the picture on the white border in red marker.

The tree in the photograph shook. Shark Gregory, Butch's kid brother, Sarah's uncle, climbed fast on his brother's heels. He'd finally caught up to the object of his adoration and affection. Sarah could see it in the boy's eyes. He loved Butch, but that wasn't unique or special. Everyone loved Butch. But he had more than love. Butch was his hero. Shark worshipped his brother in the way of young boys, which is to say he imitated Butch, chased Butch, taunted Butch, and never wanted to be more than two feet away. Most of all, he wanted to impress Butch with his strength, bravery, and courage. She plucked the thoughts from her uncle's mind through time and space and across the self-contained universe on display in the trophy case.

Sarah cringed when the move came. She knew it was coming but couldn't stop it. It was the move that still caused her father moments of regret and pain and kept him up some winter nights. Shark turned upside down on the tree limb, dangling like a trapeze acrobat in the circus. His knees clasped over the limb, his hair dangling from his head as gravity pulled it toward the ground. She can hear him. He says, "You're upside down, Butchy! The tree is upside down. The whole world is upside down."

Wait! What is that? Sarah jumped when she saw another person on the limb with Uncle Shark. Not a person. Definitely not a person. There was a hint of arms and legs, and something like a face, but it was more like a shadow, but a shadow made not from black and darkness. It was a shadow made from orange, red, yellow and putrid green.

The fire-demon looked out of the picture directly at Sarah. It made eye contact and cackled. When the laughter was fully formed, and the evil intent signified, he brought from behind him a cloven tail and slammed it into the tree limb Shark Gregory hung from.

The fire-demon disappeared.

The limb snapped.

Shark fell.

In the same manner as she had heard the thoughts of John Kennedy's wife in the motorcade in Dallas, Sarah now heard the thoughts of Shark as he fell.

Surprise.

Fear.

Panic.

Then with an icy bite she perceived the cold bite of betrayal at the moment when Shark realized his brother could not save him. He trusted Butchy and believed Butchy could do anything. But Butchy hadn't saved him. Butchy let him fall. Butchy let him die.

The blackness came again for Sarah and she was once more on the floor.

XVI

"This is gonna kill her," Wyoming said louder than his normal speech, but he did not shout it. "We need to leave here as soon as possible."

"We can't." Terence said. "This is why we are here."

115

"But she can't take any more. Whatever is going on with her and that mental voodoo she has now, it is affecting her differently than us." Wyoming was again sitting on the floor Indian style with Sarah's head on his jacket in his lap. Terence knelt beside her.

"Last time she wasn't out this long," Wyoming said. "What if she doesn't wake up?"

"She'll wake up," Terence said. He rubbed Sarah's hand between his two large, tender hands, "she is too strong not to. Besides, the Lord is too good to not have her wake up. He wouldn't have brought her this far only to let it fall apart here." Terence brought his gaze up from Sarah and looked at Wyoming. He intentionally slowed his breath, dropped his voice to a near whisper, and did what good pastors have always done. He worked at being calm when others were decidedly anxious. "Wyoming, why are you so disturbed? This is not like you. Your demeanor is normally unflappable. For some reason, you are acting more like a rookie than a veteran."

"I don't know." Wyoming turned away from Terence's stare and looked down at Sarah. "Maybe it is because I feel out of control. I don't like it."

Terence kept rubbing Sarah's hand, but his eyes were on Wyoming. "No one likes being out of control." Terence took a deep breath. "Part of it could be because this is a dream, and we have no control. We are three unfortunate Alices in this unWonderland. But another part might be the growth in your heart and the opening of your spiritual eyes." Terence tapped at his own heart with his left fist as he spoke. "In here. The biggest step is admitting we have no control, except for the decision we can make to follow The Truth or not. Feeling like you're out of control is a key step for recognizing who is in control."

Wyoming didn't say anything. He didn't grunt or humph. He didn't exhale or huff. There was only the real and metaphorical silence eternally omnipresent before the cacophony of truth.

Terence took his right hand and placed it on Sarah's forehead. "History can be either a great teacher or a terrible depressor." Tears formed in the corner of his eyes, "Sometimes the bad guys win. That's how it goes. But don't lose heart. For every Julius Caesar there is a St. Augustine. For every Nietzsche there is an Alvin Plantinga. For every Oswald there is a Nelson Mandela." Terence swallowed hard, then added. "The faith you and I share teaches us wrongs will be made right, and all things will be made new. This is true in the big picture, but also in your father's life. Butch Gregory is a wonderful man. Don't let evil rewrite what your heart knows. Evil is already defeated, but the end hasn't yet come."

When Sarah's eyes opened, Wyoming checked them immediately for signs of dilation or concussion. There were none.

"This time," Sarah said from the ground, "it was personal." She rubbed her forehead. "Did you see the fire-demon in the tree?" Reading their blank stares, she asked, "Either of you? Did you see it? In the tree?"

"No," Terence said.

Wyoming shook his head. "What tree?"

Sarah stood up and pointed to the Polaroid of the tree in the backyard. This time when she looked at it, she heard no thoughts, felt no betrayal, and saw no figure causing the tree limb to break.

That didn't stop her from telling Wyoming and Terence what she'd experienced in her mind.

"So now I'm supposed to believe your uncle was murdered by the devil?" Wyoming said. His incredulity was enforced by his sardonic tone.

"Of course," Terence said. "The devil is a murderer and a thief. He killed Shark and he tried to steal Butch. Completely within character for him. I see nothing unbelievable about that claim."

"Devil might be too simple an answer," Sarah said. Her eyes were now bright with insight. "Remember what Mel told us. These are not The Devil. This place is Hepta High—Home Of The Fighting Demons. What we are seeing in this room is the work of one of the seven."

Wyoming raised his hand and pumped it, "Rah rah sis boom bah. Go Team!"

"This is Molech." Terence said this with a confidence he rarely demonstrated. "This is the demon-god who wants to defile one generation while destroying the next."

Wyoming shook his head. Sarah tried to explain. "It's like a game of recognition," Sarah put her arms on Wyoming's shoulders and faced him. "Our challenge in this place, our test, our crucible and furnace, is to survive the different challenges and recognize what is at play. Who is in play." She dropped her voice to a lower register, "We have to find out what's at stake."

"So, you think," Wyoming said, "we have seven levels of this. Each level is a different one of those demons the old geezer with the grocery cart was talking about?"

"Exactly." Terence was exuberant with clarity.

The lights in the room went dark. On the floor, arrows illuminated pointing them to the right.

"Good morning, class" a male voice with a distinctively middle-eastern accent said. "Congratulations on passing genealogy. We hope it wasn't too much of a bullet to the brain for you." A cackling chuckle came over the intercom. "Sorry, I couldn't help laughing at my own joke. As for you, you might want to take a deep breath before we move onto second period."

The floor continued to pulsate with illuminated arrows.

Terence remembered the directional lines on the Haunted Mansion ride at Disneyland.

Sarah remembered the lights on the floor toward the exit at the movie theater after the other lights are turned out.

Wyoming remembered an airplane he was on that made an emergency landing in the middle of the night in Minneapolis.

They entered a gymnasium.

Metal doors slammed shut behind them. Sarah jumped. They hadn't opened any doors to enter the gym, but once they moved through, they all heard the distinctive sound.

"What do you want to bet," Wyoming's voice was above a whisper, but only barely. "Those doors are locked?"

Terence nodded his head in agreement.

The three of them walked underneath the basketball goal and stood on the baseline of the hardwood floor. The bleacher sections were darkened, but bright spotlights glared from above onto the floor's shiny surface. The light was uneven in its dispersal, though. Spotlights on the sides of the arena pointed toward center court, where one would expect the team mascot or logo to be.

"Are you still taking bets?" Terence looked at Wyoming. "Because I'd like to wager, we're supposed to walk to the middle."

"Ya think?" Sarah said with all the sarcasm of a typical smart-mouthed teenager.

Wyoming took the first step, and the other two followed. Terence's fancy dress shoes clacked against the floor. They echoed throughout the hall with each step.

As soon as they reached the free throw line, the gymnasium erupted in sound. It was the shouts and cheers of thousands of people, if not more. They came to a stop and looked around the bleacher section. They saw no people. Those sections were pitch black, as if walled off in a great darkness. Nevertheless, shouts rained down upon them. At first it sounded like cheers. Soon they recognized the noise as jeers and boos.

118

"Looks like we're not the home team. We're the away team." Wyoming started out again toward the center.

The walk took much longer than it should. Basketball courts are not that big. Sarah and Wyoming both felt fatigued when they arrived at the middle.

Terence was not winded, but his narrow eyes and tilted head indicated he was perplexed. He put his hands on his hips and said, "I expected it to be a devil emblem, like the Duke Blue Devils, or a pitchfork like Arizona State's Sun Devils. I didn't expect this. Never in a million years."

Wyoming chuckled, "Figures."

Sarah's mouth was wide open as she looked at the giant, round picture of her father on the floor at center court. It was not a flattering picture, either. It was in full color, and his blotchy skin looked irritated. His hair was both thin and out of place, and he looked puffy with glasses askew. His eyes were red, like he'd been weeping. Stubble covered his face. His lips were an emotionless line with a slight downturn at the corners. Fear was in his eyes, or it might have been anger. It could have been both.

When? —Sarah shot the question to her two companions telepathically. It was easier than shouting over the noise. She felt for their response. None of them knew it was taken in the secret holding cell years ago, when Agent Lapp-Bench held Butch after Amber was killed in San Diego on the day Butch, Amber, and Wyoming rescued Tamara Rey, and all those other children, from the sex-traffickers.

Wyoming walked to the middle, about where Butch's nose was, extended his arms, and shrugged his shoulders. "Why?" He said. "What now?"

"I don't know," Terence shouted over the jeers. "Maybe some contest is about to happen. A game of some kind." He walked toward Wyoming and stopped on Butch's cheek. "Perhaps we will have to play each other?"

Sarah said nothing. She walked around the ring of the circle, looking down at her father's image, but she didn't walk onto it.

Terence tried to whisper to Wyoming, "This has got to be some serious psychological trauma for her," and he turned his back to Sarah and pointed at her.

Wyoming nodded, but he could see Sarah frown.

"I can hear what you think, you know." Sarah said. But Terence noted she didn't disagree with what he'd said, nor did she fight the sentiment.

She kept circling around, making two full orbits until she stopped at her father's chin. Wyoming walked toward her, standing on Butch's bottom lip, and asked, "You know what we're thinking. You know what he said, and you know I believe this is some kind of trap. You know we're both worried about you. You know our thoughts. But we don't know yours. What are you thinking?"

"I think," she said, and stepped onto the circle. When her second foot, her left foot, found its place on the picture, there was a great shaking and sudden movement. The circular picture rose up off the floor, as if it were on a rocket—zooming upward. Sarah stumbled when it jostled. She fell backward went over the edge of the circular platform that looked like her father's distressed face. She fell sideways, hitting the edge in such a way her upper body was too far over the surface, and she flipped right off. The platform was at least two hundred feet above the hardwood floor at this point, and Sarah was falling to her death, like her Uncle Shark.

But Wyoming grabbed her. As she had lurched over, he dropped flat to his stomach and snatched both of her legs. Before he could call for help, Terence was already beside him, pulling Sarah back onto the circle.

The arena had gotten larger as they ascended. It was now larger than any stadium imaginable, but the bleachers were close to the circle they stood on, as if the building was shaped like beehive. The higher they went, the narrower the building was and the closer they were to the edges.

The people in the stands were now visible, as bright light flooded them from above. Below them was a dark abyss. They couldn't see the floor.

They were going up, but their speed had slowed. With a clamor and a shake, Butch Gregory's face stopped its climb, and the three contestants stood an unknown distance from the floor beneath.

The people in the bleachers were growing in number. They cursed at them, jeered them, and mocked them. Terence said, "I feel like I'm at a Philadelphia Eagles game when the Dallas Cowboys visit." He shook his head and said, "No. That's not quite right. This must be how the early Christians felt in the Colosseum when the Roman emperors made sport of them."

Wyoming scanned the crowd with his eyes, "I don't know about any of that, but it is hard for my brain to understand. There are so many of them. And they feel so close. And we are high—like, I'm guessing a mile high, and yet somehow we're inside a gymnasium."

Sarah, who had now gotten to her feet, looked out into the hostile crowd as well. She not only heard their words, but she felt their hatred and blind anger. The psychic wave of insult harried her heart, twisting the ever-present dagger of rejection and inadequacy, until she thought she would burst. Her eyes swelled with tears, and that was when she felt the greatest pain she would ever feel in her life. It happened as she held her arms across her chest in a futile attempt to protect herself from the pain and saw in one of the front rows her father Butch, her mother Lucy, and her brother Paul. All three of them booed her. She could hear her father, the same one whose face she stood on. He said, "I am so disappointed in you. What a failure you turned out to be. I can only hope your brother will make the family proud." Her mother said nothing to her. She simply looked at her daughter with the disapproving scowl that said more than words ever could. Paul stood beside Lucy Gregory and chanted, "Loser! Loser! Loser!" getting louder and louder each time. She kept looking through the audience and saw everyone she'd ever known—teachers, friends, neighbors. Jessica was there, but it was her bloodied corpse which accused Sarah of letting her down. "You let me die," she screamed.

Sarah collapsed to her knees and doubled over, as if retching. She put her hands over her ears, but it didn't stop the voices around her from crawling into her mind and eating away at her sanity like spiritual termites.

Terence saw something similar. His own family was in the front row. He saw his children and heard their taunts. They each one proclaimed, "You put the church before us!" and "We were never good enough for you" and other such jibes. It was the visage of his wife Muriel which stung the most. He saw her, not as she looked now, but as she looked thirty years previous when they were dating. She was not looking at Terence at all but looked at another man who was standing beside her. At first, he didn't understand. Then recognition came.

The other man was Darren Stahls. Darren had dated Muriel a few months before Terence met her. Darren and Muriel had ended their relationship, and she'd never spoken about him, but he'd existed. He also knew Darren had tried to woo her back three weeks after Terence asked Muriel to marry him.

The Muriel in the stands turned her head toward Terence in the most nonchalant manner possible and said, "I made the wrong choice." She embraced Darren and gave him the longest, most romantic, and erotic kiss Terence had ever seen.

The crowd section Wyoming saw was not filled with family members. It was a gallery of ghosts. Many were the bodies of dead Iraqis who had been mostly faceless for him. The little girl, Leylah, was there. Her body was covered in bullet holes, and a never-ending supply of blood spurted out of each one.

She spoke to him, but it was in a language he didn't understand. At the start it sounded like a plea for help. It turned into something else. Leylah raised her right hand, made a fist, and pumped it rhythmically up and down as she shouted. Soon everyone else in that section, all the dead Iraqis, did the same thing with their hands and their shouts. The language shifted, and they were saying in clear English, "Death to Wyoming Wallace! Death to America! Let the world burn."

This chanting made him angry, and he almost pulled out his pistol to show them how angry, but he saw her, one section over. Amber. She looked at him, her eyes inflamed. Wyoming didn't know why she was angry with him. Those others at least made sense to him. But why would Amber be mad? He wished she would speak to him, but all she gave was the most intense "I hate you" look Wyoming had ever seen.

"Don't you get it?" Sarah said to Wyoming. She was on her knees, but she'd recovered from her own relational nightmare enough to hear again.

"Get what?" Wyoming shouted, more in frustration than a need to be heard.

"I don't know how I can hear her, because all the others are more like pictures or video images to me, I can't hear their thoughts. Except hers. I hear her loud and clear, like I hear the two of you."

"I don't know what that means," Terence said.

Wyoming walked over to Sarah. "I don't care what it means, I care what she is saying. Tell me. What? Why is she mad at me?"

Sarah stood up and took Wyoming's hands in hers. "She loved you. She loved you in life, and you never returned her love." Sarah closed her eyes and concentrated. "She loved you so much and thought so highly of you, which is why when Amber and my father needed help, you were the only one she could think of."

"But it doesn't explain why she's mad?" Wyoming's eyebrows lifted; his cheeks pushed upward.

"You never returned her love. Then she died. You need to understand this, Wyoming. Love was not lost, it was squandered. That is why she is angry."

Before Wyoming could adjust to this splash of cold water, a booming voice, the same one that had come over the intercom earlier

122

in the hallway, spoke. This time, the voice was like an announcer at a prize fight. The voice said, "There is only room for two on the ring, someone has to go!" When the voice finished, there was an explosion of sorts, and the outer third of Butch Gregory's face burst into flames and disintegrated. Terence, Wyoming, and Sarah moved in closer toward Butch's nose.

"What on earth does that mean?" Terence said.

"I'm not certain this is, strictly speaking, earth." Sarah said.

Wyoming grabbed Terence and Sarah's arms. "It means this platform we're on is going to keep getting smaller and smaller until only two people can fit."

"Oh," Terence and Sarah said at the same time.

There was another explosion and another ring section burst into flames and disappeared.

"What if we stand on each other's shoulders," Sarah said. She was shouting at the top of her voice because the crowd cheered wildly with each shrinkage of the platform, as if it were a last second winning touchdown at a Seahawks home game.

Wyoming looked around as if trying to find a better plan. Not finding any, he said, "Okay, let's go with it. You can't weigh but about a buck-o-five, so climb onto my shoulders." He knelt down on a knee. "Terence, hurry up and help her. We don't know how much time we have before another kaboom."

Without argument, Terence grabbed Sarah with his strong arms and hands and put her atop Wyoming's shoulders. He was squarely on Butch's nose, the center of the platform with Terence standing beside him, helping Sarah stay on.

"This will work," Wyoming said. "And you're not heavy at all. In fact, I'd say you need to eat a burger and a milkshake or two."

"I'm vegan," Sarah said.

"Of course, you are. Of course, you are." He tilted his head up toward Terence, "That's the problem with kids these days. They don't eat!"

The booming voice returned. "Lawbreaker!" it shouted. "No cheating."

A glass circle appeared above them. It was the same shape as the platform that held them, and it moved downward.

"We're about to run out of headroom," Terence said, screaming even louder because the crowd went beyond bonkers with the appearance of the glass ceiling. "They are not allowing for our interpretation of the rules, I'm afraid."

"But you're taller than me on Wyoming's back?" Sarah genuinely looked puzzled, as if she were being treated unfairly at a game of gaga ball at church camp.

"A minor detail," Wyoming said. "They want one of us to go over the edge. I suspect they want us to fight about it and push someone off to save our own skin."

"That's exactly what they want," Terence said. "But I will not let them get their wish. I'm jumping. Goodbye." Terence turned around and took a step off the ledge, which was only two feet away.

Wyoming, however, reached out and grabbed his coat collar and dragged him back onto what was left of Butch's left eye. "Oh no you don't! Just because you're a holy-man and all, that doesn't mean you're the only one who gets to make decisions for the rest of us. I'm jumping." And he did.

Or at least he tried to. Sarah, who'd dismounted from Wyoming's shoulders seconds earlier, did the same thing to him he'd done to Terence, except she grabbed him by the belt loop on his jeans. She yanked him backwards onto what was left of the platform in the split second before gravity took full effect on his step off the ledge, just before that moment where momentum would have pulled them both off.

A strong curse flew from his mouth. "Don't ever do that again."

Without opening her mouth, she told him from her mind through to his mind that he couldn't tell her what to do. She then added her owns wear word for punctuation.

"The glass ceiling has stopped," Terence said, pointing upward.

"As soon as I get back on Wyoming's shoulders, it will start down again."

There was another explosion and more platform disintegrated. They stood on what remained, which was Butch's nose tip.

"So, what do we do?" Wyoming pulled his ball cap off and ran his hand through his curly hair. "I won't let the Doc jump, you won't let me jump, and we're not about to let you jump."

Sarah smiled. "I have an idea." She took them both by the hand. "Do you trust me?"

"Do we have a choice?" Wyoming said.

"I'll take that as a yes," she said. "This whole business is about them either making us kill someone, or someone killing themselves to save us, thereby leaving guilt behind for the survivor. I say we turn the tables. I say we all three jump together. At the same time. Let's see what happens."

"It's bold," Wyoming said.

"Illogical," Terence said. "But it might be what is needed." He squeezed Sarah's hand, and grabbed Wyoming's. "We better do it before they blow the whole thing up."

Both Wyoming and Sarah nodded agreement.

"In the name of the Father, Son, and Holy Spirit" Terence prayed as they all three leaped off the platform and fell over the side into darkness.

XVII

There was no sensation of falling.

There was no spiraling uncontrollably in space like bad special effects from the old black and white Twilight Zone.

They simply appeared in the hallway of Hepta High as if they'd come through a door.

"Not what I expected." Wyoming Wallace said these words as slow as a human could and be engaged in spoken communication.

"I guess Sarah called their bluff." Terence brushed off his shoulders and arms as if he should be dirty, but there was no dirt. He felt like he should be sweaty and out of breath, but he wasn't either. Sarah and Wyoming both looked as though they'd been through the proverbial ringer. It was a puzzle, but he didn't know if he wanted the solution. He turned his thoughts back toward the arena. "How did you come up with that solution?" He bent down and looked directly at Sarah's face.

"I figured," She began, "their goal was to divide us. I remembered Mel talked about the seven demons, and most work at dividing people up or turning them against each other. With the rules they'd given, I figured the only way to overcome was to stay united. The only way to stay united was to jump together. I know it doesn't make much sense, but in the moment, it felt like the right course of action."

"Clearly," Wyoming said, "it was. Good job. The question now is, where are we?"

As if in direct answer to his question, the intercom voice clicked in again. "After an exciting game, it is time to hit the showers."

The lights went out. Sarah grabbed Terence's arm and pulled herself close to him. There was a swoosh, and the sound of Wyoming's pistol being cocked.

Terence was the first one to smell it, but he didn't say anything.

Wyoming did. "I'd hoped never to smell that again. Ever." The tangy, putrid earthy smell of a mildew filled bathroom combined with the distinct odor of sweaty gym clothes swirled with teenage body odor.

Sarah made a slight gagging sound.

Wyoming Wallace again added commentary. "Smells like Teen Spirit."

Overcoming her gag, Sarah added to the conversation in the dark, "Nevermind."

"What are the you guys talking about?" Terence's voice was raised with excitement and frustration.

"It's a Seattle thing. You spent so much on the east coast, you might not understand," Sarah said.

The lights came on and grew from dull to dim, and finally to full on fluorescent brightness. They were in a locker room. Six showers were in the middle with no dividers or shower curtains. Open urinals and toilets were on the back wall. The other three sides each had lockers with wooden benches in front. Pad locks were on all the lockers. Motivational posters hung above the lockers and the in-between spaces. One said, "The moment you commit yourself, you have accomplished your goal," and it had a picture of a basketball player grabbing a rebound. Another one said, "There is no 'I' in team." The accompanying picture was a football squad huddled up. There was one other poster that was black and in tiny white letters said, "What we really mean is" and then below in large red letters, "Kill! Kill! Kill!"

Wyoming pointed it out to the other two. "One of these is not like the other," he said. "Is it sarcasm, or is the reality for this particular team?" While he waited for an answer, he gently laid the hammer back down on his revolver and holstered it.

"It might be both sarcasm and reality." Terence felt the need to qualify his answer. "What I mean is, there are elements of truth the devil likes to exploit. Athletic competition in many ways is a substitute for blood sport, with a pedigree going back to the ancient gladiators. Americans love to watch athletes in the prime of their lives spend their youth and vitality smashing into one another, tearing muscle, breaking bones, and damaging the brain. For the most part, they don't care as long as the game continues." He exhaled and kissed the air as is his custom, but this particular kiss lacked Terence's normal precision. "It is not lost on many of us that the vast majority of the athletes are people of color—Black, Latino, Asian—and most coaches and owners are old white men. It is a type of exploitation of the minority races by

126

the majority."

Wyoming took off his Seattle Mariners baseball cap and looked at it. He asked Terence, "I thought you were a big Philadelphia Eagles fan?"

"I didn't say I was immune to it." Terence grinned. "But it doesn't mean, either, there isn't at least a smattering of truth to the situation."

"I suppose we all are hypocrites in some area or another." Wyoming put his hat back on his head. He began a security sweep of the room, more out of habit than out of necessity. He tugged on all the padlocks he came by and opened one that was unlocked and empty. In the far corner of the other side he found something.

"Whoa," He said. "You two better come here."

"What is it?" Sarah asked.

"I swear, why do you have to be so difficult? Can you trust me and come here?"

She walked toward him. Terence followed. Sarah mumbled as she approached, "Maybe I'd trust you more if you weren't such a jerk to me."

"It is only out of respect for your father I am holding my tongue, for if you were anyone else, I'd put you in your place."

"Enough," Terence said. "This is no time for squabbles, because what we have here is fascinating."

"I thought you'd like it," Wyoming said, moving on to the task at hand. Sarah however, wasn't ready to relinquish her seething anger.

But the anger turned from Wyoming to Terence. "Who made you boss? Why do you get off telling me 'enough' like you're my dad or boss?"

Terence lifted his hands in surrender. "I give up. I didn't intend to come off as authoritarian. I only wanted to be a peacemaker between you two."

Wyoming punched Terence in the arm. It wasn't the kind of punch that would make a person hurt or fall back, but it was strong enough for Terence to know Wyoming wasn't playing. "What's that about?" Terence shouted as he rubbed his sore spot.

"Why did you give up so easy when she questioned you? I can stand many things, but I can't handle a man who backs down at any sign of trouble. You need to stand up to her. You didn't mean nothing by what you said, and you can't let her live like she's Queen Bee because she can read our minds."

"Shove off," Sarah said. She shoved Wyoming.

Wyoming shoved back, but not hard. It was enough of a shove to communicate that Sarah should watch herself.

"What is going on?" Terence said, stepping between the two. "Why are you acting like this? It's like you're both spoiling for a fight."

"She started it," Wyoming said.

"No, I didn't," Sarah crossed her arms. "He was being mean to me first."

Terence's eyes softened with amusement. He let out a laugh, took a step backward, and sat down on the wooden bench.

Sarah and Wyoming stopped their antagonisms and glared at the man on the bench.

"What's so funny?" Wyoming said.

"You're acting like my children—which is out of character for both of you. Wyoming, you are severely adult, and Sarah is the most mature young woman I've ever met. So, something must be going on. That was when it hit me. Our demon friends are cheating. This locker room is too small for a high school gym class or athletics department. It is a middle school."

"You mean junior high?" Sarah sat down next to Terence.

"Yeah, that is what they call it here in Sydney. Back where I grew up, they called it middle school. Some kind of spirit, or energy, or vibe or something is affecting the both of you. And that is when I started laughing. We are being tested with some seriously bad ju-ju."

"Ju-ju," Wyoming said. He pointed at the locker in front of him. "This is your test. This is your ju-ju."

By this time Sarah had seen it, and all three were wondering what it might signify.

The locker in front of them was a different color. Whereas every other locker was purple, this one was mostly red, but a tiny white box was painted in the middle where the vents were. A strip of white masking tape stuck on the top part of the door. Written in black marker on the tape was one word.

HARRISON

There was a pad lock on it.

Wyoming grabbed the lock and pulled. It didn't budge.

Terence remained seated, and Wyoming joined him as all three looked at it.

"That is my locker," Terence said. "At least, it looks like mine. Our school colors were red and white. Let me amend that. They were red and white in middle school. In high school, they were red and black. Our mascot was a panther."

128

"So, you played sports?" Sarah asked. Something in her demeanor had changed, and she now looked at him with concern.

"Technically, yes. I was never any good."

"Really?" Wyoming said. "You've got such an athletic build. I mean, my goodness, your hands are huge and your shoulders are broad. I bet you could have played linebacker or running back, and dated every last cheerleader."

"It always goes back to sex with you, doesn't it?" Sarah was indignant, and for a moment Terence was concerned the anger might flare again.

Wyoming giggled. The moment passed.

Terence ignored it and went on to address Wyoming's inquiry. "My father was a literature professor. I am a reader, always have been. When I was in middle school, I was more likely to have my nose between the pages of Asimov or L'engle. Everyone thought I should be an athlete, for the reasons you mentioned. Even then I was taller than all the other boys. The problem was I didn't have the heart for it. Yeah, today I am active and exercise, but I don't like to play sports. I'm okay watching it, but not playing it."

"So why did you play?" Sarah's eyes narrowed and her mouth puckered.

"It was required. If you were a boy, you had to play at least one year of a team sport in the eighth grade. So, I played football." He took a deep breath. "And this is my locker."

"Why are we here?" Wyoming pulled out his gun. "I bet we have to look inside your locker, so I might as well shoot the lock off now and get it over with."

"That's not necessary," Terence said. "If it's my locker, this is my lock, and I know my combination."

"You remember your combination from junior high?" Wyoming took a step back and put his hands on his hips.

"It is the same combination, or code, I've used for locks and PIN's all my life. The variations and order changes, but the essential number is always the same."

Terence stood and approached the locker like a novitiate at a pagan altar. Terror filled him, but he knew Wyoming was right. This is why they were here. "Three rings for the Elven- kings." Terence turned the knob to three. "Seven for the dwarf-lords" he turned the knob back to the left to the number seven. "Nine for mortal men doomed to die." The knob spun under Terence's fingers back the other direction to nine. "One for the dark lord on his dark throne." The dial spun back to one. Terence pulled the tumbler downward and it unlocked. He pulled it from the eyeholes.

"What are those numbers from?" Wyoming said.

Terence turned around. "You don't know?"

Wyoming shrugged.

"How about you?" Terence pointed to Sarah.

"It sounds familiar, but I can't put my finger on it."

"It's from the Bible, right?" Wyoming guessed. "You're a preacher man, and all you preacher men ever think about is the Bible."

"It's not from the Bible," Sarah said. "I can't put my finger on it, but it is definitely not from the Bible."

"Not the Bible. At least not the Holy Bible. It is from the bible of all literary boys everywhere. It is the number of rings from the Lord of the Rings. Three, seven, nine, and one."

"I've changed my mind. I bet you didn't date much in school," Wyoming said.

"That," Terence said, "is righter than you can possibly know."

Terence Harrison took off the lock, then he opened the door to the locker.

He heard the music, then realized his eyes were closed. He opened them to see he was staring into the locker. But he was not with Sarah and Wyoming, and he was not in the make-believe dreamworld. He was in his middle school. He turned around and saw himself in the large mirror behind him. He couldn't believe it. It was him, but he was thirteen-years old. His hair was high in a classic afro, and he had on the solid white practice football uniform and pads. In his left hand was a red football helmet with a snarling white panther decal on the sides.

The music came from a boom box on the wooden bench behind him. A cassette tape played Earth, Wind, and Fire.

"Harrison," an angry voice came from across the room. He cringed.

"Yeah, Coach?" He shouted, a muscle memory.

"Hit the showers, kid. You can't go to English class smelling as bad as you do right now."

"But, Coach, I'm fine." He pleaded.

"Now, Harrison, or I'll have to strip you down and scrub you with the giant brush." He pointed to the infamous scrub brush that hung on the inside wall of the coaches' office. The office was glass paned, so the students could see inside, and the coaches could see everything outside. Ostensibly this was a safety issue, to make certain the students didn't do anything dangerous or harmful. Years later, Terence

130

wondered if grotesque voyeurism and the rampant pedophilia of the 70s and 80s didn't have something to do with it. But now he was faced with the same moment again.

The coach shouted, "And turn that street music off."

He hated this place.

Yet he loved Butch Gregory. Down deep, he knew this all had something to do with his friend. The middle-aged mind stuck inside the pubescent body of a young boy reached for courage. He glanced around one more time to see if Sarah or Wyoming were around.

No sign of them at all.

It took him some time to remember how to take the pads off. The other boys on the team had already gotten out of their pads and headed for the showers. Most would not shower, which was his goal, too. It was the unspoken plan they all employed. Only about four or five of their teammates had matured, and the rest were still very much boys, whereas the others were more like men. Those boys who were man-like relished the shower, for they were able to flaunt their manliness. The others went back to where the showers were, turned on the water, wet their hair, and came out drying off. The coaches were not that observant, and not that smart.

Terence had successfully used that trick many times.

He would try it again today.

Soon, he'd stripped down to his underwear, which he didn't take off. He grabbed the bar of soap and his mostly unused towel. Before he could turn around from the lockers, he felt the sting against his backside. He jumped around in reflex, and Coach stood over him with the scrub brush. He brought it down one more time and wacked him on the side of his right thigh.

"You can't shower in your undies, Harrison. You know that. Now get those panties off right now."

The other boys erupted in laughter when Coach called Terence's underwear panties.

God, help me. Not this day. Not this day. He'd done his best to forget about that day. For over three decades it was a blank spot in his mind that he never visited. But today it was thrown back into his face, whether he wanted to or not. Only God can choose to forget. The rest of us must live with the memories. This was a memory Terence wanted to never have again.

Coach swatted him again on the side of his thigh, but this time with the brush's bristly end. "What's the matter with you—don't you understand plain English, or should I speak African monkey talk to you?"

Terence said, "I hear you, Sir."

"Take those panties off right now then get in the shower."

Against his better judgment, Terence did what he was told. He covered his midsection with his towel, holding it with a grip so tight his black hands were turning red. The racism made grown-up Terence seethe. Kid Terence was numb to it, which in time would carry its own separate pain. But he didn't have time for that now. Thirteen-year old Terence was angry at Coach's indifference to the ridicule he'd condemned him to. He knew it was coming, and he knew Coach knew it was coming. Either Coach didn't care, or Coach thought it was something natural that had to be endured. These were the thoughts of adult middle-aged Terence's mind in the body of the boy Terence, walking as slow as possible toward his punishment. It was punishment, that was certain. But punishment for what? For being a boy? For being a boy who still looked like a boy? For not having hair under his arms or on his testicles? For being a boy in a country that built a shameful public-school system? For being a boy not quick enough to run through the water before he got Coach's attention? For choosing football over track?

Punishment is awful, especially when a person is not certain exactly what he or she is being punished for. Perhaps the worst part is the sense of injustice which stays with a soul long after the punishment is served.

As soon as Terence walked into the steaming shower area, the laughter started. A big, freckled boy, one of the running backs for the team, pointed right at Terence and said, "Here comes the boy in the panties." His name was Davey, and his red hair was lathered up with soap. Davey grabbed a handful of the soap from his head. The surety of his movement toward Terence was so confident and swift Terence did not process what was happening—even though he'd lived this before—he was unprepared to react. It was as if he was stuck in the loop. Knowing what the outcome was to be did not change his actions in the moment. He knew Davey was coming with the soap, but he was helpless against it.

Davey grabbed him by his tall afro and pulled his head back and rubbed the soap into his eyes. Terence remembered the smell, and now he experienced it again. It was the harsh, chemical, green scent of Prell shampoo. His eyes burned, and he had the incredible instinct to rub them. Davey released Terence's hair, so he brought his arms up to rub his eyes. When he did, the towel covering his midsection fell to the wet floor.

Laughter again erupted from the boys in the shower. Terence couldn't see them all, but he knew them all by name. There were four. Davey was the most obnoxious, but there was also Fred, who was black like Terence, and another white boy named Mark. Mark was the quarterback. He often bragged openly he'd already slept with three cheerleaders and had gotten to second base with a high school twirler. Davey was the most obnoxious, but Mark was the leader. Enrique was a Mexican boy who usually didn't say much. Sometimes Terence thought of him as a friend, but there were days like this which reminded him otherwise. It didn't help Terence at all, not in this moment of complete powerlessness, to know Davey died in a motorcycle accident in Los Angles before he reached the age of eighteen, or Mark spent twenty years in prison for armed robbery, Fred turned things around and by the time he left high school had a career lined out in the military and eventually became an officer, or that Enrique gave his heart to Jesus at summer camp in his sophomore year of high school and owns a car dealership outside of Anaheim and is a deacon in his church. None of it helps Terence rationalize or justify what he knows is about to happen. Again.

Enrique made the next move. He grabbed Terence's arms and pulled them behind his back, holding him tight. Davey shouted, "Look at that tiny thing between those scrawny legs. We need to get a microscope from the science lab to find it."

Mark pointed, "Maybe it's not a thing at all. Maybe's he's not a boy. Maybe he's a girl."

"He does wear panties; Coach said it himself," Fred said. They were all getting in on the act now. Terence had become what every shy, bookworm boy is most terrified of—the focus of attention for a group of jocks.

"He is crying," Mark said. "Crying like a girl."

"Come on guys," Terence shouted. "It's the soap! It's the soap!" Terence remembered the logic inside his mind when he'd spoken it. His first thought was the twisted logic every victim feels in some way. It is the twisted yet hopeful thought—if the oppressor would simply understand the situation of the victim—perhaps the oppressor would see reason and stop. Although this has almost never happened in the history of persecution, it nonetheless is what comes from the mind and the mouth of victims. It happens, middle-aged Terence knew, as a desperate act of hope. People, even victims in the midst of being victimized, can't actually believe another human being would do these things to someone else, so the mind assumes the problem is a lack of information. If only the oppressor understood I am indeed not a girl, but I have soap in my eyes. In another context, the question might be different. I am a black man who only wants a fair shake, but that doesn't mean you have to hang me. I am a Jew, but that doesn't mean you have to exterminate me in your ovens. I am a Christian, but that doesn't mean you have to drown me in a trough full of urine. If only you understood I wasn't a threat to you and would never hurt you then you would stop this awful nightmare and not mock, maim, or murder me. I'm a human being with feelings, can't you see that?

The second thing Terence remembered thinking in that moment was if he shouted loud enough, some of the other boys, or perhaps even Coach, might come intervene. He came close to shouting for help, but didn't. It would have been a sign of weakness. At least that is what pubescent Terence thought.

He did not shout.

Help did not come.

The boys kept laughing. Their mockery became intensely personal. They called him every filthy name school age boys use or can imagine. Insults flew against his family, his sisters, and his race. Those were bad enough, but it got worse.

The excitement aroused Mark sexually—something which frightened and terrified Terence. Terence was too young and ignorant to understand the link between violence and sexuality. Clearly, Mark, was not. He'd done this before. So too had the other boys.

Like a gangster in a movie, Mark ordered the other three. "Hold him down on his knees." As obedient accomplices they pushed him to the ground. Mark forced himself upon Terence's face until the moment passed.

Seconds later he was alone in the shower, naked and shaken on the floor, his eyes shut tight, afraid to look.

When they finally opened, he was standing in front of the locker again, with Sarah on his left and Wyoming on his right.

"How long was I gone?"

"Gone where?" Wyoming said.

"No, no, I've been back there for what feels like hours."

"You've been right here," Wyoming said.

Sarah gasped. "Oh no. Oh no." She reached up onto her tip toes and hugged Terence. "I can't believe they did that to you."

"What?" Wyoming raised his voice.

"Let's sit down," Terence said. "I need to rest a minute."

Over the next five minutes, Terence retold the story. Sarah, who had psychically grabbed the images in Terence's mind, now heard his interpretation of events and also felt the order and logic flowing from his thought process. It came from years and years of telling stories and making arguments. Wyoming listened like a child at story time.

When he finished, he said, "I have never told anyone what happened."

"You didn't call the police?" Sarah said. "You were raped!"

"Back in those days, we rarely, if ever, called the police for things. I didn't have the words, or the wherewithal, to even tell my parents, much less strangers in uniforms. Yes, today I know that should have been reported, and," Terence wiped the tears from his eyes, "I am afraid."

"They can't hurt you anymore," Wyoming said. "Don't be afraid."

"Thank you," Terence said. "But I'm not afraid of them. Not now. I am a grown man. What I am afraid of," and again there was a pause and he wiped tears, "is the untold number of other people they abused after me. How many other boys and girls? Mark, especially, had a mean streak. I wonder. If I had told the police, or told someone, maybe they would have been stopped. Maybe they'd have gotten help that could have saved some of them before they ruined their own lives, too. But all I'm left with now is that gnawing feeling of unfinished business."

"What will you do?" Sarah said.

"The only thing I know to do."

"I vote for you hunting them down and exacting revenge." Wyoming was ready with a plan. "You say one is in prison. I bet we can take care of him from on the inside. I know a guy or two on the inside. And the car salesman, that one will be easy—" Wyoming, whose normal pace of speech reminded most people of a snail or turtle, was speaking at quite the excitable rate. Yet Terence cut him off.

"No, there will be no revenge." Terence turned his palms upward. "I will do the only thing I know to do. I have told you the story. I will tell my wife. I will tell my children. If for no other reason to give them courage to speak up." Terence trembled. "Dear God, please spare them . . ." There was a great gasp from the preacher as he prayed, "Please spare them."

The remainder of his prayer was not formed with syllables, consonants, or words. It was the ancient prayer of tears, deep breaths, and sobs. When he finished his lament, he grabbed both Wyoming and Sarah by the hands and said, "I will do the only thing I know to do. I will forgive them." He named them one by one. "I forgive Davey for

135

bullying me. I forgive Fred and Enrique for hurting me. I forgive Mark for violating me." Terence took another deep breath and added. "I forgive Coach for neglect and insensitivity. I forgive the school for such a broken system. I forgive my parents for not taking better care that things like this weren't happening in my life."

"What about God?" Wyoming said. "Shouldn't you forgive God. He let it happen."

"Forgive God," Terence looked at him as if he'd uttered something in a foreign language. "I am afraid you have it all wrong, my friend. There is nothing to forgive God. It is quite the contrary, The Lord is the one who got me through it."

The lights flashed three times, and on the last flash they stayed dark. How long? Who knows, for in this world time was different. Even if time did matter, keeping it was imprecise.

XVIII

When the lights came back up, they no longer sat on the wooden benches of the musty locker room. New scents surrounded them. These odors were different from the nasty mildew, but it would be hard to say they were more pleasant. The distinct aroma of frozen pizza, meatloaf, peanut butter and jelly sandwiches, nacho cheese chips, fried chicken strips, instant mashed potatoes, and bleach water wafted through the air.

"I was afraid one of the stops would be here," Sarah said.

"It doesn't matter the generation. The cafeteria always poses problems." Wyoming Wallace was not happy.

Terence said, "Every teen angst movie, from *Napoleon Dynamite*, to *Mean Girls*, to *Animal House* has at least one socially awkward cafeteria scene? It is because we all hated it, somehow." Terence narrowed his eyes. Sarah could have read his mind, but she didn't need to probe his thoughts to know a lecture was coming. "The irony is food is a blessing. Notice how it is often shared at the most intimate times of our lives. We eat the rehearsal dinner before a wedding and eat the cake after. Funerals are usually punctuated with food. Civic gatherings such as picnics and honorary banquets all involve beloved foods. This is modeled best in the church, where Holy Communion is the sacred meal which holds the body together in fellowship." He put his hands in the air and shook them, "Yet somehow, we haul our children into cafeterias and feed them like swine before they are gutted."

136

"You think about things too hard," Wyoming said. "I remember I hated always having to eat in the lunch line, because I got free lunches because my folks were poor. I never had fancy lunch boxes or clever, prepackaged deserts, or cheese sticks, or fruit rolls. It is hard to believe now how envious I was of kids with Jell-O pudding cups and Fruit Roll-Ups."

"See, that is what I'm talking about, Wyoming." Terence wouldn't let it go. "You were a kid, but you somehow knew there was a social barrier between you and the other kids. It wasn't about the food. It was about the differences. And the problem is after all these years and all our advancements, we continue to mess kids up with that kind of social division. Then we wonder why we have blue and red America, left and right America, and a divided culture."

"I hated being made to drink white milk." Sarah didn't elaborate.

Wyoming started his usual perimeter sweep of the area. The room was large, but he pointed out to the other two the chairs were smaller than high school age. Terence hypothesized that, like the locker room was about middle school, this was actually at elementary school.

Sarah said, "Yay. White milk." She spun her finger in the air and rolled her eyes to emphasize the sarcasm so apparent it didn't need emphasis.

The hall was a large square with a serving line running along the back wall. Wyoming jumped over the rail and investigated the kitchen area, which was a complete array of stainless-steel. Cheap plastic plates and clear glass tumblers were stacked and sorted in rows, ready for the coming lunch crowd. To his surprise, there was food in the hot pans. He saw the foods he'd sniffed earlier---fried chicken tenders, mashed potatoes, green beans, ketchup dispensers, dinner rolls, and steaming white instant gravy. A small office was in the back, and Wyoming checked it out too. It was as boring as the lunch room. It had three filing cabinets, an old wooden desk, and opened ledger books which he looked through. It was the names of students and what their balance was for their lunch bill. He saw his own name there, and beside it was written the word, "Free." He closed the book and stuck it into the top drawer of the desk. Then he pulled the book out of the desk, opened it to his page, and spit on it. Then he threw it in the wastebasket.

Three staplers sat on the desk, along with a hole punch, a ruler, a metal cup filled with pencils and pens, a glass paperweight shaped like a hamburger, and a three hundred count box of unopened hairnets. Pink and yellow receipts were spiked onto a metal rod. Wyoming's first thought was what a useful weapon it could be in the right situation. An oversized obligatory food pyramid poster hung on the wall.

It took Wyoming a moment to see it, and when he did, he cursed himself for not seeing it sooner. There was a window behind the desk. The blind was pulled over it. He snapped the blind up, catching his breath at the expectation of what he might see through the window.

He was disappointed. The window showed only darkness outside. Pitch black. Wyoming couldn't tell if it was because there was only darkness outside, or if the window itself was dark. There was no latch to open it and see out. He considered breaking it. He could use the stapler from the desk, or perhaps shoot it.

He heard Terence shout his name, followed by, "Are you okay back there?"

He shouted back. Deciding to leave the window alone for now. He came from the office and joined Sarah and Terence in the refectory. They were not where he'd left them. They had moved over to the opposite wall. "We found the snack bar." Sarah said. "Which is where I would have been every day."

Wyoming walked over to them. They both leaned against the wall, with their left knee bent and foot flat against the wall's surface. Terence had his thumbs in belt loops. Sarah had her hands in the pockets of her athletic pants.

The snack bar was a hole cut out of the wall with a door that led back into the main kitchen area. Like the main serving line, food was prepared and ready to eat. Frozen pizza warmed under a hot plate, as was hotdogs, nachos—complete with nasty plastic cheese sauce, bagged Lays potato chips, candy bars, and Pepsi products. He grunted again.

"Did you find anything back there?" Terence said.

"No. Same as in here. Cafeteria food, ready to eat. And hairnets. Lots of hairnets." He didn't tell them about the window. He never did figure out why. It seemed like something he should have shared.

"Hairnets?" Sarah said. "Gross," pronouncing it as "Ga-Roe-Sa" for exaggerated effect.

"What is the right reply to that?" Terence said. "Wasn't it, 'gag me with a spoon' or something like that?"

Wyoming and Sarah ignored him, but Terence turned serious. "Did you notice the colors on the wall in here?"

"Was there something to notice?" Sarah said.

Wyoming shrugged, as if it was a detail which wasn't vital.

"I did." Terence stepped away from the wall. This wall is purple. The other one is white," he pointed to the front wall, "and the back wall is also purple. The fascia around the serving line and this snack bar is checkered purple and white."

"So?" Sarah said.

"I get it," Wyoming said. "The locker rooms were purple too, except for your one locker. It was red."

"True," Terence nodded. "My school colors were red and white. I know what Sarah's school colors are. Sydney High is blue and white. Wyoming, what were your high school colors?"

"It was a light kind of maroon and white. Not quite dark maroon like the color of the Washington D.C. football team, but a light, almost creamy maroon. Perhaps the way a woman's hair might look who had dyed it but didn't want it red. Almost autumn colored, I would say."

"Gasp!" Sarah shouted. "Now I see where you're going." She too came away from the wall and looked around the room with eyes wide opened. "If you mix red and blue you get purple, and if you were to add a creamy maroon, the hue you would get would be almost exactly this shade of purple."

Wyoming shook his head. "Now they are just messin' with us."

Wyoming started strolling around the tables and chairs. "So now we know this is designed especially for us. If we didn't already know that, then we should have." He kicked a chair and turned over a table. Sarah started to reach out for him to calm him down, but Terence held her back.

"I know you can read his thoughts," Terence whispered to her. "I can too, right now. He's sorting things out. Let him be."

She obliged, but she didn't appreciate being told what to do.

Wyoming, however, continued to walk around. He was standing in the middle when he turned back toward the other two. "I wonder what this test will be?" Wyoming mumbled to himself, but they both heard him. He got louder with his speculation. "The first was a psychic test on the nature of history," he held up one finger. "The second was a test of unity in an athletic contest," he held up another finger. He lifted the third finger, "The third was a psychotic and cruel memory about shame and violence." He held up his left hand with four fingers now lifted. "I wonder what is in store for us here in the cafeteria."

"Monsters?" Sarah said.

"I have a feeling the monsters are being saved for last." Wyoming answered her.

Sarah probed Wyoming's mind to see what he meant by monsters, and what she saw was his mental vision of The Rab-Shakeh with a fiery lasso in one hand and the biggest gun she'd ever seen in the other. She shuddered and left that image alone by itself.

"So far, we've seen no indication as to what is going on or how this plays out." Wyoming looked around. "However, if the other three levels are any indication, we will know soon enough. What I was thinking, though, is whoever these things are that created this place, they've made us lunch. We should probably eat."

"Are you serious?" Sarah said. "What if it is poisoned?"

Wyoming nodded. "If they wanted us dead, they would have already done it. They could poison the air we're breathing, for that matter. If this is air. I remind you, we don't know where we are or for how long we're going to be here. We should eat."

"Well then, if I'm going to die eating, I'm getting pizza and a Pepsi," Sarah said.

"What, no white milk?" Wyoming said. "I was about to get twenty from the fridge over there for your dining enjoyment."

"Ha, ha, ha," Sarah said.

Wyoming lifted his ballcap and ran his hand through his curly hair. "So, are you gonna eat the cheese pizza or the pepperoni?"

"I'm a vegan," Sarah said. "So, cheese all the way."

"But," Wyoming raised his hands, "it's not pepperoni because this is a dream world. No pig died. Why not go ahead and splurge a little and have the imaginary meat?"

Sarah looked at Wyoming with large eyes and said, "But in my heart a pig did die."

"Cheese or otherwise, the pizza looks nasty to me," Terence chimed in. "I'll have nachos and a Snickers bar. And a Coke."

"Sorry, there is no Coke here." Sarah said. She had already hopped the counter and began to gather her food. She put down her plate of pizza and started working on Terence's nachos. "There are only Pepsi products in here, and the cans all look funny, too. You can have a Diet Pepsi, Pepsi, and something called a Pepsi Free."

"Give me a plain old Pepsi," Terence said. "Calories are the least of my problems today."

Just as Sarah and Terence sat down at a table, Wyoming Wallace returned with a tray filled with food. He had a plate of chicken strips, gravy, two dinner rolls, and a whole separate plate of green beans and four tiny cartons of chocolate milk.

"That's a lot of green beans," Sarah pointed. "Hungry?"

"I like green beans. What's it to you?"

"To each his or her own," Terence said. Without warning, he bowed his head and prayed. "Dear Lord Jesus, we are in the strangest

140

of places. Yet you have provided this food for our nourishment and for our fellowship. Strengthen us with it. I ask you to hold us tight in the bonds of friendship. Protect us from whatever the evil voice has planned. In Jesus' Name. Amen."

Sarah added an amen.

Wyoming had opened his first chocolate milk during the prayer.

"Sarah, you said earlier the cans of soda looked funny." Terence began, "They do not look funny. They look perfect." He held up his can of Pepsi—the mostly white can with the blue trademark dot in the middle swirled by red. "This is what a can of Pepsi should look like. I guess you would call it retro. I'd put it somewhere in the mid-80s before they started tinkering with all the cans and making them darker." He took a loud sip. "In fact, everything feels so much darker these days."

"Cynical, much?" Sarah drank form her own Pepsi can.

"The older I get, the more cynical I become." Terence popped a jalapeno pepper in his mouth. "Symbols matter, and what I've noticed is over the past decade, probably since 2001, marketing campaigns have adopted darker colors, darker styles, and far less brightness." He held up the can. "Notice how much brighter this can is? There is more white on it, and this may sound like I'm reading too much into it, but this can looks happier and more vibrant than the mostly blue, and dark blue at that, cans of today. Coke has done the same thing, as have most soft drink companies. Check it out sometime." Terence stuck a cheese-soaked nacho chip in his mouth and continued. "It's not only in marketing. It is everything and everywhere. Movies are darker now. The villains are more villainy, but the good guys are more villainy too. Everything is morally tainted. Plus," he wiped his mouth with a paper napkin, "the actual images on the screen are dark. The movies aren't only metaphorically darker, they are literally darker. Every director out there wants to show the moodiness of the theme, so the thing is shot in such shaded lighting it is often hard to see what is going on. You know I'm right."

"About what?" Wyoming stuck a fork full of green beans into his mouth. He chewed as he spoke. "All I hear is an old man complaining about those young whipper snappers. I get it from my folks all the time."

Sarah laughed. "You're old like Terence."

"I am not," Wyoming pointed the chicken strip at Sarah like it was a weapon. "Terence and I are from two different generations. I guess he was born sometime around 1962, maybe 63. How close am I?"

"Not bad, young whipper snapper." Terence laughed at his own joke. No one else did. "I was born in June of 1962." He took a long look at Wyoming, "You, on the other hand, are a child of the 80s. Let me guess. Was it 84 or 85?"

"Neither," Wyoming stuck an entire chicken strip into his mouth. "I was born on Easter Sunday, 1982. That makes us almost twenty years apart."

"And that," Terence smiled with self-satisfaction at Sarah, "means that we are two completely different generations. I grew up with bomb shelters, Cold War, Woodstock, Watergate, and Disco. He grew up with the shopping malls, Live-Aid, the fall of communism, computers, Clinton-Lewinsky, and MTV."

Wyoming nodded. "Roger that." He stuck another chicken strip in his mouth. He asked Sarah, "So what year were you born?"

"2002."

Terence's eyes popped. "That means we are each twenty years apart. Three completely different generations."

Sarah tore open the wrapper to her candy bar. "I guess. But you guys are old. It doesn't matter if you're older than Wyoming, you're still two old men."

"Rude, much," Terence said in the same tone Sarah had earlier used to mock his cynicism. He pushed back his chair. The scraping sound of metal on tile echoed.

Wyoming said, "Calm down, grandpa. She's joking with us, unless she is one of those self-entitled vain millennials more concerned about a selfie and making sure the barista gets her drink order perfect."

"Ah," Terence leaned back toward the table. "We have to remember her generation. She grew up with Obama, gay pride, safe spaces, trigger warnings, and constant updates on the smartphone."

Wyoming drank an entire carton of chocolate milk in one swig. He wiped his mouth with his sleeve. "She might need a place to go cry."

Sarah glared at Wyoming. "At least I am aware of my emotions, unlike you emotionally stunted boys." She turned her attention now to Terence. "And you. Remember those insults of yours the next time you have to get your daughter to help you update your iPhone."

"She's got a point there, Doc. But I know where my emotions are, they are right where I buried them."

"And where would that be?" Sarah snapped the words at him like a towel.

"In the middle of the godforsaken Iraqi desert while I was fighting to make sure you and the other snowflakes could sleep safe at night. I dug the hole with my backbone, because I would need that to be strong to carry the weight of my responsibilities. I covered the hole with my willpower, because that is what it would take to accomplish the mission. Then I marked the spot with the helmets and boots of my brothers-in-arms who never came home."

"Thank you for your service," Terence said as he put his arm on Wyoming's shoulder.

"Oh, don't even," Wyoming, who sat directly to the right of Terence, pushed his arm off. "The reason I had to go to war was because of your worthless generation. You created all the problems, elected all the bad leaders, made all the wrong decisions, and handed us a worldwide dumpster fire. Good job, Baby-Boomers."

"I didn't do it! I didn't start the fire." Terence brought his hands up and patted himself on the chest. "I didn't do any of it. But you need to remember your place, whipper snapper. You talk about Iraq, but my big brother gave his life on some anonymous and unimportant hill in Vietnam. He left behind a wife and a baby." Terence's anger hit the flashpoint. "You volunteered to go into the military. Not my brother. He was drafted. No deferments for the black kids, the Mexican kids, or the poor white kids. No country club connections for us. My brother had earned a place in the freshmen class at UCLA and Stanford. He wanted to be a biologist. Who knows, he might have discovered a cure for cancer by now or for AIDS or Alzheimer's. But no. He was black, so he was sent to fight the wars of the white man—white men like you, Mr. Wallace. Population control at its finest—that is what war is all about. The powerful people keeping their power." Terence took a deep breath put his hands palm down on the table. "I appreciate your service and sacrifice, but don't you dare sit there and act like you are the only person who has hurt, because you're not."

Sarah had enough. "The problem with both of you, and your generation, is you want to solve every problem with authoritarian solutions backed up by war and power." She pointed at Terence, "I wish you could hear yourself. You tend to take control of every situation as if you are the final say." She turned her head to look at Wyoming, "And your first instinct is to pull a blasphemous piece of steel from under your arm. You're both warmongers. You do it different, but the result is always the same. People die. Innocent people. In your own separate ways, you and those like you are all drunk with power."

"Everybody dies," Wyoming said. "Nothing is going to fix that. It is the nature of things. What is not the nature of things is for one

143

generation to be as incompetent as yours. You don't know how to do anything. If it doesn't come easy, you whine and complain about how unfair and hard life is." Now Wyoming pointed to Terence. "His generation fouled everything up, your generation doesn't have a clue and can't get your head up from your phone, so that leaves my generation to fix everything. And I mean fix every last thing."

"Fix this." Sarah threw her half-empty potato chip bag at Wyoming. The bag glanced off his shoulder and went flying behind him, spilling junk food onto the ground. Wyoming returned fire by launching a handful of green beans at Sarah. She ducked, and most of them missed. She picked one of the beans out of her lap and hurled it toward Terence. It hit him in the face and stuck in his beard. The ridiculous image made Sarah erupt in laughter. Soon Terence was laughing, and so too was Wyoming. Milk cartons, nachos, candy bars, and chicken flew through the air amongst the three. They were covered in each other's meals, and they continued to reuse the artillery. The beans splintered into fragments from the projectile pounding. Chicken strips were all over the place, and cheese sauce dripped in varying degree on each of them. Wyoming came out the worse, for at some point in the battle Terence and Sarah ganged up on him.

Static crackled over the intercom. The disembodied voice that was becoming too familiar to the threesome spoke. "Lunch is over. Time to get back to class."

The lights in the hall dimmed but didn't go totally dark. The same arrows on the ground lit up, as the floor did when they first entered Hepta High.

"Wait, that's it? That's all?" Wyoming stood up and brushed debris from his clothing. "Where is the monster?"

Sarah looked at him with kind eyes as she smiled at his protest. "I almost believe you." She told him. "I almost believe you are upset there wasn't something horribly dangerous and terrible here for us to face."

He adjusted his Mariners cap. "I am. I was expecting some kind of monster."

"I know." She said, remembering The Rab-Shakeh image in Wyoming's mind. Sarah stood up, joining Wyoming and Terence, who had also stood when the lights went dim. She asked Terence, "What do you make of this? I'm thinking like Wyoming. I was expecting a challenge, or a monster."

"We were the monsters," Terence said.

Sarah and Wyoming gave him the same confused look.

"What I mean is, we were close to the brink there with our discussions. We crossed the line on our judgment, our generational biases, and the anger we carry deep inside?" He shook his head. "How we handled it was the test. When you threw the chip bag, and we all realized how silly the arguing was, our concern and care for each other overcame whatever ill-temper was going on inside us. But if we look inside ourselves, each of us knows it could have gone a different direction. It could have gotten ugly—the ugly that tears families to pieces or divides nations."

"Like our nation." Wyoming said.

"Jesus said a house divided against itself will fall. We need to remember, as often as that line is quoted, that the Lord said it in the context of demonic activity."

"I didn't know that," Sarah said.

"All grandpas know things like that, you whipper snapper." Wyoming delivered the line matter-of-fact.

Terence continued his analysis. "The spiritual reality of joy filled our background and we became one again. That was the test. And we passed."

"By my math," Wyoming held up four fingers, "we're about to move into the fifth challenge."

"Three more, probably." Terence said. "Unless there is something like a bonus round."

The lights on the floor flashed, as if impatient with their slowness in moving on. The voice on the intercom came on again. "Hurry along, students. Tardiness will not be tolerated."

"Sounds like he means business," Wyoming walked onto the path. Terence and Sarah moved in behind him. "I wonder what detention is like here?"

Sarah probed his mind and saw the image of a room filled with scorpions and snakes.

They followed the lights pulsating on the floor out to the back wall, then to the center of the room, and out the doorway. The hallway was pitch black except for the walkway lights. Wyoming did not slow down. They emerged out of the darkness into a bright light, but it was no room; it was the same hallway, but now it shined with brilliant illumination.

"Hey," Sarah shouted from the rear. "Check your clothes."

"What do you know about that?" Wyoming said, amazed.

Their clothing was refreshed. The cheese sauce was gone, as was the spilled soda, and the smell of abused vegetables. The light was brighter now, so bright Wyoming pulled his ball cap brim down over his eyes. Sarah and Terence raised their hands to their eyes. It didn't help.

There was no single light source. It came from everywhere. A constant baseline hum rose from the floor beneath their feet and swept over their bodies. The sound was not so much audible in their ears as they felt the vibrations throughout their flesh. Shadows had disappeared. Everything was effervescent, like they were inside the light.

XIX

They were inside the light.

Wyoming was now no longer leading the group through the walkway as they had bunched up together, walking *en masse* forward through the light. In one motion, without interruption or transition, they emerged from the light and found themselves floating in the air, as if they were microscopic dust particles. Wyoming, who had experience jumping out of airplanes, grabbed his friend's hands. They began to tumble down toward the ground. At first it was a freefall, head over feet and out of control.

The closer they got to the ground, the bigger they became. Their growth was so rapid, they never did hit the ground. They went from tiny specs falling out of control to standing upright on the floor. Hands held tight, they looked at each other in disbelief.

Wyoming shook his head. "You guys want to hear a bad joke?"

"No." Sarah said. "Not now."

Wyoming, undeterred, went ahead. "What does Geronimo yell when he parachutes from an airplane?"

Terence looked at Wyoming with his hands open, begging for the answer.

Sarah said, "Native American jokes are not funny."

Wyoming spread his arms out as though he were falling and said, "Meeeeeeeeee."

Terence smiled. Sarah looked away. What she looked away to was difficult for her to tell. There was no room, or at least anything they would recognize as a room. They stood in a blur. Things were in motion, but unrecognizable and indistinct, because the motion was fast.

"Do you hear it?" Terence said.

146

"Yes, I do." Wyoming said.

"Me, too." Sarah whispered, as if confiding a deep secret to a bestie.

"Donna Summer. I haven't heard this song in years." Terence began to dance a bit, and he kept shouting, in some kind of rhythm, "Hot stuff, baby."

"You've got the wrong song, Doc. I guess the fall must have messed with your ears. Or maybe it is old age catching up with you." Wyoming patted Terence on the back in consolation. "What you hear is Eminem. I'd recognize Slim Shady anywhere."

"I hear Ed Sheeran."

Terence stopped dancing. "I know what I hear. The queen of disco is coming through loud and clear."

"Sames," Sarah said. "I hear Ed Sheeran, and I bet Wyoming is really hearing whomever he is hearing. What did you say the name was?"

"Unbelievable," Wyoming through his hands up. "Eminem. He was the first real white hip hop artist."

"Negativo on that," Terence said. He'd started dancing again. "You're thinking about the Beastie Boys. Those were the first white rappers. Everyone knows that."

"Beastie Boys. I've actually heard of them," Sarah said. "*Licensed To Ill,*

right?"

"Right on," Terence said, still dancing. "But they were never my thing. I'm a Motown man."

The room started to clear up. It was filled with people. Couples were dancing, music was playing, and there were tables with punch and refreshment. Pictures were being snapped. Everyone was dressed up in tuxedos and formals.

"Prom. They brought me to my prom." Wyoming looked up and saw blue and white balloons hanging from the ceiling. The room looked exactly the way he remembered it. His senior prom was held at an old civic center. The floor had new carpet, but the walls and ceiling were dingy and old. The decoration committee had decided to cover the old part of the room with balloons. He and about four other boys had spent the better part of a week blowing up all those balloons during fifth period Spanish class.

"This is just like I remember," Terence said. For the first time since they'd entered this world, Terence looked happy. Terence

Harrison, in the real world, was the kind of man who made everyone around him feel at ease. His internal strength, intelligence, and abiding spiritual strength made people trust him. The counter to this, was Terence rarely felt comfortable. He always felt responsible for everyone else and everything else. Dancing to the music of his youth had a therapeutic effect on him, the way a massage or a day at the beach might have for someone else.

"What do you mean, like you remember?" Wyoming said. "You've lost your mind, Doc. This is my high school senior prom."

"No, it's not. It's mine. Don't you see the banner over there." He pointed in rhythm with the beat, "It says, 'Class of 1980' hanging on the wall? If nothing else, can't you tell by the haircuts people have and these awful yet glorious polyester clothes?"

"I don't see any of that." Wyoming looked for the banner Terence described, but he only saw the images they hung up to commemorate the new millennium. Several posters and banners had the abbreviation 'Y2K' and such. It hit Wyoming like a panting in his soul. He had a glimpse of nostalgia, where he could remember the optimism, hope, and feeling of invincibility they'd all had back then. Nothing turned out as he thought it would.

Terence stopped dancing when the song he heard changed. It went from Donna Summer to *Mr. Blue Sky* by ELO. In the hesitation he noticed the dumbfounded look on Sarah's face. "What do you see, Sarah?"

"My future."

Wyoming heard her say it, and it pulled him away from his reflective thoughts about the year 2000. He scratched his beard. "Yes, of course. You'll be starting your senior year this year. You are the class of 2020, and it hasn't happened yet."

"Interesting," Terence said. "Wyoming and I are reliving our memories. These are things that have happened. But you—this is all the future. The question is, is it a real future that you have time traveled to, or is it a conjectured future from your own mind."

"I don't know," she said. Her eyes sparkled with a girlish pleasure which looked unnatural to her normal countenance. Her usual steely resolve and cold ambition turned soft and nonchalant. A gleam. A sparkle. A euphoria.

"She's high." Wyoming said.

"What do you see?" Terence asked her as he looked around the room.

"I see." She said.

148

In this dream landscape which Sarah, Wyoming, and Terence occupied, all three were at their senior prom at the same time but twenty years difference between them, spanning three generations and multiple locations containing both complete and incomplete action. They occupied the same space beside one another but saw different people. They stood right next to one another but heard different music. They saw one another standing there, but each one saw the others surrounded by different décor and different styles.

Sarah was the first to walk away.

It wasn't long before Terence walked away.

Wyoming was the last, but he had good reason. He'd seen her in the corner of his eye when the blur first faded but didn't trust his senses. The mood eventually convinced even him this was an alright moment. Her name was Angela, a petite redhead who played trombone in the band. She'd never given Wyoming the time of day, but he'd chased her since his freshman year. In a month they would all graduate, and he wanted to go out in a blaze of glory.

The DJ has shifted songs and was now playing "You're Still the One" by Shania Twain. Angela was all alone, and this was his chance. He didn't say a word to her. He came up from behind, put his arm around her waist, pulled her tight, and started to slow dance.

In this world crowded with dreams and temptations, she didn't resist. She melted into his arms and draped hers around his neck. It was all he ever wanted. He didn't have to be a tough guy, or save the day, or fight the wars, or find the criminals. No one had to die. It didn't matter to him if the young woman he danced with was make-believe, without a personality, a will, or a soul in an illusory dream world. She accepted him, and he could relax there with her.

In the real world, in the real year 2000 at his high school prom, he tried the same move with Angela. Except the real Angela, who had personality, free will, and a soul laughed at him and said, "I don't think so" as she snapped her fingers four times in the air making a circle before she walked away to rejoin her friends and make fun of the creepy loner in the funny looking boots. The singular moment of rejection left a relationship scar on Wyoming which never healed. He always needed to prove his worth to the next woman. This was especially true if the next woman was redheaded—the unattainable goal.

But here in this room in which he'd floated in as a particle of light, everything was perfect. The scars were healed. His heart was warm. She smelled like strawberries.

149

A voice spoke to him. It was Angela. She whispered in his ear. Or was he hearing it inside his heart? "You don't have to leave. Stay with me. We can dance forever. We will dance until we can't dance anymore. We'll kiss, and make love, and be together, forever. You never have to hurt again. Stay with me. Don't leave me. You can stay right here, forever."

"Forever," he whispered.

Terence had a different experience when he walked away. His high school prom occurred long before he met Muriel, but he always knew high school girls weren't his thing. At eighteen years old, he was a shy young man who had not the courage to even ask anyone on a date. But music, music was his groove. It was to be so his whole life. As a scholar, he enjoyed jazz to study by. In the car it was 80s hits. When he was enjoying himself at home, he liked the Motown sound. But any beat with a good rhythm made his hips sway and his feet stomp. This make-believe prom was everything he'd ever wanted. Time became irrelevant to him as he lost himself in the music. The turntable played one disco dance tune after another—The Bee Gees, Sister Sledge, Teena Marie and ABBA played on and on. He danced with every girl in the room, whether they were pretty or not. He knew some, some he didn't. He didn't care. He wanted to dance.

In the real world of 1980, Terence Harrison stood in the corner of the gym with his buddies during prom. Although the music had called to him even then, his fear and social awkwardness kept him from enjoying the moment. It wasn't until he went to college, met Muriel, and decided life was too short to live in fear, that he discovered how much music and dancing meant to him. Here in this dream landscape, he was able to live the prom he never had. The prom he wanted.

Underneath the song, he heard a whisper. It was as if an angel, or the great Elven queen Galadriel, were giving him a secret message backmasked onto the music. The enchantress told him, "You can dance forever. You never have to leave here. You can stay with the music, with all these beautiful girls who adore and accept you. You can be the hero of the moment, of every moment, in this place. Forever."

He heard the promise in his heart, and he accepted the terms gladly.

Sarah's make-believe future was different from the make-believe pasts Terence and Wyoming relived. She was the first to walk away, the first to enter into the ether of the other. Hers was the promise of prom future and it was a future which had been stolen from her. What she saw that beckoned her was Jessica. She saw Jessica, who was dead but was now alive before her eyes. She was lost but now found.

Sarah stepped back to take it in. Her breathing was quick and shallow. She felt a brush from behind as someone approached. It was Roberto. He moved quickly toward Jessica and took her in his arms. He drew her close and they slow danced as the song played.

> I found a love, to carry more than just my secrets
> To carry love, to carry children of our own
> We are still kids, but we're so in love
> Fighting against all odds
> I know we'll be alright this time
> Darling, just hold my hand

They held each other tight as they danced, and to Sarah it was the most beautiful thing she'd ever seen. She mumbled the words of the song, "Fighting against all odds, I know we'll be alright this time, Darling, just hold my hand." The words traveled from her mouth to her heart. This time they could make everything alright. It felt like a second chance. Romeo and Juliet risen from the grave.

Sarah called out to her resurrected friend. "Jessica! Jessica!" On the second call Jessica heard her name, turned and smiled. Sarah hugged her so tight Jessica should have said something about it. But she didn't. Jessica didn't say anything. She only smiled. Her blond hair was in an updo with a tiara nestled into it. Her long neck and athletic shoulders highlighted a string of pearls that caught the blush of her pink prom dress. A white orchid was delicately pinned over her bosom.

"You know," Roberto said to Sarah. "We can all be together, forever. No one has to die or hurt. There doesn't have to be any more pain or problems. You'll never have to study or work again. All the problems in the world can be someone else's problems. You can stay right here if you want to. You can stay right here with us. Forever."

There was nothing Sarah wanted more. She was all for giving up on hurt and disappointment. She was ready to be happy with her friends. She didn't want life to be hard anymore.

The song changed. Sheeran's nasally voice stopped, and the new song the DJ played echoed. A new tune, but it felt as old as the Olympic Mountains out on the peninsula. It was a tune Sarah knew. She'd heard it before. But where?

Sarah's mind exploded. She remembered. She remembered Jessica dead in her arms with the song looping over and over again. This was the same song, here at the prom. With Jessica. And Roberto. Her body stiffened, and she stepped away.

151

She remembered Wyoming.

She remembered Terence.

She remembered her father, and how he needed her. She remembered her mother, and brother.

She remembered who she was.

Her prom was completely different from Terence and Wyoming's, but she could see them. Terence was dancing like a crazy man, and Wyoming had some girl in his arms. She started with Wyoming, calling out his name. He didn't answer because he couldn't hear her. She tried to shake him but wasn't able to. She couldn't touch him. She could see him, and they occupied the same dimension, but it was as if he was sealed off from her. Her third attempt was to yank the girl away. She figured that would get his attention if nothing else did.

But it didn't work the way she thought it would. When she reached out to touch the ginger Wyoming danced with, there was nothing there. Sarah realized Wyoming was actually dancing with what looked like a cardboard cut-out of a person. It wasn't an actual person.

But he kept dancing.

Sarah screamed at him. She jumped up and down. She cursed at him.

No luck.

She decided to try Terence. She had almost the exact same result. There was one slight difference. When Sarah called him the first three times, he ignored her. She couldn't touch him, the same as it was with Wyoming. Terence wasn't dancing with anyone specific, as he was much more promiscuous with his groove. At first, they looked like people to her the same way Jessica and Roberto did. The closer she got, and at different angles, it was apparent they were cardboard too.

She shouted his name again, to no effect. Something her father told her once about whispering in a crowded room came to mind. Butch had told his daughter that in a room filled with noise the most successful tactic to being heard was not to scream over the crowd but to lower your voice. Butch told Sarah there was something magical and mystical about a word discreetly shared that wanted to be heard.

Sarah whispered, "Pastor Terence." When she did, he glanced her way and smiled right at her. She'd broken through the spell, but it was short lived. He went back to dancing.

Despair was close at hand. Sarah sat down on the floor and thought. What was quieter and more discreet than a whisper? What was a more discreet way to get Terence's attention? She remembered what she had forgotten since they entered the prom. She had a gift she could use.

Sarah closed her mind, pushed back the suicide song playing in her heart from her prom, and reached out to touch Terence and Wyoming. In this world it was as easy to reach them both at the same time as individually. She sent them an image. It was a memory of her father—an image of him with her and Paul at the Sydney Diner eating pancakes.

She felt something push back against her, something she'd never felt before. She recalled when they first came upon Hepta High she'd told the other two she felt someone else. Now she knew whoever was pushing back on her attempt to reach Terence and Wyoming was the same presence she'd felt at the beginning. She imagined this was the person who had designed the curriculum. Person might not be the right word, but definitely a personality.

The pushback was not in her mind, but it was in the mind of Terence and Wyoming. The other entity was buttressing their delusions. Sarah pushed harder with the image of her father, but it kept getting reflected back at her. The entity had put mirrors around them.

Instead of forcing a thought, she decided to listen. She temporarily chose to forget about Wyoming. She concentrated on Terence. She opened up her mind and imagined a cable connecting her mind to his. It wasn't quick, but the connection came. She could hear his thoughts. He was happy. She could hear his happy thoughts as he lived inside the music. The song he heard was "YMCA" by The Village People. It didn't take long before Terence's joy rubbed off on her and she was smiling and tapping along to the rhythm.

Stop it! She needed to concentrate. She slapped her wrist.

She reached out again to Terence. This time she moved beyond his momentary thoughts and worked down to his inner self. She did this by seeing herself standing on Terence's head and drilling into his brain with a jackhammer. After she'd imagined this, she transitioned the mental image to an archaeologist sifting through the detritus. She looked for artifacts left behind by the real Terence.

Tiny Sarah excavated atop Terence's imaginary head casting away rocks, gems, and a book or two until she found what she knew was her best bet. She grabbed it and stuck it into the oversized pocket of her jogging jacket. She imagined herself walking down Terence's forehead and standing at a ninety-degree angle to his face, with his eyeglasses right below her heel. She pulled out the artifact from her pocket and held it up for Terence to see. Tiny Sarah shouted "See!" while actual Sarah whispered, "See. See this picture of your wife Muriel. See her

153

and love her. Remember your real self. Don't forget who you are. The real. She is real. The music is not."

The mirror shattered. It had been blocking her thoughts, reflecting them all, but now it was gone. When it did, Sarah again sent out the mental image of her father to Terence along with the message to him that he needed to come back to her. She tried to show him how the girls were all cardboard and the music was only in his mind.

It was working, but it drained her. She could feel herself losing control of her own thoughts. She was becoming caught up in the two minds at once. She could feel Terence's heart mingling with hers, and her own mind couldn't take more. When she felt him respond, Wyoming's mind also opened up to her. The mirror that guarded one had guarded both. Yet like Terence, the delusion's power warped his mind. She pushed to him Butch's image, the message for help, and the need to remember who he was.

Wyoming did not stir.

She sent him the sight she'd seen of the redheaded girl as being only a piece of painted cardboard.

There was no movement from his side.

She was losing. Terence stirred, but he'd not come fully back to her, and Wyoming hadn't responded. Sarah doubted she'd make it. She was sending thoughts to Terence, but now was attempting to break through to Wyoming. She didn't know how, but she knew all three of them had to make it or else they would fail.

Muriel is what Terence needed. What did Wyoming need? What would break through? What could she use to get him back?

The last cognitive thought she had before the end was duty. She projected that one word, duty, toward him. She whispered, "Do your duty, soldier." Screaming curses came rushing at her from Wyoming at the same time the shrill of Donna Summer's voice from inside Terence's brain while her own ghost suicide song thumped in her heart. She was overloaded from far too much input. A swirling menagerie cascaded through her: Jackhammers, artifacts, dancing girls, Jessica, Roberto, Wyoming's pistol, her father's face, green beans, JFK, shopping carts, banana slugs, and a lighthouse crashed into her and she felt gravity itself shove her brain right out of her skull. She saw it floating in the air, like a scene from an Arthur C. Clarke novel.

All went dark. Sarah stopped.

* * *

154

"Relax." It wasn't a command, but a kind suggestion. A gentle suggestion that carried empathy and love. The word communicated understanding. It cradled, nurtured, and fed. The spoken word "relax" echoed, like a mechanic's wrench echoes in an empty car garage, or the way an empty soda can rattles on a tile floor, or the way a young boy's voice bounces off the placid water of Crescent Lake after dark. "Relax" the word was only spoken once but it moved around, exploding first over there and now over here. It pinged all over like a movie theater demonstrating the stereophonics of the sound system before the film begins. The echo of the word "relax" felt eternal.

No origin. No beginning. No ending.

Then something changed. The sounds of the word "relax" fell apart. The disentangled letter "r" and the syllable "lax" along with the vowel "e" then the sound "re" bounced around the "x" sound. There was no choreography to the sounds. The lack of order was more than random; it was an eternal and ancient chaos. The disassociation continued until the echo wasn't recognizable sounds but broken grunts.

The grunts further disintegrated into resonance that devolved into a dissonance leaving only a vacuuming silence that sucked itself back into the audible realm.

The echo's iterations overlapped until the variant sounds re-formed into letters. The letters echoed the deconstructed letters and syllables of "relax" until it became one actual word again, spoken from one woman.

Sarah heard all this, but she couldn't see.

"Relax," the word came again. But this time it was followed by more words. "Your brain needs to reorder itself. It is a disturbing process. You'll need to relax."

"Who are you?" Sarah said. Or did she think it only? She hadn't heard herself say the words.

"Who I am doesn't matter right now." The voice said. "What matters is who you are. Try not to think right now. Listen. Wait."

"But—"

"Shhhh. Listen. You almost tore yourself into shreds. It was brave, and that bravery is noble, but the damage was actual. We needed to heal you so that you could go on. The other two are waiting for you right now. You can rejoin them soon."

Other two? Sarah didn't know who she meant.

"You are almost finished with the quest. Only two more levels left. Actually, only one more because the last one is special."

155

"No bonus round?" Sarah thought of Wyoming's speculation. Then she remembered who the other two the woman was talking about.

"See," the voice said, "you are already getting your mind back. Humans are complicated entities. It takes more than a moment to resort, so please try to listen. And wait."

Sarah tried to listen and wait. The voice she could hear but couldn't see sounded familiar. Who was it? It wasn't her mother, was it? Maybe it was? No, she wouldn't have to guess if it was her mother. A girl always knows her mother's voice, like the time when she was seven years old and got lost in the Nordstrom's in downtown Seattle. Her mother cupped her hand and screamed Sarah's name, and Sarah heard it and came running.

Sarah remembered swimming in warm water and being cold. She felt bright lights but couldn't see them.

Her thoughts returned to her mother. Could she ever forget the sound of her mother's voice? No, she could never forget the sound of her mother's voice. Could she? She tried to remember what her mother looked like. She couldn't. Panic swept over Sarah. She couldn't remember what her mother looked like. What kind of daughter was she? What happened? Was this death? Was this hell—to not be able to remember something important to you, for the thought to be on the edge of your ability to grab it but to not be able to, always and forever on the verge of the discovery that would change reality, or somehow make sense of everything? It would be a fitting hell indeed, a place with only questions but no answers.

Sarah accepted she had died at her senior prom and this was hell. Everything here was. Terence, Wyoming, the challenges, all pure hell. No, she decided it was not the senior prom. She died at Jessica's house the day she committed suicide. Everything else she remembered afterward was her mind firing random neurons and the closing synapses working for one more time to create some sense. She was only gears and motors coming to a stop and throwing off random sparks before the eventual shut down. Her computer was going off line and spewing disjointed lines of code and images. She tried to accept this as fate, but the panic swelled again.

Her mother's image came to her. Her father. Paul. She didn't see them with her eyes, but imagined them, because she as yet could not see anything. She must be dead, and thus would never see her family again.

The panic turned to sorrow.

156

"Relax" the soothing, strong voice again said. "The more you try to use your mind, the harder it is to re-sort. It doesn't make sense, the things you are thinking. The memories. The frightening ideas. Those are natural and normal, but whatever you believe is happening, you are wrong. You must relax. Be still. This will be over sooner if you relax and let the moment do its work."

Sarah smelled something. It smelled like the medicine cabinet at home.

The woman's voice spoke again. "In a moment your eyes will open, and your mind will be repaired. Remember, you are not alone, and I don't mean your two other friends. The three of you are not alone. We are with you, but you must face these temptations. You must pass through the fire. Once that is over, you'll perceive."

"Perceive what?" Sarah thought.

"Darling, you'll perceive some of what this all has been about. It will not be full perception. Things are often so muddled and dark you might not understand it all, but you will be able to have some level of comprehension. Your eyes, though spiritual now, will dull after you return."

XX

Her eyes popped open. The world was blurry. An odor of chemicals and rubbing alcohol overwhelmed her. She squished her face up in reaction to the odor. Satisfied at feeling the muscles in her face, she brought her arms up to her chest. Feeling her corporeal self with her own appendages gave her the confidence to sit up. When she did, her head spun.

"Welcome back," Terence said, steadying her by placing his hands on her back.

"Where are we?" She said.

"Uncertain," Wyoming said. "Our best guess is that it is time for biology lab. Can you smell the chemicals?"

"It smells like a funeral home."

"No, funeral homes smell different." Terence shook his head. "They cover up the smell with flowers and peppermints. When those sweet smells are combined with the aroma of moth balls from old ladies, perfumes, and the invariable appearance of an Old Spice Man, you get the unique soul killing smell of a funeral parlor."

Wyoming Wallace said, "Sounds like you have some resentment

issues, there."

"Like you wouldn't believe."

"How long have I been out?" Sarah rubbed her throbbing forehead.

"Not long. We got here seconds before." Wyoming looked at his wrist to check the watch that wasn't there. "But what was time in this place, anyway. What was the last thing you remember?"

"I remember feeling both of you in my head as you escaped the prom. But, then," She stammered. "I can't." She exhaled. "I remember feeling like I was going to explode, and there was darkness." She held up a single finger. "Wait, there was something. No, it was someone."

"Someone?" Terence said. "Who?"

"I can't remember. I feel like I know who it was, but I can't remember. I don't know."

"Did he threaten you?" Wyoming said.

"No. She comforted me."

"She?" Terence said.

Sarah smiled at Terence. "Are you gonna turn everything I say into a question?"

"Maybe?" he said. "Good to see you're back to your old self."

"It was a woman who talked to you," Wyoming was processing. "Where were you at? What did she look like?"

"I couldn't see her. I don't know. I can't even remember what she said. But I remember her being there, wherever there was."

"Isn't that the biggest question—where are we, or perhaps what is this place?" Terence took off his glasses and rubbed his eyes. He stood beside Sarah, who was laying on a lab table in what looked like a high school biology lab. "I can't decide if this is a Jungian nightmare or a Freudian one. Every single step we take there is some kind of Jungian archetype that haunts us. But just when I decide that is what is happening, we get a psychoanalysis that rattles me to the core, and which smells decidedly Freudian."

"Maybe it is a Cartesian nightmare?" Wyoming said.

"How do you mean?" Terence said. "But before you answer, let me say how impressed I am. I would never have thought you to be versed in such."

"People often underestimate me." Wyoming's face was steel. "Usually to their peril." He stroked his bearded chin. "I was thinking about the nature of existence. This whole charade feels like a play on existence itself. What is real? None of this is real or all of it is real. There is no middle ground. And what does it mean to be real? Does something need to have occurred in linear time to be real? Is this," he held his arms open wide, "Any less real than me driving my jeep down the shoreline of Sinclair Inlet? Is it any less authentic than when I hold a woman in my arms in the dark?"

"What you're asking," Terence said, "is since we are thinking this, then it is real whether it actually occurred outside our minds or not?"

"Pretty much."

Sarah felt left out, so she popped off the table she sat on. "You guys are suggesting we are in a battle for our existence." She realized her shoes were untied, so she bent over and tied them. When she rose up, she picked up where she left off. "I don't buy it. We exist. We don't have to prove it. We are real, whether we are in a body or not. This is not about us at all. It is about my father."

"Perhaps, but after what we went through in the prom nightmare, I know it is more about us." Terence focused his eyes on the floor before he looked back up at the teenage girl. "Sarah, I need to tell you something." He looked down at the floor again. "Thank you. Thank you for risking your life to remind me who I am. I don't know how you did it, but you found a way to break through to the real me. I can't even begin to tell you how grateful I am."

"Ditto," Wyoming said.

"Really!" Sarah tilted her head sideways. "Ditto. I know you're not all mushy and emotive, but you can't find something more than ditto?"

"No. Because if I say anything more, I'll have my own little neurotic crisis, and as they say, 'aint nobody got time for that." Wyoming stretched his neck and looked around. "We have a job to do. Or how did you put it in the thought you sent me: Duty. We are on duty."

For reasons she would never be able to explain, Sarah gave Wyoming Wallace a hug. It was a spontaneous demonstration of connectivity and empathy. Before she knew it, Terence had wrapped his long arms and big hands around them both and pulled them close.

They cried, together.

The hug broke up, and Wyoming asked Terence, "How long have we been at this? What does your fancy dancy Rolex watch say?"

Terence said, "You know, I haven't even looked at it in a while. The last time I checked it, in the cafeteria, it was going backward." He extended his arm and pulled back his coat sleeve. "It shows the same time I saw when we first arrived, 3:16 PM." He stared at it more, "The funny thing is the second hand keeps spinning around. The watch thinks it works."

Sarah retreated inside her mind. The numbers 3:16 must mean something. She didn't know what it meant, but it had to mean something. The seconds matter, but the hours don't. The answer to the puzzle was before her, but she couldn't access it. Tantalizing, like the secret to everything was hers to own and share, that it all would make sense. Yet it was also unknowable, ineffable, as if the cosmos was playing games with her by showing her what she needed but telling her the price was more than she could ever pay.

"It's not fair!" she screamed at the top of her lungs.

Terence and Wyoming jumped.

"What's not fair?" Wyoming said.

Sarah wasn't ready to share. She never would be. She reached down inside herself to find strength. What she found was the word, "Relax." That single word wiggled up her spine and burrowed into her head. It helped her feel better.

"I'm fine. It was nothing," she told the two men. "I'm fine."

"If you say so," Wyoming said. "But none of us are fine."

The intercom voice came on again. "Well done, students. We are surprised you have mastered all your lessons. Now it is time for . . ." the intercom crackled with a devilish chortle, "dissection."

The lights inside the lab dimmed. To their left a panel slid away revealing an enclave lit from both above and below. Glass jars filled it. Some were small, some were large, and some were gigantic. Wyoming, typical for *genus gladiator*, stepped out first. He started on the left with the smaller jars. Terence and Sarah came up behind him.

A flashing digital display sign appeared on the ceiling above where the enclave opened. It read "The Great Ape Exhibit."

The smaller jars held brains floating in what looked like liquid. Each jar was labeled with names: Einstein, Manson, Aristotle, Khan, and Hitler.

Sarah said, "I'm assuming the Khan brain belonged to the Mongolian ruler Genghis and not Khan Noonien Singh."

On cue, Terence looked up toward the ceiling and yelled, "Khannnnnnnn".

Sarah applauded. "I assumed anyone who nerded out about the one ring to rule them all would get the reference. My dad made me watch those when I was a kid. I hated it, but that was a pretty good William Shatner impersonation."

"Thanks." Terence continued the Shatner impersonation by putting his hands out, palms up, and jerking them around while speaking. "Your dad," he paused, "is a good," another pause, "man."

Terence said. "He," another pause, "prepared you for," pause, "life."

"You may have taken it too far with the whole Shatner pause thing."

Wyoming ignored their folly. He investigated the specimens. "Notice the dark spots on some of the brains?"

"Those lesions might explain their aberrant behavior." Terence said. "Those dark spots are only on the three evil ones. Hitler's brain is completely covered in them. By contrast, see how much bigger the Einstein and Aristotle brains are?" Terence now leaned in to examine closer as he talked.

"Did that move?" Sarah said. "Did you see it?"

"What moved?" Wyoming asked.

"The dark squigglies on Hitler's brain." She pointed, and when she did some moved again.

"Whoa," Wyoming said. "That probably shouldn't happen."

"They're alive," Terence watched one wiggle away from an area on the frontal lobe of Hitler's brain only to push itself between the folds of another section. "I wonder if the dark spots are living entities. Living spiritual parasites that corrupt the human mind." Speaking to no one specific, he completed the thought. "It makes sense, especially when you consider the biblical account of demon possession and the medical work of neurology."

Sarah heard Terence's thought before he ever spoke, so she was quick with a reply. "Wouldn't medical scanners, or autopsies, show these living dark spots?"

"Not if they were in another dimension. No. These evil entities perhaps exist in several dimensions at once, the way we always assumed angels existed."

Wyoming Wallace pushed his face up against the top of Khan's jar. "But these brains are dead. If these lesions are alive, wouldn't they move on to a living host?"

Terence kissed the air. "Evil always endures longer than the one who perpetuated it. If these lesions are living in different dimensions, they might also live in different times." He pulled off his glasses and said, "They are both here and there, in real time with Hitler, Khan, and Manson all at once."

They moved along to the next set. These jars were about the same size as the brain specimen containers. The difference is the brain containers were waist high and they looked down into the jar. In this exhibit, the jars were on elevated pedestals eye level to Wyoming, which meant Sarah had to stand up on tip-toes to see, and Terence had to bend his knees.

The lighting didn't activate until they were close to the jars. They could tell they were specimen jars from a distance but couldn't see inside them. As soon as they got close, the lights came on and all three gasped.

"Embryos." Wyoming said.

"Babies," Terence said.

Again, there were five jars, each labeled. The first one was labeled "Aborted December 9, 1974, Would Have Cured Cancer in 1999." The other four were labeled in the same fashion.

> Aborted: July 22, 1968, Would Have Brought Peace to Islam.
>
> Aborted: July 7, 1980, Would Have Invented Water-Powered Automobile.
>
> Aborted: November 12, 1977, Would Have Cured AIDS.
>
> Aborted: April 4, 2002, Would Have Saved Roberto and Jessica.

Terence put his hand against the first jar labeled 'Would Have Cured Cancer'. "If this person had lived, my father would not have died so young."

Wyoming squinted. "Peace to Islam means I never would have gone to war. No Bin Laden. No Al-Qaeda. No Jihadis."

Sarah's lip trembled. It was a thought that had come to her two or three times in the past year. Not specifically about Jessica and Roberto, but abortion in general. Had her best friend been aborted? Had her future husband been aborted? Had the person who discovered how to live on Mars been aborted? But to see it put before her in such dramatic terms was shocking.

Her lip trembled, so she bit it until it bled. The iron focused her thoughts and fed her anger. She reached out her mind to find the same consciousness that had pushed back against her when she tried to break through to Terence and Wyoming at the proms. She knew it was out there, watching. She reached out and found it. When she did, she said, "Not this time. I am a woman, and I am strong."

Terence and Wyoming both felt the psychic episode, but they didn't understand what had happened. It felt to them like a deep base guitar thumping. When they looked over at Sarah, the hair in her pony tail flapped as if it were in a strong breeze. Her clothes rippled. The two men stepped back from Sarah and the jars back into the main biology lab behind them.

When the episode ended, Sarah looked at the two men and said,

162

"What?"

"That is what we wanted to ask you." Wyoming said.

She turned her lips upward. "Someone else is watching us, and I'm pretty sure that person, or thing, knows we are not falling for his dirty tricks." She rocked back and forth on her feet from heel to toe, then said, "Let's keep moving. Nothing more to see here."

"Wait first," Terence said.

Sarah didn't argue. She could feel his intention, but not his exact motive.

Terence put his hands on two of the baby jars, closed his eyes, and looked up. "Lord, we never knew these people, and it is our loss. We trust them to you who was the one who gathered all the little children around you. We commend them to you, as sheep of your flock, and ask they, and all those who suffered the same fate, be welcomed into your arms, where there is light everlasting, and suffering is no more." He gulped before he could continue on with the prayer. "I offer also, prayers for their mothers. Who knows what events happened in their lives to bring them to this decision, but I pray they found healing, hope, and restoration."

Tears came down his cheeks, and he finished the liturgy. "The Lord gives, and the Lord takes away. Blessed be the name of the Lord."

"Amen," said both Sarah and Wyoming at the same time.

The holy moment abated as Sarah moved on down the row. When they were all close enough the lights came up on these jars. They were gigantic, standing taller than Terence with a diameter greater than the three of them standing side by side. There were only three of these jars, and each one was again labeled.

Being three jars, and three of them, they each took up a position in front of an individual jar. Sarah was the farthest down the walkway, and she read the label out loud. "Hiroshima." Wyoming was beside her, and he followed her lead and read the single word written on his. "Stalingrad." The next up was Terence. He whispered, "Gettysburg."

Wyoming stepped closer to his jar. "This goes from weird, to morbid, to sick." He stuck his face up closer to the glass to see inside. He could see bodies of soldiers, tiny bodies, floating in the liquid. Some were bleeding from wounds in their chest. Others had body parts shattered by artillery. Some were headless, others were cut in two. As Wyoming was about to pull back, for he had seen enough war in his lifetime, the liquid inside the jar glimmered. The blue hue that was the jar became a plasma screen projecting images. He saw Nazi tanks obliterating walls and people. From the top of the jar airplanes swooped down and bombed women and children. His ears heard Russian commanders ordering people into hopeless, untenable positions as fodder for German artillery. He saw shoeless and coatless German and Italian soldiers frozen in the snow.

Sarah had a similar experience with the atomic bomb.

Terence, likewise, could see Pickett's infamous cavalry charge. He smelled the gunpowder from the cannons, heard the moaning of the dying soldiers in blue and gray, calling for their mother, their children, their lovers, and the Lord. He stepped back.

"I can't take this." He said.

"Do we have a choice?" Wyoming said.

"There is always a choice," Terence dropped his gaze. "Life is all about the choices we make."

Sarah said, "We have three choices. Bad, worse, and worser."

"Bad," Wyoming mumbled, "would be moving on to see what horror show is waiting for us down the line."

Terence picked up the thought. "Worse is staying right here and dwelling on the carnage we have inflicted on each other in the name of nations, gods, and greed."

Sarah finished the logic. "Worser is failing to realize this is all a test."

"You are wise beyond your years," Terence said. "And you are right. Nevertheless, the things we see are not make believe. They happened—we never moved away from Cain killing his brother Abel." He had put his hand against the jar, but now took it off. "The bad choice is best right now. Let's move on and see what happens, if it's okay with the two of you."

Wyoming stepped by Sarah and took the point again. He could see there was one specimen jar ahead. It wasn't as big as the battle jars, but it was larger than the specimens. When they got close enough the lights came on. What they saw was not anything they could have expected. It was a man, or something like a man. The specimen was at least eight feet tall. Muscles bulged. The head was bigger than a typical human head, but it was elongated like the Egyptian pharaohs of old. Ridges of sharp bone extended beyond the flesh from the elbow joint down to the tip of the pinky finger. The brow was furrowed. Fangs extended from incisors below the lower lip. In the middle of the chest was an electrical display, flashing with red, green, and yellow lights with the occasional flicker of blue. The eyes did not look fleshy. They were metal. The creature's skin was a brownish tone, like someone from the

Indian subcontinent, but the facial features were definitely Anglo, except the ears. The ears were tiny and shaped in an inverted funnel.

"This guy is covered in muscle," Wyoming said. "He would do well at cage fighting."

Sarah asked. "Terence, is that a label in front of you? What does it say?"

"Yes," he said. "You're not going to believe what it says."

"What does it say?" Wyoming hadn't taken his eyes off of the specimen.

"It says Human Male, Year 5020"

"No way," Wyoming said. "People don't have fangs."

The Other nudged Sarah's mind. The message came in full sentences, like she was reading text messages on her phone. She called out to Terence and Wyoming, "Listen, someone is talking to me." She started to read what the messages said. "In the next three thousand years the humans who survive your wars, your disease, and your broken politics will be stronger, faster, deadlier, and enhanced. No morals, no scruples, no religious mumbo jumbo. Only survival. Only physical. Life or death."

She stopped. "That's it, that's the message. That's all there is."

Wyoming said. "Worst. Message. Ever."

"Can it be true?" She looked at Terence.

"Sure." He wiped his brow as he stared at future human. "Consider the size people were four hundred years ago, or even two thousand years ago. We are taller now, bigger, and stronger. Most of that comes from better diet and medicine. But you throw in some unnatural selection of warfare and murder, and the surviving human stock, just like cattle or wheat, will be bigger and stronger. Now add in some technology and implants, especially if you started at birth, and you could end up with something like this."

"What about the morality part?" Sarah said. "Does this thing have a soul? And if it doesn't, is it human?"

"Theologically, it has the *imago dei*. The question is, does it listen to the conscience the Lord put there at creation, or has it been intentionally muted? A person, even today, can numb themselves with drugs, activity, and violence to the point where they don't hear the still small voice." Terence kissed the air. "But this place is a demon place, remember that. The devil is the father of lies. So, this is a kind of half-truth. What we see here is a human from three thousand years from now, but it is not the only kind of human in three thousand years. Perhaps there are humans more like us, or maybe they have positive

165

advancements and not these," he waved his hand, "these, these, abominations. It is more likely what we see before us is only one human from one possible version of the future."

"I wouldn't want to live in a world where these things were roaming around." Sarah said.

Terence replied, "A prairie girl from two hundred years ago would have said the same thing about living in a world with fast automobiles, airplanes, microwaves, and nuclear weapons."

Wyoming laughed, "Yeah, but cars don't come after you. I get the feeling this guy would track you down and drink your blood while making your wife and kids watch."

"Why do you laugh at such a horrible thought?" Sarah said.

"Because it does," was all he said.

"Hey, look!" Terence pointed. "Do you see the lights on the chest?"

Both Wyoming and Sarah came in closer to where Terence stood. The red, green, and yellow lights on the creature's chest flashed faster, and in a different sequence. The interval for the flashing blue lights increased.

There was an orange light and a purple one. A display screen under the lights flickered to life.

"What is happening?" Sarah said. She stepped backward. The other two did as well.

"It is more alive than those brown squiggles on the brains," Wyoming said. "Very much alive."

They backed up out of the enclave and into the biology lab behind them until they bumped into a table.

"I feel like we should run," Terence said. "But I don't know where we would run to."

"This is not the world we know, so, I doubt we can get away" Wyoming said. "Remember how they reacted when we tried to change the rules in the arena on the platform?"

"This feels more dangerous than the arena," Sarah said.

"Only by degrees." Wyoming said.

The glass jar cracked. The crack splintered, webbed, and fluid poured onto the floor. The future human brought up his arms, pushing through the liquid and the glass and stepped out onto the floor. He shook his naked body like a dog, as the shoulder length hair flapped around.

"Wyoming," Terence whispered.

"Yeah, Doc!" Wyoming said.

166

"This is definitely a Jungian nightmare—complete with monsters."

Wyoming said, "You're right."

Sarah stepped out in front, putting herself between the future human and her friends.

"What are you doing?" Wyoming said.

"I'm going to try to communicate. There is no reason for us to assume it wants to hurt us. It might be scared."

"It doesn't look scared," Terence said. "It looks scary."

She reached out to see if she could hear its thoughts. "My name is Sarah" she told it telepathically. "We don't want to hurt you." She sent the future human a mental picture of the four of them holding hands. She realized how lame and hippy that was as soon as she'd done it, but she was deficient in a vocabulary of word pictures for peace and friendship.

To her amazement, future human responded back using his own mental pathway.

She told Wyoming and Terence, "His name is 871HTH."

"He must be named after his father," Wyoming said. "What else does he say?"

871HTH continued toward them, but it was a slow walk.

"Sarah?" Terence shouted. "Give us something. Is he communicating? Is he talking?"

"Yeah, but it's not good," Sarah said. "He says he's going to drink Wyoming's blood while me and you watch."

"Told ya," Wyoming said. He reached under his left arm and brought out the six-shooter. "Drink this," he said, intentionally mimicking Sarah's words from the cafeteria. He aimed for the flashing lights on 871HTH's chest. He pulled the trigger.

"You missed," Terence said.

"No way I missed." He aimed for 871HTH's head, as he was only about ten feet away now. "You might want to pray for these bullets, Doc." Then he again squeezed off two rounds.

It happened so fast Wyoming barely saw it, but see it he surely did. 871HTH moved his head out of the path of each shot.

"Doc, did you see that?" he asked.

"See, yes. Believe, no." Terence's mouth was wide open.

Sarah didn't see anything. She lifted the memory from Wyoming's thoughts. "Wow," she said as she backed up.

Future human 871HTH turned toward Wyoming Wallace.

"Here it goes," Wyoming shouted as he went down onto the floor, preparing to leg sweep his adversary. Before he got there, Terence leaped out to tackle 871HTH.

It was a brave move, but ineffective. 871HTH pushed Terence away. The sharp bone ridge on his arm sliced through Terence's jacket and gouged him under his ribcage. Blood spurted out of him as he fell onto Bunsen burners stacked on the floor at the front of the lab.

Wyoming brought his leg sweep, but it was useless on the muscular and firmly planted 871HTH.

871HTH kicked Wyoming in the chest, flinging him across the room. He landed right beside Terence.

Wyoming and Terence shook their heads at each other.

"This guy reminds me of someone I met in Anchorage a few years back." Wyoming rubbed his chest. "he was about as tall, but a lot uglier."

"You meet some interesting people, don't you?" Terence took a pained breath. "He reminds me of a deacon back in Philly. That guy was bad news."

"Well, this guy is bad news as well."

While they chatted, 871HTH began a slow walk toward them.

Sarah threw a chair at him, which glanced off and skidded across the floor. She ran full speed and jumped onto his back. She tried to claw at his face, but 871HTH swatted her off his back with no regard or respect for her ability to injure or hamper him.

Wyoming told Terence, "You go low, Doc, and I'll go high."

"It will not work," Terence said.

Wyoming was in motion by the time Terence said it. He jumped from the floor and lunged right at 871HTH's face. Terence was behind him, lunging from the ground toward the thighs of the naked hulk. He was careful to stay below the arms, where the boney ridge meant the business end of the future.

Wyoming didn't show the same kind of care. As all three of them tumbled toward the tiled floor, Wyoming threw one successive punch after another into 871HTH's midsection. It was all muscle under there, but he jabbed and jibbed anyway.

Terence didn't have a clue as to what course of action to take down below, so he contented himself with merely laying on top of the beast so as to keep him on the ground.

This arrangement didn't last long. 871HTH kicked Terence off with a powerful thrust of his thigh, and took Wyoming by his shoulders and hurled him again across the room in the opposite direction from which he'd kicked Terence.

Sarah was now back in action. This time she picked up the chair and held on to it. Running at full speed, she lifted the plastic chair over her head and smashed it against the right flank of 871HTH. She did it again, and then a third time. The future human kept walking toward Wyoming. She yelled at him and hit him with the chair, which did not register with 871HTH in the slightest.

Terence swooped in from behind, careful to avoid those exposed bones, and took 871HTH to the ground again. Sarah jumped on top of the dogpile.

"I think we got him," Terence said.

In a refute of Terence's assertion, 871HTH unleashed another part of his arsenal. He accessed the circuitry moving from his brain to his digital enhancements. He found the one which controlled auditory commands. In that file were various language prompts, animal sounds, and tactical routines. It was the tactical routines which he accessed. He whisked through several options until he found the perfect one for this situation.

No words came from Sarah or Terence. The sound attacking their ears and head paralyzed them. It was more than a tormenting sound, it was a neurological blocker that matched the exact brainwave of the opponent and brought him or her to an immobilizing moment of agony. It would have felt better for both Terence and Sarah to have been able to squirm, curl up into the fetal position, put their hands over their ears, or otherwise get some relief from simple movements. But movement was impossible.

They rolled off 871HTH and hit the ground with a thud. Sarah expected the comforting voice on the other side telling her to relax, because she was certain she had died, again. But the only thing she heard was every nerve in her body screaming in pain. Her head was facing Terence, and they could see each other, but neither one could speak, move, or talk. She tried to reach out to him mentally, but the fire in her body burned so hot the thought was eradicated before it ever achieved fullness.

There was a moment when she decided this was hell. She'd been mistaken earlier when she thought the echoing word was hell. This was it.

But the moment passed. It passed because 871HTH stood and walked away. The range of his auditory weapon was limited, and it was also temporary. As impressive as his advancements were, he was not able to maintain his offensive tactic for anything other than short bursts. When he walked away, Sarah and Terence regained control of their body, and the pain ceased.

871HTH moved onto his primary target, Wyoming Wallace. He grabbed Wyoming by the right leg, and lifted him high, dangling upside down, facing Sarah and Terence. Sarah, who had stood up, gasped. She was certain he would break the cowboy in half like a raw spaghetti noodle. She saw the next few moments as if it were still framed photography. The monster would bring Wyoming down over his knee. She could hear the bones in her friend's spine snap. She could see the pain and surprise on his face. His body limp on the ground. It was too much.

But Wyoming remembered.

He reached up against the gravity to his belt. In one motion, he unsheathed his knife with his left hand, then twisted his body as he plunged the blade into the 871HTH's side. The blade found soft, vulnerable flesh and stuck fully into the torso. 871HTH let out a wail, dropping Wyoming. Wyoming pressed the attack. He slashed the blade across his opponent's legs, then again tried to sweep them out from underneath his attacker. This time it worked, and 871HTH fell to the ground.

Wyoming scrambled to his feet. He stomped 871HTH in the face and put the barrel of his pistol against 871HTH's temple. "Even you aren't fast enough to swivel around this," as he pulled back the hammer.

Sarah saw the next few moments from here in her mind as well. She saw Wyoming pull the trigger. She saw the head of 871HTH explode. Bits of brain and sinew, along with wires and processors, flew everywhere. The thought made her sad, and she realized what Wyoming was doing was wrong.

"Wait!" she screamed again.

Wyoming didn't stand down, but he didn't pull the trigger either. "What?" He said. It was a question, but it was also a complaint.

"We can't kill him."

"Sure, we can."

"I'm not talking about ability. I am talking about morality."

Terence stood beside Wyoming. He held his side where his own wound bled. "She's right."

"Of course, you do. Preachers never want to hurt anyone."

"True, for the most part," Terence grimaced as he spoke, "but it's not the conundrum we have here. We saw back there in the gallery," he pointed to the enclave, "the violence, greed, and spiritual darkness we are all capable of. The only way to change the circle is to stop it." Terence shook his head, as if arguing with himself. "Put the gun down."

"What if he tries to kill us again, which I am sure he will?"

"He's injured. You beat him once. You can do it again, if you need to." Sarah's voice was not as strong or confident as she'd hoped it would sound.

"Maybe," Wyoming said. "The problem is, by my math, I only have one bullet left. I have no other shells. This might be our only chance. If we don't do something now, it might be the end for us."

"I understand." Sarah said. "You trusted me in the arena when we jumped. Trust me now. This is the right thing."

"That was different. We had no other options. I've got a good one in my hand right now with the finger on the trigger. And it is an option which doesn't involve trust at all."

"Wyoming," Sarah lowered her voice. "I need you to trust me."

"Trust doesn't come easy for me." Wyoming never took his eyes off of 871HTH.

Terence spoke up, "That is a cliché, Wyoming. Trust doesn't come easy for anyone. It's a rare opportunity to have the luxury of trust, as well as a gift to have people in your life to trust."

"I trust her," Wyoming pointed with the bloody knife in his left hand, but still not looking away from 871HTH. "But not him."

"Do you trust God?"

"That's a loaded question, Doc."

"I don't think it is a loaded question. And I don't think you believe it is either, do you? You know this is the choice for you right now and probably for the time and age in which we live. To trust or not trust."

"I only have one bullet left and this is point-blank range." Wyoming, who was now on his knees over 871HTH, shoved the barrel of the gun harder into the skin. "Look at his eyes, guys. He knows this is a gun, and he knows his time is up. He only understands violence and power. He's wondering right now what is taking so long. There is only one logical thing to do and it is shoot him."

"No." Sarah said. She didn't shout, but she was firm. "There is only one thing to do. Put the gun away. You will not need it, not now, anyway."

Wyoming cursed. He disengaged his weapon and brought it shoulder high pointing at the ceiling. "I guess we'll see."

They did not know if it was out of fear or surprise, but 871HTH did not attempt to stand. He sat up, pressing his right hand against the wound on his left side. Wyoming looked at Terence with a look that said, "What now?"

Terence shrugged a reply.

Sarah sat down beside 871HTH, aware that even in this injured condition, he could snap her neck or slice her jugular before she would know what happened. She pushed those thoughts away. With her right hand, the one closest to him, she touched his hand. She hadn't tried to reach him telepathically, yet. First, she wanted to be human.

He shivered when she touched him. She wondered if he was cold since he was naked and bleeding. She also thought how he had been in the fluid, as a kind of hostage. Now he was in the open air. Surely, he was cold.

She sent a mental image to Wyoming and Terence of a blanket. Terence looked around the room, seeing nothing usable. He remembered he was wearing a coat. He took it off and with great care and intentional slowness draped it over 871HTH's shoulders. It fit like his youngest daughter's coat would fit Terence, but it covered him and gave some warmth.

They sat for a long time, but maybe it wasn't that long at all. Who knows?

At some point, Sarah tapped into 871HTH's mind. She said one word to him. Friend. He responded, almost before Sarah had completed her own message. He was confused. He didn't understand. Her mind searched for something helpful and she found it. She sent him a mental picture of the sunrise side of Mt. Rainier in the summer. The lush greenery, clear water, blue skies, and abundant sunshine communicated from her heart to his peace. 'Peace for you' she whispered, then tossed the thought at him as a feather drifting through the air and floating right into his consciousness.

She couldn't prove it, but she thought she saw a smile before he stood up. He wrapped Terence's coat around his shoulders like a cape. Both men bristled and took guard, but it was unnecessary.

871HTH looked one more time at Sarah. With the look he sent an image of her in a white summer dress with garlands in her hair. He also transmitted to her the thought, "Brave and beautiful" but the words weren't exactly English. It was something like "Bratis kun stanrioy." It sounded in her mind like a strange mix of German and Japanese. In this odd world she was in, she found a way to know what the words meant. "Brave and beautiful." She treasured the words in her heart, and never shared it with the other two. "Brave and beautiful."

871HTH turned from them and walked across the room, opened the classroom door, and left.

"Just when this place can't get any weirder," Wyoming pulled off

172

his ball cap and pointed it toward the now open door and said, "that! You get something like that."

"Weird begets weird," Terence said. "I thought it was weird when you wished for a knife. I can't tell you how glad I am you wished for the knife."

Wyoming said, "I'm always good like that."

The intercom crackled. "Sarah Gregory, Wyoming Wallace, and Terence Harrison please report to the principal's office."

"Looks like we're in trouble." Terence said.

"We better hurry. I don't want to be tardy for this because it feels like the grand finale." Wyoming rubbed his hands together in glee.

"I can't tell if you're joking or not," Terence said.

"Come on," Sarah said. The typical sequence of earlier transitions began. The lights went dim, and walkway arrows appeared on the floor. Once they left the lab, Terence checked the wound on his side. He expected it to be gone, given their earlier experiences.

It wasn't. Neither did his jacket reappear.

"Hey, Wyoming," Terence said. "Check your pistol. How many bullets do you have now?"

Wyoming checked. "One. Why?"

"Just wondering."

Sarah said, "I don't have to read your mind to know what you're thinking. I don't believe we are getting freshened up this time. Wyoming is right. We're about to end this. Now."

"Good," Terence said. "It's been interesting and all, but I feel like Dorothy, and I want to click my heels three times and wake up back in Sydney. Our Sydney. My Sydney."

"Home, sweet home," Wyoming nodded, giving his head a quick folksy jerk to the left.

"We're not going to see a wizard." Sarah said. "We're going to see a demon."

"Pretty much the same thing, I think." Terence said.

There was no more talking for a long time after that.

XXI

The principal's office was not a principal's office, or at least nothing like what the three dreamers thought of as an office. There was no desk. No chairs. No books. No bookshelves. No diplomas on the wall. There was no fish tank in the corner. No American flag. No maps. Nothing educational, inspirational, or encouraging.

The hallway from the biology lab was the same bright fluorescent light as the room, but the further they went, and they went far, it got darker. It wasn't long before they were completely in the dark. Sarah reached for her cellphone as a light. It was the first time since they arrived she'd reached for it, and then it was as a primitive tool for light and not a technological device. But the phone was not there. It had not made the journey to the nightmare world. She considered trying to conjure it, as Terence's had his watch and Wyoming his knife. She didn't try, though. She knew it wouldn't work. Not at this level.

They kept walking in the dark. Their walk was slow.

Somewhere along their walk the sounds started. The first sound was the screech of an owl, but if anyone would have asked Terence, he would have told you the owl sounded like a Godzilla sized owl with laser eyes and broken glass for feathers. There were roars from creatures none of them recognized as well as the hissing sound of vipers. Wyoming was certain he felt cold air swirl around him as batwings moved above and beside and the odor of guano overpowered his senses. It even felt like they were below him, if that were possible.

The darkness panicked Sarah more than she wanted the other two to know. It felt to her like the upstairs at Jessica's house. The same enclosing darkness pulsated. Despair dug into her heart with razor claws. Hopelessness settled into her mind. It was the same feeling all over again. It choked her individuality. It squeezed her spirit from the inside out. The outer darkness was an echo, an outward projection of the internal darkness of her own condition. The void that surrounded them came from her, oozing from her pores, breathing its devilish dark.

Back in Jessica's house, it was only the glowing light of divine intervention which saved her from giving into the darkness. There was no light now, and she was afraid nothing would save her. She became sad, not for herself but for her friends, Terence and Wyoming. She'd learned to love them. Her fear was they would die here in the black hole which arose from her own soul and surrounded them.

"Stop it!" Wyoming shouted the thought at Sarah. It was so loud Sarah actually jumped when she perceived the words, but nothing audible had actually been said. "We all feel the same, but different," he continued his thought.

"What he said." Terence's thoughts rattled inside of Sarah's mind. He sent his own image of him standing in a cemetery.

Terence reached out his hand and took Sarah's. He reached for

Wyoming's, and the cowboy didn't fight the idea.

The three of them held hands as they walked on in the darkness. It was impossible to tell how long they walked. There were intervals where the sounds, roars, and hisses were louder and more varied. There were also long periods of silence—a species of silence that sucked every attempt at sound into a vacuum of nothingness. Their journey may have been exaggerated minutes that feel much longer than actuality because the terror is so great, or it might have been days upon days of moving forward. Throughout their journey, not one of them ever thought of turning around. It was only forward to whatever awaited.

Light appeared. It wasn't a gradual increase in light as one might expect when you get closer and closer. Two blazing pillars appeared out of nowhere, but they had always been there. They approached those two pillars and kept walking on. Eventually they came by two more, and by four more until they stood holding hands, in the midst of seven blazing pillars.

Sarah, Wyoming and Terence stood at wrought iron doors. The doors were tall, taller than they could see. Each door had intricate silver latticework pressed into the iron. The silver spun into dazzling circles, ever moving and changing, forming occultic symbols for a moment of recognition before it moved on to form something else. Sarah flinched when she saw the pentagram. Terence spotted several swastikas, an ankh, and an ancient symbol for chaos. Wyoming saw the all-seeing eye inside a pyramid and a nazar.

The door had no handle, knob, or knocker.

Wyoming pushed it. It didn't move.

Sarah sent out a mental question. "How do we open it?"

She heard Terence think, "Password."

Wyoming's thoughts agreed.

"What?" She shrugged as she thought.

Several words went through Terence's mind. He thought of his old locker code, three, seven, nine, and one. Surely that wouldn't be it. His mind raced—and the other two heard every thought as they raced through his mind: Ali baba. Sesame. Then Joshua.

Wyoming interrupted Terence's thoughts with one thought/word: Rab-Shakeh.

The iron part of the door snapped sideways and slid into the wall like a pocket door. The silver latticework peeled off the door and hung in the air on both sides. It shimmered as moonlight on the winter solstice. The left-side portion of the silver formed a circle doorway.

175

The right-side silver spelled out a sentence that hung above the doorway.

Lasciate ogne speranza, voi ch'intrate

Terence translated the Latin from Dante in his head. "Abandon all hope, ye who enter here."

When Wyoming heard the rendering in his own head, he smirked and walked through the portal. As always, the other two followed without hesitation.

The floor inside the next room was black marble. A swirling red compass rose was etched in the marble. When the three of them approached, it lifted from the floor and became an inflamed three-dimensional object. Where north would have been on a normal compass rose, "Hell" was written in a gothic script. Instead of south the word was "Desolation," for west, "Sin," and for east, "Death." The glow from the evil compass was the only apparent light in the room.

The four walls were translucent, yet dark. Wyoming put his hand against the wall to his left. It was frozen. Lightening flashed outside. The light from the lightning allowed them to see. They were atop a great pinnacle. The sides went straight down, at least several thousand feet on each side. Above them a half-moon hung in the sky alongside a brilliant planet Venus, but no stars shown in the sky. They could hear the wind howling, although they could not feel it. There was no ceiling.

The Rab-Shakeh stood behind the compass rose. Sarah gasped when she recognized him as her psychology teacher, The Rab. He was dressed in black robes. Had he worn a collar, he'd have looked like a Roman Catholic priest in a formal setting at the Vatican. Around his neck he wore a thick pewter necklace, and hanging from it were tiny, severed shrunken heads. Sarah recognized one of them as Jessica's. Beside it was Roberto. A six-foot upside down cross levitated behind him.

"Hello, Sarah" The Rab-Shakeh said. "Welcome, shaman," he nodded toward Terence. "And a hearty welcome to you, warrior." His teeth glowed a supernatural white when he smiled at Wyoming Wallace. "I feel compelled to admit something. I didn't believe you'd make it beyond the dance, and I can't tell if I am pleased you made it this far or not. My ambivalence amazes even me."

He paced back and forth in front of them, hands clasped in front. He reminded Wyoming of the drill sergeant at basic training. To Terence he was a slimy television evangelist. Sarah thought of an old movie she saw once about Russia, and the character Rasputin.

"Once you realize how this ends," The Rab-Shakeh opened his hands and spread his arms wide emphasizing the room, "you probably will wish you could go back to the dance. At least there your puny brains could enjoy the ecstasy of illusion—the joy of the dance, the affirmation of romance, or" he turned specifically to Sarah, "the gladsome reunion with old friends." He now walked around them, like a shark circling divers in a cage. "Yes, you would have died, that much is certain, but you would have died in the comfort of ignorant bliss."

He was now right behind Terence, who was praying. "Your cute magic spells will not be effective here in my lair, holy man." He came around to look at Terence face to face. "El Elyon has no authority here. This is my home—mine. Sydney High School is mine, too. Soon the whole city will be mine. I own it and I own you." He rubbed his hands together with glee. "After I kill you, I am coming after your father," he whipped around and grabbed Sarah by the face. His large hands cupped her cheeks and he pulled her toward his own face.

Wyoming lunged toward him, but The Rab-Shakeh reached out his left hand and snapped his fingers. Wyoming froze in place before he could even get his feet off the ground. The Rab- Shakeh returned to his subject of the moment.

"Sarah Gregory, I will eat your father's spleen and share his entrails with all my best friends. Oh, how I have sought to destroy him. So long has he been a thorn in my flesh."

He squeezed her face harder, but it didn't hurt her. It was only uncomfortable. "Once you die, here, with his two friends, he will wallow in even greater self-pity, loathing, doubt, and fear. Within only a year or two I can drive the wedge between him and your whore mother. I see a delightful future indeed. Lucy will leave him. After all, she is younger and more vibrant than him. She wants a man, not a weasel. Yes, she will find a man who will thrill her and fulfill her. As she chases of after Belial, your brother Paul, distraught over his sister's death, will turn to drugs and dropouts. I'll make sure he finds plenty of both. Oh, I bet he has a taste for the rock candy." The Rab-Shakeh stuck out his tongue and flickered it with vulgar delight.

"Can you see him, Sarah?" he continued his invective. "See him in his black clothing, painted eyes, black nail polish, and purple lipstick. Can you hear his language? The profanity? The blasphemy? The nihilism?" The Rab-Shakeh's lips shivered in excitement and his eyes twinkled. "Can you see him at the tender age of twenty-four drowning in his own vomit at the meth house located four blocks down the road from Sydney Community Church? Can you see it, Sarah? I know you can. Can you smell the puke? Has the odor of death reached your nostrils? Do you taste the stale antifreeze in the air? Can you feel the hopelessness? I know that you do, don't lie to me or yourself. Welcome to a little thing called Fate—and this is Paul's."

And she did. Her mind formed the image. Sarah wasn't able to discern if it was her own image, or if The Rab-Shakeh had implanted it there, but she could see it. She saw all of it.

"Ooh, but it gets better, my dear Sarah." The way he said the word Sarah was as if he'd spit the word. "The moment he dies, the moment he expires from this glorious world, your mother will be in the arms of her latest boyfriend, and, oh this is delicious, the guilt of that knowledge will haunt her in a way nothing else could ever do, sad to say even more than your death. She will grow into despair. She will live to be an old woman, but an old woman filled with such bitterness and regret that her life will be misery."

The Rab-Shakeh squealed in delight at these thoughts. "She will make for herself a far greater prison than I could ever build. Isn't the human condition delightful? I will feed on her misery for decades. Her morose melancholy will be nourishing me long after your body has rotted in its cheap pauper's casket. I tell you, the quality and depth of her pain and depression will be a delightful source of nourishment for years. Decades!"

He released her face and took a step back. Now he could see all three of them together. "But that is not the best part, not by far." His energy levels now kicked up exponentially and he was playing the part of salesman—selling them on his joy for the future destruction he was creating in this exact moment. "The best part is Butch Gregory. I have taken away his church. I am about to take away his daughter, friend, and protector all at once. He has alluded me for years. Now, at last, I have him. I will take away his wife and his son, but slowly. T'will be a slow cancer that eats away at him every night and day until finally, in a moment of despair, after Paul is dead and his wife has her soul sucked out, he will take Wyoming Wallace's beautiful killing tool in his hand. Butch will have it because Wyoming will be dead, and Wyoming has no other friends to have his things. So, in a box in the garage is the pistol and a handful of shells. But he only needs one." The Rab-Shakeh was writhing in orgasmic delight as the words came from his lips. "Can you see it, Sarah? Can you see it? He will take Wyoming's gun, while holding, yes, yes, while holding Terence's old Bible and a picture of your family taken when you were young children." The Rab-Shakeh bounced up and down in anticipation. "He will put the barrel into his mouth, say a pathetic prayer to his jealous and unreasonable Jew-god, then blow his brains out. Can you see it?"

Sarah saw it.

Wyoming and Terence also saw.

The Rab-Shakeh again stepped backward.

Terence came free from his temporary immobility.

The area of the marble floor beneath The Rab-Shakeh rose seven feet into the air, creating a dais. "The only thing in doubt is how do you die?" His hands were again clasped in front of him, feigning control of his raw emotions. "We could feed you to wild animals? How positively Roman it would be. The Pontifex Maximus would no doubt approve." He shook with delight, then yelled, "No doubt!" He raised his arms, then finished the thought, "I might even get my toga out and wear it. My pet dragon needs feeding, but it would require us traveling to Scandinavia for the celebration. Grendel would be overjoyed. It's been a long time since we've been to the mead hall together. We could always use a crucifixion. Or my personal favorite—we can skin you alive and stake you to the hot sand and watch as the ants eat you alive and the sun bakes you dry as jerky. I miss the old ways. The Assyrians weren't smart, but they certainly knew how to kill people. Their thoroughness should be admired by all."

While he spoke, Terence had gathered Sarah and Wyoming together around him, and they held hands. They didn't need to speak because the mental link between them had grown in intensity. Their thoughts were interwoven. If one of them thought it, the other two heard the thought as if it was his or her own. Sarah's ability grew, enveloping all three of them, bringing the three into one mind.

From Terence, they felt the rightness of not looking at The Rab-Shakeh. He wanted a spectacle and an audience. They should not give him one. They instead looked at each other in a tight prayer circle. From Sarah, they each understood this was a chamber of lies. The truth was twisted, as was time and the future. Nothing the demon said was actuality. The compass here was broken. This was a place without a true-north. Out of Wyoming flowed strength and dignity; a perseverance of the will that would not surrender to the darkness. He gave them backbone and fortitude.

Wisdom, truth, and strength enveloped and sealed them with a protection The Rab-Shakeh could not see or perceive for he is spiritually color-blinded. He, and those like him, cannot see or perceive noble characteristics. Virtue is beyond his field of vision.

The Rab-Shakeh was talking in the background about stoning them

179

when he realized his audience ignored him. He screeched like an owl, leaped off the dais and landed behind Wyoming. "Stop that! Resistance is not allowed in here. I will not be ignored."

His words carried weight toward them, and there was a powerful urge to break their bond and look at him. But Wyoming's strength held them together. Wyoming told the other two they must hold firm because The Rab-Shakeh wanted to break them up. They had to be strong.

Now The Rab-Shakeh circled them as he had earlier, but this time his pace was faster. He brought out from his capes a staff. With the flourish of a pro-wrestler, he spun the staff around and brought it down upon Terence's head. The staff never reached its target. A pulse of light, bright light, originated with Sarah then surged outward to repel the staff. The energy knocked it from The Rab-Shakeh's hands, hurled it across the room, and smashed it against the translucent walls where it disintegrated.

The Rab-Shakeh cursed in more languages than Terence knew, but he heard Latin, Greek, and Hebrew. He guessed the other phrases were from long dead languages of the Babylonians, Persians, Sumerians, and Egyptians. Terence's mind wandered to thoughts about how ancient this demon was, the things he'd seen and done, and what he might learn about humanity's past from him. Likewise, Sarah's heart wandered. She longed for her mom and dad. She was ready for this to be over. She was losing strength and focus.

Their bond weakened, and the evil one circling them felt it. He increased his antics of distraction. He cursed ever louder and more creatively. He danced and gyrated. He threw out mental images of fatigue and rest toward Sarah. He found the lingering question about the Tower of Babel inside Terence's mind and gave him an answer he wanted—yes it was a technology-filled tower far more sophisticated than anything in the 21st century.

They had made a valiant stand, but defeat was at hand.

Except, Wyoming would not allow defeat. He screwed his courage to the sticking place. He brought all the energy of his will upon his friends. An electric green aura appeared on him, then it swallowed Sarah and Terence. The energy formed a surrounding sphere. It was a tiny sphere which blocked out the words being spoken in accusation against them or the attempts to weaken them. It was a bubble in which only the three of them existed. They were no longer in the principal's office, not in the tower, and not in the darkened room. Somewhere else is where they went.

The Rab-Shakeh disappeared.

Music filled their ears, but nothing they recognized. The intensity dissolved. Wyoming relaxed, as did Sarah and Terence. The music was in the background; but something was missing.

Sarah figured it out first. "I can't hear your thoughts," she said.

"We've lost the connection," Terence was sad at the thought. "I feel like someone died."

Wyoming didn't comment. His eyes said it all.

"Where are we?" Sarah said.

"There is no telling," Wyoming chuckled. "I haven't figured out where we've been since we got here, wherever here is." He squinted, "But I see someone in the distance, walking this way. Maybe he or she knows where we are."

"It's not—" Sarah said turning around to look at what Wyoming saw.

"Relax," Wyoming cut her off. "It's not the bad guy. This looks like someone else. Someone completely different."

The person walking came closer, but he didn't get much bigger. As he came, however, he brought colors and scenery with him.

It was a boy. He wore a white vee-necked t-shirt, blue jeans, and old-fashioned high-top Converse shoes. His hair was cut in a buzz.

The scenery came with him, and soon he was in their midst, as were trees, with one particularly large tree, a grassy yard, blue sky, and beautiful sunshine. The scene warmed all three of them from the inside out. It felt as if it had been forever since they'd been anywhere except the dungeon of Hepta High or in the soupy fog of Shadow Sydney.

The little boy looked at Sarah and said, "I'm your uncle."

"You look like my brother." Sarah's reply came without any hesitation. "His name is Paul."

"I know Paul," the boy said. "And you look like my mother."

"Daddy tells me the same thing, but he never told me how much you looked like Paul."

The boy glanced away from Sarah and introduced himself. "Hello Terence and Wyoming. My name is Shark. I am Butch Gregory's brother."

Sarah blurted, "He died when he was a kid. I saw him in the tree when we first came here, or there, or wherever this place is. I saw that the devil is the one who broke the limb." Sarah put her index finger in her mouth and chewed the fingernail. "Uncle Shark, what is going on? Are we dead?"

"No, you're not dead," Shark said. "It was close back there, I have

181

to admit. However, you are very much alive and safe, for now at least."

Terence went down to one knee and looked Shark in the face. "Where are we?" He asked the question with a deliberate slowness that made Sarah wonder if he'd spent too much time around Wyoming.

"The easiest answer is you are with me."

"Unsatisfactory," Terence pointed a finger at Shark. "I need more to work with. Give me the complicated answer."

"Your bodies are where you left them. Sarah is in her room. Terence is in the recliner in his living room. Wyoming is in the bed. When you went to sleep, your minds connected to bring you to this rarely visited expression of reality."

"So, our minds are here," Sarah said.

"Don't be silly, Sarah." Shark shook his head. "You're as literal as your father. Your mind is with your body. A mind can't operate without a body, which is something everyone knows. Your minds are connected, which is a perfectly normal thing. People's minds connect all the time. Married people, twins, close friends, even sometimes mortal enemies become connected. Most humans don't believe in such things, so it goes unrecognized or explained away."

"Wait a minute," Terence raised back up, but he put out one palm as if stopping Shark. "What we've gone through is not the same thing as twins who report being able to feel their sibling's pain or joy."

"True, but it is the same principle. Same kind, different intensity." Shark smiled. "Someday, you'll understand. For now, you are looking at things through a shadowy haze, but in the future, you'll see clearly."

"Face to face," Terence said.

"Face to face," Shark antiphoned. "And know as you are known."

A shiver ran down Terence's spine.

"Does this place have a name?" Sarah wasn't following the moment which Terence and Shark shared. "Is it on a map?"

"No maps. Not ones on paper or computer screens, anyway. It has several names. It was once called Abaddon, but that name came to mean something else. The Greeks thought of it as Tartarus, but again, it got slippery. There is a word we've started using of late, but you couldn't pronounce it. It means In-Between. The three of you were In-Between."

"In between what?" Terence asked.

"Life and death. Heaven and hell. Future and past. In the world you live in, the physical realm is the dominant reality. The spiritual is negated, forgotten, or denied. Even those who believe in true spirituality can only briefly access it in fits and starts. In-Between is the opposite. The spiritual is the dominant, and the physical is negated."

"What I want to know," Wyoming Wallace spoke to Shark for the first time, "what was the purpose?" Wyoming asked him. "Because, to be honest, that was the hardest thing I've ever gone through." He shuddered. "It was not pleasant."

"It is hard to explain in human words," Shark said, "but a good answer is revelation. This whole process for you was about revelation."

"Self-revelation?" Terence said? "Or the impartation of necessary knowledge?"

"You are a sharp and precise theologian," Shark said. "The answer is both."

"And you," Terence smirked, "are slippery with your rhetoric."

"Thanks. I've been working on it." The playful glee on Shark's face reminded them of someone else they loved. Someone who had lost his playful look.

"Why was it so nasty? So mean, violent and ugly? Why so wicked? Surely God is not wicked?" Sarah was looking for the words to describe the experience at Hepta High. "It was so dirty. Mean."

Terence helped her. "Why did we have to experience the evil in our past? That can't be from God. We know that has been forgiven."

"Forgiven, yes." Shark brought his hands out in front. "In-Between is complicated. It is spiritual, but not all spiritual is from the Lord. It was the demons who brought you here. The Lord allowed it. He let them. They wanted to destroy you with your past, with anger, with hatred, with despair, but The Lord had other intentions. He knew it would make you stronger. Stronger, together."

Terence put his hands in his pockets. "That means this place is like the life we all live and experience every day. It is filled with darkness, heartache, and pain. The trick is to hold on to goodness."

"At least it's over," Wyoming said.

"Oh, I'm sorry to tell you. It is not over." Shark again shook his head.

"What?" a unison interrogative flew from their lips.

"What do you mean it's not over?" Sarah's tone pounded with agitation.

"The journey in the In-Between is over. Your work is not. I have to send you back so you can finish."

"What are we supposed to do?" Wyoming asked.

"I can't tell you." Shark said. "Rules. You know."

"Whose rules?" Sarah was incredulous.

Shark nodded his head, "You are so much like my brother. I'll tell you what I told him a few years ago. He rules, and these are his rules. They are good rules for the sake of freedom and choice. There is no one predetermined ending to make, but all endings serve the final predetermined ending.

"Is it to be a trial by fire again?" Terence looked at Shark.

"I can't tell you," Shark said.

"I knew you were going to say that," Terence kissed the air. "Can you answer this—because this is the question I think that has formed on all of our minds. Why? Why did we have to go through this? When we began we assumed it was about Butch, but, I have to be honest, this felt personal, like it was about me. Is this about Butch or not?"

"Yes," Shark said. "It is about you. It is personal. But it is also about Butchy. The best way to destroy my brother is to destroy the people who mean so much to him." Shark waived his hand at all three of them. "The three of you are some of those whom he cares about most, along with the church he loved—" Shark cut off his sentence midway, the way a person does when he or she realizes too much has been said

"So, what do we do?" Terence asked.

"You'll know what to do. But what does your heart tell you?"

"My heart?" Terence stammered, clutching at his chest. "I dare not trust my heart."

184

PART THREE

I have refined you
But not like silver;
I have tried you
In the furnace of affliction.

Isaiah 48:10

XXII

He was glad she was with him.

Nothing made Butch Gregory as happy as when Lucy was by his side. It wasn't only the comfort level they shared, because they'd been married for nearly twenty years. It was a joy he'd had even when they were dating. Her presence made him feel like a whole person. Butch had never thought much of Greek philosophy, but the way he felt around Lucy was more than enough pause for him to consider the old Platonic idea each person was half of a whole, and the journey of love was finding the other half. He had decided he'd found his other half, and he was whole with her. Even though everything else in his life might be broken and busted, when he was with her, he was whole.

He believed she felt the same way. He hoped she did.

They sat in a country diner eating what was quite possibly the most delicious breakfast to be found in the whole world. It was a far cry from Butch's favorite greasy spoon, The Sydney Diner. This gem, named The Peeled Apple, was nestled in the foothills of the Olympic Mountains on the backbend of Highway 101 as it headed toward Olympia. It was famous for the size of its food. The pancakes were as big as Frisbees, the burgers stacked higher than a person could fit into a mouth, and the plate of biscuits and gravy could have been confused for a wheelbarrow at a construction site. They served gourmet style coffee, but in unpretentious 1970s coffee mugs. A pastry chef came in every day and made fresh pies, sweetbreads, tarts, and even chocolate éclairs unlike anything else. The servers made a big deal about calling patrons by pet names like sugar, hon, sweetie, beauty, and doll. The parking lot was always full.

Butch and his family had driven out here many times for dinner or a Saturday lunch, even though it was almost forty-five minutes away from their home in Sydney. They had never been there on a Sunday morning. He'd always been busy.

Lucy swirled the bit of chocolate-chip pancake at the end of her fork into the maple syrup. "What time does the worship service at Lighthouse start?"

"The usual—11am," Butch sipped his coffee to wash down the biscuit. "They have what they call Sunday School at 10. So very traditional." He shoved in another mouthful of biscuit, ham and egg. "They are good people, though. Interesting, but good." Butch looked at his watch. "We have plenty of time. The church building is only about fifteen minutes from here. And, so what. If I'm late for Sunday School, what are they going to do, fire me?"

She gave him a sideways glare. "Probably not. But it doesn't mean you should take advantage." She licked syrup from her lips, "Remember, your boss is not the people at this church. Your boss is the Lord."

Butch hadn't told Lucy about the weird stuff with the woman and the crying in the parking lot. He chalked the odd encounter up to his own despair, depression, and over-active imagination. He was quite certain everything was normal. Everything was fine. It was all in his head. He was a middle-aged man going through typical crisis. It was all psychological.

He did believe Lucy coming to Lighthouse Church with him would help.

"Have you heard from Paul yet?" Butch changed the subject.

"Let me check." Lucy pulled her phone from her purse. "Yeah, he texted me. Him and Ryan are awake, showered, and on their way to Ryan's church with his parents." She scrolled down. "He says their folks got them breakfast at McDonalds."

"Don't tell him we're here. It would make him jealous." Butch thought it over, "On second thought, tell him where we are because it will make him jealous."

Lucy obliged. She took a picture of Butch holding up his half-eaten plate.

"Should I send it to Sarah too?"

"Nah," Butch said. "She's hasn't been in a playful mood lately." Several thoughts ran through his mind. "Did you check in on her before we left?"

"She was sound asleep in her bed. She'd left the light on when she dozed off. Looks like she was studying."

"Did we do the right thing by not even offering to bring her with us?" Butch pulled off his glasses. "We are in such uncharted waters with her. With everything that happened to Jessica, maybe we shouldn't leave her alone."

"She's fine." Lucy said without equivocation. "She is a strong young woman. She is our daughter, after all. You've got to trust her. We've raised her to endure the storms. Sarah is not as fragile as you suspect she is. I know you can only see her in your mind's eye as a baby sitting in your lap, or a kindergarten kid bringing home macaroni noodles glued to blue construction paper. That is how I see her sometimes, too, but that is not who Sarah is. Not anymore. It is who she was, not who she is." Lucy put the last bite of breakfast in her mouth. "In fact," she said as she chewed, "she is exactly like you: stubborn, contemplative, reflective, irritating, and capable of great compassion."

"I know," he said. "But I worry."

"Worry is a sin."

"Don't preach to me, woman."

"Someone needs to."

"Why?"

"Because preachers aren't always right."

"You and Tommy Bothers would agree on that count."

"That's not fair."

"You're right. I'm sorry. I guess I'm still a little stung by it." He raised his hands in a pantomimed surrender.

"Who wouldn't be?" she took a long drink of her grapefruit juice. "You were railroaded from a job you loved and away from people you had invested yourself into. But it doesn't mean you're broken, or your calling has been changed, or somehow expired."

"You believe God's call is irrevocable?"

"That's what the book says, doesn't it?"

"Yeah, but there are other ways of understanding it."

"Shut up, preacher boy. Eat your breakfast then take me to church or lose me forever. I don't want to hear any theological waffling today. Today is a day for certainty."

XXIII

Frank was waiting for Butch at the door. Butch noticed the welcome team was wearing the exact same clothes he'd worn the week before. This time, though, Butch didn't notice the patina of moss on the roof, the rust on the walls, plastic bags buried in the parking lot gravel, or the victimized smiley face.

Frank was true to form. He didn't say a word to either of the Gregorys. Butch did notice he looked at Lucy for two beats longer than was appropriate. He didn't blame Frank, though. His wife was beautiful. He sometimes forgot she was a decade younger than him, and that she was a looker.

Frank handed Lucy a quarterly Sunday school book, but not Butch. He puzzled over this as they walked down the hallway. Frank had given him one last week. Did Lighthouse church have a one book per

189

person rule, no exceptions, not even for the preacher? Probably.

They were half-way to the room of doom when Lucy whispered in his ear, "This place smells like my childhood."

"Smells like my nightmares," he whispered back.

"Stop it," she smacked him on the arm. "Be nice."

"That was nice. I didn't say I was thinking it smelled like middle school gym class."

The room was as Butch remembered from his previous week. Same fluorescent lighting. Same hum. Same unbelievably high temperature. Same faces. Same ridiculous names. It wasn't until he stood in the doorway that he remembered how there had been barely enough room for last week. Now there were two of them. He wondered what would happen.

"Don't just stand there, boy" Rue barked at Frank. "Put it in gear and get the preacher and his bride chairs."

Butch introduced is wife. "This is Lucy. We've been married for almost twenty years. She is much nicer than I am." He giggled, but no one else did.

Rue stood up and shook Lucy's hand. He introduced everyone in the room in the exact same tone and inflection he'd done the previous week with him—with all of the Sprocket, Bobby, Emcee—all of it. Frank arrived with two chairs, but not identical ones. Frank handed Butch a metal folding chair like he'd sat in the week before. For Lucy, Frank opened up a newer plastic chair with a Washington State Cougars seat cushion tied to it.

"Thank you, Frank." Lucy demonstrated her superior pastor-wife skills by not only remembering his name, but by extending her hand and touching him on the shoulder when she said it. It had been a long time since Butch had observed, carefully observed, the effect his wife had on other people. It was something to behold.

Rue and Lucy hit it off. Whereas Butch's introduction to the group had been sterile and professional, Lucy immediately engaged Rue about how old his children, Frank and Sprocket, were and the unique challenges of their age differences growing up. She asked about family life, their home, and somehow before Butch had even gotten comfortable in his uncomfortable chair, she'd discovered both their mothers were named Iris. Lucy's dazzling persona was so brilliant before his eyes he never noticed the door was shut, and the claustrophobic panic never came. She not only set everyone in the room at ease, but she set him at ease as well.

Prayer requests came, and several asked about Sarah. The

weirdness with the woman in the sanctuary had caused him to forget his involuntary emotional vomiting of the week before when he'd asked for prayers for Sarah. This line of inquiry confused Lucy, Butch could tell, although no one else would have picked up on it. He felt bad for not having told her. It wasn't a willful omission. Having gone this far down the line, he decided to go ahead and tell them everything. He shared how he thanked them for the prayers then told about Jessica, Roberto, and how it was Sarah who found the whole situation. He didn't tell them any supernatural elements in the story. Those kinds of details were a Gregory family thing. As much as he might trust these odd folks, they were not family. He'd trusted Sydney Community as family, and the results had been devastating. He wouldn't make the same mistake twice.

Lucy held his hand while he spoke.

The class was uneventful. He and Lucy kept their mouths closed. He didn't correct the one line of thought that was leading to a Unitarian concept of the Trinity, and she didn't offer a differing point of view regarding how to interact with transgendered people. They were guests here, and this was something they understood. The hard part was functioning as the guest. For most of their adult life together they had been at Sydney Community, and had felt liberty and freedom to be who they were without fear or the need of clarification. Here they were something different, and they didn't have freedom to be authentic. It wasn't something the two of them had talked about before coming to Lighthouse. They didn't need to. They both understood it.

The thought tugged at Butch, like an annoying mosquito, that his failure at Sydney Community was due to the presence of perceived liberty and freedom, but that liberty was not real and that is why he was fired.

Later, the sermon went well, but Butch couldn't wait to talk to Lucy about the song service. He didn't speak to her about it at all ahead of time, wanting instead to let her experience it fresh the way he did the previous week. He sat on the platform during the song time, therefore he could see from her eyes she'd have much to share later. This became especially apparent when they sang "When the Roll Is Called Up Yonder" twice in a row. There was some hymn Butch thought was "Alas, And Did My Savior Bleed" but the tune coming out of the karaoke machine was either off or the song leader was singing different words. It was such a confusing moment in the worship service Butch thought there was a tiny chance it had switched gears and become a Pentecostal moment and there was no one to interpret.

Butch preached yet another sermon which an objective outside observer might label as self-therapy. This time he preached an obscure passage from the Old Testament where Samuel the prophet is addressing the people of Israel. The old crusty prophet tells them they have made a mistake in wanting a king. He tells them they have rejected God and chosen the ways of the other nations. He tells them he will soon be leaving, and they will be on their own. Butch's energy level elevated as he approached the mid-sermon, the part where he told his hearers the majority might rule in a democratic institution like the modern church, but the majority wasn't always right. From there he pointed out all the ways the monarchy eventually led to the destruction of Israel and the exploitation of the people. Butch was particularly hard on Solomon, whom he accidentally almost referred to as Tommy.

When the sermon was over, and the traditional "Invitation" hymn had been endured, he and Lucy spoke with Rue, Emcee, and a few of the other people who had only come to the worship service. Lucy's presence made everyone feel warmer toward him. There were more hugs and fewer handshakes. Rue invited them to lunch at a local Chinese buffet, but they politely declined saying, "We need to get back to the kids."

"Bring 'em next week," Rue said.

"Thanks," was all Butch said in reply. He knew better than to promise anything right now. His life was not stable enough to guarantee his kids would be here next week. He winced when he realized, walking down the steps of the church, he couldn't promise he'd be here next week.

Lucy held his hand. "This is nice."

"What's nice?"

"Walking leisurely with you at church. We were both always so busy at Sydney Community. We never got to walk out after worship together, sit together in small group, or giggle about how horrible the music was."

"Wasn't it, though?" Butch turned around to see if anyone was near enough to hear him. "You might find this hard to believe, but this week was far better than last."

"No way." Lucy grinned from ear to ear. "I'll get you one of those music box thingies for Christmas."

"Please don't."

They were laughing when they neared the car, and Butch popped

192

the trunk open with the key fob. He put his satchel and suitcoat in the trunk and Lucy put her purse in as well. The surprise was waiting when he shut the trunk.

To his left stood The Omen, the frightening woman from the week before. Butch's knees wobbled. His stomach tremored. Her eyes looked to him like fire. The wind gusted, swirling her hair in a paranormal tempest.

She said to him, "937 Stonebriar."

"Excuse me," Lucy said.

Butch looked to his wife. "The music wasn't the only thing I didn't tell you about." He turned his shoulder back around to address The Omen, but she was gone.

"You saw it, right?" Butch said. He wanted to know if this was a shared experience, or if what he saw, and had seen last week, were symptoms of a hyperactive imagination under too much stress. Part of him actually hoped that was the situation.

Lucy nodded. Her eyes were wide.

"What did you see?" Butch said.

"What did I see?"

"I'm not going to tell you what you saw," Butch was insistent. "You need to tell me what you saw." He waved his hands, "Quick, before the moment passes."

"I saw," she said, "a wispy, thin, middle-aged woman with long hair tell you what sounded like an address."

"What else did you see?"

"Nothing. She ran off."

"Did you see her run off?"

"No, not really. Honey, you were talking to me. I couldn't see anything through you."

"She couldn't have run off real fast without us seeing?"

"What are you getting at?" Lucy chewed her left index fingernail.

Butch said, "I'm not getting at anything, except, I didn't see her leave. She was there one moment and not there the next." Butch looked around, "And it's the 'not there' part that bothers me most."

"She must have run off," Lucy said. "What other explanation is there?"

"Not everything has an explanation," Butch said, thinking of the whale, the Nevada desert, and salmon. "But I can't feel my tongue. My mouth is dry. I need a soda."

They stopped at one of their favorite convenience stores outside of Olympia on the way home named Kamilche Trading Post. It was owned and operated on by the Squaxin Island Tribe and everyone always stopped there traveling through. Butch wasn't hungry, but Lucy ordered a fish sandwich and also bought a dreamcatcher. She said she'd give it to Wyoming the next time she saw him.

Lucy drove home while Butch told the story of what had happened with The Omen the previous week and how it had shaken him. He also told her about the odd prayer moment in the class.

"So that's why you wanted to make nice as a family again when you got back?"

"I suppose. Yeah." He felt guilt.

"What do you think she is?" Lucy asked.

"I don't know."

"Yes, you do."

"No, I don't."

"You are the worst liar in the world." Lucy hit him in the arm. "You have an idea, or at least a thought. I can see it."

Butch sucked 7-UP through his straw. "She is either a friend or a foe. I don't know which. Maybe she is both? But I do know she is operating at a different level from me."

"So, she is spiritual."

"I guess you could say so."

"I did say so. Do you say so?"

"I suppose."

The conversation went on in the same way the entire thirty minutes from the Trading Post to their home. All the while, there was a strong suspicion in both of them something had changed. There were things going on to which they had been blind, or too self-centered to notice. Because of this growing reality, neither one was surprised to see Wyoming and Terence's cars parked on the street in front of their house.

XXIV

"What's going on?" Butch asked out loud when he walked into his home.

Wyoming Wallace sat on the sofa. Terence sat in a rocking chair in front of the big bay window. Sarah was on the floor, her knees drawn up under her chin.

"The usual," Wyoming said.

"That bad?" Butch plopped into his recliner while Lucy sat down next to Wyoming.

Terence Harrison puckered his lips and kissed the air. "The last time the three of us—Wyoming, Butch, and myself—were in this room together was the day that crazy lady tried to blow us up."

"Why did you have to bring her up, Doc?" Wyoming didn't smile.

"The day my house blew up. Someday, for sure." Butch tried to smile, but it wouldn't come. He leaned forward in his chair and put his hand on Sarah's shoulder. "Honey, there might be some things your mom and I need to talk about with our friends. Can you run along upstairs and maybe do some homework or something?"

Sarah didn't say anything. She glared at him.

"Um, Reverend," Wyoming said. "I don't know what you think, but she's as much a part of what we need to talk about as anyone else, if not more so."

"Oh no," Lucy said. The blood flowed from her face. "What has happened?"

Sarah had not spoken. She moved closer to her mother and sat at her feet. Terence was the one who spun the tale of what they had encountered the night before as they slept. He started with the end. "When we woke up this morning, we all knew we had to meet with you. It was easier for Sarah and Wyoming, because they didn't have commitments. We talked about it, and Sarah believed it was best if I went ahead and preached this morning at Ebenezer. We didn't want to cause any alarm bells to go off."

"What kind of alarm bells?" Lucy asked.

"Any," Wyoming said, "Any at all. We are at a place where alarm bells are definitely not a good sign. No bells. No sirens. No alarms."

"Right," Terence said. "We don't yet know what the entire scope of this situation is, so it is better to keep things quiet." He cleared his throat, "But we did have a hard time talking Wyoming out of driving down to Olympia and personally escorting you back to Sydney."

"Why didn't you tell us before we left?" Butch ran his hands through his thinning hair.

"You left early," Sarah said. "We slept late, if you want to call it sleep."

"I certainly don't feel rested," Wyoming said.

Lucy turned her head, speaking directly to Wyoming. "I don't understand. Where did you go last night? What did you do?"

"That's what we need to talk about," Terence said.

To say Terence was a master storyteller is underselling the skillset at his disposal. The events that happened in the dream landscape were exciting on their own merit. Nevertheless, there was something in the way he told the tale, without embellishing what happened, that made it so much more suspenseful. His attention to detail, to lighting, to smell, to dialogue, and the way he drew the line toward an awareness of a maleficent presence behind the endeavor demonstrated what made him a great preacher and communicator.

When Terence arrived at the end of the account, Butch jumped when he was told his brother Shark had spoken to them.

"I don't know what we're supposed to do now?" Sarah said. "In the other place, we knew we were supposed to keep going, like some kind of stupid video game where you complete one level and then there is the next. But sitting here, I have no feel for what comes next." She looked up from the floor at Terence and Wyoming, "Do either one of you?"

They both shook their head. "Not a clue," Wyoming added.

"I do," Lucy said.

"Me too," Butch was not happy. He told his briefer, and decidedly less exciting story about The Omen in Olympia. He finished by saying, "It is an address, and we should go to 937 Stonebriar."

"Right now?" Sarah said.

"There is no time like the present." Terence stood up, indicating with his actions and his words what his preference was.

"What will we find?" Butch said.

"Trouble," Wyoming said.

"The real question," Terence said, "Is do all five of us go? It might be a little much."

"Why wouldn't all five of us go?" Lucy was already holding her purse and her keys.

"Well," Terence stammered, "It's just—"

Butch cut him off. "It's just that I'm not liking the idea of my wife and daughter putting themselves into possible danger. They've been there before, and it was awful. And Terence knows he wouldn't either."

"Tough," Sarah said. "Mom and I are in this as much as you are, so let's get going." Sarah pulled out her phone while her parents marveled at her aggressiveness. Wyoming, by contrast, thought nothing of Sarah's actions. He was standing beside her, and the two of them were looking at her cell phone.

"Sarah's already found the place," Wyoming said. "Guess what? It's about" he counted under his breath, "seven blocks from the high school."

"Of course," Terence nodded. "Hepta High."

Butch looked at his daughter. "I guess I have no real say in who goes and who stays? So, if we're all going, how about we take two different cars. How about us Gregorys go in our sedan," he pointed at Wyoming and Terence, "and you two take Wyoming's Jeep?"

"Fair enough," Wyoming said.

"Should we call the police?" Terence asked.

"For what?" Wyoming said the words like a curse.

"Not yet," Lucy said. "We might need to later."

XXV

Butch and Lucy sat in the front seat of the blue sedan while Sarah sat in the back. It was an eight-minute drive from the Gregory home to 937 Stonebriar, but it might as well have been in a different universe. "I know the house," Sarah said.

"Have you been there?" Butch's words came out high pitched and agitated.

"No, not exactly. Everyone in school knows about that house."

"Why?" Lucy turned around from the front seat to talk to her daughter.

"It is where kids go."

"Which kids?" Lucy asked.

"Kids. I don't know, I guess just kids. Probably kids who don't want to go home. Kids who don't have a home. Just kids."

Butch's expression betrayed his anxiety about the situation. "Has that ever been you? You didn't want to come home?"

"No. Yes. But not the same way." Sarah huffed. "This house is where kids go to drop out of everything. But I never went there. I've never wanted to fade away."

"Who lives there?" Lucy said.

"No one," Sarah said. "Everyone."

"I see." Butch made a left turn onto the street that ran along the high school. "Did Jessica ever go there?"

"I don't know." Sarah chewed on her fingernail. "I guess. Probably."

"Would you describe it as a meth house?"

"Maybe. Pretty much. Yeah."

Butch hesitated, "I don't mean to sound cruel. All this hurts." He brought his hands up off the steering wheel and made a universal gesture, then brought them down hard almost slamming them onto the wheel. "I know it is hard and I probably sound like a jerk. We don't know what we're walking into, and any information might help. If it is a meth house, it is something we should know." He hesitated again. "And what's more, I wish you weren't here with us. It makes me nervous."

Lucy turned her head from backward to look now at her husband. Her eyes were unsure. "What do you think we'll find there?"

Sarah didn't wait for her father to answer. She unbuckled her seatbelt and leaned up through the middle of the sedan seats, "Whatever you think you'll find, it will not be that, and whatever you could never imagine, it will be more."

Before either Butch or Lucy could answer, they arrived at their destination.

* * *

Wyoming drove behind Butch in his black Jeep. They had left in such a hurry, they hadn't talked about who would follow whom. Wyoming decided to follow the Gregorys so he could scan things with a better perspective.

"I know this house," Terence said. He held onto the panic bar with a firm grip.

"If it is the one I think it is, I do, too." Wyoming shifted gears. "It is not a good place."

"No, not good at all," Terence said.

"About seven months ago a kid from the Ebenezer youth group overdosed. It happened there at this house on Stonebriar. An elder drove me by it and we prayed in the car. At the time, it felt like a pathetic gesture of weakness, like something which didn't matter all that much." He stared out the window, his eyes empty. "Now," he shook his head, "I'm beginning to wonder if it might have been much more. Actually, it might be how all this got started."

"In what way is that, Doc?" Wyoming gave Terence a pained look. He couldn't figure out where the conversation was going.

Terence kissed the air, "It is a lesson I learned long ago. I should have known better. But sometimes we forget the fundamentals. We get busy with life. We get sloppy. I didn't guard myself, or my people. When we decide to go after the devil, he comes back at us with fury. He is a counter-puncher." The preacher paused before starting again. "When I was a young minister, I once went to the worst part of

Philadelphia, downtown in the old abandoned areas. This was in the late 80s when things were especially bad in the inner cities. I stood on a corner in the middle of the night. In my spiritual haste and naiveté, I didn't pray to God. Instead, I talked to the devil."

"Sounds like a Van Halen song." Wyoming noticed Terence didn't even smirk so much as smirk at his joke, he straightened up and said, "Well, what did you tell him? What did you tell the devil?"

"I told him to get out of town and go back to hell. I told him I was claiming this neighborhood in the name of Jesus and he had no right here. I told him he was already defeated, but if he wanted to, he could give me his best shot."

"But isn't that stuff true?" Wyoming said. "From what I understand of the Bible, what you say is true."

"It is true, in a way." Terence said as he leaned into the right turn Wyoming made. "But I am a servant. I should have been talking to the Lord and not talking to the devil. It is hard to explain, but what I did was instigate a fight with the evil one. I poked the bear." Terence poked at the air with his left hand. "What followed was the hardest year of ministry. One bad thing after another, and I have come to believe that bad year is correlated with me trying to take on the devil single handedly that night. It was arrogant, and costly."

"So, we shouldn't battle evil?" Wyoming pulled up behind Butch as he parked his sedan.

"I didn't say that." Terence shook his head. "We must battle evil. What we shouldn't do is personally go after the evil one. We shouldn't go looking for trouble. There is enough trouble in the world that comes to us. My job is to be faithful to the Lord. I should let him take care of the evil one. My work is to love people and tell them the truth. There are boundaries."

Wyoming pulled out his pistol from his holster. "You're thinking a few months back maybe you and the old man who prayed here might have opened up the can of worms again." Wyoming popped the cylinder on his pistol. He let out a long, slow whistle.

"What's wrong?" Terence said.

"Weird."

"What's weird?"

"This pistol was loaded. I always keep it loaded. But right now, it only has one round in it."

"No way," Terence said.

"Apparently, there is a way. Those shots I fired in the dream had to have been real. In some way or another." He reached across

Terence and opened the compartment on the dashboard. He grabbed a box of Remington shells, reloaded, and stuck a handful in each coat pocket. "Did the kid who overdosed survive?"

"Yes," Terence said. The question snapped him back from thoughts about the dream world. "But he jumped off the Narrows Bridge three months ago. The family was so upset they didn't even have a funeral for him."

"Devil or not," Wyoming opened the Jeep door, "it is time to put a stop to this. We can't keep letting him have these kids."

Terence opened his door and got out. "Hey, Wyoming. You said you knew this house. How?"

"I'd rather not say." He slammed the door. "It wasn't pleasant." He looked ahead and saw the three Gregorys getting out of their car. "Maybe call the old man, the elder, and tell him to start praying. I feel like now would be a good time."

"I would, but he died a week after we were here."

"It shouldn't surprise me. But it does."

"Heart attack in his sleep. We didn't give it much thought at the time. He was in his early 70s. It happens. But now, I wonder what dream he went through? Was he stuck in a world like we were? And didn't make it out?"

"Good question," Wyoming said. "What I want to know is, why don't people put these pieces together before it's too late? If you folks believe so strongly in a spiritual world, why does it take us having to go to hell and back before you believe the effect it has upon us in this world? And why are all these kids dying and no one is doing anything about it? Do they think suicide is natural? Do they care? Shouldn't someone be investigating this bull? Why does it come down to two preachers, their families and me? You'd think there would be some kind of governmental agency to handle this."

"We wrestle not against flesh and blood." Terence said. "Governments are probably part of the problem. Not completely, but the system kills. The letter kills. God sent us, and if he is with us, well, he is all we need."

Wyoming shook his head as the five of them joined up.

Butch spoke first. "Sarah says there is a back door which is easier to get in and out of. Apparently, the front stays locked."

"You can bet he knows we're coming." Sarah added.

"Good." Wyoming snapped. "I'm ready to help him pack his bags." He looked around the group. "I was thinking Butch, Lucy and I would go in the back door. Terence and Sarah can go in the front."

Wyoming nodded at Sarah. "For some reason, I feel like you're the leader here. Does the plan make sense?"

"It does," She said. "We should have a pastor in each group, and we should split up my mom and me, but mom and dad should be together because they are two halves of the same person."

"Those were my thoughts exactly," Wyoming said.

"I know." Sarah nodded.

Terence touched Wyoming on the shoulder, but the cowboy did not look up. They both knew what happened, because it had happened before.

XXVI

Wyoming and the two Gregory parents walked toward the backyard. They made no appearance of being careful, trying to hide, or attempting any subterfuge.

The house was a dilapidated nightmare. There were no neighboring homes around it. The road leading to it passed through a thicket of alder trees, salal, underbrush, and wild blackberries, with several zigs and zags. Like so many homes in this part of the country, if you were not looking for it, you'd never have known it was there, even though it was less than seven or eight city blocks from Sydney High School. A left turn off the main thoroughfare, another left, a right and the road becomes a dirty trail that winds through the woods, and up to the house.

Once upon a time, the siding had been white with blue trim. Moss had turned the white into green and the blue trim slimy black. Decades ago a young couple probably built the three-bedroom, two-bath rambler with dreams of a future. They planted a yard—grew flowers— paid bills—cooked dinner—watched television—made love—raised children. This had been their home, a place of peace, joy, and hope. Even in its current disrepair, the house held an echo of a happy past life. An architectural memory lingered. A rusted swing set with a sad, broken slide told the tale of warm spring days spent in the sunshine with chubby cheeks grinning and curly hair blowing in the breeze. Weathered rocks outlined overgrown flower beds along the exterior wall where tulips and roses used to reach up and try to drink the golden rays of life. Bare windows with cracked glass at one time were covered with handmade curtains from which warm light from lamps used to glow through at night as a mother crocheted blankets and a father read the news while the sweet smell of cinnamon and apples wafted from the pie baking in the oven.

Those happy memories were murdered by an ancient maleficent force who destroyed and killed anything good. The Rab-Shakeh brought a gloomy pallor over the entire property. The unkempt trees blocked out the sun's natural light, making the lonely lot to resemble the shadowland of winter's twilight, even though it was midday in late spring. A cold wind blew from both the east and the west, swirling around the house as a spiritual sentinel keeping guard. Every sound echoed. The blowing leaves hitting the side of the house, the sound of people's breath, the creak of a rusty chain all resounded over and over again as an infinite loop. No other sounds came from the outside world because 937 Stonebriar was a forsaken island where anything of human goodness or divine love had become ghosts from the past.

* * *

"I'll go first," Wyoming put his hand on the knob. It wasn't locked.

Butch said, "Hold on a second."

"What for?"

Butch didn't answer. He took Lucy by one hand and put the other hand on Wyoming's shoulder. "Lord, we don't know what is inside this spooky house. What we do believe is you have brought us here. I pray you protect us, and especially by us I mean my daughter. Grant her strength and allow her to see the truth. In Jesus' name. Amen."

"Amen," Lucy added.

"I should've known," Wyoming whispered as he turned the doorknob. "You people pray all the time."

The smell of human filth was the first sensory effect. The second was the dim lighting. They were standing in the kitchen. A refrigerator sat to their left, as did a crumbling Formica counter with a sink, a microwave, and even a knife block. There were no knives. An open doorway that led into a den was in front of them. The hallway running the length of the house was partially visible. To the right was a pantry door.

Wyoming flipped a light switch to his right. Nothing happened.

"It's been a long time since power flowed through these wires," He said.

A figure stepped from the shadows in the hall and stood in the doorway. "You don't know what real power is," the shadow spoke.

Wyoming couldn't discern any distinct facial features, clothing, or corporeal characteristics. He was about to reply with something smart-mouthed, like "I'll show you power" or "If you had real power, the lights would be on" or some other inane retort.

Butch beat him to it.

"We know all about real power," the preacher said. "And we know you don't have any."

The shadow fluttered, rippling like a curtain in the wind. It broke into three large refracted pieces before reassembling itself.

"Is that so," the phantom said. "Let's see whose power is greatest right now."

There was a hydraulic sound before the shadow rose from the floor and flew at the three of them. Wyoming reached for his pistol, not sure hot lead was the right solution, but it always felt like the right solution to him. Before he could act, Butch Gregory took a stand between them and the shadow. "Light dispels darkness," he said simply and plainly. When he did, there was a burst of pulsating light throughout the room.

The shadow shrieked and was no more.

Lucy came up from behind her husband and kissed his cheek. "Good one, honey. Where did you learn to do it?"

"It was a breakout session, some kind of learning annex they had last year at the annual denominational meeting in Portland."

"Not likely," she said, kissing his cheek again.

Wyoming stepped in front and stuck his head in the doorway that served as the juncture between the kitchen, the den, and the hall. "We should expect more trouble."

"Can you hear Sarah and Terence? We should be able to hear them, you'd think." Lucy put her hands in her coat pocket.

"Not necessarily," Wyoming said. He was thinking about the dream world. This house felt like the dream world to him. "Should, could, and would are not the kind of things we can count on right now." His speech slowed. He said, "The rules are not the same in here as they are out there," he pointed to the backdoor. "Our friends could be right beside us and we might not even know it."

The pantry door behind Wyoming flung open. A man sprung out of it and jumped onto Wyoming's back, carrying both of them to the ground. Two other figures ran from their hidden holes in the den. Another attacker came storming down the hallway and into the kitchen.

Wyoming and his attacker were at Lucy's feet. She kicked Wyoming's opponent directly in the head. He rolled off Wyoming, which is when Wyoming put an elbow hard into his throat, crushing his esophagus.

The first one coming from the den lunged at Butch, but he dodged, causing the attacker to slam his head straight into the dead refrigerator. The tiny kitchen was filling up with people and bodies. The second attacker tried to reach for Lucy, but he stumbled over the man lying on the floor clutching at his shattered throat. When he did, she kicked him in the groin, then immediately said to him, "I'm so sorry."

"No, you're not," Butch said. "At least I'm not."

The fourth attacker never got close. As he rounded the awkward corner from the hallway into the kitchen, Wyoming Wallace put a hollow point bullet in the middle of his gaunt, yellow, meth-addled face.

"Did you have to kill him?" Butch said. "I mean, they didn't seem like much of a threat."

"I didn't have to," Wyoming said. "But I wanted to. Does that count for anything?"

Butch let it go.

The three attackers on the ground were all groaning.

"They are only babies," Lucy said. "I bet the oldest is maybe seventeen."

"What do you want to do with them?" Wyoming said as he got to his feet.

"Don't kill them," Lucy said.

"I'm not," Wyoming grinned. "At least not yet. But I don't want them sneaking up behind us later."

"Do we have any duct tape?" Butch said. "We've used the gray tape in the past with good effect."

"I am fresh out." Wyoming shrugged.

Lucy turned around behind her, opened a drawer, and pulled out a giant roll of bright orange duct tape. "It's not gray but should do the trick."

Working together, it didn't take long to secure the three surviving goons.

"I oughta go ahead and put a bullet in this one with the crushed windpipe. He aint gonna survive much longer anyway."

"No," Butch said. "You never know what might happen."

"Have it your way," Wyoming muttered.

"I'm concerned we haven't heard from Terence or Sarah yet." Lucy bit at her fingernail.

Butch put his arm around Lucy. "I'm sure Sarah is fine. She is with Terence."

"Terence is a pussycat." Lucy said.

"More like a teddy bear," Butch's face bobbed up and down as he said, with a smirk on his lips.

Wyoming said, "You don't know him as well as you think you do. Doc is made of steel." He shook his head again. "Besides, Sarah can take care of herself."

* * *

Terence and Sarah did not have the same trepidation as the other three about entering the house. They didn't knock, pause, crouch, or pray. Terence pointed at two backpacks on the porch. Sarah said, "There are two people inside the door. They know we're coming."

"Perfect," Terence said. "I wouldn't have it any other way."

"Your sarcasm is duly noted." Sarah said.

"Who said I was being sarcastic?"

Sarah walked up the crumbling stone steps and opened the door.

"You were wrong," Was the first thought Terence had upon entering. Neither he or Sarah knew if he'd actually said it out loud.

"I was wrong?" she said, raising the pitch of her voice to form it as a question.

"But it is more of a wrong in kind rather than number. You were mostly right. Not the way you thought you were right. But right nonetheless."

Their witty conversation emerged from the fact there were indeed two waiting for them, but what waited was not people, at least not as they expected. In what was once a living room, two creatures stared at them. They both looked hungry. The creature on the left was something from a werewolf story. It stood on two legs, wore blue jeans, but hunched over as if it wanted to walk on all fours. It had a snout like a wolf, a mouth full of teeth, and two long arms complete with claws at the hands. It was covered in black and silver hair which was noticeably thicker around the head, forming a lush mane.

It wore a Panama Jack hat.

The creature to the left was a great snake. It sat coiled on the floor with its head perched in the air. The eyes were yellow. Its tongue flickered. The serpent's diameter was at least three feet, and its length might have been twenty or twenty-five feet. The scaling on the snake was golden, red, and black. The Egyptian ankh symbol was

205

emblazoned between its eyes on its flat brow.

"He told us was five of you." The serpent said. His voice was not what she expected. The snake did not hiss. It spoke with perfect diction in a rich baritone. "Where are the other three people?"

"What other three?" Sarah said. "It's me and my old friend, Terence."

"Nonsense," The werewolf said. His voice sounded like a thunderstorm. "He promised us five."

"Does he always keep his promises?" Terence said. When neither responded, Terence continued, "Liars will always lie, twist the truth, and manipulate. I feel like he's probably done it to both of you your whole lives."

The serpent lifted its head to look eye to eye with Terence. "We are the Guardians, and your slick words will not deter us."

"Perhaps," Terence said, "But more is going on here."

Sarah plunged deep into Terence's thoughts. It had been so easy in the dream world, but here it was harder in the real world. Or maybe it was harder in this particular house. Maybe this place was fighting her. She pushed hard, and eventually she was able to reach into Terence's mind and deliver a message. It was a simple one. What are you doing?

The only answer he gave her was that he could see.

She trusted him, but she kept her eyes on the werewolf.

Terence asked the serpent, "You are a Guardian. I respect that. I am a guardian, too. I guard secrets and protect people. My name is Terence. What is your name?"

"I am Guardian," the serpent snapped.

"That is your function. That is your job, but that is not what I'm asking. I'm asking you, what is your name?"

To Sarah, it looked like the snake shrank. The same was true of the werewolf.

"My name?" The serpent said. His voice was clear and diction perfect, but the timbre of the sound was not as rich.

"Yes, your name. What is it? Who are you?"

"I am Guardian?" The serpent said.

"No, that is what he has made you be. It is your slave name." Terence now stood tall over the serpent as its diminished size became more pronounced. "What is the name your mother gave you? The name your father spoke over you when you were yet in the womb? Who are you?"

The serpent shrieked. It trembled. No longer coiled, it now lay long ways on the ground, flailing about in a seizure. Its tail flipped and flopped, hitting the floor hard enough to cause the dirt to fly up. The head of the creature twisted as the whole being writhed in pain. The mouth foamed. Some kind of liquid oozed from under it, like it was melting. The shrieks transformed to howls.

White light exploded all around the room, and the serpent was no more. Where it had been, lay a boy of about fourteen years old. He was naked, and unconscious. Terence took off his jacket and covered him.

The boy told Terence, "My name is Samuel." Having said it once, he kept saying it over and over again. "My name is Samuel. My name is Samuel." Each time he said it, he emphasized a different word in the sentence.

"Hi, Samuel," Terence and Sarah both said at the same time.

The werewolf, though smaller and decidedly more curious looking than frightening, ran through the door and across the yard.

Samuel stood up, wrapping Terence's coat around him. "I'm going home now. I want to see my mama."

They watched him leave and walk up the road toward the high school.

"Will the wolf thing harm him?" Sarah said.

"No. Samuel's biggest concern is finding home. But that is good for him. By contrast, Mr. Werewolf will undoubtedly run all the way to Tacoma, unless he comes to his senses first. The first instinct is often flight, but I suspect the demonic possession on that one is tenuous and temporary right now."

XXVII

Terence and Sarah heard the gunshot from Wyoming's revolver when the werewolf ran out. They ignored it until they stood in the doorway watching Samuel, the half-naked boy who had been a serpent, walk up the road.

"I wonder what the gunshot means?" Sarah said.

"It means Wyoming is being Wyoming." Terence turned around and looked into the dim cavern of the Stonebriar house. "I suppose we need to find them. Can you reach them, telepathically?"

"No. I can sorta feel them, though. I know they are here in the house, and I know they are alright. At least they believe they are alright. But I can't communicate with them."

"I bet he is blocking you." Terence shrugged. "Oh well. I guess we have to go find them."

"Absolutely," Sarah said. "I feel his presence like a person might feel a hot fireplace in a cold house. Even if you can't see it, you can smell it. You can feel the house getting warmer."

"Are we getting warmer?" Terence's eyes were wide.

"Yes. But we're not hot yet."

Terence used the flashlight app on his cellphone to illuminate the dark interior. They walked through the short hallway connecting the front living room to another hallway that ran down the length of the house. They saw Butch, Lucy, and Wyoming coming toward them.

"Mom," Sarah said.

"Sarah," Lucy said.

But neither one could hear the other. Sarah walked toward her mother, but there was a barrier between them where the two paths met. It was invisible, but as solid as steel. The five human beings could see each other, but they couldn't reach one another or hear across the chasm.

"Oddest thing I've ever seen," Wyoming said. He put his hand up to the barrier. "It feels like cold metal."

"Like glass?" Butch said. He reached up to touch it. "No, not like glass at all."

On their side, Terence was conducting the same touch experiments. Sarah tried to break through it with her mind.

"Want me to shoot it?" Wyoming asked Butch.

"No. That wouldn't work." Butch said.

"Come on, it's worth a try."

"Hold your fire, cowboy." Lucy winked at Wyoming. She approached the barrier and put her left hand on it. "I feel something." She spread out her fingers on the barrier. With her other hand, she pointed to Sarah, then to her own hand. She hoped Sarah understood.

And so, it was. Sarah understood what her mother was communicating to her. She took her right hand and placed it directly across from her mother's hand. Neither woman knew what to expect, but they were driven by instinct more than knowledge. But what is instinct other than secret knowledge, knowledge that comes not from mind or imagination, but knowledge stored in bone, muscle, and gland.

The first sensation they felt was warmth in their hands against the coldness of the barrier. Their hands sweat the way hands do when two people hold hands for a long time. A tingle came next. The tingle startled Sarah, but her mom's resolve gave her strength.

No one said anything, not even Wyoming.

The warming sensation grew until it was uncomfortably hot.

Electric arcs danced off their hands. Neither woman let go of the connection, though both were in pain.

Butch grabbed Lucy's free hand and started to pull her away. She waved him off. Her eyes were closed, but she raised her bowed head his direction and shook it.

Their hands glowed. No one could tell if they were burning or dissolving. The air was perfumed with sweet ozone and acid fire. Sarah screamed. Tears came down her face. Lucy was stoic silence, but her lips trembled. Her body became rigid, working to hold on.

Terence and Butch prayed.

Wyoming stared in disbelief.

Lucy cried out for the first time as the sound of thunder filled the tiny hallway juncture. The thunder came at the moment mother and daughter touched each other and the barrier melted. The pain went away, and they knew what to do.

Sarah followed her mother's lead.

Where their palms touched, the barrier disappeared. They moved their hands in ever growing circles making a bigger hole with each revolution. The two of them erased the barrier separating the two groups until there was a large enough space for Sarah to step through.

When she did, their hands stopped glowing and they fell into one another's embrace.

Butch checked their hands, and both looked fine. No burns, no scars, no injuries.

Terence wiggled through the hole in the barrier. "I hate to sound ungrateful, but maybe you could have cut the doorway bigger? We're not all tiny high school girls around here, you know."

"We heard gunshots," Sarah said, looking at Wyoming.

"We ran into some old friends," he said. "How about you guys, did you find anything?"

"Some major somethings," Terence said, finally through the hole. "About halfway through that, whatever that was, I wondered why we didn't go out the front door and come in the back to meet you."

"It wouldn't have worked," Lucy said. "The barrier would have moved, keeping us separated until we learned how to overcome it."

"Ya think," Wyoming said. "Because Terence's fix would have been much simpler."

"Mom's right," Sarah said. "The barrier was real, but it was not locked into this spot. It would have shifted its location and moved anywhere to keep us apart."

They heard a loud obscenity come from the kitchen area, and two more attackers ran down the hallway toward them. Simultaneously, three attackers came up the out of the dark hallway from the front living room where Terence and Sarah had met the snake and werewolf.

"I guess we'll have to compare notes later," Wyoming shouted. He fired a shot at the one in front. His first shot missed, the second found a thighbone. The teenage boy fell to the ground with a yelp. The other attacker, coming from the kitchen, jumped on top of Terence and took him to the ground.

The three Gregory's, Butch, Lucy and Sarah turned around and took the three coming from the living room. Butch went low on the lead attacker, for the hallway was narrow. There was only room for one at a time. The second attacker fell on top of Butch. The three of them struggled to get leverage as they squirmed in a pile on the filthy floor. Lucy and Sarah looked into the eyes of the third one, who had somehow navigated the sprawling, writhing, ganglion of legs and arms and was right in front of them.

Sarah realized they were cut off from the rest of the group. She put herself between her mom and the attacker.

Sarah ducked as he took a wild swing.

She could hear his thoughts. He wanted drugs. He was told if he took care of Sarah and her friends, he could get another fix or two for his efforts. Sarah listened for anything else, but that was the only thought going through his mind. She was able to anticipate his movements easily.

After the attacker's third failed swing, she got a good look at his face. She knew him. He'd been a senior when she was a freshman. There had been a bright future for him. She looked for his name in her memory. He'd been on the football team. He was smart. Didn't he get a scholarship to Oregon State? His girlfriend's name was Violet. He was Keith. She smiled when she remembered his name.

"What happened to you, Keith? How did you end up like this?"

She'd hoped her question would snap him out of his mindlessness. The opposite happened. When he heard his own name, it angered him further and he jumped at her, intending to claw her eyes out. The hallway was narrow, and when he lunged for her, she stepped sideways into an open door.

That was when everything changed.

XXVIII

The door didn't close behind her. It dissolved into the wall, or what the wall had become. She was separated from everyone else. The place where the door had been turned into limestone. She was bathed in reddish orange light, like the glow of a fireplace on a cold January morning when all the other lights in the house are off. The room was hot. It was a humid, wet, moist heat and drops of perspiration formed on her brown and under her arms.

She turned around from looking at where the door had been and looked toward the center. Her eyes could not process the reality she was inside the house, for she was now in what looked like a giant hall, or cavern. The ceiling looked infinitely high, and the room was larger than the sanctuary at Sydney Community Church.

"Hello, Sarah, daughter of Butch and Lucy Gregory. I've been expecting you."

The Rab-Shakeh's presence filled the cavern. Sarah felt the ambient personality of his evil intentions vibrate against her flesh. It wanted to get inside her, the way it had gotten inside Jessica, Roberto, those kids who attacked them, and who knows how many others. It, he, tried to get into her heart and mind. But he couldn't.

The Rab-Shakeh spoke. It wasn't the kind, gentle voice of the teacher Mr. Raba, or even the creepy voice of the dream Rab-Shakeh from Hepta High. Mr. Raba was a prop, and the dream experience was as a partial product of Sarah's own consciousness. But this voice was the real voice of the ancient foe. The sound escaped from his mouth, but his lips never really moved. The words sounded like he was under water. Even though the monster was right in front of her, the sound, the words, came from somewhere else, as if even this presence were yet another layer, another façade, while the real Rab-Shakeh dwelled somewhere other.

This thought burdened her mind more than it should have. She wondered where his physical self was. The person—thing, standing here challenging her, trying to destroy her was merely another avatar. The genuine essence of what she faced was behind a curtain somewhere else pulling levers and switches. Evil might not be eternal, but it was crafty.

"Sarah Gregory, you are mine," he said to her. "You did not give yourself to me, like your friends did. Nevertheless, I have taken you in my trap. You are now mine, forever."

"You've told me that lie before," She shifted her weight from one foot to the other, rocking back and forth with pent up energy. "Twice, actually. Neither time did I believe you, and I don't believe you now. I will never belong to you."

"Lie?" His head drooped. "Would I lie to you? It hurts me so much you would think so little of me and accuse me of such a treachery. I only want the best for you. Only the best." He blew her an air kiss.

Sarah roared with laughter. "Now that is a whopper of a lie. You called yourself The Destroyer. You want to destroy me." She bit her lower lip. "You want to destroy my friends, my family, my school, and my community."

"No, no," he almost purred as he denied her words. "That is not what I mean. It is not you I want to destroy. No, no. I want to help you transcend this unholy existence you're trapped in. I want to destroy the powers which hold you captive. I want you to joyfully escape into eternity where all your questions will be answered. Your friends are there waiting for you. I only seek to give you goodness and love, belonging and acceptance, peace and joy."

Sarah knew this wasn't right, but he was inside her head now. Ideas of surrender, hopelessness, and doubt washed over her. She was so tired of this trip.

The Rab-Shakeh took two steps toward her and extended his arms. "Sarah, my daughter, why do you struggle?" He looked into her eyes. "What if you've been on the wrong side all along? You know it's possible. Only an arrogant soul would never admit the impossibility of being right all the time. What if your father, as noble as his intentions are, has been on the wrong side? Could it be God himself has been keeping you and the human family from its fullest potential all along?

"Consider the possibility, for just a moment, he wants to push you down into a constraining morality. He has been withholding the truth from your kind since the dawn of the cosmos. He does nothing to stop the eventual faint whisper of a sad and pathetic death. Children die from starvation. War ravages civilizations. Disease strips away dignity, and the god of your father does nothing about it—doesn't even lift a finger. And you worship him for it. I tell you the truth, Sarah Gregory, such a god is not worthy of worship at all." His voice rose in indignation with each accusation. "I, on the other hand, have come to destroy his intentions and his shackles. I have come to break the chains of small mindedness and intolerance. I intend to crush the prison of religious false hope." His voice was now so loud Sarah could feel the soundwaves vibrating against her, then lowered the decibels to a near whisper. "That is why I am The Destroyer, because I want to free you. I destroy the prison holding you and all people back in the dark ages of belief. I want to liberate you. I want to free your mind and your body. I want to free your soul and your libido. You belong to me, you belong with me."

Sarah heard the drum rhythms from the song. The song that played in Jessica's bedroom. The song that had played when Roberto died. The same song that woke her up out of the daydream within the dream at the imaginary prom of Hepta High.

Here it was again.

The wickedness came at her straight on. She didn't know if she could hold on through it.

I can't win. But I have to win.

He is too strong.

I am all alone. There is no one to help me.

"Help me," she whispered. Her whole body were paralyzed, but she forced out that tiniest and quickest of all prayers. The desperate two-word plea floated from her lips straight to the ears of the one who always listens and always hears.

How can I win? How can anyone defeat evil?

"Help me."

A conversation she had with her father came to her mind. She replayed it. She'd asked her father how to defeat evil. They were talking about a silly book. She was angry at him and was trying to trap him in his own words. She didn't really want the answer to the question. Her goal was to make him feel bad. She'd wanted to make him feel inadequate. So, she asked him how to defeat evil. She didn't esteem much of his answer then. It had sounded like way too much preacher talk. Now she needed those words. She was trying to remember what he'd said. She closed her eyes and focused. But it was no use. The memory didn't form. She could see him standing there in her doorway. She saw the book cover. She felt her anger at him. She saw his disappointment, how his face was crestfallen. The wound in his eyes at how she had talked to her father pierced her soul.

But she couldn't remember the words.

"Help me," she whispered again. A tear crawled down her cheek.

He had told her it was what you believe. He said if we focus on ourselves, evil wins. If we focus on evil, evil wins. But if we focus on our beliefs and who we believe in, evil doesn't stand a chance.

He'd said something else, though. She tried to remember. There was something else. She couldn't remember.

The Rab-Shakeh was three feet away from her now. She could feel the heat coming from his avatar. Her mind wandered. Focus eluded her. She tried to imagine where The Rab-Shakeh truly was? Was it hell? Was it heaven? Was it the gymnasium of Sydney High? Was it in a bunker in Iraq? Was it in Jerusalem?

All she could think about was him.

"Am I not here?" he said. "Oh yes, I can feel your questions. Most people have similar thoughts. When they behold my glory and power, it is impossible to not ponder my greatness. You want to know where I am, but am I not here?"

Sarah tried to talk, but the words were slow in coming. "Your true self is not here," she said. "I wonder where you are."

He roared, "Am I not everywhere?" In his right hand was a rod of gold. He slammed it into her abdomen. "Did you feel it, snarky child? Is the precious metal of kings and emperors real enough for you, peasant girl?"

The rod pressed into her, and now he twisted it counterclockwise. "I could push my scepter through your flimsy shirt, puncture thin, pathetic skin, jam it through the intestines, until I snap the spinal cord. You wouldn't be the first. You wouldn't be the last. Not by far."

"I thought you said you were here to free me. I guess it was just another lie."

"Lies? Oh, Sarah, your words are so hurtful and mean spirited. Why have you become so intolerant and judgmental? I would never lie to you. These are alternative facts, and alternative facts are the zeitgeist of the age, my dear." He licked his lips. "I will free you from this body and send you on to the next world. Doesn't it sound delightful?" He opened his eyes wide and looked into hers. In his gaze, she beheld the cosmos. It was an infinite reservoir of awe and wonder.

But she blinked. She didn't blink because she wanted to. His hypnotic stare was powerful. She didn't blink because she was strong. She didn't blink because she knew she needed to. She blinked because she heard the voice of her father.

Was it his voice, or hers? She couldn't tell. What she heard was him instructing her how to defeat evil. She was focusing too much on The Rab-Shakeh. "If you focus on evil, evil wins." That was what he told her that Sunday afternoon in her bedroom, when she had provoked a fight with him.

What can I do right now?

The Rab-Shakeh shook himself when he realized the metaphysical

214

connection he'd established with his prey had been lost. He stumbled backwards, which did not go unnoticed by Sarah. She could defeat him. She had just made him weak enough to stumble. What could she do? What leverage could she make? Was there a magic formula, a specific prayer, the right words to say? If she amassed all her cleverness, perhaps she could riddle her way out.

She was young and strong. There must be some way for her to get untangled and run away or kill him. She was resourceful.

She could do this.

In her mind's eye she imagined herself running around The Rab-Shakeh, exhausting him until he finally collapsed of fatigue. She visualized herself using his very scepter to bludgeon his head. Yes, she could do this. The first step to success was always a positive attitude.

"A positive attitude," The Rab-Shakeh mumbled in mockery at her. "I invented that one, too."

She shook her head in denial. But she knew it was true.

"I invented it about a hundred years ago, long before you were born. It rates amongst my highest achievements. But I must admit my friend Gaia has done more work of late in psycho-babble. She has a real gift for it. Her latest nugget is, 'The heart wants what the heart wants.' Perfect, isn't it?"

Hope's flicker perished. She accepted the reality of her fate. She would die here, as would her father, mother, Wyoming, and Terence. Eventually, The Rab-Shakeh would come for Paul and claim him too just as he predicted he would when they were stuck in Hepta High. And all her friends at school. There was nothing she could do about it. She was too weak, pathetic, and helpless to do anything in the face of such great evil.

The Rab-Shakeh had taken a position behind her. She wanted to run. She couldn't. That she didn't know why she couldn't run irritated her.

He pressed in close to her from behind. He ran his scaly hand through her hair. He inhaled deeply.

"In your own way, you are quite beautiful. Not stunning and gorgeous like your friend Jessica. Yes, Jessica was as magnificent as a Hollywood starlet or a runway model. Her genes were good where it counted. True, she wasn't smart, but smarts don't matter in the bedroom." He pulled her hair, yanking it backward so he could look into her eyes. "You have an athletic, muscular physique which is attractive. You could be appealing, but you must learn how to use it." He leaned his lower body against hers. "Perhaps death is not what is best for you right now. You could be made to serve. Taught your place in the real world." He let go her hair but did not step away. "It would be my pleasure to teach you."

Fatalism filled her heart. He would abuse her, then he would send her out to who knows where to be abused over and over again. The things she imagined were beyond horrific. Her skin grew clammy. She felt a million hands touching and groping her. It wasn't enough for him to kill her, he wanted to humiliate her. He wanted to destroy her.

He must have heard her thoughts, for he shouted, "I am The Destroyer! You are the destroyed!"

How could this happen? Where had she gone wrong? What had she done wrong to deserve this?

At the bottom of her despair, she heard her father's voice again. Or was it hers?

The voice told her she was focusing too much on herself. She was only a tool.

Sarah heard the words, but she failed to grasp the meaning. Of course, she was focused on herself. A demon older than dirt promised to send her into sex slavery. Who wouldn't?

She darted her eyes and saw The Rab-Shakeh. She looked at him to see if he could tell she was hearing voices. He was unaware. These thoughts were guarded from his awareness.

Interesting. But she didn't have time to think about why.

She took a chance and talked back to the voice in her head. "What do you mean? Tool? He sees me as a tool, what are you telling me to do?"

The voice again spoke to her. It told her she couldn't defeat evil. If she focused on The Rab-Shakeh, he wins. If she focuses on herself, The Rab-Shakeh wins. The only way to win was to focus on what she believed. She couldn't defeat the evil. She could, indeed she must, let herself be a tool in the hands of the one who has already beaten every evil.

Sarah heard those thoughts as words, but they oozed out of her soul and into her mind in a way she'd never quite experienced before. She felt them into reality. This was the third time she'd faced him. The first time was in Jessica's house, then the second time in the dream world. Each time she had survived by realizing things around her weren't exactly what they appeared. Those experiences gave her insight into what she needed to do.

XXIX

"I believe," Sarah said in a soft voice. "I believe you don't have the power to abuse me."

"What?" he said, snapping himself around to stare directly at her.

"I believe my family loves me, and I know I love them."

"What are you talking about? Your family is dead!"

"I don't believe you. I believe they are alive, because I can hear my father's voice. And I believe you can't hear him at all."

"Butch Gregory is dead! Dead! Dead! Dead! Dead!"

"He is not dead. Yet, even if he were, I believe he would be more alive than he's ever been, because he would be with the Lord."

"Don't talk about him anymore," The Rab-Shakeh raised his scepter to her throat.

"I believe I would prefer you kill me now, right here, than let you win. Because if I die, I win. If I die, you lose. You know it, too. But you can't take life, can you? Yes, I believe you can't take life. All you can do is lie, swindle, persuade, and cheat people into giving up their lives. It is why Jessica, Roberto, and who knows how many others killed themselves. You can't do it. They have to do it themselves." She huffed, "Some do it quickly, like my friends, and others do it slowly over time with addictions and dangerous living, compromise and comfort."

Sarah's voice grew stronger.

"I believe you are nothing more than a bully." She spit right between his eyes as she spoke.

"I believe you are a coward. I believe there is good in this world, and that is what bothers you the most. I believe in love. I believe in God the Father Almighty, Creator of Heaven and Earth."

The line felt good to her. It felt right. It felt the rightest she'd ever felt. Her mind took over her mouth, and she remembered the rest of the creed.

"I believe in Jesus Christ his only son, our Lord. He was conceived by the Holy Spirit. Born of the virgin Mary, suffered under Pontius Pilate, was crucified, dead and buried. He descended into hell. The third day he rose again. He ascended into heaven, where he sits at the right hand of God the Father Almighty."

She kept getting louder as she spoke. The Rab-Shakeh diminished in size. What Sarah didn't realize was she'd started to move. The restraints on her, of whatever nature they were, fell away. She moved her left hand and pointed right at him, "He is coming again to judge the quick," she jabbed her finger in the air, "and the dead." The moment was so natural and fluid to her she didn't realize it, but the look in The Rab-Shakeh's eyes indicated he knew what had happened and what was coming next.

She continued with the creed.

"I believe in the Holy Spirit. One holy church. The communion of saints. The forgiveness of sin. The resurrection of the body. The life ever-lasting."

She was standing over The Rab-Shakeh. He'd shrunk to two feet tall. His scepter had disappeared, and his color had changed. Instead of the bright, fiery red he was the color of old leather. His skin wrinkled. His eyes bulged. For a fleeting moment, he reminded Sarah of an insect.

Her eyes narrowed. Her brow bent. Her lips full of scorn. She knelt down to look at him in the face. She whispered the last word of the ancient affirmation of faith. "Amen."

An explosion of activity commenced on the word "Amen." The roof of the house blew off like a hurricane ripping shingles from a beach home. Sarah had forgotten there was a roof. The light in the lair had been such to her it felt like a dungeon or a subterranean cave. Now, with perfected vision, she could see it had all been smoke and mirrors. She'd been in the master bedroom the whole time. The roof gone, natural sunlight illuminated the rotting home. The walls were covered in green mold. The floor was infested with slugs, bugs, and even some trees grew out of the thick layer of dirt. Used needles, dirty clothes, and what looked to her like skeletons laid about.

The Rab-Shakeh shrieked. His voice now sounded like a shrill child. "No!" he kept repeating. "This can't be. I'm not ready."

But what he wanted didn't matter. Not anymore. Fire swept down from the sky above and devoured him. It started at his hands, which had been uplifted in defiance. Sarah saw them melt like wax. Fire continued to stream from the sky onto the demon. It burned his chest, lower body, and feet. His head remained, hovering in the air like a Mylar balloon.

"This isn't over," he said. "It's never over."

Sarah said, "Maybe, but you're a liar. But here is some more truth: I am so over you."

Another flaming flash came through the gaping hole where the ceiling once was. It hit what was left of The Rab-Shakeh. The disembodied head shook, fighting the heavenly fire with all its might. There as a screech, a curse, the ugliest profanity in the universe, then silence. Sarah jumped when the head fell to the floor with a thud. It smoldered like a log pulled from the fire. It was charred such that it no longer looked anything like the ferocious creature who had tortured her and those she loved.

The smell was next. It was an unholy putrid odor that caused an immediate, violent physical response. She vomited.

When the retching abated, she heard the sound. It was the sound of people. At first it sounded like the voices were far away in the distance. They got closer and she realized they were near, but her ability to hear had been hindered. Perhaps from the fire? Maybe from the burning? It could have been from the magic of The Rab-Shakeh? Now the voices were close, but they suddenly stopped.

"What is that smell?" Wyoming Wallace said. He was the first one to enter the room. He covered his nose and mouth with his Mariner's ball cap.

"Ahhh," was all Terence could say. He had stepped into the room, but he stepped back out.

Lucy and Butch stopped when the smell caught them off guard. The pause was only slight. They pressed on through it when they made eye contact with Sarah. The three of them embraced like never before over the destroyed remains of The Destroyer.

"The three of you," Wyoming said, "Are gonna putrify and rot if you don't get out of this room soon."

"He might be right," Butch said. He took Sarah by one hand and Lucy by the other. The three walked toward the doorway.

At the threshold, the floor shook.

"An earthquake?" Lucy said.

"Nope." Wyoming's certainty overrode Lucy's uncertainty. "I've seen this movie before. We better get clear."

Before he could finish his sentence, the outside wall of the bedroom collapsed inward, smashing the remains of The Rab-Shakeh's head like a berry thrown against a wooden fence. The sheetrock on the walls cracked from floor to ceiling. It peeled off and fell in large chunks. Wind swirled, picking up the pieces of wall, floor, ceiling, and whatever furniture there was swirling it around.

The visual was too strong for the five of them to leave. Sarah felt this lingering was dangerous, but she couldn't help herself.

She jolted back to the moment when the floor of the back half of the house snapped in two, pushing up from the bottom.

"It's time to go," she shouted.

"I'm with her," Terence said.

The five of them stepped over three dead bodies in the hallway by the kitchen.

As they cleared the back door, the house erupted in an explosion. Each individual particle of home—floor, trusses, siding, shingle, electrical wire, plumbing, concrete slab, everything—shot upward into the sky far above the tree line. The swing set, the picnic table, the mailbox, the rusted propane tank, even the septic system from the ground joined the floating debris of The Rab-Shakeh's lair. The ground beneath where the house had been trembled and split open.

Green light came from the hole in the earth. It hummed before it turned hot and vaporized every bit of the house. Everything that had been was gone forever. The ground closed.

There was not one shred of physical evidence any of it had ever existed. It was erased.

They stood, mouths open wide, in awe.

"Perfect," Wyoming said. "We don't have to call the police. There is no crime scene. No evidence. As far as the peaceful village of Sydney is concerned, nothing happened here at all."

"Don't be silly," Lucy said. "Someone will miss the house. And those people. All those people we fought off in the beginning are—were—still in there."

"No one will miss the house." Terence held his hands out in front of him, palms down. "I'm quite certain it has been off the grid and hidden from view and from people's minds so long it was completely forgotten." He pivoted and looked at Lucy, "Sadly, the same is probably true of those kids that were in there. They are victims as well. Anonymous, forgotten victims."

"How long were we separated?" Sarah asked her father.

"I don't know. What do you think, Wyoming? It wasn't long."

"Let me think," Wyoming stroked his chin whiskers as he walked back from his Jeep. He cut the end off of a cigar and lit it with his Zippo. "You're right, Reverend. We weren't in the house long at all, at least it didn't feel that way. What do you think, Doc?"

Terence checked his watch. "I'll be dill pickled."

"What?" Lucy asked.

"My watch. This is not my watch." He pulled up his sleeve so they all could see. "This is the fancy Rolex I had at Hepta High."

"Stop gawking and tell us how long we were in there." Wyoming spit on the ground.

"No more than twenty minutes total from the time we pulled up."

Butch looked at Sarah, "We were separated for maybe a minute.

Maybe."

It felt like an eternity.

XXX

"No," Butch Gregory said. It was one of the firmest things he'd ever said.

"No?" Gerald repeated, but added an interrogative tone.

"No," Butch said. "This isn't right. I can't accept."

"Shouldn't you talk to Lucy about it?"

"We've already talked. She suspected this is why you wanted to see me."

It was Wednesday morning, the Wednesday after the Sunday of the showdown at The Rab-Shakeh's lair. Gerald sat in the Sydney Diner and outlined what had happened the night before at the board meeting of Sydney Community Church.

They had booted out Tommy Bothers as chairman and elected Gerald.

They recanted their vote of no-confidence. Then they went further still by admitting it was sin and confessed it as such.

They presented evidence proving Tommy had doctored the information and fabricated the complaints.

Someone had checked, after all.

They also voted to bring Butch back as pastor, and even agreed to let him keep the parachute salary package as a bonus for coming back.

But Butch wasn't buying it. "This isn't right. As much as I'd like to come back to Sydney, things in my life have changed. I don't know what the future holds for my family, but I definitely feel like it is time for me to turn the page."

Gerald's shoulders drooped. His face fell.

"Look," Butch said. "I know you're disappointed."

"Understatement of the year, Butch. I fought hard to get you back. I thought it was what you wanted."

"It is, I mean, it was. Three weeks ago, I would have jumped at it and been ready to start back right away. And I am grateful. Yet, you know what is true, two wrongs don't make a right. It was wrong what the board did to me, and what the church allowed them to get away with, and in my understanding of things Sydney Community will be held accountable for how they threw away their responsibility. But this board meeting last night is nothing more than a knee-jerk reaction.

221

Those of you who are there need to clean house, seek the Lord, and move forward. Your next pastor is out there somewhere, and he or she is being prepared by the Lord for the work."

"What if you're the next pastor?" Gerald doused his hash browns with ketchup before shoveling a mouthful.

"I am not. I am the old pastor."

"Can't you be both? The old pastor and the new pastor."

"It don't work that way, Gerald. You know it, too. It hurt so bad, what they did. It was like they cut out my heart with a letter opener and made me watch them slice it with a paper cutter until it stopped beating. They didn't terminate me from a job, they kicked me out of my family, stole my friends, and hurt my wife and kids. I've given everything I've got for almost twenty years, and it didn't account for anything in their eyes."

"Can't you forgive us," Gerald said. "I mean, how many times have you preached about forgiveness. This would be your greatest sermon ever."

"I do forgive them," Butch said. "And I realize it wasn't everyone, but I could never trust Sydney Community again. Forgiveness is one thing. Lining up to be hurt again is something else."

Butch looked out the window and watched a tandem bicycle ride by on the busy city street. "It is impossible to pastor without trust. I don't know if I'll ever be able to trust any church again, much less Sydney Community. I don't even know if I will ever be able to pastor again."

"How can you say such?" Gerald spit his coffee. "You were born to pastor."

"I've come to believe I was born to pastor Sydney Community. It was my one true calling. But now it is over." He shook his head at Gerald. "There is a difference between being born to pastor in general and having been born, or created, to pastor a specific place. I don't know if I can make the adjustment to leading anywhere else. I'd always be guilty of comparing the two." He glanced up at the ceiling, then back at his friend. "It will take thought, self-evaluation, prayer, silence, and probably a few awkward moments to figure out what is next for Lucy and me. But one thing is for certain, I know Sydney Community is my past, not my future. I also know I must spend time with my son. I almost lost my family, and it had nothing to do with Tommy Bothers, or anything else, except that I was dumb." Butch was careful with his words. He had not spoken of The Rab-Shakeh or the dreamworld to anyone other than those involved, and he intended to keep it so.

"Sarah and I have come through the darkest moments of our relationship. I don't want to make the same mistakes with Paul I made with her. I may not be able to pastor a church and rebuild my family at the same time. In the future, perhaps, but right now I have more important things to do."

"Are you going to stay in town?"

"We have no plans to leave. It is not exactly like other churches are beating down my door wanting me to come lead them. I mean, after all, I am used and washed up. Churches only want cool, hip-and-with-it guys wearing untucked shirts and goatees with a solid Reformed theology. That's a prescription I could never fill. It is time for me to ride off into the sunset, or out to pasture, or something. Old pastors are not a hot commodity."

"What will you do for money? I mean, you've got to live."

"We will come up with something. The house is paid for. The kids are older and will not be around much longer. Our needs are low. Maybe I'll go into business for myself and only do weddings and funerals. It could be good. The dead don't complain, and newlyweds disappear."

"You'd die of boredom."

"Boredom might be what I need. What we need. Who knows, the small church I'm filling in at on Sundays down in Olympia might become permanent. All I'd have to do is show up and preach. That's not bad work."

"At the beginning, but it wouldn't be long before you started tinkering with the church like an old mechanic and a fixer-upper. You'll want to pop the hood and look at the engine. Soon you'd be moving around this, changing up that, and people would start to fill up the small church. You'd be right back in the middle of the action again."

"Maybe," Butch sipped his coffee. "Maybe."

* * *

"So, were they connected?" Butch asked Terence.

"Who? Who is connected?"

"The Rab-Shakeh and Tommy Bothers, that's who." Butch brought both his hands out in front of him and bobbed them up and down to punctuate his frustration at Terence's lack of understanding.

Terence puckered his lips in his habitual way then stroked the whiskers on his chin. "No. Not in any direct way, at least."

Butch shook his head, "But as soon as The Rab-Shakeh died, Tommy's power, his hold over Sydney Community, vanished. Surely it can't be coincidence."

"I didn't say it was coincidence, Butch. I said they weren't connected. At least not directly connected. Coincidence and connection aren't necessarily the only choices we have. But first let's back up your words. Who said The Rab-Shakeh was dead?"

Butch said, "We saw it. We all did. With our very own eyes."

"We saw the spiritual entity who has tormented people for at least three millennia, and probably longer, vanish. We saw the human representation of the entity, in the form of Mr. Raba, The Rab, burn out in a fiery sulfur vapor. We saw the threat to our immediate selves go away because we, with the help of the Lord above, overcame. We saw everything, I grant it. But it is not the same thing as the death of The Rab-Shakeh."

"You don't believe he is dead?" Butch's face sank as the words came out of his mouth.

"Not for a moment." Terence almost added that neither did Sarah or Wyoming, but to explain how he knew it would take too long. "It would be mighty presumptuous to believe that out here in Sydney, two preachers, a high school girl, and a gunslinger were able to vanquish one of Lucifer's A-Number One Beasties? The Rab-Shakeh is alive and well. He simply moved on. He was not welcome here. He was exposed, just like when Hezekiah and Isaiah exposed him through the Holy Spirit long ago. He's left, but has moved on to somewhere else. So, while we are comfortable and secure for the time being, I am quite certain in the fall, in some small town, outside Tampa or in the heart of Phoenix, maybe up around Detroit or down in Mexico City, a new psychology teacher is making himself at home and quickly becoming the favorite among all the cool kids. His charisma will win them over and destruction and death will be the result. Evil is not stronger than God, and Jesus defeated the devil forever on the cross, but evil has not been erased from the human experience. Not yet."

"It makes me shudder." Butch sat down. He fidgeted with his glasses. "I guess I'd hoped there would be relief, that at least what we went through would secure a better future for the world. I suppose I was naive."

"Butch Gregory, why can't you stay in the middle? Why do you have to always go to such extremes in your thinking. The logic is muddled. Because The Rab-Shakeh is not dead doesn't mean we didn't secure a better future. We did; indeed, we did for those nearest us,

224

those who mean the most. I suppose Sydney, though not immune from evil altogether, will have a long fallow time of peace and prosperity. For now, we know The Rab-Shakeh was at work all along here. It is why the child traffickers you dealt with ten years ago were so strong. It is why The Judys were able to cause such mischief. The Rab-Shakeh was paving a broad avenue for evil in general. Sin begets sin. He didn't bring the child traffickers. He didn't create the Judys. He didn't encourage Tommy Bothers, either. What he did was spread spiritual fecal matter all over the region, thus allowing infection, for it is an infection, to grow and metastasize. Just like an unhealthy person who doesn't heal tends to develop other kinds of illnesses over time, so it was with Sydney. It explains the collapse of Tommy Bothers. Once The Rab-Shakeh was eradicated from his stronghold, people's vision cleared up. In our dreamworld—Wyoming, Sarah, and I could never see very far. Our vision was blocked. People were operating around here with blocked vision. It clouded their judgment. Some of those elders who voted to remove you would never have done such a cowardly thing with a clear head. But The Rab-Shakeh magnified malevolence, thus giving Tommy more power than he ordinarily would have held. The result was you, as the emissary of God, were without support and without cover as the infection spread even into the church body. Lord knows there was and perhaps still is a fair amount of it in Ebenezer, too."

Terence bowed his head, as if praying. When his moment passed, he looked up at his old friend. "I've got a couple of questions of my own. What is happening at the church in Olympia?"

"Well," Butch stammered, "Yesterday was peaceful." He stood up and refilled his coffee mug from the tiny coffee pot sitting on Terence's desk. He didn't return to his chair, but instead looked at some of the titles on Terence's bookshelf. He finally continued, "Yesterday was peaceful. No omens, no visions, nothing traumatic. Lucy and both kids came with me. It was nice."

"Have you talked to anyone about the omen woman?"

"Yes, I have. The main leader there, Rue, told me the woman I described was kind of a local legend. She didn't belong to Lighthouse Church or any church for that matter. She drifted in and out, and had for as long as anyone could remember. Her name is Madeline." Butch fingered the spine of a Hans Kung book. "Rue told me no one ever paid any attention to her ramblings."

"Interesting," Terence said. "Are you going back down there again next Sunday?"

"Yes," Butch sighed. "They are drawing up a six-month contract. It's not much money, but it is enough, particularly given what I received from Sydney Community when they canned me."

Terence leaned back in his chair and propped his feet up on his desk. "You should invest all the money you got from Sydney Community in some hot tech stock. You might become an overnight millionaire and be able to retire and do something you love. You and Lucy could open a soup kitchen here in town or some kind of homeless shelter. Heaven knows there is a need for it."

"Lucy would certainly love that. But you know, if you invested the money, you'd become a millionaire. Not me. I am not fortunate. I would lose my shirt and become a homeless waif. I'd be the person people would see at the intersection with a cardboard sign. My sign would say, 'WILL PRAY FOR FOOD' and people will lock the doors on their car when they see me."

"Over-dramatic much, don't you think?"

"No." Butch didn't turn around. He kept looking at the books. He was now in Terence's preaching section and Butch's lips moved as he read authors names, Craddock, Miller, Smith, Mitchell, Robinson, Broadus.

"You've got a John Broadus in your library?" Butch sat his coffee down and pulled it from the shelf. He held *On The Preparation And Delivery Of Sermons* the way a pilgrim would hold a holy relic.

Terence ignored it. He knew this game Butch played. He didn't want to focus on the subject of their conversation, so he changed it. Terence allowed it, for it was a kind of answer, so he changed the subject again.

"My second question. Have you heard from Wyoming?"

"Yes." Butch put the book back into the shelf, picked up his coffee, and returned to the uncomfortable chair. "He sent me a text message three days ago saying he had some unfinished business in Texas. He told me he would explain everything later and he'd be back before July Fourth."

"Do you believe him?"

"I believe those are his intentions." Butch shrugged. "Why do you ask?"

"Because I feel like he is in trouble."

Butch sipped his coffee. "Sarah said the same thing yesterday."

Epilogue

Two Years Later

Sarah Gregory pedaled her bicycle across the University of Washington campus. It was late at night, but she wasn't afraid. After all she'd been through, she didn't fear much at all. The one exception was her calculus class. She was afraid of that, but otherwise her freshmen year at college had been uneventful and pleasant.

She didn't realize how late it was. She'd come back to her room to study, but after a quick bite of dinner and a hot shower, she decided it was time for sleep. Her Communist roommate wasn't back yet, and Sarah hoped to be asleep before she did because the roommate was obnoxious. It wasn't long before Sarah's eyes closed.

In her sleep, she was sitting in a hotel lounge. There were no people around, and she sat at a bar nursing a Pepsi. The hair rose on the back of her neck. Sarah got up from her seat and walked around a corner. She could see two high-backed leather chairs. Someone was sitting in them, and smoke billowed from the top of one.

She came around from behind them, knowing exactly what she'd find.

It was Wyoming Wallace and Terence Harrison.

"I always knew we'd meet like this again." Sarah sat down in the third, empty chair that wasn't there before, but now was.

A fourth figure walked upon them. The tall, thin, long haired woman said, "We've got work to do."

"Who the deuce are you?" Wyoming said, sticking his stogie back into his mouth with a sense of satisfaction.

"My name is Madeline, and I am the one who has called you here."

CPSIA information can be obtained
at www.ICGtesting.com
Printed in the USA
BVHW070946020619
549903BV00002B/140/P